About the author

Julian Stockwin was sent at the age of fourteen to *Indefatigable*, a tough sea-training school. He joined the Royal Navy at fifteen before transferring to the Royal Australian Navy, where he served for eight years in the Far East, Antarctic waters and the South Seas. In Vietnam he saw active service in a carrier task force.

After leaving the Navy (rated Petty Officer), Julian practised as an educational psychologist. He lived for some time in Hong Kong, where he was commissioned into the Royal Naval Reserve. He was awarded the MBE and retired with the rank of Lieutenant Commander. He now lives in Devon with his wife Kathy, and as well as his Kydd series he has recently published a non-fiction work called *Stockwin's Maritime Miscellany: A Ditty Bag of Wonders from the Golden Age of Sail*, which contains fascinating facts and sea lore from that period. More information about Julian Stockwin and all his books can be found on his website at www.JulianStockwin.com.

JULIAN STOCKWIN

TREACHERY

HODDER

First published in Great Britain in 2008 by Hodder & Stoughton
An Hachette UK company

First published in paperback in 2009

3

A CIP catalogue record for this title is available from the British Library.

ISBN 978 0 340 96113 1

Typeset in Garamond MT by Palimpsest Book Production Limited,
Grangemouth, Stirlingshire
Printed and bound in Great Britain by Clays Ltd, St Ives plc

Hodder & Stoughton policy is to use papers that are natural, renewable
and recyclable products and made from wood grown in sustainable forests.
The logging and manufacturing processes are expected to conform to the
environmental regulations of the country of origin.

Hodder & Stoughton Ltd
338 Euston Road
London NW1 3BH

www.hodder.co.uk

To Admiral Sir James Saumarez

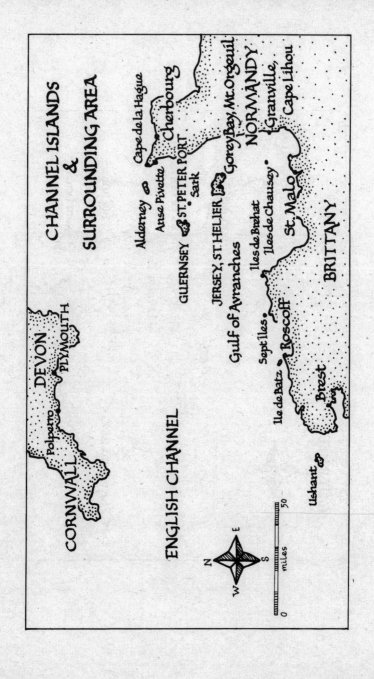

CHANNEL ISLANDS
&
SURROUNDING AREA

Alderney ⬠ Cape de la Hague
Anse Pivette ● Cherbourg

GUERNSEY ⬠ST.PETER PORT
Sark ●

Gorey Bay, Mt. Orgueil
JERSEY, ST HELIER 🏰
Gulf of Avranches NORMANDY
Granville,
Iles de Brehat Cape Lihou
Iles de Chausey
Sept Iles St. Malo
Ile de Batz ● Roscoff BRITTANY

Brest

CORNWALL
DEVON
Polperro PLYMOUTH

ENGLISH CHANNEL

N
W E
S

miles
0   50

Ushant ⬠

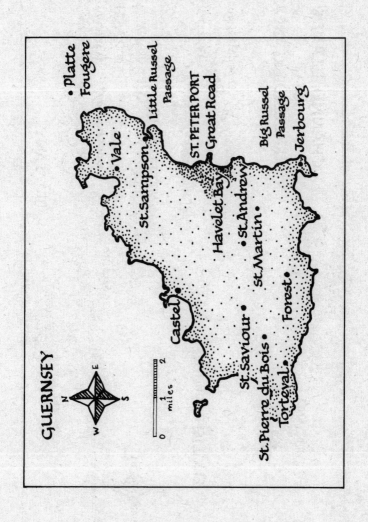

GUERNSEY

N
W E
S

0   1   2
miles

Platte
Fougère

Little Russel
Passage

Vale

St.Sampson

ST. PETER PORT
Great Road

Havelet Bay

St.Andrew

St.Martin

Big Russel
Passage

Jerbourg

Castel

St.Saviour

St.Pierre du Bois

Torteval

Forest

Chapter 1

His Majesty's brig-sloop *Teazer* eased sheets and came round prettily for the last leg of the short passage from Polperro eastwards to Plymouth Sound. The ship's clerk knocked softly at the captain's cabin door. There was no reply so, from long friendship, Nicholas Renzi entered quietly. Commander Thomas Kydd was sitting rigid at the stern windows staring out. He turned, his face a bleak mask. 'Tom, dear fellow? I've brought you this,' Renzi said, proffering a glass. 'The natives hereabouts do swear by its power to lay demons and recruit the spirit.'

Kydd accepted the offering but it remained untouched in his hand. 'Fine nor'-westerly blow,' Renzi went on brightly. 'We should raise the Sound on this tack, I'd venture.' There was no response from the fine and ambitious sea officer, who had made the incredible journey from the fo'c'sle to the quarterdeck, then achieved his own command, now brought so low.

It had been so sudden. Returning triumphant after a rousing cruise, Kydd had decided to snatch a few moments in

Polperro, the home of his newly betrothed, Rosalynd. There, he had learned of her tragic death, just days before.

Renzi drew a chair close. There was little to be said – grief was such a private thing, but in this Renzi knew guilt. His closest friend had stood alone when he had followed his heart and asked a country lass to be his bride, not Persephone Lockwood, the admiral's daughter. There had never been a formal understanding between Kydd and Miss Lockwood, but society – and Renzi – had been outraged nevertheless.

'You should know this, dear friend, I – I own myself shamed by my actions, you must understand,' Renzi said, in a low voice. 'It was unpardonable not to recognise that it was – that your sentiments sprang from the noblest and purest . . .'

His words went unheard but he vowed that whatever lay ahead for Kydd he would be at his side. Especially when he tried to re-enter the world that had turned its back on him. But there were more pressing concerns now. 'We dock in so little time I have to ask, shall you prepare to take the deck again?'

Kydd's face turned slowly. His eyes filled as he tried to speak and his fists clenched.

Renzi knew for the sake of the future that Kydd should be the one to take *Teazer* to her rest. 'You are the captain still, and duty is a stern mistress. Shall I . . . ?' He let it hang.

As the words penetrated, Kydd rose from his chair like an old man and made his way to his inner cabin. After a few minutes he emerged and took a last long look through the windows at the receding wake.

'I have th' ship, Mr Standish,' Kydd mumbled to his first lieutenant, and stood alone, face set and pale, staring ahead. Rame Head passed abeam; *Teazer* hauled her wind for the

Sound and home. Hands went to stations for mooring ship and she came gently to single anchor at Barn Pool.

The early-autumn sunshine had a fragile, poignant quality as the sloop's gig pulled across the short distance to the dock-yard; at Kydd's side, Renzi held ship's papers. The boat nuzzled into the landing stage and Kydd stepped out, seeming lost and bewildered. 'This way, old fellow,' Renzi said, glaring at passers-by, who stopped to gape at the subject of the so-recent scandal.

It was not far to the offices; the flag-lieutenant hurried away to inform the port admiral of their arrival. Lockwood himself came stalking out to the waiting room but halted in surprise at the sight of Kydd's ashen face. News of the tragedy had apparently not yet reached him. 'I'm astonished you have the temerity to cut short your cruise, Mr Kydd. There are matters, it seems—'

'Sir, I beg t' report m' full success in y'r mission.'

Lockwood blinked.

'*Teazer*'s report,' Renzi said, handing over the details of Kydd's twin victories – success against the notorious Bloody Jacques, the renegade privateer who had terrorised the Devon and Cornish coasts, and the unmasking of Zephaniah Job as the man behind the smuggling ring.

The admiral flicked through the papers. 'I, er . . . It would appear I must offer my congratulations, Commander,' he said, and looked up, but Kydd had left.

When the news was broken at number eighteen Durnford Street, the residence Kydd and Renzi shared, a pall of silence descended. Shocked, Mrs Bargus the housekeeper cast about for things to do that might in some little way comfort her employer. A cheerful fire was soon ablaze and the cook was set to prepare his favourite braised duck. Becky, the maid,

3

came in timidly to light the candles but departed quickly, leaving Kydd and Renzi alone.

'If there's anything . . .' Renzi started hesitantly, but stopped as racking sobs seized his friend.

He waited patiently until they eased.

'I never reckoned it could hurt s' much,' Kydd choked.

'Yes, brother,' Renzi murmured.

'Rosalynd's gone. F'r ever. So innocent an' young, an' she – she never knew—'

'I have to return to the ship, Tom,' Renzi said gently. 'There's things will need . . . arranging.' Unless someone was there to head off troubles arising in a temporarily captainless vessel chaos might ensure: the ambitious Standish would probably not see it as in his best interest to take a firm hand.

'Do remain here, dear fellow, and I'll be back when I can.' Renzi found the brandy and placed a glass before Kydd.

It was no easy matter but a flow of fictitious captain's orders relayed by Renzi saw the larboard watch stream happily ashore and a suspicious Standish set to turning up the hands for restowing the hold. It was dark before Renzi could make his way ashore again, and he hurried to Durnford Street.

Mrs Bargus answered the door, flustered and apprehensive. 'Oh, Mr Renzi! I'm s' glad you're here! It's the captain – he's in such a state! All those things he's saying, it's not right, Mr Renzi . . .'

Kydd was slumped in the same chair in his shirtsleeves, gazing fixedly into the fire, the brandy bottle nearly empty beside him. He jerked round when Renzi entered. 'Ahoy there, ol' shipmate!' he called bitterly. 'Bring y'r arse t' anchor an' let y'r logic tell me why – why scrovy bastards like Lockwood still strut abou' while my Rosalynd . . . while she's . . .' His face crumpled.

4

Renzi went to him and touched his arm. 'I'm going to the apothecary, my friend. He'll have much more efficacious medicines for your pain.' It was chilling to witness: never in all their years together had he seen Kydd in such a condition – save, perhaps, in the early days in the old *Duke William*.

'No!' Kydd's hoarse cry pierced him. 'St-stay wi' me, Nicholas.'

'Of course, brother.' Renzi stoked the fire and drew up his chair. With a forced laugh he went on, 'You should have no care for *Teazer*, old fellow. There's half the ship's company rollicking ashore and Kit Standish believing you gravely concerned with the stowage of the hold.'

Kydd took no notice. Instead he turned to Renzi and said hollowly, 'It's – it's that I can't face it, Nicholas – life wi'out her.' His hands writhed. 'I saw all m' days in the future wi' her, plans an' course all set fair, an' now – there's . . . no point.'

Carefully, Renzi replied, 'Not at all! I see a fine officer who is captain of a ship that needs him, one with the most illustrious of sea careers to come.'

Kydd grabbed his arm and leered at him. 'Don't y' see, Nicholas,' he slurred, 'it's th' sea right enough. It's taken m' Rosalynd as it can't abide a rival!'

'What? Such nonsense.'

Kydd slumped in his chair. 'I knew ye'd not unnerstan' it,' he said, almost inaudibly, and closed his eyes before Renzi could continue. 'No point,' he mumbled, 'no point a-tall.'

'Tom, I have to slip out for a space,' Renzi said. 'I'll be back directly.'

For a long minute Kydd said nothing. Then, with his eyes still closed, he said, with intense weariness, 'As y' have to, m' frien'.'

* * *

'Why, Nicholas! What a surprise!' Sensing the gravity of the visit, Cecilia added hastily, 'Do come in. Mrs Mullins is engaged at the moment – the drawing room will be available to us, I believe.'

Renzi followed Kydd's sister into the home of her old friend, whom she was visiting. She turned to face him. 'It's Thomas, isn't it?'

'Yes . . .' Renzi hesitated. 'I'm truly sorry to have to say that Rosalynd . . . has been taken from us. She was drowned when a packet boat overset on the way to Plymouth.'

Cecilia gasped. 'No! It can't be! And – and poor Thomas. He – he must be feeling . . .'

'I rather believe it is worse than that. His intellects are perturbed. He's not seeing the point of life without Rosalynd and I fear for his future.'

'Then I must go to him this instant, poor lamb. Pray wait for me, sir, I shall accompany you presently.'

'No! That is to say, it might not be suitable, Miss Cecilia. You see, he is at this moment, er, disguised in drink and he—'

'He might be, um, flustered, Nicholas, but he needs us. I shall go to him,' she said, with unanswerable determination.

The night was cool as they hurried through the streets, but when they reached number eighteen they were met outside by a distraught Mrs Bargus and a wide-eyed Becky clutching her from behind. 'I didn't know what t' do, Mr Renzi! All of a sudden I hears this great roar fr'm upstairs – fair set m' heart a-flutter, it did. I goes up t' see, an' then down comes th' captain in a pelt. He pushes past me an' out on the street. An' he just in his shirtsleeves an' all.'

It was past enduring: the shock of the news had given way to the spreading desolation of grief, then the firming certainty that he wanted no part of a world that did not include Rosalynd. Whichever way Kydd faced there was pain and mockery, heartbreak and futility. Blind hopelessness had demanded release, and exploded into an overwhelming compulsion to escape the prison of his hurt.

He stumbled on into the night; some instinct had made him snatch up his sea-worn grego as he left, which kept him warm and anonymous over his shirtsleeves. Setting his path away from the sea, his thoughts tumbled on, a tiny thread of reason struggling against the maudlin embrace of the liquor.

Suddenly he had a theory: every mortal had a measure of happiness allotted to them and his had just run out. Did this mean he should resign himself to dreariness for what remained of his days? Was this something to do with the Fates? Renzi always set his face against them, something to do with . . . with 'terminism – deter . . . something . . . Damn it! Who cared about Renzi and his high ideas? Tears stung and no answers came.

A gentleman of age saw him and frostily made much of crossing the street to avoid him. Kydd glared drunkenly at him: how he'd suffered at the hands of so-called gentle society. In the hard days as a newly promoted officer from before the mast he had been ignored until he had learned their fancy ways. There had been ill-disguised scorn for his origins even in far Nova Scotia until he had earned admiration in a social coup when he had unwittingly invited the mistress of Prince Edward to a ball. It had been seen as a cunning move for advancement in high society, and here in England they had been ready enough to see him court one of their own but could not accept that his heart had finally been taken . . . by another.

Bitterness welled. Now when he so needed those who

cared and understood to rally to his support there was no one. Not a soul. Cecilia could not be seen with him for the social stigma and Renzi, well, he had been so disapproving about Rosalynd in the past . . . Be damned to it – be damned to all of them! When he had been a common foremast jack it had never been like this – he remembered the comradely understanding, the rough kindnesses . . . Then there had been no judgements, and all was plain speaking, square playing. The memories flooded his brain fuzzily, the drink in him only intensifying his loneliness. He yearned to exchange his hard-won status for the careless warmth of the fo'c'sle. But never again would he—

A sudden thought came – seductive, challenging and glorious. He had lost everything, was alone in the world now and nobody cared. What if he left Commander Thomas Kydd to his misery and became once more Tom Kydd, carefree mariner, shipping out on a deep-sea voyage to the other side of the world? There were ocean-going merchantmen a-plenty in Plymouth, taking on last stores and cargo – they would snap up a prime hand.

Such a voyage would give him time to heal, find a new self. He gulped at the thought. After all these years, would he be able to hand a staysail, tuck a long-splice, stomach the burgoo and hard tack? He knew the answer instantly.

Yes.

He tried to focus on the details, muzzily aware that he was in no fit state to walk the mile or two back to Plymouth. He drew himself up with drunken dignity and hailed an approaching public diligence. The only other occupant stared in astonishment at his worn, tar-smelling grego over the lace-trimmed shirt and stylish breeches, then averted his head.

He was deposited outside the King's Arms in Old Town

Street, on the heights above Sutton Cove and well clear of the insalubrious sailors' haunts – but that was where he was headed, down the narrow streets, alleys and passageways into the jumble of rickety buildings around the waterfront. He knew that Cockside on the opposite side of the Pool was most favoured by the merchant seamen so he made his way there, spurred on by the roars of jollity from a nearby taphouse.

A memory – a reflex from a life long ago – came back: he removed one shoe gravely, placed a few coins in it then put it on again it. This old sailor's trick would ensure that whatever condition he was in later he would not be a burden to his shipmates in returning to his ship. Whichever it would be . . .

He lurched upright and continued down the steep, unlit street towards the glittering pool of darkness. What was waiting below? What adventure would follow? Every time he had been to sea it had always been into some wild experience or other. Since he'd left the shore life and—

A blow to the side of his head sent him staggering, disoriented. He turned— Another from behind knocked him to his knees. 'Scrag 'im then, mate!' he heard.

Footpads! He scrabbled for his sword but, of course, it was not there. Grog-fuddled he was easy meat. A blackjack smacked into his head and sent him sprawling.

Then the two were on him, expertly riffling his pockets, taking his purse, a small ring, the fob watch Cecilia had proudly given him when he had achieved the quarterdeck. He was helpless while they ransacked his body with savage, invasive hands.

'Dick – I'm 'avin' them kicks. Help me get 'em off th' bastard.'

They had seen his breeches, the sign of a gentleman, and these were his finest, worn for the admiral. He struggled but was held while they were viciously stripped off. 'An' the shirt, cully!'

He caught one a glancing blow but it was no use. Before they had robbed him of stockings and shoes, too, something made them scurry off, leaving him prostrate in the dirty alley, sore and shivering with cold and shame.

Kydd sat up, head swimming. A bout of heaving seized him and he fell sideways, sliming his undervest. He got to his feet unsteadily, then saw that one of the robbers had thrown aside his own garments to run off in his. A rank pair of trousers and a ragged black waistcoat; they would have to cover him as he made his way back to ... his old life?

No! If there was one thing he was not, it was a craven-hearted lobcock. He would see through what he'd set out to do. With pathetic dignity he hauled on the malodorous trousers, the fat-streaked waistcoat, and his old grego, which the footpads had disdained. It had seen many a stormy night in the past and no doubt would in whatever lay ahead ...

Kydd set course stubbornly for Cockside. He reached the cobblestones of the quay, the bowsprits of silent ships spearing high above him in the still darkness. On the far wharf others were moored broadside to, with cargo working gear rigged, waiting for the next day. A lone shipkeeper wandered morosely about the deck of his vessel.

The sailors' taverns were beacons of light and noise and he made for the nearest. His mouth tasted vile, his head throbbed – but a gage of bowse with the splicings would soon set him to rights. Kydd pushed open the door and a sickly sweet smell of liquored sawdust and warm humanity hit him. A few turned, then resumed their conversations.

Across the room a serving maid looked at him speculatively and made her way through the tables. 'A hard time, sailor?' she said sympathetically. It was not uncommon after a rough voyage and the hard carousing that followed for a sailor to sell his clothes. Kydd's heart warmed to her and he gave a shy smile. 'Ye're welcome here, shipmate,' she continued. 'An' what c'n I find f'r you as will chase away y'r mem'ries, m' dear?'

Kydd's face clouded. 'Thank 'ee, Miss – but there isn't a med'cine made as will settle that. Er, I have m' hopes of a long voyage t' come, though,' he concluded weakly. His expression eased. 'But a muzzler o' y'r right true sort is wha' I'd take kindly.'

'Look, come over an' sit wi' these gennelmen,' she said and waved a pot towards a cosy group about a table in the corner. 'They's in from the Indies, eleven weeks 'cross the Western Ocean wi' a sprung foremast an' aught t' eat but belaying-pin soup an' handspike hash.'

The beer was dark, honest and spread the glow of inebriation once more. His new friends had glanced at him curiously just once and then, as was the way of the sea, had accepted him for what he was. 'Yez must've had a time of it, Tom, m' skiddy cock. Which hooker?' one asked.

'Save y'r kindness, mates, an' it's something I – I don't wan' t' talk of,' Kydd said gruffly, and took refuge in his tankard.

'Right b' us, ain't it?' the oldest in the group said hastily to the others and called for another pint. 'An' if ye're not flush in the fob . . .' he muttered kindly.

'Ah, "everybody's mess an' no one's watch"?' Kydd snorted, 'No, cuffin, I has m' cobbs as will pay m' way.'

He fumbled with his shoe while the others looked away politely. He found the coins – in his careless haste he had slipped in three half-guineas and a florin, a princely sum for a seaman. Embarrassed, he mumbled something and ordered a drink for each man.

They had not questioned Kydd's reticence – many went to sea for a good enough reason – but they told him willingly of their own hard passage. Seeing Kydd relax a little, they asked what he had in mind for the future and, head spinning, he tried to explain his great need for far voyaging. They nodded: it was the ambition of most seamen when reaching port to spend all their hard-won pay in one glorious spree and, penniless, sign on for another hard voyage.

'Well, matey, we's not f'r south o' the Line, but y' might want t' think about *Barbadoes Packet*. Sailin' soon f'r Batavia in hardwares. Her mate'll be about lookin' f'r hands tonight, I shouldn't wonder.'

Kydd tried blearily to take it in.

'Th' mate?' said another, with feeling. 'Ye're forgettin' it's Hellyer, a right bucko as ever I seen! You ship out in that there—'

A splintering crash and female screams slammed into Kydd's consciousness followed by urgent shouts and a strident bellow from the door. Reeling, he tried to make sense of it as his companions shot to their feet and yelled at him, 'The press! Skin out while y' can, Tom – *jowla*, *jowla*, matey!' They disappeared hurriedly into the scrimmage and Kydd tried clumsily to follow but fell headlong. Before he could rise he felt knees in his back, his thumbs secured with ropeyarns, and he was yanked to his feet.

'Got a rough knot 'ere, sir,' the press-gang seaman called, his hand firmly on the scruff of Kydd's neck as he tried to writhe free.

A young lieutenant was approaching and Kydd hung his head in stupefied dejection, waiting for recognition. 'Ah, yes. Looks fit enough. Hey, you – which ship? What rate o' seaman?'

Kydd struggled with his befuddled mind. 'Er, there's a mistake,' he mumbled.

'That's "sir" t' you, cully,' the seaman said, with a sharp cuff to Kydd's head.

'Um, sir, y' can't take me, I'm . . . er, that is t' say, I'm . . .' He trailed off weakly.

'And, pray, what are you, then? A gentleman?' the officer said sarcastically, eyeing Kydd's appearance. 'Or possibly the captain of your ship as can't be spared.'

The seaman tittered.

Kydd said nothing, overcome with mortification. The lieutenant changed his tone. 'Now there's nothing to be ashamed of. Should you show willing, in the King's service, we can make a man of you. Proud to serve! Who knows, there's been those who've been rated full petty officer in just a few years.'

Numb, Kydd was led off with the others by the Impress Service, the regular organisation for supplying the fleet with men. He knew they were going to the receiving ship, an old, no longer fit-for-service hulk moored well out.

There, they were herded into the darkness of the hold, and the gratings slid into place with hopeless finality. Two dim lanthorns revealed dirty straw and pitiful bodies, a pail of water in the corner. In the morning he would be cleaned up to go before the regulating captain who, he recalled, was Byam, honourably wounded at the Nile. Without question he would be recognised.

The drink-haze fled, leaving him in full knowledge of the horror of his situation. He would be laughed out of the Navy. Even the merchant sailors would chortle with glee at the story of his downfall. To the disgrace of his family, he would be pointed out wherever he went as the captain who had been pressed by his own press-gang.

The long night passed in self-condemnation, recrimination and torturing images of his shocked friends and relations as they heard the news. How could he bear the shame? What excuse could he offer? He lay sleepless on the rank straw, dreading the day to come.

At first light the guards took up position at the grating. Kydd heard footsteps approaching and saw figures peering down. He shrank away. There were muffled voices, then a guard lifted away the grating and swung over a lanthorn. 'Hey! Yair, you wi' the grego!'

Kydd looked up miserably.

'Yes, that's him, the villain,' came a cultured voice. Another loomed next to him.

The ladder was slid down. 'Up 'n' out, matey, an' no tricks!'

Kydd climbed slowly, misery overflowing. He reached the top and raised his eyes – to be met with the grave face of Nicholas Renzi, who said, with a sigh, 'It's him. Tom Brown, gunner's mate. Never to be trusted ashore. I dare to say that *Teazer*'s captain will know what to do with him.' He turned to the lieutenant. 'I do thank you for securing him – we'll have him back aboard immediately. I don't believe Captain Byam need be troubled.' Then he ordered the thick-set seaman next to him, 'Hale him into the longboat directly, if you please.'

Tobias Stirk grinned mirthlessly and frogmarched Kydd away.

Chapter 2

Hearing movement in the other bedroom, Renzi sat up. Although he was very tired, he rose quickly and dressed. It had been a long, distressing night. After frantically searching for Kydd for hours, he had gone to *Teazer* and found Stirk. Together, with Stirk sworn to secrecy, they had scoured the dockyard and town. Then, despairing, they had thought to check the press-gang catch.

Renzi knocked softly. Kydd's pain was heartbreaking and he was clearly not responsible for his actions: who knew what he might do next?

'Tom?' he called gently. 'Are you awake, brother?'

There was an indistinct murmur. Renzi entered. To his surprise Kydd was shaved, dressed and tying his neckcloth. 'Do I see you well, my friend?' Renzi ventured.

'As ye'd expect.' Kydd did not take his eyes from the mirror.

'Believe me, brother, you have my every understanding. When one's wits are askew with grief there is no telling where the mind will stray.'

'Spare me y'r pity, Nicholas,' Kydd said. 'It happened.'

'I'm saying that I've yet to meet the man who, trapped in a pit, is able to fix on far horizons. What you did—'

'What I did was weak an' foolish. I could've brought th' Service t' contempt an' ridicule.' He paused. 'I'm t' be – I'm beholden t' ye, Nicholas, f'r what ye did last night.'

'It was nothing more than a friend would do, dear fellow.'

Kydd resumed at the mirror. 'I'm goin' back aboard. This is m' duty an' this I must obey above all things.' He paused. 'It was th' last thing she spoke t' me, o' course,' he added, swallowing hard.

'A noble sentiment, Thomas. Fitting for a gentleman of the first rank.'

Kydd found his waistcoat. 'Ye'll oblige me b' tellin' how many – er, who saw me last night.'

'Why, none of acquaintance, I believe,' Renzi answered equably. 'The quarter is not favoured by King's men.'

'But there was Stirk.'

'It was Toby Stirk who thought to summon a waterman, once we were landed, and even gave you his coat to wear over yours on the way back. Do you think he would be the kind of man to glory in his captain's abasement? There is none who—'

'And Cecilia?'

'She will now be in possession of my note detailing how you were cruelly set upon by footpads while taking the night air to clear your head, and that visitors are discouraged.'

Kydd finished dressing. 'I'm returnin' t' *Teazer* now,' he said abruptly. 'Do ye wish t' come?'

'If that is my duty, Captain.'

'It is.'

*   *   *

16

The waterman, under the tight-lipped grimace of his passenger, bent to his oars and sent the wherry skimming across to the little brig in Barn Pool. Rounding the pretty stern windows he brought it expertly alongside her side-steps, and Kydd boarded briskly.

'You, sir!' he roared, at Prosser, the lounging mate-of-the-watch, who straightened in dismay at Kydd's sudden appearance. 'What kind o' watch can't sight their captain returnin' on board?'

Prosser snatched off his hat. 'Er, you're not in uniform, sir,' he said weakly.

Further forward the boatswain faltered under Kydd's glare. 'We – we weren't told ye was comin', sir,' he said.

Hurriedly the watch found things that needed attention round the decks. 'This is not a King's ship, it's a Dutch scow. What are th' men doin' for'ard?' Kydd said angrily. 'Hangin' out th' washing? If 'n ye can't take charge properly, Mr Prosser, I'll find someone who will.'

He stalked down to his cabin. Renzi paused, then descended the after hatchway to his own tiny hideaway to wait out the mood.

The morning wore on: he usually worked by the clear light of the stern windows in the captain's cabin. He gathered up his papers and made his way aft, knocked softly and waited.

'Yes?'

The impatient tone made him hesitate.

Kydd was at his desk, his face stony. 'Is there anything y' need?'

'Oh – er, you wished to sight the quarterly return on casks shaken,' Renzi said, thinking quickly. 'Will this be the right time, do you think?'

'Not now. Ask th' bosun to step aft, if y' please.'

The afternoon watch came to an end and the starboard watch for liberty mustered. There would be the usual sore heads in the morning after their time ashore. Standish paid his respects warily and was off as smartly, leaving the ship to its evening rest. Renzi waited a little longer, then went up.

Kydd was sitting motionless by the stern windows, gazing out at the shadowed waters. 'I – I'll be stayin' with *Teazer* for now, Nicholas,' he said stiffly. 'Ye're at liberty t' use number eighteen as y' see fit.'

'Thank you, my friend,' Renzi said quietly. 'But, as you'll know, we've been at sixes and sevens in recent days. I need to take some quiet time to bring things to order. I shall stay aboard.' Without asking, he sat down in the opposite chair.

Kydd stirred and cleared his throat. 'Ship's business? Then do y' care t' share m' dinner?'

It was a cheerless meal: not so much Kydd's halting conversation or his silences but the contrast with what had been before. Kydd's face was drawn, his eyes dull, and there was no light-hearted taking up of Renzi's witty sallies.

As soon as he decently could, Renzi excused himself.

The next day Kydd kept to his cabin. Life aboard *Teazer* settled to a dreary stasis at her mooring, the entire ship affected by the solitary and melancholy figure in the captain's cabin.

Renzi knew the cause of the flares of temper, the distracted silences: Kydd had seized on *duty* as salvation – the stern call to a code of conduct that was plain, uncompromising and immediate. A pathway out, which would offer a clear and unthinking course to follow that was sure and secure. And it was denied him while *Teazer* lay idle.

What would Admiral Lockwood plan for them? he wondered. It was an embarrassment now to have Kydd in his command, despite his recent successful cruise. Another anti-smuggling patrol? Worthy but dull, with possibly the Admiralty questioning continued employment of such a proven asset in this way. It would probably be a vague order to keep the seas as far from Plymouth as could be contrived; in any event, the sooner they got under way the better.

On the fifth day, Standish went ashore to the dockyard and returned with packages. He disappeared into Kydd's cabin and soon the ship was alive with rumour – orders had arrived at last.

The ship's clerk reported with the others. While the cabin filled with animated chatter, Renzi picked up the single sheet: '. . . and agreeable to an Admiralty Order . . . you are detached from duty in the Plymouth Command and shall proceed forthwith to join the Channel Islands Squadron . . .'

Renzi smiled cynically. Not only had Lockwood rid himself of his embarrassment but had even managed to have them consigned to the quiet backwater guarding those lonely English outposts, the tiny Channel Islands near the French coast. He had never heard of any stirring battles in that quarter – in fact, nothing of note in all the years of war. It was exile for Kydd.

He looked again. The date was a good seven months earlier. Lockwood had been asked then to provide a vessel but had held on jealously to his small fleet – until now.

'We're near ready t' sail. What's to do about our marines?' Kydd exploded, as though it was Renzi's fault.

'We'll hear back soon, I'm sure of it,' Renzi responded, although he felt that Kydd had enough on his hands without insisting they ship the complement of marines to which they were entitled since they were now proceeding to a 'foreign' station.

He had himself worded the application, which had been duly acknowledged, but Kydd was in a dangerous mood. 'Don't th' marines barrack in Stonehouse? I've a mind t' go ashore an' stir the idle swabs.'

There was no dissuading him and Renzi found himself hurrying behind as Kydd stalked the short distance from Stonehouse Pool to the massive light grey stonework of the barracks. A sentry snapped to attention and slapped his musket, bringing a lieutenant strolling out from the gatehouse. 'Sir,' he said, saluting smartly, 'what can I do—'

'Commander Kydd, HMS *Teazer*. An' where are our marines?'

The lieutenant blinked. 'Sir?'

'I've not time t' discuss th' matter. Please t' conduct us to y'r general in charge.'

'The colonel commandant,' the lieutenant said, clearly pained. 'This is irregular, sir. Perhaps the adjutant might satisfy.'

They headed across the parade ground, passing several drill squads of marines executing complex manoeuvres.

Kydd did not waste time. 'Kydd, HMS *Teazer*. We're t' sail soon an' I've heard nothing of our marines, sir.'

The adjutant steepled his fingers, then glanced up at the ramrod-straight colour sergeant at his side. 'Then I'm to understand that you seek a company of marines to make up the complement of your fine vessel before you sail?'

'Yes.'

The adjutant barked, 'Sar'nt, go outside and find this officer some marines.'

'Sah!' bellowed the man, with a quivering salute, and marched noisily away. In a suspiciously short time he marched back in and crashed to attention with another salute. 'Sah! No *marines*. Sah!'

'None?'

'No *marines* a-tall. Sah!'

The adjutant assumed an expression of saintly sorrow. 'There, Commander, you see? We cannot help you – there are no marines left, I regret to say.' Sounds of screamed orders on the parade ground outside echoed in the office.

Kydd took a deep breath. 'You flam me, sir, an' I'll not stand f'r it,' he snarled. 'What are th' men outside? A flock o' goats? If I don't get m' men an' that main quickly, I'll—'

'Commander! There seems to be a misunderstanding!' the adjutant said smoothly. 'We may yet find you some men.' He pointed at the colour sergeant. 'Tell me, what do you see there?'

'A marine?' Kydd grated, without humour.

'No, sir. If you will observe, the man bears facings and cuffs of royal blue. This to the knowing signifies a royal regiment. Sir, he is a *Royal* Marine and has been since His Majesty in the year two did us the signal honour of recognising our services to the Crown of the last century or so.'

'Sah!' the colour sergeant blurted in satisfaction. 'Loyal an' royal it is. Sah!'

'So, you see, these are proud men and are entitled to their honours. Should you take aboard *Royal* Marines you will find no more loyal and courageous a band of men anywhere.'

Kydd glowered.

'Now, let me see, I have the current sea roster here. Pray tell, where do you see your service mainly? What rate of ship? It does matter, you know.'

'Brig-sloop, Channel Islands Squadron,' Kydd snapped.

The officer sighed. 'Not as who might say an active station.' He leafed through the book. 'A brig-sloop, ship's company of eighty – a hundred? Then you'll be looking to a company of a sergeant, corporal and a score of privates.'

'No officer?' Kydd came back testily. Even a junior lieutenant would be better than none for no one in *Teazer* could talk soldier lingo enough to take charge.

'None. But you'll find a Royal Marine is different from your regular soldier – more initiative, more reliable on his own.' He leaned back. 'I'll find you a long-service sergeant you might rely on, Commander. As for the men, it takes some two hundred Royal Marines to get a ship-o'-the-line to sea and I rather fancy you'll have to be satisfied at this time with near a dozen.'

'Have no fear, sir, the men will be found. The barrack-master will need the details, of course, and I'm assuming you have made application for complement in the usual form. Our quartermaster will kit them for service and you shall have them before you sail. Good luck and good day to you, sir.'

'Our marines at last, thank God,' Standish muttered peevishly, spying *Teazer*'s longboat putting out from Stonehouse Pool.

'I rather think they would wish to be referred to as *Royal* Marines, Mr Standish,' Renzi murmured, watching the boat full of red coats approach.

'Lobsterbacks,' Standish said. 'Well, as long as they're inboard and victualled in by noon we'll be in a fair way of putting to sea before dark. Our lord and master is in a right taking, I tell you – wants to up hook and bowting the briny without losing a minute.'

'You've applied for a removal out of *Teazer*,' Renzi said quietly.

Standish looked at him sharply. 'Who told you that?' His gaze swung back to the boat. 'But it's true enough. Since he's crossed the admiral's hawse there's no hope o' *Teazer* being put in the way of a good fight and chance of distinction – the Channel Islands, I ask you!' He continued moodily, 'And it's got to be said, since his dolly had the bad grace to get drowned he's been knocked athwart and no use to any. I fear our Mr Kydd's appetite for glory has gone, and with it any desire I have to stay in this ark of misery.'

Renzi did not reply. The rot was setting in. Only the previous day they had lost Boyd, one of their only two midshipmen. There had been a rambling letter from his father about a fortunate placement in a ship-of-the-line but the real reason was obvious: society was unwilling for their sons and heirs to learn their officer-like qualities from someone of Kydd's reputation. And none had come forward to take Boyd's place; this was unfortunate for a midshipman counted as a petty officer and, among other things, could stand a watch in harbour under the mate-of-the-watch. It would not improve Prosser's attitude.

From his tiny cabin Renzi could not fail to overhear mess-deck conversations: at the moment the men were generally understanding of their captain's grief but he would quickly lose sympathy if he could not soon come to himself and give the ship and her company the attention they deserved.

Word was passed of the marines' imminent arrival, then Kydd appeared and stood motionless with a look of inward distraction. Renzi noted the resulting movement of officers and men: they were crossing the deck to keep their distance, not out of respect.

The boat's coxswain hooked on abreast the side-steps. Renzi moved unobtrusively to watch. After the sergeant and corporal had swung themselves inboard less than half seemed confident in their movements boarding a ship of war. However, the sight of so many identical red-coated uniforms was striking beside the individual dress of the seamen.

When the men had been drawn up to satisfaction by the corporal, the sergeant swung about and marched down the deck. He had strong, confident features with an easy cheerfulness. 'Sar'nt Ambrose, sah! Corporal Jay, sah! An' twelve privates come t' join,' he reported.

'An' not before time, Sergeant,' Kydd said. 'We're t' sea directly.'

'With only one midshipman?' murmured Renzi beside him. 'A mort hard on Mr Prosser, I believe.'

'Do him good, th' lazy villain!' Kydd flared. But he knew this was no minor quibble: the lack of a midshipman in the opposite watch was going to affect more than just the watch-keepers for in any kind of action they were effective in standing between officers and men.

He rounded on Renzi: 'So, if y'r polite society doesn't see *Teazer* a fit berth f'r their sons, why, I'm th' captain, an' it's m' right to set on the quarterdeck as midshipman any I please!' he retorted. He turned back with a sardonic smile. 'Send Able Seaman Calloway aft, if y' please.'

Teazer put to sea on the tide and stood out into the Channel. Seen from the rolling green hills of Devon, there was nothing to suggest that this was anything other than one of the many small men-o'-war going about their vital business in great waters. Her spars and rigging properly a-taunto, her pennant streaming out, sails trimmed to perfection, she was a picture of grace and warlike beauty – but on her quarterdeck, with the marks of grief and misery on his face, a figure stared astern over the widening seas at the receding coast.

Renzi watched Kydd unnoticed. It would be long months before England was sighted once more. Was there a chance that his friend could heal, away from the memories? He made his way below, guiltily aware that for himself the exile would not be wasted: he had heard enough of the Channel Islands, with their neither truly English nor certainly French character, to be looking forward keenly to his time there. An earnest guidebook was waiting on the bookshelf and opportunities in the future for exemplary ethnical comparisons would be limitless.

At daybreak they raised the south-west of Guernsey and, with the customary pilot aboard for entry into harbour, rounded the south-eastern tip. The island itself was only a few miles long, but a dismaying number of vicious rocks, reefs and islets were visible in the approaches to the harbour, scores of black fangs waiting on every hand.

St Peter Port was guarded by the brooding mass of Herm offshore, and closer to, a squat castle on a rocky islet before an inner harbour. Between, there was a broad expanse of clear water, sheltered from the prevailing westerlies. There, upwards of thirty ships were moored, including three warships riding to anchor.

'Ye'll be wantin' the two-decker, o' course,' the pilot said respectfully. '*Diomede*, an' flagship o' y'r admiral.' She was only a 50 but boasted a splendid gallery with a real, old-fashioned stern-walk. *Teazer*'s small swivel cracked in salute as six marines – all that could be found room for on the afterdeck – were drawn up and, with much stamping and slapping of muskets, brought proudly to attention.

'Away the gig.' Kydd, in full dress uniform, stepped gravely into the boat. Renzi watched it stroke smartly away for the flagship. The twittering of pipes carried over the water as Kydd mounted the side and was gone.

'I'll be below,' Standish announced, a bored look on his face. He clattered down the hatchway, leaving Renzi with the pilot, whose work would not be done until *Teazer* had anchored safely.

'This is Admiral Saumarez,' Renzi pondered aloud to the pilot.

'Aye, it is.'

'And something of a hero, I believe,' Renzi added. 'Was it not *Orion* at St Vincent and the Nile? And, of course, Algeciras . . .'

'A Guernseyman first an' always,' the pilot said stoutly.

'This is his *fleet*?' Renzi said, gesturing at the other two ships, both frigates of some maturity. Even the small flagship *Diomede* was of an obsolete and derided class, not big enough to fight in the line of battle or fast enough to stay with frigates.

'Well, an' there's another two frigates out on a cruise, like,' the pilot said defensively. 'Plenty an' enough for Sir James t' see away Johnny Frenchman, I'll believe.'

To Renzi it was unsettling: at a time when England stood in such peril why consign one of Nelson's band of brothers, a proven leader and experienced admiral, to be a full commander-in-chief of a tiny island or two and a handful of frigates?

He held his doubts, but that didn't stop the boatswain pressing the case: 'As it may be, cully, but it don't say why such a right copper-bottomed fightin' man as him tops it the admiral-in-chief here when a little one'll do, does it?'

The pilot drew himself up. 'No mystery, m' friend. He's a

Guern', as I said, an' he's come back t' stand by his people in their time o' need. Anything y' can see wrong wi' that?'

Kydd returned, his face set. 'Great Road, astern o' *Cerberus*,' he ordered Standish, who had come back on deck and was awaiting the order to moor. 'Mr Renzi, please t' attend on me,' he added, and disappeared below.

There was a marine on duty outside the captain's cabin. As a naval officer, Renzi had been accustomed to due obeisance but as a ship's clerk he was not to be noticed; Kydd, however, received the respect of a musket clash as they passed into *Teazer*'s great cabin.

Kydd emptied his dispatch case of papers. 'I'd be obliged if ye'd see t' these. Orders o' the station as will touch on *Teazer*'s standin' orders, forms o' the sort as y' will see bear on our new standing.'

'New standing?'

'Aye,' Kydd snarled. 'As second t' *Cerberus* 32. Attached t' her for victuals an' stores, f'r duties as her captain will fr'm time t' time direct.'

'Attached? This will—'

'It means no cruisin' on our own any more.'

Renzi frowned. Apart from the obvious loss of independence, the natural assumption of honours for the senior in any combat that might eventuate and the halving or less of any prize money, there would be little chance now for challenges and diversions to lift Kydd from the pit of despair. 'My commiserations, dear fellow. How shall you—'

Kydd's expression was hard. 'I shall do m' *duty*, as will you, an' every man aboard this barky. Those orders t' be transcribed directly, an' the purser t' lay aft now.' Kydd's eyes gleamed fiercely, his drawn features bleak and forbidding – almost callous in their estrangement from the world. Renzi felt deep disquiet.

The papers complete, Kydd left for *Cerberus* to make his number with her captain. He returned quickly, without comment, in time to receive the seven local men coming aboard who had volunteered. Unlike the general run of seamen in England they could be sure that service would be in their home waters, defending their own kith and kin.

At six bells Mr Queripel, a small but well-built man in nondescript old-fashioned dress, arrived aboard. His certificate showed him approved by the commander-in-chief to act locally as a form of on-board permanent pilot, insisted upon by Saumarez for all non-native naval vessels in his command. Renzi saw Dowse, their own sailing-master, take wary measure of him.

Standish turned to Kydd. 'Sir, might I ask—'

'When *Cerberus* puts t' sea, so does *Teazer*,' Kydd grated. 'Until then we remain in attendance at anchor. Is that clear?'

'Aye aye, sir,' Standish said sulkily.

That night there was no invitation for Renzi to dine with the captain; he supped with Standish and the others in what passed for a wardroom, the cramped space outside the cabins below.

'Tut, tut,' the master said, after the meal had advanced sufficiently for tongues to be loosened. 'Where are our spirits? Why are we cast down? Th' chances are we'll soon have our heart torn out on some Godforsaken rock and out o' this 'un quick enough.'

'Mr Dowse! F'r shame!' said the boatswain, Purchet. 'Could be th' Frogs are out an' then—'

'And then they fall on these pawky islands?' Standish

sneered, from the head of the table. 'I don't think so, Mr Hellfire Bosun. No, if they've got a handful of hours to crowd across the Channel, they'll not waste time here.' He tossed back his wine.

'Then why's his grandevity Sir James o' Algeciras sent here?' Dowse asked. 'Must be f'r a very good reason.'

'*Ha!*' Standish came back instantly. 'You really can't smoke it? He's here for just the same reason as we are.' He glanced quickly at Renzi, who had taken no part in the discussion, then went on, 'In course, he's run afoul of some higher and sent here to keep the natives quiet!' He went on strongly, 'Stands to reason, dammit – commander-in-chief of an island four miles thick and not a ship-o'-the-line in his command? What other reason than he's been exiled too?' he said bitterly.

'What's *your* opinion, if y' please, Mr Renzi?' Dowse asked politely.

By now, in this company, Renzi had been accepted for what he was – an enigma, but no threat. He had kept to himself, scrupulously careful never to take anyone's part, his relationship with Kydd seen as that of an eccentric and needy scholiast taking advantage of the free board and lodging due a ship's clerk. A quiet and amiable manner, however, had ensured him the warmth of these men. 'Why, I've seen nothing so far that might lead us to suppose there has been some form of alienation, but this presents a mystery. I fear that without facts I'm as much at a loss as you are.'

Standish snorted. 'If you insist on making it a mystery, sir, I do not.' He banged down his glass. 'Rather more to the point is our predicament.'

'Our which?' said Renzi, mildly. Over time they had come to see that he did not carry tales to Kydd and were increasingly open in his presence. With his ear to mess-deck gossip and to the confidences of the commander, he was in a unique position – which might well end in an impossible situation if he did not tread circumspectly.

'You do not call this a predicament that we're to spend the rest o' the war flogging up and down this coast while all the victories are won elsewhere? I have my hopes of a sea career, gentlemen, as won't be found here. Remember, out of sight, out of mind. We'll not be noticed in *this* pawky scow.' He took a savage pull at his wine. 'And,' he paused for breath, 'I asked to be appointed into *Teazer* because I'd heard Tom Cutlass was to be her owner and we'd ride to glory together in some famous mauling. In just six months he's thrown the lot away! In with the admiral's daughter and set fair to be made post into a frigate for his trouble, me as his premier, and he takes up with some country milkmaid!'

The table remained silent. 'And the worst is, the looby lost the wench and has clearly taken leave of his wits, been touched in the headpiece. God knows what he'll do next – do you?' he threw at Renzi.

Renzi cleared his throat. 'The man is to be pitied at this moment, I believe. He confided to me something of his feelings for the young lady and his present state is perfectly understandable, given—'

'So we must all suffer while he comes to his senses.'

Dowse stirred uncomfortably. 'Er-hum. Them's strong words, sir,' he said quietly. 'Th' man only needs time.'

'Which we ain't got!' Purchet came in unexpectedly. 'I don't mind sayin' it before yez all but I'm afeared. He's comin' down hard f'r no reason an' unsettlin' the hands, then forgets things as are needful. If he is, um, not as who should say, square in his reason, then God help us if ever we come up wi' a Frenchy.'

*　　*　　*

A day later a lieutenant from *Cerberus* brought orders for sea: a neutral had sighted two French corvettes heading west. To the open Atlantic – or Brest? Either way, Saumarez wanted this immediately investigated by *Cerberus* to the south and another frigate to the north, to sail without delay.

Throughout *Teazer* there was a quickening of pace, a lightening of spirit. A corvette would be easy prey for a frigate but the other must be theirs. It would be a rare match and hard fought – unless *Cerberus*'s bird tamely gave in the fight early and *Cerberus* turned to claim both.

There was point now to the mindless cleaning and blacking of guns, the make-work tasks of a ship in harbour. Kydd could be seen everywhere about the decks, and when *Cerberus*'s signal to unmoor was bent on, *Teazer* was ready. The hoist went close up, and at the midships capstan men placed themselves at the bars, seamen and marines both.

'Stir those mumpin' dawdlers!' Kydd bawled down the deck to Standish. 'If we're still hook down when *Cerberus* weighs, I'll – I'll make 'em rue it!'

To the reedy sound of a fife and the stolid thump of a drum they set to the task with renewed determination. Well before the frigate won her anchor, *Teazer*'s was clear of the seabed and coming in rapidly. Renzi, on the quarterdeck at the ready with his notebook, pursed his lips. They must now throw sails aback to keep from running down the still-tethered frigate; on the more senior ship, would this be seen as a brazen attempt to do them down?

Eventually the Union Flag at the jack of *Cerberus* whipped down to indicate her anchor was aweigh and, with a flurry of flapping and banging, *Teazer* set her sails loose to the wind and settled to follow in her wake.

'Two cables astern, until th' open sea,' Kydd told Standish.

The low coast slipped past but more of the appalling rocks showed until it seemed they were surrounded by them. For the moment they would be in no danger, in the wake of the experienced bigger ship.

Queripel came forward and stood next to Kydd. 'It's not th' rocks ye should be most concerned of,' he began, 'y' can see 'em. It's the tide set an' currents round 'em that c'n vex even th' most experienced. When th' tide state is—'

'Stand down, Mr Queripel,' Kydd said. 'Ye're not required.'

The man's eyebrows rose but he said nothing and retired to the wheel. Renzi knew better than to interpose and concentrated on the low sea coast to larboard and the endless dark crags and fissures that protruded from the water on all sides.

Clear of the Brayes the vessels stood on out to sea northward, taking advantage of the steady west-north-westerly. Standish made much of trimming sail, demanding a foot of fore-tack here, checking out a main-topsail sheet by two feet there, until *Teazer*'s bowsprit rose and fell dead in line with *Cerberus*'s stern and at the required distance.

Kydd did not interfere, and when the activity had died away he left the deck, to Standish's clear relief. However, he returned almost immediately, carrying his octant. He paced deliberately to the foredeck, braced, and sighted with the instrument, bringing the main topmast truck of *Cerberus* to the waterline. Then he strode aft and confronted Standish. 'Our orders are t' take station two cables clear, as well y' know, sir. What's this, that you believe it t' mean a full twenty yards closer?'

The lieutenant remained silent.

'I'll not have *Cerberus* think us laggardly in our duty. I'll trouble ye to fetch y'r instrument. T' save you the figuring it'll be six degrees an' forty-four minutes ye'll set.' He stared

Standish down, and an abashed midshipman was sent below for Standish's sextant, which, like many officers, he preferred to the more old-fashioned octant.

Kydd waited until Standish was on the foredeck sighting, then stumped off. As soon as he had gone Standish abandoned the task and returned aft, his face murderous. 'Get for 'ard with this, you,' he demanded of Prosser, shoving the sextant at him. 'The sooner I'm quit o' this madness I swear, the better.'

Mid-afternoon the signal to tack was thrown out from *Cerberus*, with the amplification that the two would advance in line-abreast by the same distance. Kydd had been expecting this, and from noon had both watches on deck and lines ranged along ready for the manoeuvre. The hoist jerked down – the execute. In frenzied excitement *Teazer* hauled and braced, spinning about handily under her brig rig full minutes before the frigate, surging ahead in a fluster of foam but quickly finding need to brail her courses and idle until *Cerberus* had steadied on her new track.

The waning sun brought with it brisker winds: oceanic westerlies that had a fetch of thousands of miles and a steady pressure that drove unwary sailors staggering across the deck. It was exhilarating sailing – men came from below to watch *Teazer* take the combers on her bow in a crunch of seas, a dizzying swoop and lift, while out there on their beam to windward was the thrilling picture of a thoroughbred frigate snoring along in a smother of white, close-hauled under a full press of sail.

Purchet came aft and touched his hat, leaning forward to make himself heard. 'She's like t' wring her topmasts, sir,' he said respectfully. Aloft, every sail was as taut as a board, thrumming with nervous tension and with edges in a mad flutter. The boatswain crossed to a sheet and thumped it with a closed fist. It was as unyielding as an iron bar. He looked back significantly.

Kydd did not speak at first; his gaze went to the topsails, which shivered on the point of going aback where the apprehensive helmsman was luffing up, spilling wind to avert disaster. 'Single reef in th' courses,' he allowed grudgingly.

Out on their beam the frigate was making splendid sailing, her wake racing past and with only the occasional graceful nod and sway in answer to the lively conditions. *Teazer*, however, was now taking the seas heavily forward, the straining impulse of her sails sending her into steep oncoming waves with an explosion of white sea and then the shock of a sudden slowing. Courses were double-reefed and topsails to a precautionary single.

'Signal, sir,' reported a midshipman. *Cerberus* was visibly pulling ahead. 'Our pennant, keep better station!' The flags streamed out high and clear. It was, no doubt, something of a sweet revenge for the frigate captain, for as *Teazer* struggled to keep up *Cerberus* increased her lead, all the while keeping the signal flying.

It was not until dusk, and *Teazer* floundering miles astern, that the frigate relented and, with a fine show, brought to until the little sloop could come up.

It had been a fruitless chase, the French long gone and nothing to show.

When they had cast anchor again in St Peter Port, Kydd had been summoned by Captain Selby to *Cerberus*; what had been said Renzi did not know, but Kydd had retired immediately to his cabin, ejecting him. As he left, Renzi caught sight of Kydd slumping in his chair, staring unseeingly out of the stern windows.

Allowing an hour to pass he had returned under some pretence of letters to be signed at the same time as Tysoe, Kydd's servant, had under his advice brought in wine and left quickly. Kydd said nothing but accepted a glass.

'A drollery to reflect that Guernsey is undoubtedly the chief supplier to our smuggling fraternity in Cornwall, and here we are to consider them our charges to protect,' Renzi said lightly.

Kydd stared into his wine.

'And such a singular part of the realm, I've read. The guide-book tells that they still converse in a species of ancient Norman French, which your Parisian would find it a sore puzzle to understand.' He inspected his wine. 'A visit ashore should prove most diverting . . .'

'Go, then.'

'I had rather hoped for your company in such an interesting place, as we may talk about at a later time.'

'Understand that I only have th' one interest – *to do my duty, an' no other!*'

Renzi tried once more. 'It might prove restorative to the spirit to accept something of the kindness and hospitality that is undoubtedly on offer to the heroes who defend these shores. To taste something of the delicacies peculiar to these climes – it seems the *gâche* alone will reward the asking.'

'I'm stayin' aboard.' Kydd's voice was flat and spiritless.

Standish returned bubbling with tales of St Peter Port and its social attractions; it seemed that, as a colourful landfall, it was fulfilling every expectation.

Renzi was sorely tempted: what he had read so far in the guidebook had been explicit about the remarkable differences in social attributes to be experienced on the island, neither a colony nor a contiguous moiety of either England or France. They were stationed here, true, but for how long? Better to snatch a glimpse now.

It was not hard to conceive of an excuse that must take him ashore, two papers needed the signature of the civil authority, and soon he was in *Teazer*'s boat heading for St Peter Port, the town above the enfolding arms of a north and south pier set about a tidal harbour.

The shore rose steeply behind, buildings crowding along irregular streets, and directly at the fore, a long and busy waterfront lined with tall warehouses that took in goods directly from the ships alongside. The port was remarkably busy, the flags of a dozen nations visible from the many ships now settling on the mud. This was no maritime backwater.

He was left at North Pier and, remembering the directions he had been given, pushed past the noisy porters and wharfingers and squeezed up the narrow passages between the buildings to emerge on the main street.

He looked about. Here was a quality of building that would not disgrace Bath or Weymouth. The shops of a perfumier, a stay-maker and an importer of carpets from London, all evidence of a level of society on the tiny island that was no stranger to wealth, a diverting ethnographical study. Was it purely economics at the root of their success or was it true there were other aspects to their culture?

High Street was choked with people, carts and carriages in rowdy contention. He found his way to Smith Street, a steep road that led him up to quite another purlieu: imposing new buildings that looked out above the hurly-burly of the town to the sweeping prospect of the harbour, castle islet and distant islands.

He found the government offices easily enough and it took minutes only to complete his duty, but as he wandered back down to High Street and its lively crowds he felt reluctant to return to *Teazer* straight away. He decided to walk the length of the thoroughfare, revelling in the riotous sounds and smells after so long in the small ship with its bleak atmosphere. At the end was a church and, beyond, a rookery of decaying medieval houses crowded on the steep slopes above boatyards on the strand.

He turned to go back; but on noticing a raised level with the crush and animation of a market, he was drawn irresistibly to the cheerful din. At the far end was a noble arch, and to the right a stone building with, in the upper storey, the unmistakable lofty windows of an assembly hall.

Renzi crossed to admire it; on the end wall there were posters, theatre notices and, to one side, a beautifully handwritten one. He bent to read: 'The Cists and Dolmens of Ancient Sarnia newly considered. A public lecture to be given at the Royal College of Elizabeth . . . Revd Dr Carey, MA Oxon etc., etc. . . .'

Dolmens! Of course! Were these in any way related to the cromlechs of Brittany? What manner of mysterious peoples had created those great stone monoliths? Had their civilisation wilted and crumbled from the immense effort – or had they failed to meet some overwhelming economic challenge and subsequently disappeared from the face of the earth?

His excitement mounted. What fortune to have come ashore the very day it was to be delivered. A wave of guilt rushed in: he had vowed to stand by Kydd in his grief and travail. But at this particular time he was not so immediately needed, and this lecture, given by a passing savant, would not be repeated.

He would go! He had plenty of time to discover the where-abouts of the Royal College as the event would take place this evening so until then he could wander the narrow streets agreeably and possibly the rocky shore. His means did not extend to a meal but there were sights enough for an enquiring mind. Feeling like an errant schoolboy, he set out.

With evening drawing in Renzi topped the rise above the town, footsore and hungry, looking for the ancient college. The town was giving way to country; on the left-hand side, for some distance, he saw a series of newer, more handsome houses, and on the right, open fields and a dilapidated struc-ture of uncertain antiquity.

Where were the college and the people flocking to the lecture? He stopped a passing tradesman. 'Elizabeth College? Ye're looking at it!' he was told.

It was an academy of sorts, much decayed but still in possession of extensive grounds and with only one glimmer of light showing. Renzi entered hesitantly.

'Welcome, welcome! Do come in, sir!' The broad room was musty with age and gloomy with dark panelling. There were but six sitting among the rows of school chairs facing the lectern from which a diminutive cleric beamed at him.

He settled in the second row. Chairs scraped and coughs tailed off in the silence until it became evident that no more would arrive. The man picked up his papers and introduced himself; the talk was pleasantly delivered and competent, the material stimulating. At the conclusion Renzi applauded enthusiastically but he subsided at the thin handclaps from the rest of the stolid audience.

Renzi offered a question or two, which were gratefully received, then the meeting concluded, most quickly making for the door – all but one gentleman. 'A good evening to you, sir,' he said, 'and I do not believe I have seen you before.'

'Mr Renzi, er, of the Navy. Just visiting.'

'Then I should thank you for supporting the reverend doctor with your presence. Are you by any chance an old scholar of the college?'

'No, sir.' So the lecture had been a noble attempt by the dominie to attract the public, the gentleman speaking with him an old boy loyally present. Judging by the painfully chalked Latin epigrams still on the board, Renzi surmised that the lecture would not seem to be typical of the kind of instruction normally carried on.

'Then . . . ?' the man asked politely.

'I have a penchant for the outworkings of human culture of any age, sir.'

'An unusual inclination for a sea officer, if I might remark it.' The man's bearing was aristocratic, his eyes shrewd.

'I – I am not a naval officer, sir. My situation is fortunate, being that of a man of some learning afforded the felicity of board and lodging, while I undertake my investigations, for the trifling price of acting as ship's clerk.'

'How curious!' The man hesitated, then held out his hand. 'My name is Vauvert, and it is my pleasure to make your acquaintance, Mr . . . ?'

'Renzi.'

'My carriage is at present in use, else I should offer to transport you back to your ship, but my house is near and no doubt you will appreciate refreshment before you return.'

Vauvert's house was one of the large, handsome buildings on the other side of the road. 'I'm by way of being an *écuyer*, that is to say a *négociant*, a merchant investor, and my name is not unknown in these islands.'

Renzi took in the fashionable adornments of the drawing room. 'Mr Vauvert, it would gratify me considerably to know how it is that a distant island, barely five miles across, can display such wealth and success, when others . . .'

'The reason is simple. We are left to our own devices, Mr Renzi. Parliament in London plays no part in our affairs and our loyalty is not to the English King but to the Duke of Normandy.'

'I'm astonished to hear it,' Renzi murmured uneasily.

'This is so,' Vauvert said firmly. 'Our islands were anciently in the fiefdom of Normandy and we see no reason to shift our allegiance to the Crown of England.'

Renzi held still. In the face of the revolutionary madness sweeping Europe, savage laws had been forced through by the prime minister William Pitt with swift and dire penalties for illegal and treasonable association. If—

'Therefore our loyal toast will always remain to the Duke of Normandy – who, since his subsequent conquest of England in 1066, now occupies the throne in the person of His Majesty King George.'

At Renzi's expression he continued smoothly, 'Which confers considerable benefits, chief of which is an independence in matters of trade and law – for instance, we are outside the remit of English Customs and Excise . . .'

'I have heard the term "smuggling" used in that connection,' Renzi said delicately. *Teazer*'s days of guarding the Cornish coast were still fresh in his memory.

'Never in these islands!' Vauvert said stoutly. 'We are the suppliers of goods only. If our clients choose to evade payment of duty on subsequent import then this cannot be our concern. It has served us well over the centuries, in truth.'

'And privateering, I've been led to believe.'

40

'*And* privateering. It must be confessed that many fine houses along Grange Road here were raised on the profits therefrom. But, pray, do not be deceived. It is our trading that has made us what we are. That and our independence. You will want to hear of our Bailiff and Constable who in this land hold powers higher than a prime minister, our jurats, States and Royal Courts – but I fear you will not wish to be delayed.'

Renzi gave a polite bow and murmured a farewell.

'It is however an unlettered place,' Vauvert added. 'I would very much like to hear of the progress of your studies here, Mr Renzi, perhaps at a later date . . .'

Chapter 3

As Renzi entered the captain's cabin, Kydd threw him a dark look. 'Th' ship in th' state y' see her, and y' step ashore on the ran-tan like some jackanapes wi' not a care in th' world? I'm surprised at ye, Nicholas!'

'It was ship's business,' Renzi replied, 'and there being no boat going inshore after dark, as you'll recall.' He had spent a cold night on the foreshore, waiting for *Teazer*'s milk-boat at dawn, and did not need a lecture.

'There's some who'd say as ye're guilty of being absent fr'm place o' duty,' Kydd said hotly. 'How c'n I keep discipline if'n you're straggling ashore as it pleases ye?'

Renzi paused. 'I feel you're not yourself, my friend. Perhaps you should—'

'Don't y' understand me?' Kydd said harshly. 'You're ship's clerk an' have a duty t' the ship. Y' know, I c'n have ye in irons f'r breaking out o' the ship – desertion!'

Angry now, Renzi took a moment to control himself. 'My dear fellow, your words cannot help but strike me as somewhat intemperate, not to say provocative, and hardly justified. You've been under strain lately, I know, and—'

'Ye're not t' go ashore again without I say so.'

'As you wish,' Renzi said. 'Yet I'll have you know that I understand and have much sympathy for you in your loss . . .'

'F' give me f'r sayin' it,' Kydd said sarcastically, 'but I don't see how y' can. Until y' cares enough f'r someone, loves 'em as I do – did . . .' he said thickly. He faced away suddenly, then turned back with a wooden expression. 'But, then, it's of no account to you, o' course.'

Renzi felt his control slipping. 'Confound it, man – do you think you're the only one who's loved and lost? Death is part of life, and others find ways to deal with it.' He was breathing deeply. 'You're not the same man I knew, Tom. It's knocked you askew, touched your human judgement – where's your spirit? You've changed – and not for the better.'

Kydd did not respond and stared down at his hands. Then he said, 'You're in th' right of it. I'm changed.' With a heavy sigh he went on, 'I'm now empty – quite empty, y' see, an' there's only duty now in m' life.'

Renzi bit his lip. 'This won't do, Tom. You must come up with a round turn – see yourself, what you're becoming. Do I need to lay it out before you? Be a *man*, for God's sake!'

Kydd stiffened. 'An' you're th' one t' tell *me*? If *you* were a man you'd not have run off fr'm Cecilia to New South Wales.'

With a deadly ferocity, Renzi swept Kydd's papers off his desk. He leaned down, inches from his face. 'How *dare* you?'

Kydd did not flinch, staring back with equal intensity, and said slowly, 'Pick up th' papers – or leave my ship now!'

Renzi bit off what he was about to say and made to walk

44

away, then turned back abruptly to face Kydd again. 'I will *not* leave the ship. You don't realise it but, at this moment, there is not a soul whom you may call friend. And I solemnly warn you, as surely as the sun will set this day, very soon you will most certainly need one.'

'Do try the buttered crab, Mr Kydd,' Lady Saumarez pressed. 'You really should – Guernsey is not to be outshone in the article of fruits of the sea.'

'Yes, yes, my dear,' the admiral murmured. He turned to Kydd and chuckled. 'She's local-born, as was I, and will not rest until you are as a fatted calf on the good produce of our island.'

Kydd sat quietly, toying with his food.

'Now, I always like to invite my new captains to a little dinner *en famille* like this – less formal and allows us to talk freely, learn about each other, as it were.'

'Aye, sir,' Kydd said respectfully.

'Tell me, your service history is sparse in its detail – you were at the Nile, were you not?'

'Sir. Fifth of *Tenacious*.'

'Come, come, sir! You are much too coy. I happen to know that you were out in the boats when *L'Orient* blew up. That must have been such a fearful sight close to. Did you suffer much on your own account?'

'No, sir. I had th' boat's crew under coats an' sails. Th' big wreckage went over th' top of us.'

Saumarez waited but Kydd did not elaborate. 'And this is how you won your step to commander?'

'No, sir. That was later, just before th' peace.' He resumed his meal.

Saumarez threw an amused look of resignation at his wife,

who simpered encouragement at Kydd. 'Who placed you on your own quarterdeck?'

'It was Adm'ral Keith, sir.'

'For a fine action, no doubt.'

'Off Toulon, Captain Rowley desired I be removed fr'm his ship, sir, an' so Adm'ral Keith sent me t' Malta to commission a new brig jus' built.'

Saumarez sat back in amazement. 'Well – 'pon my soul! For an officer of record you are a quiet one. Have you any family?'

'No, sir.'

'Ah, well, then, perhaps you should. There is nothing on this earth to compare with the love of a good woman to set the cares of the world to naught.' His warm look at his wife was returned with an affection that was as tender as it was private. He turned back to Kydd. 'May we know if you have any hopes at all – in the connubial sense, I mean?'

Kydd sat rigid and unspeaking.

Saumarez went on, 'Sea officers, I fear, are so much at a disadvantage when it comes to affairs of the heart. I remember once when . . .' Then his words trailed off and astonishment was replaced by dismay as tears coursed down Kydd's face. Lady Saumarez stared open-mouthed.

Saumarez jumped up, stupefied by the sight but caught himself quickly. 'Er, my dear, Commander Kydd is, um – and will be retiring with me to the red drawing room – for brandy, that is.'

He hurried round the table, helped Kydd to his feet and led him into a large room with a cheerful fire. 'Now, what is this, sir?' Saumarez asked, in a kindly tone.

'I – I can only apologise f'r m' conduct, s-sir,' Kydd choked. 'Y'see, I've – I've just this month lost m' intended t' drowning—'

He fought down the tears and added stiffly, 'If you desire, sir, I shall leave y' house immediately, o' course.'

'Good heavens, no. I had no idea – here, you shall have a good brandy directly.' He hurried to the decanter. 'It's one of the faults of our modern society that a man cannot in any wight allow his feelings to display. Do sit, sir – my wife will fully understand when I tell her of your sad loss.'

'Sir.'

'It will, of course, be a grievous ordeal for you, but remember that for those who trust in the Lord's goodness it will be seen that there is a reason, however hard it is to apprehend at this time.' He drew his chair closer and confided, 'You will perhaps not at this point easily entertain the notion, but it has been said that my nature is one that in its sensitivity might more readily be seen in a man of the cloth. I can assure you that any distress in my fellow creature I do feel for myself.' He touched Kydd's arm lightly. 'Therefore I trust you will not take it amiss when I offer my advice. It is that you do seek the humanity and warmth of your fellow man in the healing – the well-springs of charity are deep, and within us all.'

Kydd's expression did not change.

'I'm only too aware that for the captain of a ship this might prove . . . difficult, but there is a means to this end. I'm referring in this to the Mermaid's Club, which is a retreat for naval officers in St Peter Port. There you may find solace with your brothers of the sea.'

At Kydd's silence his forehead creased in concern. 'In fact, you may take it as a species of command, sir. I shall have a word in the right place as will see you introduced. Dwelling on your hurts in the privacy of your cabin is not to be countenanced. Now, I will be bending my mind to the task of finding ways to keep you and your command as active as I can contrive. Never doubt it, Mr Kydd, all things will pass in God's good time.'

The room was broad but low, and dominated at the far end by windows that extended the entire width to provide a fine prospect of the busy harbour below. 'Ho there, the stranger!' a voice called from the group at ease round a mahogany table towards the back.

Kydd handed his cloak to a steward, stepped forward and bowed. 'Kydd, brig-sloop *Teazer.*' A few in armchairs nearby looked up curiously from their newspapers, then nodded politely.

Kydd was the only one in uniform; the others wore shore clothes. He approached the group. 'Gentlemen.'

'Come to join, I take it,' a large man, older than Kydd, said. 'Aye.'

'Umm. Of good standing, polite to your betters, not afraid of the bottle? Any habits, vices we should know about?' His eyes were shrewd.

'No.'

'A pity. We can do with men o' spirit. Right. Ten livres a month – that's less'n a guinea – feast-days extra, commensal brandy extra. Are you game?'

'Aye.'

'Then you're in. I'm Carthew of *Scorpion* ship-sloop, and chairman o' the Mermaid. This is O'Brien out of *Harpy* brig and the rest you'll get to know soon enough.'

He sat back in his chair and contemplated Kydd. 'Sit your-self down, then, Kydd. O'Brien, get the young man a rummer. Now, sir, we'll know more of you. What did you do to be banished to this benighted corner o' the world?'

'I was detached fr'm the Plymouth command o' Admiral Lockwood, agreeable to an Admiralty request—'

'Ding dong bell, man, and what's that meant to say? That you—'

'I received m' orders an' I did my duty, Mr Carthew,' Kydd rapped.

Faces turned elsewhere in the room and the talking died away for a space. 'Well, well! Do I see a discontented fire-eater before me? If so, you have my condolences, my dear sir. You'll have to work hard to chase up some sport here.'

O'Brien murmured something indistinct and Carthew laughed cynically. 'Then my best advice to him is to get used to it – the only way he's getting out of here now is to contrive to be wrecked or become the admiral's élève when there's to be a promotion!' He continued to appraise Kydd coolly. 'Is it right that you were at the Nile?'

'I was.'

'I see. And Saumarez here second-in-command under Our Nel. Fortunate for you, not to say useful,' he said smoothly.

'I was fifth in *Tenacious*, signal luff, an' never clapped eyes on him but the once, if that's y'r meaning.'

'Do ease sheets, Mr Fire-eater,' Carthew said evenly. 'This is a small command and we all have to live with each other.'

As the hard night softened with the first intimations of dawn, Kydd readied his boats' crews. It was a hastily planned operation with all the potential to go wrong. During the night they had been towed within striking distance by *Teazer*. He was in the first boat, about to lead the shore party, which included others who had been sent in reinforcement from the squadron.

An oar clunked awkwardly as the men took up position

49

for the coming assault. 'Hold y' noise, oaf,' Kydd hissed savagely, 'or I swear I'll see y' liver at the gangway tomorrow!' The man stared at him resentfully.

All hinged on surprise – getting the men ashore and to the top of the two-hundred-foot cliffs before troops, roused by sentries, could arrive from further up and down the coast. Once on the heights there was level ground into the interior countryside, and if they could establish a well-defended position reinforcements could flood ashore.

The coast materialised ahead from the dove-grey mists, high, craggy and forbidding. There might be pickets even now concerned by the odd cluster of shapes out to sea, finding a telescope and . . . Kydd scanned the area feverishly, looking for the features he must locate in order to land in the right place: an offshore scatter of rocks that guarded a small coomb, not much more than a fissure but which would give them a chance to reach the top. There! At the right distance from the unmistakable high headland to the south-west he saw the betraying white of sea-washed rocks extending out in a distinctive pattern, Les Lieuses, Sept Boues and the rest.

'Stretch out!' Kydd roared. 'Stretch out f'r y'lives!' The need for caution was past – now everything depended on speed. Oars thumped and strained as men leaned into the the task. Astern, the other boats surged and flew to bellows and threats from their coxswains.

At the periphery of his vision Kydd saw movement at the high cliff-edge. It was a figure on horseback! The alarm would now be given speedily – their margin of time was perilously small. The figure fell back and disappeared.

They reached the first rocks. The assumption was that those defending would believe these lofty crags would prevent any seaward onslaught – this would certainly be true for a ship-of-war under sail but well-handled boats could thread their way through and make a landing.

As they approached, the cliffs towered impossibly high above them but their information had been correct: a fold in the cliff-face lay away at an angle; bare rock, scrubby bushes and the occasional scree slope – but a way up!

And praise be! Queripel had the tides precisely calculated in these parts. The rocky plateau at the base was all but submerged, allowing the boats to ground close in. Kydd clambered over the side, all pretensions to dignity abandoned, and splashed into the shallows. 'Move y'selves!' he bellowed.

Men started to gather on the rocky strand, many staring up anxiously at the precipitous heights. 'Light along th' tackles – get going, then!' Kydd barked irritably. This was his trump card: numbers of nimble-footed topmen would work in relays, advancing upward to secure a block and tackle, which would then be used to sway up swivel guns and their improvised mounts in stages. Only a light weapon at sea, on land in these wild parts they would be the only artillery in the field, and would give pause to even the finest infantry arrayed against them.

'Now!' Kydd gestured to Ambrose, and the marines began to climb up the slope, disappearing quickly into the scrubby undergrowth in clouds of reddish dust. At the top they would throw up a defensive perimeter for the rest. The stolid sergeant had grasped immediately what had to be done.

It seemed to be going well – too well? Nearly two hundred men were massing at the foot of the cliff, each encumbered with a musket slung over his back and others with ungainly packs of ammunition. As more landed, they were getting increasingly in each other's way.

Kydd drew his sword hastily. 'Forward!' he yelled, and led them upwards in a rush. So much had to go right! There were those who were detailed to haul on the tackles, unarmed topmen swarming up to secure the blocks, more still to fleet the blocks once close up, others to keep together for gun-crew when on the level . . .

At any moment lines of soldiers might appear along the edge of the cliff – and it would be all over very quickly. Panting with effort, Kydd yanked on bushes to heave himself up the craggy heights, muscles burning and his world contracting to the untidy slither of dust and rubble that was their path.

Out of sight above them the marines must have reached the top – would they be met with naked bayonets or . . . ? But there had been no sudden shouts so they were still in with a chance.

When he drew near to the top Ambrose scrambled over to him. Breathless, Kydd heard that the perimeter was secure with outlying sentries concealed and the defenders not yet in sight. Keeping his head down, the marine pointed out the salient features: a far-distant cluster of buildings, probably a farm, and further still the tip of a steeple. For the rest it was open fields and curious cows in a gently rolling rural tranquillity.

'We post th' guns here – an' over there,' Kydd gasped.

'Sah.' Ambrose pointed suddenly. Following the outstretched arm Kydd saw mass movement at the edge of a small wood a mile or so away. Without a telescope he could only squint. Then, as the activity extended to each side, there could be no mistake. Troops were deploying.

'Get those guns up here at th' rush!' he bawled, and heaved on a line himself. The swivels with their clumsy frame mountings were manhandled up and hurried into position. Men fanned out to either side. It was sobering how few two hundred looked when occupying a battlefield.

But they were in time. Dusty and weary, chests heaving with exertion, they stood ready.

Trumpets could be heard faintly as the soldiers opposite formed a line and, to the thin rattle of drums, advanced on them. 'Give 'em a swivel,' Kydd ordered. They were not within range but it would show them what they'd be up against.

At the spiteful *crack* there was wavering in the ranks, and screamed orders carried across to them. The lines came to a stop and a white flag rose. It was brought forward by an officer. Kydd grinned savagely: the day was theirs – and so easily.

The man trudged over, red and angry. 'Damn it, sir, no one told us o' artillery in the field. Rather unsportin', I would have thought. Where the devil did they come from?'

'Show him, Sergeant,' Kydd grunted, and watched while the officer was escorted to the cliff-edge and peered down.

When he returned he mopped his forehead. 'Well, sir, an' I declare m'self well and truly at a stand.' It had been a hard march for the soldiers from the redoubts to the west but they had been too late.

'I give ye victory, sir,' the officer said in admiration. 'Those ship guns were a master-stroke.' He advanced to shake Kydd's hand. 'Major Jevons, o' the Guernsey Militia. Might I hope t' see you at Fort George one day, sir?'

It had started as a difference of opinion between Lieutenant Governor, General Sir John Doyle, and Rear Admiral Saumarez as to the adequacy of the military defences in the south of the island. Kydd had taken up Saumarez's conjecture that they were not impregnable and now there was proof positive for all to see.

HMS *Teazer* had closed with the land the better to view proceedings and had the singular distinction of flying the colours of Rear Admiral Saumarez with the standard of the Lieutenant Governor.

In a little over an hour Kydd was back aboard. 'Well done, sir!' Saumarez said genially, when introductions had been made on the quarterdeck to Doyle. 'Showed 'em what the Navy can do, by Jove.' He looked benignly upon Kydd. 'And what an active and enterprising officer might be trusted to achieve.'

Chapter 4

The chamber of the House of Lords was in an uproar. Baron Grenville, a former foreign secretary, was on his feet and in full cry: 'In fact I'm led to believe that this government has no idea – *no idea* – of the dire threat the kingdom now faces! Allow me, my noble lords, to attempt to arouse some measure of urgency in this supine Tory ministry.'

Seated on the Woolsack before the empty throne, the lord chancellor frowned but made no move to intervene.

Grenville waited for the noise to lessen then pronounced, 'I can now say for a certainty that Bonaparte no longer menaces Great Britain with invasion.' Having the august chamber's full attention, he went on, 'This is just so: the threats have now been withdrawn!' There was puzzled murmuring. Then he continued, with quiet venom, 'My noble lords, the empty threats have gone, and in their place is the awful reality. From Dunkirk in the east to Granville in the west, in every French harbour and port opposite us, there are now being built hundreds – nay, thousands – of invasion craft whose only purpose is to throw one hundred and fifty thousand men on the English shore.'

Lord Hobart fidgeted in his seat. As secretary of state for war in a beleaguered administration, his would be the task of replying to the unanswerable.

'This realm, at great cost to its treasure, has created and maintains a navy whose chief purpose is the safeguarding of our islands. We have a right to see it arrayed in all its might along our coasts, resolutely facing the enemy, as it has done so gloriously from long before.' Grenville gestured at the wall panels, each of which depicted a scene of some heroic sea battle from England's long past.

He paused, then asked, 'But where is it now? Apart from Lord Keith in the Downs it always seems to be away on some distant errand – dissipating its strength on some foreign adventure. It should be *here*, standing four-square before Bonaparte's hordes.'

Turning sharply, he looked straight at Hobart. 'I beg this House do remain attentive while the noble lord does enlighten us as to why we should not be *terrified* at this moment!'

Rising slowly, Hobart tried to marshal his thoughts. 'My lords, er, there is—'

There was a stir at the door and the lord chancellor got to his feet. 'The Earl St Vincent,' he intoned.

A buzz of interest broke out. The bluff man in the splendid robes of a peer of the realm was Jervis. Honoured by his sovereign, he was a sea hero whose service dated back to before Nelson was born. It had been he who, in the year of the Great Mutiny, had led the fleet against the combined might of the French and Spanish to spectacular success. He now stood at the pinnacle of his sea profession as First Lord of the Admiralty and strategic head of the Navy, feared and respected.

His wintry eyes took in the excited peers as he paced slowly to the centre of the chamber. 'My noble lords!' he said, in a voice that had in past days carried through winter gales. 'I do not deny that we are faced with a determined and dangerous foe who is undoubtedly resolved on the conquest of Great Britain. You are right to be concerned, to question the power of the Royal Navy to withstand the tyrant.'

He paused. 'It is not in me to find you agreeable words of comfort – that is not my way. You ask me to assure you that Bonaparte will not prevail. That cannot be in my power to guarantee to you.' In the utter silence Earl St Vincent added grimly, 'This only am I sure upon: I do not say, my lords, that the French will not come. I say only they will not come by sea.'

'Sir, *Teazer*'s number at the signal tower,' Standish said, to the motionless figure on the quarterdeck. A ship's pennants hung out meant a summons for her captain to attend immediately upon the commander-in-chief. Standish tried to hide his curiosity.

'Aye,' Kydd acknowledged dully. 'Th' gig t' be alongside in fifteen minutes.'

'Thank you, Flags. I'll ring when you're needed.' Saumarez turned to Kydd. 'Do sit, sir,' he said formally. He picked up a paper from his desk and regarded Kydd gravely. 'There are two matters that I wish to discuss, the first of which is causing me some distress. I think it fair to inform you that I have received a most unusual, that is to say disturbing, communication from the port admiral at Plymouth.' He regarded Kydd steadily. 'In it Admiral Lockwood has seen fit to disclose to me his views on your moral worth while serving in his command, which are not necessarily to your credit.'

'Sir? This is—'

'The wording need not concern you, but it should be understood that I myself hold personal probity and the strictures of honour among gentlemen at the highest possible value, especially so in any of my commanding officers whose moral example will naturally be followed by those serving aboard his ship.

'Now, Mr Kydd, please know that I propose to decide for myself your fitness of character for the dignity of captain of your vessel, as is only right and proper. However, the nature of these views implies a moral transgression of some weight and I therefore do beg you to acquaint me now with the substance of—'

'I have naught t' regret,' Kydd whispered, his face pale.

'Why, surely Admiral Lockwood did not—'

'He— There's nothing I've done f'r which I need be ashamed. Nothing!'

'It's very odd, then, that—'

'I swear!'

Saumarez leaned back, plainly mystified. He seemed to come to a conclusion and sat forward. 'Er, very well, sir. Then I'm minded to take your word on it.' He put down the paper firmly. 'And therefore, unless I learn of something to the contrary, you shall hear no more of it.

'Now, may I know if you've been able to find a measure of companionship at the Mermaid's Club?'

'Thank you, sir, I have,' Kydd said stiffly.

'Again, you do have my sincere condolences, Mr Kydd, and my wife wishes you to know that she perfectly understands your—'

'Sir.'

'Yes, well, perhaps we shall move on to matters more of

the moment.' He reached across and rang the desk bell. 'Ah, Flags. If we could have the Gulf of Avranches charts.'

He turned to Kydd with a sombre expression. 'You're no doubt aware of the preparations the Corsican tyrant is undertaking for his enterprise against England. I have this day received more news of these evil works, which must not be suffered to continue with impunity.' Saumarez selected the large-scale chart and laid it on his desk. 'I have not forgotten my pledge to make your command an active one, Mr Kydd, and now I have a mission for you.'

He moved the chart round to face Kydd, tapping his finger at a point on the coast of Normandy, a bare forty leagues from England. 'I wish you to look into Granville to discover a count of invasion craft and similar assembling there. Should your report warrant, I shall have no alternative but to contemplate action against them.'

Granville was one of the few harbours of that iron-bound coast, lying to the south-east beyond the vast reef plateaux and vicious half-tide rocks and could only be approached at particular states of the tide. The harbour was in the lee of a long peninsula, an ancient town atop its length and long, enfolding stone piers providing capacious shelter below.

'I understand, sir.'

'It will not be an easy task – the waters in approach are shallow and treacherous and the tidal streams prodigious. I believe that spring equinoctial ranges exceeding forty feet are often experienced there,' he added, with a thin smile. 'And you will discover Granville to be so situated that only the closest approach will answer.'

'I'll do m' duty, sir.'

'I'm sure you will, Mr Kydd,' Saumarez said. 'There may be others who may feel that their greater familiarity with these waters entitles them to this important task. I'm confident, however, that you will secure the intelligence without overly hazarding your ship or taking unnecessary risks, and it only remains for me to wish you good fortune.'

'Where's Queripel?' Kydd demanded.

Standish, startled by Kydd's sudden appearance on deck in the midst of the upheaval necessary in a rush to sea, turned to Prosser. 'Pass the word for Mr Queripel.'

'My cabin!' Kydd said irritably, and left.

The lieutenant scowled. 'Where the devil's Quez?' he said to Prosser. 'I don't know what all the fuss is about, this only a reconnaissance – action to be avoided at all costs. Where is the rogue, dammit?'

The little man puffed up, buttoning his waistcoat. 'As I was a-mustering m' charts,' he said, with dignity.

'Captain wants your company,' Standish grunted.

Kydd looked up as Queripel entered the great cabin. 'What do ye know of Granville?'

'Granville! Not y' harbour of notice – dries at low water, miles o' reefs and sandbanks afore you come up with it. C'n get a nasty lop over the shallows if'n the wind's in the sou'-west on the ebb and—'

'I mean t' look into it directly,' Kydd said flatly. 'How . . . ?'

Queripel hesitated, then said defensively, 'An' if it please ye, 'twould oblige me should Mr Dowse be heard an' all.' Queripel was clearly conscious that his position aboard was local and irregular: a hired pilot would in the nature of things assume responsibility for the ship, but his position was ill-defined and he did not want difficulties with the sailing-master later.

Dowse was summoned and Kydd gestured him to one side

as a chart was spread. 'I'll hear *your* opinions afterwards. Get on with it, then, Mr Queripel.'

'From the suth'ard, Mr Kydd,' Dowse came in, before Queripel could speak, pointing to the long peninsula set out to the south-west from the north–south-trending coast. To see directly into the port it did seem obvious they would have to make their approach more from the south.

'Won't be possible, Mr Dowse,' Queripel said firmly, 'what with Banc de Tombelaine an' the shoalest water of all t' the sou'-sou'-west. We has t' come at it by the same course as all do take, from the west, an' lay Le Videcocq rocks no more'n a couple o' cables distant.'

'From th' west?' Kydd said sourly. 'An' under eye the whole time?'

'Can't be helped, sir,' said Queripel.

Teazer had lain uneasily to anchor overnight to the east of Îles Chausey, a six-mile desolation of countless rocks and reefs that were a bare ten miles from the Normandy coast and Granville. At dawn the winds were fair, the day bright and no sail in sight. But the sloop remained stubbornly at anchor: there would be no sudden descent on the port, for Queripel had been insistent. The tides had to be right.

It was not until after nine that *Teazer* got under weigh. The tide-set had been quite apparent while they were moored; the ship had soon swung into the ebb and the rapid current had gurgled urgently along her hull until in the early hours it had lessened. After the vessel had veered right about, the busy swirling had begun again in the opposite direction.

On a strengthening flood tide *Teazer*, with doubled look-outs, raised the coast, an uneven ripple of blue-grey firming quickly to a sweep of craggy coastline interspersed with sandhills and beaches. The pale blobs of sail close inshore changed aspect one after another as the far-off craft, recognising an approaching man-o'-war, fled for their lives.

The Granville peninsula, Cape Lihou, lay dead ahead. Ending in a prominent lofty headland, it angled across and half concealed the harbour. The sheltering stone piers of the port sweeping the vessels into its embrace were dozens of feet high, in deference to the vast tidal range. And they hid the harbour completely, with everything it contained.

'They enters b' keeping in wi' the land from the south,' Queripel murmured. This lie of the piers would give the best protection from harsh westerlies, but meant that their one and only chance to see past the high stone walls was to close right in with the land, then make a hard turn to the left until they could peer inside the two pier-heads.

'Take us in, Mr Dowse,' Kydd ordered, lifting his telescope to scrutinise the panorama. The distant last sail was even now disappearing within the enfolding piers as they approached, leaving the whole coast in both directions clear and somnolent in the autumn sunshine.

The headland gained clarity, but as they neared and shaped course to its southward there was a gust of white on the bluff tip and, seconds later, a double thump. Cannon balls plumed and skittered towards them.

'Ranging fire only,' murmured Standish, coming up to stand next to Kydd. 'The villains'll have to do better'n that.'

Kydd didn't reply. Another rumble, and a shot passed the length of the ship before meeting spectacularly with a wave crest to send spray sheeting and rattling over the quarterdeck. 'Stand on, Mr Dowse,' he said, with a cold grin. 'We'll tack about opposite the harbour entrance as quick as y' please an' out again.'

Teazer edged away to make sea-room, but Queripel said anxiously, 'An' nothing t' starb'd.' At the same time a distant avalanche of thuds sounded and the sea was alive with rising plumes. Boxed in as they were by sand-shoals to the south and the peninsula to the north, their approach track left precious little space for manoeuvre – and of a certainty the gunners in the old fort were well aware of it. No inquisitive British warship was to be allowed sight of the harbour.

A ball slapped through the fore topsail, leaving a ragged hole, another parted a backstay with a musical twang, and they were not yet within a mile or so of the harbour. Dowse whispered to Standish, 'Action t' be avoided, did ye say, sir?'

'Hold y' course!' snarled Kydd, as the helmsman allowed the ship to fall off the wind.

Standish whipped up his glass. 'Sir – I see . . . two, no, three and more craft under sail and leaving.'

Kydd raised his own telescope, then lowered it. 'Gunboats,' he said heavily.

It altered everything. Small lug-rigged open craft they each mounted a cannon in their bows. One, two – possibly four or five – *Teazer* could take on but, well-handled, a swarm together could bring the broadside of a frigate to bear. It was time to retreat.

Renzi entered the cabin noiselessly to see Kydd at his desk, head in his hands. He stood by the stern windows for a moment, then turned. 'An unfortunate situation,' he said softly. His friend did not look up. 'As would vex the saintliest,' he added.

Kydd raised his head and mumbled something, but Renzi was shocked by the red-rimmed, puffy eyes. Kydd gestured wearily at a chair and Renzi sat quietly.

'I'll not quit,' Kydd croaked.

'It would seem we have little choice,' Renzi said.

'Standish wants t' land a party an' scale th' heights t' look down the other side into th' harbour.'

'With the old town all along the top and roused by our presence? I think not.'

'A boat in th' night? But they'd never see anything.'

Renzi pursed his lips. No course of action suggested itself and in going on he was only humouring Kydd. 'Then possibly some sort of . . . spy, agent who, when landed, will mingle unnoticed and . . .'

Kydd's head lifted. 'You?' he said, and smiled.

Renzi treasured the look for the memory of shared times now past, but said wryly, 'The character of a Norman townsman might well be beyond my powers, I fear.'

The light died in Kydd's eyes more and he slumped back. 'I shall think on it,' he said finally. 'Tell Mr Queripel t' present himself with his charts, if y' would.'

Shortly, HMS *Teazer* got under way from where she had been lying hove-to and made away to the west, yet another frustrated English man-o'-war thwarted in her mission to uncover Bonaparte's secrets. No doubt there were those in Granville seeing her fade away over the horizon who were blessing the port's odd topography for repelling the foe so easily.

But among the islands of Chausey *Teazer* ceased her retreat and rounded to in a channel east of the larger. Renzi and Standish waited at the conn, the rich stink of seaweed drifting out from the scatter of rocky islets. A desolate cluster of sod huts was the only sign of life.

'It sounds a right madness,' Standish said sullenly. Renzi forebore to reply, for Kydd had been curt and unfeeling: he

64

alone would carry out the plan. Any other conversation was stilled by Kydd's arrival on deck.

'Sir, you've given thought to what this means for the customary usages of war?'

'Yes.' Kydd was apparently in no mood to discuss matters. 'Ye have y'r orders, Mr Standish. Mind you fail me not, sir,' he added grimly. 'You have th' ship.'

The lieutenant stepped forward. 'Aye aye, sir.'

The yards came round and, taking the pleasant wind on her quarter, *Teazer*'s forefoot chuckled contentedly as she began to circle the forlorn group of rocks. Before long she found what she was looking for.

'It'll do,' Kydd said shortly. 'Mr Andrews, go below an' find a notebook,' he told the young midshipman. 'I'll be telling ye what to write.'

The white-faced lad hesitated. What Kydd contemplated was causing consternation round the ship. Renzi motioned the lad to one side. 'I do believe, sir, that any clerkly duty belongs rightfully to me,' he said to Kydd. 'And, as it happens, my notebook is ready by me.'

The little fishing-boat bobbed disconsolately under *Teazer*'s guns while the pinnace pulled out to it. By common consent in wartime the fisher-folk were left alone to go about their business but now Kydd had seen fit to capture one. If it resulted in reprisals and the sea fisheries of Britain suffered . . .

The three-man crew had little choice: they were relieved of their rank-smelling fishing smocks and headgear and sent back to *Teazer* while Stirk and Renzi set about acquainting themselves with the rigging of the little two-master that reeked so of eel and shellfish.

It was a simple but effective lugsail rig, the Breton *chasse-marée*, a 'tide-chaser' that was fast and agile in these shallow waters, but Renzi had a considerable sense of foreboding. Trespassing in French waters out of uniform they could be taken up as spies – and the French would stop at nothing to prevent information about their invasion preparations getting out.

And the only way their stratagem would work was if they sailed right up to the entrance, ignoring the heavy cannon of the fort and the gunboats at readiness inside. He swallowed and glanced at Stirk, who sat impassively forward next to the foremast stepped so close to the stem. There were distinct advantages to those not cursed with a vivid imagination, he thought ruefully.

The frayed brown sails fluttered then tautened and the boat leaned willingly into the wind, heading back to Granville and its home while Renzi wedged himself against the gunwale. All depended on things having settled down after the English ship had been seen to give up. But was Kydd to be trusted in his judgements? It was so troubling, his obsession with duty. Did his headstrong daring mask carelessness with others' lives?

Cape Lihou loomed ahead; sail were dotted here and there, issuing out from between the pier-heads, free to continue their coastal voyages. Renzi was aware that locally their little craft would be well known, and with strangers seen aboard, to answer a friendly hail might result in alarm and disaster.

They were close enough now to make out the embrasures of the fort at the tip of the peninsula, the long, defensive walls along the old town and the high stone piers extending well out, a perfect concealment.

Faint shouts came from over to starboard – another *chasse-marée*, waving for attention. Instinctively Renzi ducked and began to throw odd bits of gear to Stirk, who quickly caught on, busying himself industriously at nothing. Kydd remained stolidly at his steering oar, concentrating on the approach.

The ruse of being too occupied to talk seemed to satisfy: with several final derisory yells, the fishing vessel passed across their stern and away. The afternoon light was mellowing to early evening, but if they made it to the entrance soon, they would have no difficulty in seeing into the port. A coaster emerged and, loosing topsails, made off to the south; they were now less than a mile from the entrance. Under his fishing smock Renzi readied his notebook and pencil – they would have minutes only. He dared a glance at Kydd. His concentration was intense.

Angry voices came from astern: a French advice boat making importantly for the entrance as well. Kydd fell away from the main track to let it by. Renzi busied himself once more and caught glimpses of faces, some bored, others staring down the worthless fishermen as they overtook to make the sharp turn to pass within the piers.

'On m' mark,' Kydd whispered savagely. Their lives depended on what happened in the next few minutes. The twin pier-heads, each with the figure of a sentry atop, were now barely hundreds of yards distant, the nearer one drawing back with their advance. In seconds they would know everything.

The pier-heads drew apart and there within was what they had risked so much for – Renzi had time only for a quick impression of an inner harbour all of a quarter-mile in size and crammed with small craft before Kydd leaned on the steering oar and the boat turned sharply towards the entrance.

'Now!' Kydd rapped. Renzi was holding a bucket on a rope over the side as though scooping water but at the command let it go. Under its drag the boat lurched to a snail's pace and Kydd began his count.

'I see six – no, a full dozen o' *chaloupes canonnières*,' he hissed urgently, 'No – make it a score. An' more'n I can count o' *bateaux canonnières* – say twenty, thirty?' The piers were approaching slowly and steadily, and if they allowed themselves to be swept inside they would be trapped.

'There's six gun-brigs, an' more building on th' inner strand,' Kydd went on remorselessly.

Something in the muddy water caught Renzi's eye; a subliminal flick of paleness and mottled black. It must be desperately shallow here and—

His mind went cold: years of experience told him that the sea state had changed. The tide was now well and truly on the ebb – Queripel's calculations had been proved inaccurate in these local conditions: they had been counting on an approach with the flood and retreat on the ebb.

It might already be too late. Renzi's imagination saw them making desperately for the open sea only to grind to a sickening stop on some tidal bank. 'Er, tide's well on the ebb,' he said, with an edge in his voice.

'Take this down. A frigate – say a 24 – building t' th' north, wi' at least ten flat barges next t' it.'

'I do believe we should put about now,' Renzi said pointedly, with an odd half-smile. The piers were near enough that a sentry could be seen looking down on them curiously.

Renzi tried to catch Stirk's eye but he was doing something with the lug-yard. 'Tom, we have enough as will convince even—'

'Stand by t' go about!' Kydd hissed. A coastal brig was coming up fast astern, a marked feather of white at her forefoot and, in her relative size, indescribably menacing. Renzi stood ready with his knife.

'Lee-oh!'

The blade severed the bucket rope in one, and at the same time the steering oar dug deeply. Then Renzi understood what Stirk had done: a lugger had to dip the yard round the mast when going about, but he had furtively laid it on the wrong side at the cost of their sailing speed. When they had turned, it was already on the correct side and had gloriously filled, sending the bow seaward.

Renzi leaped to the main lug and worked furiously on the heavy yard. Distant screams of rage across the water made him look up and he saw the brig bearing down on them, frighteningly close. They had not gathered enough speed to clear its path – and the close-hauled larger vessel hemmed in by shoals clearly would not be able to avoid them.

Stirk gripped the gunwale and stared in horror at the onrushing ship but Kydd remained immovably at his post. On the brig men were running urgently to the foredeck shouting, gesticulating.

The ship plunged nearer, its bowsprit spearing the air above them and suddenly it was upon them – but the swash from the bluff bows thrust them aside and they were clear by inches, the barrelling hull towering up and rushing past almost close enough to touch, the noise of her wash sounding like a water-fall. And then it was over, the plain transom receding and men at her taffrail shaking their fists at the lunatic fishermen.

The old boat gathered way agonisingly slowly, her gear straining. Renzi knew that high above them in the fort their antics were being pointed out and probably puzzled over, especially the odd fact that they were shaping course not along the coast but heading directly out to sea.

Now all depended on speed. It would not be long before the French woke up to their audacious incursion and then . . .

The first dismaying sign was the sound of a thin crack

high up. Gunsmoke eddied away next to a signal mast at the tip of the headland, clearly to bring attention to a string of flags that had been peremptorily hoisted.

They stood on doggedly but then a deeper-throated thud sounded and, seconds later, a plume arose between them and the open sea.

Renzi looked again over the side and saw that anonymous sea-bed features were becoming visible in the murky water. Then, with a bump and slewing, they came to a halt.

It was now deadly serious: if they could not get off within minutes they would find themselves left high and dry by the receding tide, easy prey for soldiers cantering up on horses.

'Over th' side!' Kydd shouted, leaping over the low gunwale into the water. It was hard, serrated rock underfoot, the striations parallel with the coast. They manhandled the big boat, heaving until their muscles burned. It moved. Then, juddering, it found deeper water and suddenly they were dangling from the gunwale. At the limits of their strength they flung themselves inboard panting, and hauled in on the slatting and banging sails.

Stirk saw them first. 'Be buggered – they's after us!' he gasped, pointing back to the harbour entrance. One by one gunboats were issuing out. It was now all but over.

'Sheet in!' Kydd roared. The *chasse-marée* leaned and showed her breeding, perfectly suited to the shallow waters of the Brittany coast. But it would not be enough against the half-dozen vessels now in fierce pursuit.

Then quickly it *was* all over. In obedience to orders, and at the appointed time, HMS *Teazer* appeared round the headland, her colours flying and guns ablaze.

Chapter 5

The large, airy upper room at Government House, St Peter Port, with sunlight beaming in from tall windows, was ideally suited for a captains' conference. The commanding officers of His Majesty's ships in Guernsey Roads sat round the long table with, at the head, in his gold lace and decorations, Admiral Sir James Saumarez. Distinguished at St Vincent and the Nile, victor of Algeciras, he made an imposing figure.

'Gentlemen.' His grave glance took them all in – Selby, captain of the frigate *Cerberus* at the foot, with the sloop commanders on each side: Carthew of *Scorpion*, O'Brien of *Harpy*, Kydd of *Teazer* and the rest.

'I have no need to remind you of the utmost seriousness of our situation with Bonaparte adding daily to his arsenal for his enterprise against England. We have now received intelligence of a most disturbing nature directly affecting this station, concerning the harbour of Granville, which is, as you must be aware, apart from St Malo, the only anchorage worth the name in all the two hundred miles between Cherbourg and Brest.'

Studied blank looks indicated that this was old news to most.

Saumarez continued: 'It would appear that Granville is being readied to play a major role in the armament and building of invasion barges and support craft, concentrating them there in great numbers – yes, Captain Selby?'

'Sir.' The frigate captain leaned forward, 'But do we have *recent* intelligence as will—'

'This last two days Commander Kydd has returned from a reconnaissance of the harbour. By means of remarkable exertions he was able to look into the port directly and make an account of the shipping therein. I have no reason to doubt his information.'

Selby sent a quick smile of respect to Kydd, who did not acknowledge it.

'I've heard something of this daring, sir,' Carthew interjected, looking pointedly at Kydd, 'and I rather feel it would be of interest if we could hear his justification for taking prize a fishing-boat, contrary to the common usages?'

O'Brien murmured something but Saumarez cut across quickly: 'The vessel was not made prize, and was restored immediately afterwards. And I understand the master did not decline the sum that was offered him for the, er, hire of his craft. You should understand Mr Kydd has my entire approbation for the initiative he displayed in this matter.'

Carthew exchanged a significant glance with the others.

Saumarez frowned. 'And I shall be looking to more of the same from all of you in the very near future.' Heads rose as the implication of his words penetrated.

'Yes, this meeting is not one about defences, gentlemen. We are to make an assault on Granville.'

There was stunned silence, then a hubbub of excited talk.

If it went forward it would be the first real offensive operation in these waters against the French so far in the war
– and the best chance in sight of some form of distinguished action. But Granville? In so formidable a defensive
position with forts and a walled town overlooking the
harbour? It would take considerable military resources – did
Saumarez have these?

The admiral called the meeting to order and went on, 'The
essence of my plan is this. The primary objective can only
be the invasion craft: I propose to inflict such damage on
them that their sailing to join in concentration those readying
opposite England's shores cannot be in contemplation before
the winter season is upon us.

'And by no means may we consider a landing. This leaves
us in prospect of a massed boat action, which I can only
think will be a bloody affair indeed, and I will not have it.
There is, however, one possibility left us. Bombs.'

Saumarez paused while his captains took his words in. A
bomb-vessel was a specially constructed craft with a huge
mortar throwing explosive shells. If it could be manoeuvred
into position . . .

'I have therefore sent for a pair from the Downs Squadron
to assist us in the assault. *Sulphur* and *Terror* will be joining
us, with their tenders, and then we sail against the enemy.'

There was no mistaking the feeling in the pugnacious
growls round the table.

'With shoal water out beyond cannon fire before Granville,
there is limited sea-room and thus our force is constrained.
Therefore I am making the following dispositions: I will be
shifting my flag to *Cerberus* frigate from *Diomede* to close with
the coast more nearly and will, of course, be in overall
command. The two bombs will also be under my direction

and will form the core of the assault. To this end, there will be a force of three sloops and cutters whose sole duty will be the protection of the bomb-vessels.'

This was a small force to set against the might of the French but if a ship-of-the-line were present it would necessarily be compelled to remain powerless far offshore, and with the bomb-vessels warped close in only smaller craft could keep with them.

'Under whose command will the covering force be?' Carthew asked. He left unspoken his realisation that any valiant defence of the bombs would certainly be applauded but only the man in command would bear the public credit.

'For this task I will be asking Commander Kydd,' Saumarez replied levelly.

'Sir! I must protest!' Carthew said hotly. 'This officer has been in these waters only a few weeks and, besides, I feel I must draw your attention to the fact that he is considerably my junior in the list of commanders.'

'I'm not in the habit of defending my decisions, sir,' snapped the admiral. 'However, you will recall that Mr Kydd has had a recent and intimate acquaintance with the object of our expedition and has done nothing to disabuse me of his suitability for the post. He will assume charge and I expect all my captains to support him.'

Sailing with the early-morning tide the small fleet laid course for the enemy coast – the flagship *Cerberus* in the van and HMS *Teazer* immediately following, leading the close-support squadron.

However, even before Jersey was laid to larboard it was clear that the bomb *Terror* was unable to stay in the line, her broad, flat-bottomed hull making atrocious leeway in the combined south-south-westerly and strong tidal current. It was essential that she be in position before dark: her mooring arrangements were complex and technical, for it was not the mortar she aimed but the whole ship.

Her sister *Sulphur* was delayed in port. There was now every prospect that the assault would fail even before it started and there were bleak looks on every quarterdeck. Later in the afternoon *Cerberus* backed her topsails and hove-to with *Teazer*'s pennant and the signal for 'come within hail' hoisted.

Saumarez's voice sounded through the speaking trumpet, strong and calm. His orders were to go on and anchor before Granville and await the bomb-vessels, which would now necessarily be obliged to conduct a difficult night moor. A council-of-war would be called upon arrival.

Pointe du Roc was raised by five o'clock, and well before dusk *Cerberus* let go her bower anchor, a second streamed out by the stern. She settled just outside range of the guns of the fort on the louring heights. The signal for 'all captains' was immediately made.

'As you see, gentlemen, we have set ourselves a challenging task,' Saumarez opened, with a tight smile. 'I propose to place the bomb-vessels to seaward of the peninsula. Their fire will overarch and descend into the harbour the other side among the dense-packed shipping with the object of causing general damage and the utmost confusion, for there is nothing that the French might do to prevent it falling among them.' He looked meaningfully at Kydd. 'Unless, that is, they are able to make a sally against the bombs.'

'They'll not touch 'em, sir – that's m' promise.'

'Good. May I know how you plan to dispose your forces, sir?'

'*Scorpion* and *Harpy* t' take close station on the bombs, *Eling* schooner f'r communication and *Carteret* cutter with *Teazer* at th' entrance o' the harbour t' bar any who thinks t' leave.'

The captain of the schooner was visibly crestfallen and Carthew curled his lip in a barely concealed sneer. 'And if there is a concerted attack on any one position?'

'Red rocket, all vessels attend at the harbour entrance. Blue rocket, t' fall back on the bombs.'

'Very well. We lie here until the bomb-vessels reach us, at which point we close with the shore to begin the bombardment, paying particular attention to the state of the tide. If any vessel takes the ground, there will be no help for it – with this tide range there can be no relief.' Saumarez hesitated. 'It does occur to me,' he said, in a troubled voice, 'that our actions will be alarming in the extreme to the civil populace, living as they do in the town beneath the flight of the shells and in sight of them exploding. Captain Selby, do you take a flag of truce ashore and warn them of what will occur and—'

'*Warn* them? Sir! The bombs are now able to approach under cover of darkness and can achieve a fearful surprise and – and—' he spluttered.

'Nevertheless this is what you will do. Can you not conceive, sir, the mortal dread that must seize every female heart at the sudden thunder of Jove we will unleash? I will remind you that our duty is to make war against soldiers, not children and womenfolk.'

Terror had touched on a reef, which delayed her progress, and it was not until after midnight that she was reported approaching. In the wan light of a fading moon she was shepherded in.

Out of the darkness the ghost-like form of a schooner appeared and a voice hailed *Teazer*. 'Compliments from the Flag an' on account o' the tide state, *Terror* is to prepare for an immediate bombardment, an' desires ye to take position according.'

Kydd acknowledged; it was a breathtaking assumption that the little bomb-vessel could in the darkness lay out accurately her anchors and springs in readiness – not only that but to contemplate bringing forward the other vessels to their close-in positions and undertake an actual bombardment . . .

One by one the sloops abandoned the security of their anchors for the invisible urging of the tidal currents and felt cautiously for their appointed positions in the last light of a low moon, well aware of the lethal ramparts of granite beneath their keels.

The long stone piers by the low moonlight seemed strangely sinister in their stillness as *Teazer* drew nearer, the small cutter close astern. At a prudent distance she rounded to and awaited developments.

At two in the morning, the last of the moon disappeared and darkness enfolded the scene, a chuckle of water along the ship's side the only intrusion into the stillness. Then, suddenly, the night was blasted apart: a blinding sheet of flame erupted, which froze the shadows of ships and the anonymous black heights of the peninsula in stark relief. A fat thud rolled over the water while a red streak drove across the night sky, high and over the huddled town, to descend out of sight on the other side. Then there was another.

Unseen guns opened up on every side in an eruption of noise, gunflash stabbing from the embrasures of the fort, at gun-towers along the cliffs and even from field-pieces atop the piers. And all in vain. Apart from occasional small splashes out in the darkness there was nothing to show for the chaotic fusillade fired blindly into the night.

From the bomb-vessel a blazing flash and another two-hundred-pound shell was hurled into the blackness, followed by another. The shallow-draught bomb-vessel pounded away with monotonous horror in the darkness. *Teazer*'s tense watch on the harbour, however, spotted no rush to escape: the vessels within were evidently taking their chances rather than risk the unknown English warships lying outside in wait for them.

In the first creeping pre-dawn light firing ceased and all vessels fell back to their deep-water anchorages, leaving vacant the stretch of water where before there had been such warlike activity. From seaward, however, nothing could be seen of the effects of the long bombardment, and at the council-of-war Saumarez looked at his captains gravely. 'A good night's work, I believe,' he said heavily, 'yet I feel frustrated. Without certain knowledge of our success I am reluctant to quit the field while there may well be work yet to be done.'

Selby frowned. 'Sir, we've pummelled the enemy for nearly four hours continuous. Do you not think that—'

'And I believe I mentioned we have no intelligence regarding its effectiveness,' Saumarez said testily, and glanced at Kydd.

'I could not see into th' inner harbour,' Kydd said, his face drawn.

'The French are well roused b' now,' Carthew put in. 'They know what to expect an' they'll have daylight to prepare.'

'Y' want a retreat?' Kydd said tautly. '*Sulphur* will be up with us this day – we have th' chance f'r double the fire.'

'Do you want to return there without clear cause? We don't know for a fact we have failed, sir,' retorted Carthew.

'We find out,' Kydd rapped. 'Lie at anchor today, an' this night land a reconnaissance party t' settle the matter, the bombs t' await their signal.'

'A reconnaissance party? Against such odds? Pray who would be the hero you would find to accept this mission?' Carthew enquired silkily.

Saumarez rubbed his eyes in fatigue. 'Gentlemen, this discussion is to no account. In the absence of information I must decide myself if—'

'I'll lead the party!' Kydd announced, looking directly at Carthew. 'Sir, I'll be ashore at dusk – and with y'r information b' midnight.'

'Mr Kydd,' said Saumarez, weighing his words, 'am I to understand you are volunteering to lead a party of reconnaissance yourself? You must understand that in the nature of things this must be regarded in the character of a "forlorn hope". We are all wanting sleep, Mr Kydd, our judgement necessarily in question. I beg you will reconsider your offer, sir.'

Carthew leaned back, his expression unreadable.

'I will do it, sir,' Kydd said.

Renzi squinted closer at the congested typeface and brought the little brass Argand lamp nearer. It guttered for a moment: the disadvantage of having his tiny cabin so close to the main-hatchway was, however, more than offset by the relief it gave from the 'tween-decks fetor and he resumed his study.

The small volume in German, in turgid *Hochdeutsch* dealt with the Perfectibilists, who were urging the reclamation of modern society from its sordid roots, not through gross revolutions but the perfection of human nature through rigorous moral education.

On the other side of the thin partition the mess-decks were in full cry after issue of grog and the talk eddied noisily round. It did not penetrate Renzi's thoughts for he was well used to it. He was much more interested in how a source for this moral education could be found, given that Weishaupt had specifically proclaimed the abolition of all religion. Yet the *Illuminaten* could not be lightly dismissed: it was said to be a secret society of freemasonry with Goethe himself a member and—

Suddenly he became aware that the mess-deck had gone quiet, but for one deep-throated voice holding forth nearby. Despite himself he listened: it was Mawgan, petty officer and captain of the foretop, an older man and steady – Renzi could visualise the scene beyond the thin bulkhead, the others listening raptly to him.

'No, mates, I ain't! An' this is fer why. He's got th' mark about 'im. I seen it before, done somethin' evil an' has t' pay fer it. First he loses his doxy an' then it's his ship an' we with it, afore he finally goes down ter his just reward.'

There was indistinct murmuring and Poulden came in, troubled: 'Y' can't say that, mate. He's had a hard beat t' wind'd since losin' his sweetheart, bound t' bear down on 'im, like.' There was increased muttering, which did not sound like sympathy.

'There's one thing as gives me pause t' think.' Renzi knew it to be the voice of the sharp-faced Gissing, gunner's mate. 'Yer've all got him on th' wrong tack. He's not a death-or-glory boy, not he. No, it ain't that a-tall – an' I'll tell yez fer why.'

Renzi held still. Kydd's call for volunteers on his return from a council-of-war had been met with a stony silence and his own offer curtly dismissed. No more eloquent testimony was needed for the loss of moral authority that Kydd was now facing.

'Go on, cully, then tell us – *why*'s our Tom Cutlass not a-tryin' t' top it the flash hero?'

There was a moment's pause, then Mawgan said, ''Cos he's not int'rested.' Shouting down the disbelieving cries, he continued, 'He's not int'rested fer a clinkin' good reason. He's got th' death-wish.'

'Yer what?' A horrified quiet spread through the mess-deck.

'A death-wish, yer iggerant lubber. That's when y' grief is so oragious y' can't see as life's worth th' living. Y' doesn't care if yer lives or dies, an' then y' feels as if bein' dead might just be th' medicine t' cure all y'r pain . . .'

This was clearly a new and deeply disturbing thought for straight-thinking sailors to dwell upon. Renzi hesitated. If he intervened, his overhearing their private talk would be revealed and his position become impossible. But at the same time he could recognise the signs: in the absence of insight and enlightened leadership from Kydd, the malignancy of unreason and superstition was spreading among the unlettered seamen and it would not take much . . .

'So he's going t' be careless with his life – an' I ask ye this. Will he be any different wi' us?' There was a dismayed silence and he finished flatly, 'There's a-going t' be them as leaves their bones here, mates, take my word on't.'

Teazer had made one pass along the coast north with Kydd at a telescope, and as the evening was drawing in she was heading south once more. To an appalled Standish on the quarterdeck, Kydd had loudly declared that in the absence of men of spirit he was going on the mission alone. It had brought astonishment and grudging admiration but no volunteers.

Now, as the time was approaching, there was a fearful expectation about the ship: landing on an enemy coast under arms to act the spy was utterly alien to the kind of courage a seaman was normally called upon to display.

When lights began twinkling ashore and a hazy darkness descended, Kydd came up on deck, dressed in dark clothing, his face pale and set. 'Sir, may we know your intentions? If – if you—' Standish stammered.

'I shall be landin' at th' neck o' the peninsula,' Kydd said coldly, 'an' will cross quickly to th' other side, which if ye'll remember is a beach along fr'm the harbour. They won't be expectin' any t' approach fr'm the inside direction.'

'Sir.' Stirk, touched his hat respectfully but remained impassive. 'Boat's alongside.'

Poulden and three seamen were in the gig; their role would be confined to taking him ashore, perilous though that would be. 'Ready t' land, sir,' Stirk reminded.

'You have th' ship, Mr Standish,' Kydd said stiffly, and crossed to the side, looking neither to right nor left. Renzi held still, watching silently.

'Sah!' Sergeant Ambrose emerged from the main hatchway, followed by three more marines, each with blackened gaiters, signifying imminent action. 'Y'r escort present 'n' correct, sah!'

Kydd hesitated and turned to Ambrose, who saluted smartly. 'Sergeant – do you . . . ?'

'We'll be with ye, sir.'

'Thank 'ee, Sergeant, but—'

'Th' men are volunteers too, sir,' he said crisply.

There was a stirring among the men and Midshipman Calloway stepped across the deck. 'I'll come if y' wants me, Mr Kydd,' he said, twisting his hat nervously in his hands.

Stirk growled something at him but he held his ground.

'Yes, lad.' No emotion could be seen on Kydd's face.

'Sir – if you'll have me.' Andrews, the wispy midshipman, came forward too and looked at Kydd, imploring.

So junior, Renzi thought, but he would not be such a loss to the service if he failed to return.

'Very well.'

From the crowd now came cries of encouragement and further offers but Kydd cut them off. 'Th' Royal Marines an' these two. Muskets f'r the redcoats.'

In a hushed silence they boarded the gig. Renzi followed it with his eyes into the darkness but Kydd did not look back.

The oars rose and fell, dipping carefully and economically, the rowlocks stuffed with rags to muffle the thump of each stroke. Kydd sat upright, his gaze searching what could be seen of the shore until he pointed in one direction. 'Th' beach there – we land at th' northern end.' The lights of the town were along the top of the peninsula, well to the south; an anonymous rural darkness stretched away everywhere else.

Obediently Stirk moved the tiller and the boat headed in. Every sight, every sound that could not be instantly identified was a threat – betrayal and disaster could happen so quickly. The pale beach looked so exposed, a low, dark rock at the end offering the only cover.

The boat hissed to a standstill on the sand at the edge of the water and, taut with tension, the men went over the side, then splashed ashore – aware that the hard sand underfoot was the soil of the enemy. 'T' me,' Kydd whispered hoarsely, and hurried to the nearby rocks, searching for a sea-facing cove.

They scurried after him to the shelter, their boat and security already heading rapidly seawards. With the whites of eyes flashing about him, Kydd whispered, 'No more'n half a mile across here, I've measured it wi' bearings. No lights as c'n be seen, should be all farmland. We come t' a beach th' other side, work our way as close as we need. Questions?'

'If'n we get cut off by a patrol . . .' Ambrose began.

'We don't let ourselves be,' Kydd said. He raised his head cautiously above the line of granite. 'Nothing. We move.'

They crossed a straggling line of coarse grass into low dunes that soon gave way to firmer grassland, but it was now so dark that only gross shadows loomed ahead, not a light within a mile. Kydd struck out inland, the marines on either side, the midshipmen in a nervous crouch behind. The smell of cow pasture was rank after the purity of the sea air.

A stout stone wall materialised across their path with a suspiciously military-looking ditch beyond. They scrambled over and found muddy water at the bottom of the ditch before reaching, panting, the far side. Ahead the ground rose and the skyline could just be made out. Squarely athwart their track was the squat, low shape of a building.

'A sentry post,' whispered Calloway, fearfully.

'Sergeant?'

Ambrose sucked in his breath. 'Not as any might say . . .'

They waited for long minutes, seeing no signs of life, just hearing the breathy night air playing through the straggling grasses. Then Kydd said, in a hard whisper, 'We can't wait all night. We go forward. When we get to the building, we listen.' He moved quickly towards the silent shadow.

It was of rough stone but gave no other clue. They pressed up to its cold bulk, keeping an absolute quiet, their breathing seeming loud in the stillness. Nothing. 'We go—'

The wooden squeal of a door shattered the silence. It was opening on the opposite side. Then came the clink and slither of – a harness? Sword scabbard? A military accoutrement?

'A marine at each end,' hissed Kydd savagely. 'Bayonets! Take him wi' cold steel if he turns th' corner.'

Ambrose dispatched his men who silently took position, unseen in the inky blackness behind the wall. The random clinking sounded from one side, growing louder and more distinct, almost certainly the spurs of a cavalryman. The footfalls, however, seemed uncertain. Ambrose whispered cynically, 'He's bin on the doings 'n' is goin' behind to take a piss.'

The sounds drew nearer and nearer – and, in a desperate swing, a terrified young marine transfixed an indistinct figure with an audible meaty thump. The figure dropped, squealing and choking, the unmistakable clatter of a falling bucket like a thunderclap.

'It's – it's an ol' woman! I done an ol' lady!' The marine's cry of horror pierced the night. He dropped beside the frantically twisting shape on the ground, her terror-stricken frail cries turning to pathetic sobs.

Kydd swung on Ambrose. 'Sergeant!' he ordered stonily.

The man hesitated only a moment, then crossed over, took the marine's musket and thrust the bayonet expertly; once, twice. There was a last despairing wail that ended in choking and – stillness.

'We got t' go back now,' Calloway pleaded, and the other midshipman's wretched puking could be heard to one side. But there was only the serene caress of the night breeze abroad and Kydd turned on them. 'On y'r feet,' he said harshly. 'This is only a farmhouse. We're going on.'

Beyond the structure a rough-made access road gave them

fast going to the main road to town, crossing in front of them. Halfway! If it were daylight they could probably see down into the harbour from the other side. As it was—

'*Halte là – qui vive?*' In the dimness they had not noticed a foot sentry astride the road further down. '*Qui va là?*' he called again, more forcefully.

Kydd whipped round: there was only low scrub nearby, pitiful cover. 'Sergeant—'

But the sentry had yanked out a pistol and fired at them. Then, hefting his musket, he stood his ground.

'It's no good, sir,' Ambrose whispered hastily. 'He's stayin' because he knows there's others about.' More voices could be heard on the night air.

Kydd stood still for a moment, then said savagely, 'Back t' th' boat!'

They wheeled about, racing past the silent bulk of the farmhouse and to the ditch. As they clambered over the wall there was the sudden tap of a musket, then others, dismayingly close.

'Move!' Kydd bawled. There was no need now for quiet. They stumbled and rushed towards the sea, tripping and cursing in their frenzy.

Kydd stopped suddenly. 'Where's the marines?' he panted. A double crack to his rear answered him. Ambrose was behind the wall delaying the troops closing in, two firing while two reloaded. It would hold for minutes at most.

Kydd and his men made the beach. The pale sands gave nothing away – there was no boat to be seen. The end must be very near, despite Ambrose's sacrifice. Kydd traced the line of the water's edge along the beach until his eyes watered.

The firing stopped, but then out on the dunes flanking

86

them musket fire stabbed again – inland. The marines must still be doing their duty but it would not be long now.

At that moment a rocket, just half a cable offshore, soared up and burst in a bright sprinkle of stars. 'A gun!' Kydd roared. 'Any wi' a musket, fire it now!'

But, of course, there was none. In the inky darkness no sailor untrained in the art could possibly be relied on to reload a musket; the marines must do it by feel.

'There's no one?' Kydd pleaded.

'Sir! I have this,' Andrews said shamefacedly, handing over a little folding pistol. He had taken it just in case, a foolish notion, but now . . .

'Priming powder?'

It was in a little silver flask. Kydd snatched it and sprinted to the nearest rock. He shook out a large pile and, holding the pistol lock close, stood clear and pulled the trigger. The powder caught in a bright flare, which died quickly but did the job.

'Come on!' Kydd yelled hoarsely. 'For y'r lives!' He broke cover and ran to the water's edge. And there it was, their boat pulling strongly inshore, Stirk at the tiller. It grounded and Kydd stood in the waves, urging the others into it.

'We gotta leave now, sir!' Stirk pleaded. His crew were rotating the boat seaward for a fast withdrawal to the safety of the sea.

'Wait!'

All along the line of dunes the flash of muskets was increasing. Twice Kydd felt the whip of bullets close by. The boat was afloat and pointing out to sea, but he remained standing in the shallows with his hand on the gunwale.

Then there was a flurry of firing from up the beach and figures were staggering across the sand, one with another over his back. 'Ambrose an' the marines!'

Willing hands helped them into the boat and, with frantic strokes, the little craft finally won the open sea.

Troubled and depressed, Renzi stood by the main shrouds, gazing out into the hostile darkness. The talk of a death-wish was nonsense, of course, but it pointed up the core of the difficulty: since losing Rosalynd Kydd had turned hard and bitter, and no longer possessed the humanity that had informed his leadership before.

It had destabilised his men, who could not be expected to follow one whose character they could not fathom, whose human feeling was so much in doubt and who was said to be deranged by grief. Above all, the iron control and remoteness now set him apart.

There was a distant spatter of firing ashore. Renzi stiffened: the party must have been discovered, he thought. They could not last long against regular French troops and he gripped the shroud.

Standish appeared next to him. 'Seems he's got himself into a pother,' he said casually. 'To be expected. We'll give him an hour, I think.' Renzi could not trust himself to reply.

Another spasm of firing occurred further along – it grew to a crescendo, musket flashes now atop the dunes all along the beach. Then it lessened and stopped abruptly. It was not possible in the dark to make out what had happened, but Standish let out a theatrical sigh. 'It seems to be all over with Mr Kydd, I do believe.'

'You'll send another boat,' Renzi snapped.

'I will not. There's half the French army there waiting for us to blunder in to the rescue. I'll be taking *Teazer* to sea and—'

'*Boat ahoooyy!*' The fo'c'sle lookout's voice cracked with

feeling. A distant cry came out of the night. A seaman ran aft and touched his hat to Standish.

'Our boat in sight, sir,' he said, with relish.

The tired party came over the bulwark, ashen-faced, the wounded marine handed up tenderly. Kydd went straight aft to Standish. 'I'm t' see the admiral. You have th' ship till I return.' Without acknowledging Renzi he went over the side and the boat shoved off.

Renzi noted sadly that Kydd had not said a word of praise to the men or ordered a double tot for them, something inconceivable before.

The boat came back quickly; as soon as Kydd was inboard he summoned Standish. 'Th' admiral has decided t' resume th' action. We stand to at dawn.'

This time it was to be both bomb-vessels, *Sulphur* and her tenders having arrived during the night, and not only that but a daytime assault for maximum accuracy. The tides allowed for an approach at five in the morning and the two ships would pound away for as long as the tide allowed, probably until ten – or until they were overwhelmed by vessels emboldened by daylight that the French must surely have in readiness. Much would depend on Kydd's inshore squadron . . .

The two bomb-vessels crabbed in and began the elaborate preparations with three anchors and springs attached in such a way that the vessel could be oriented precisely. It was then a technical matter for the gunners: the charge exactly calculated for range and the fuse cut at the right point to explode the thirteen-inch mortar shell just above the ground for deadly effect.

As the day broke with wistful autumn sunshine the bomb-vessels opened up. Sheets of flame shrouded the small ships in a vast cloud, again the heavy concussion, and this time it was possible to glimpse a black speck hurled high in a parabola, trailing a thin spiral. Seconds later from behind the headland a muffled crash was followed by a lazy column of dirty smoke.

The provocation was extreme and there was every possibility that before long the beleaguered French would burst out of the harbour in a vengeful lunge to crush their tormentors.

The frigate moved in as close as she dared, leadsmen in the chains and kedges streamed, but there was no avoiding the fact that the bomb-vessels could only be defended by the smaller ships with a lesser draught. *Teazer* and the cutter stayed off the entrance to the harbour.

Suddenly, from the harbour mouth came a succession of gunboats – one by one in an endless stream – a growing array until a full twenty-two of the ugly craft were in view.

'"Attend at th' entrance!"' roared Kydd aft to the signal crew. All possible forces were needed, even if it stripped bare the bomb-vessel defences. 'An' give 'em a gun!' As the red-flag signal whipped up, a gun cracked out forward to lend urgency.

The other two sloops hauled their wind for the entrance, but before they arrived the gunboats were roping themselves together in a double line facing outward. 'Be damned t' it!' Standish spluttered. 'They're defending the harbour as they think we mean to cut 'em out!'

It was telling evidence of the respect and awe in which the Royal Navy was held by her enemies. Nevertheless, the battering the French were receiving was murderous and unceasing. Surely they would attempt some kind of retaliation.

In the light morning airs, powder smoke hung about the

ships in slowly roiling masses as the mortars thudded again and yet again, the dun clouds spreading gradually far and wide. There was little response from the forts, sited to overlook the port; the French were paying dearly for having ignored the possibility of an artillery strike from the sea.

Dowse pointed over the side. 'Mr Kydd, ye can see – we're makin' foul water.' The tide now fast on the ebb, their keel was stirring up sea-bed mud.

The bomb-vessels concluded their work and their windlasses heaved in their ground tackle, but it was this moment that held the greatest danger: would the enemy see the fleet in retreat and throw caution to the winds to seek revenge?

Cerberus lingered until the last possible moment to cover the withdrawal before bracing round for the run out to sea, her admiral's flag proudly aloft. Still the enemy remained out of sight. But it was time to leave: *Teazer* jockeyed round to take position astern of the flagship, the last to leave the field of battle.

Then, suddenly, the frigate slewed sharply to starboard and slowed to a crawl before stopping altogether. Her sails were let fly, then doused, the big man-o'-war now motionless. 'She's gone aground,' hissed Kydd. 'We close an' take th' admiral off.'

Things had changed catastrophically: the powerful ship was now helpless. Hard and fast with the ebb far from spent, without the means to manoeuvre, she lay easy prey.

'Sir, we stand ready t' take you off,' bellowed Kydd, through the speaking trumpet to *Cerberus*'s quarterdeck. Saumarez could be seen in serious consultation with Selby. Hard decisions must be made: to abandon ship now, in good order and no loss of life, or be forced later to a humiliating scramble over the side in the face of hostile gunfire.

Disdaining an offered hailer, Saumarez cupped his hands and roared back, 'I shall stand by the ship, Mr Kydd. Do as you see fit for the defending of the bombs – their preservation is of great importance.'

'Aye aye, sir,' Kydd acknowledged.

The bomb-vessels even now were making a slow but steady retreat to the north-west – but if any of the small squadron was detached, would the remainder be enough to discourage a determined attack on the stranded frigate? On the other hand all could be retained and deployed to prevent the enemy leaving Granville, the only threat of any consequence. But if, once out of sight, the bombs were set upon . . .

'Tell *Harpy* t' come within hail,' Kydd called. It was a moot point whether his temporary command of a squadron defending the bombs could be said still to exist in their absence but he had his orders from the admiral. *Harpy* was dispatched with the schooner *Eling* to chase after and stay with the bombs.

'*Scorpion* t' come within hail.' The bigger ship-sloop affected not to notice the signal but, at *Teazer*'s gun, went about and came up, pointedly rounding to windward off her quarter. Kydd ignored the calculated slight: the custom of service was for the senior to lie-to while the junior went round her stern to leeward and Carthew, no doubt, was making a point.

'I'd be obliged should you stay wi' the frigate,' Kydd hailed. '*Teazer* an' *Carteret* will lie off th' harbour.' There was an unintelligible acknowledgement from Carthew and the three-master curved away, leaving just one brig-sloop and one tiny cutter to meet whatever challenge would emerge from between those stone piers.

The day wore on; it was clear that *Cerberus* had lost the race against the tide – she was now visibly at an angle and unnaturally still. And the significance would not be lost on the French. With such a prize within reach, there for the taking, it could now be only a matter of time.

Another hour. Now the frigate lay heeled over at a crazy angle, her guns either in the water or impotently skyward, her green-streaked copper bulking indecently, her men moving hand over hand along the decks, the ship a picture of helplessness.

When the attack did come it was cunningly mounted and rapidly carried out. Without warning a stream of other gunboats under oars issued out, one after another. In the light winds *Teazer* and *Carteret* were too late in closing with them, and with their carronades' short range could only blaze away in futile desperation as the shallow-draught gunboats swiftly made away against the wind for the north of the Videcocq rocks, where no British ship could follow.

It was a master-stroke. The gunboats were positioned such that their weapons could bear on the helpless frigate – only one long gun each, but these were full-size eighteen- or twenty-four-pounders. Together they would have the same weight of metal as the broadside of a frigate of equal size. And *Cerberus* could do nothing but endure until the inevitable capitulation.

The guns opened with slow and deliberate fire. The first shot sent up a plume of water just short, others joining to surround the frigate with a forest of splashes – and then, aim improving, dark holes appeared in the naked hull.

Renzi watched in alarm; Kydd's squadron had failed. In just a short while the admiral's flag must be lowered in abject surrender. Then, suddenly, his friend seemed to lose his reason. He wheeled his sloop about and sent her pell-mell at the harbour itself.

In the smoke and confusion of combat a miracle happened. The gunboats abandoned their prey and retreated inside the walls of the harbour, and when the tide returned *Cerberus* was duly refloated and was able to make off to safety.

But Kydd was not of a mind to communicate his motives to anyone . . .

Chapter 6

It was galling in the extreme. Because of the gravity of the situation Renzi had overcome his scruples and resolved to warn Kydd of the ugly mood that was building, the savage opinions he had overheard and in charity forewarn him of worse to come. He had to make one last try to get through to Kydd. He entered the cabin after a polite knock and waited.

It was difficult to broach after Kydd's wild triumph, and Renzi controlled himself with effort. 'If you only knew what coming to you like this is costing me in violation of my sensibilities—'

'Then you're free t' go. An' why you should come an' waste my time with y'r mess-deck catblash I can't think,' Kydd threw over his shoulder, then resumed scratching away with his quill.

'May I know at least why we're at anchor here instead of Guernsey?'

The other vessels had retreated to the security of St Peter Port while they were again moored off Chausey Rocks, with a tired and fractious crew.

Kydd looked up, expressionless. 'Since y' ask, I'm t' keep

a distant watch on Granville f'r a few days t' see what they'll do.' His features had aged so: no sign of animation, none of the interest in things round him, only this dull, blinkered obsession with duty.

'Do you not think it wise to apprise your ship's company of this? They've been sorely tested recently, I believe, and now to be robbed of their rest . . .' The heartless dismissal of the old lady's death as the fortune of war had upset many, and the ferocious solo altercation at the harbour mouth had others questioning Kydd's sanity.

'They'll do their duty,' Kydd said shortly, and picked up his pen again.

Renzi drew breath sharply and blurted, 'Good God above! The ship is falling apart around you and still you won't see! The men need leadership – someone they can trust, that they may look up to, believe in, not a grief-stricken machine who spouts nothing but duty and—'

Kydd's fist crashed on the table. 'Rot you f'r a prating dog!' He shot to his feet. 'Who are you t' tell me about leading men?' he said. 'As we c'n all see, you've left th' world t' others an' taken refuge in y'r precious books.'

Cold with fury, Renzi bit out, 'Then, as it's clear you no longer value my services or my friendship, I shall be leaving the ship in Guernsey. Good day to you, sir!' He stormed out, pushing past the boatswain who had been about to knock. Kydd stood, breathing rapidly and gazing after the vanished Renzi.

'Um, sir?' Purchet said uncertainly. 'It's b' way of bein' urgent, like.'

'What is it, then?' he said.

Purchet stepped inside, closing the door. 'M' duty t' tell ye, sir,' he mumbled, then stopped as if recollecting himself.

'Tell me what, Mr Purchet?' Kydd snapped.

The boatswain took a deep breath. 'In m' best opinion, sir, the men are no longer reliable.'

Kydd tensed. 'Are ye telling me they're in mutiny, Mr Purchet?' Everything from this point forward, even an opinion or words spoken in haste, might well be next pronounced in the hostile confines of a court-martial.

'I cannot say that, sir.'

'Then what?'

'They's a-whisperin', thinkin' as I can't hear 'em,' he said gravely. The boatswain's cabin in the small sloop was as thin-walled as Renzi's. 'I don't take mind on it, usually, but as it's s' bad . . .'

'Tell me, if y' please,' Kydd prodded.

'Er, I have t' say it how I hears it,' Purchet said.

'Go on.'

'Well, one o' the hands has it as how you're out o' your wits wi' grievin' an' says as any doctor worth th' name would have ye out o' the ship. An' they thinks as how this makes ye not responsible, an' therefore it's not right fer them t' take y'r orders.'

'An' the others?'

'Sir, they say how as t' prove it, they seen ye change, like, fr'm their cap'n in Plymouth t' a hard-horse Tartar who doesn't hear 'em any more – them sayin' it, o' course,' he added hastily. 'They seen ye at Granville, th' last fight, an' say that if ye're careless o' your own life, what's theirs worth?'

Kydd waited, his face stony. 'Anything else?'

'Why, sir, this afternoon, when young Jacko said them things y' heard, most would say he'd had his grog an' was talkin' wry, like, no need t' seize 'im in irons like that. An' they're a-feared what ye'll do when he comes up afore ye tomorrow.'

97

'And this's y'r mutiny?'

'There's a gallows deal more, sir, as it's not fit f'r ye t' hear.' He looked at Kydd defiantly. 'I bin in a mutiny once, an' knows the signs. All it wants is f'r one chuckle-headed ninny t' set 'em off wi' hot words, an' then—'

'Thank 'ee, Mr Purchet. Y' did th' right thing,' Kydd said formally.

The boatswain shifted awkwardly and mumbled, 'Jus' wanted t' warn ye, like.'

As had Renzi.

'I'll – I'll think on it,' was all Kydd could manage.

'Then I'll be away for'ard,' Purchet said, with quiet dignity.

Kydd sat down slowly, cold with shock. Since he had first won command those few years ago in Malta, he had taken satisfaction that his origins before the mast gave him a particular insight into the thinking of his men, but now – a mutiny?

Deep down he knew the reason and it was the one he feared most.

To be brutally honest with himself, he would have to admit that he was confronting personal failure. His seizing on *duty* as the answer to his pain, a sure and trustworthy lifeline out of the pit of despair that he had grasped so eagerly; this had secured its object, the continuance of his professional functioning, but at grievous cost. By degrees it had changed him, become the master of his soul and now ruled his every action, turning him into a hard-hearted, blinkered automaton.

He balled his fists. It had been too easy – a way of keeping the world and its hurts at bay, but also an excuse not to think. And, above all, not to face things. He paced fretfully about the cabin: if it was not the answer, then what was?

The decanters were in the sideboard. He hesitated, then took out the rum. Its fire steadied him but this was no remedy. That could only be to face up to his pain, the grief . . . memories.

Since that terrible day he had instinctively shied from their immediacy. Was he ready to deal with them yet? A feeling of inevitability crept over him. He was not blessedly logical, as Renzi was, but something drew him irresistibly to focus on just one thing: the slight but constant pressure at his breast, always so warm against his skin. The locket.

He had worn it next to his heart since the day when Rosalynd's silhouette had been fashioned into a miniature – and he had never dared look upon it since he had lost her. He drew it out slowly, tenderly. For a brief moment he held it tight in his hand, fighting the flood of images, then snapped it open.

Her likeness: Rosalynd. In black crêpe paper, now a little crinkled. He held the trinket reverently, trying to relive the time when it had been new. The cheap gilt finish had now worn through to the bright steel at the edges and in places there were specks of rust, but no matter. What he held in his hands was Rosalynd, his sweetheart.

He gulped as his eyes misted, but another thought intruded, growing in strength and insistence. This was *not* Rosalynd. It was merely her likeness. It was tarnishing and fading and would eventually disintegrate. It was not her: she no longer existed in this world – except in his memory, and there she would never fade.

He knew then what he had to do. He crossed to the stern windows, opened the centre one and swung it wide. Outside there was impenetrable blackness but with it the clean tang of salt, seaweed and waves soughing mournfully against *Teazer's* counter. With only a brief hesitation he hurled the locket into the night.

It was done. With the act came a feeling of release; lovers separated by distance would eventually meet again, but when separated by time they would not. Rosalynd was of the past. There was now no need for *any* elaborate personal defences: she was safely preserved in his memory, and he had his duties to his present existence. Renzi *had* been right but it had taken the threat of mutiny to bring him to—

Mutiny! The reality flooded in and his mind snapped to full alertness. He did not fear a bloody uprising so much as the certainty that the moment an order was disobeyed, a scornful or threatening word uttered, nothing short of a court-martial and a noose at the yardarm would satisfy an Admiralty sensitive to the slightest evidence of disaffection or rebellion in the fleet. Long after the corpses were cut down *Teazer* would bear the stain of dishonour – and it would be entirely the fault of her captain.

It demanded action – and quickly. What should he do? Order the marines to stand to, heading off any moves now under way? Wake Standish and have him, with the warrant officers, armed and aft? This would stop any mutiny in its tracks but would immediately throw the ship into two camps set implacably against each other.

He couldn't do it. He would lose any regard that still remained in his men and that was too great a price to pay. Then what? Do nothing? That was not possible. Instead he would appeal directly to them. On a personal level, but not as a supplicant: as their captain. And not on the quarterdeck in the usual way . . .

His servant Tysoe had taken to keeping out of the way so Kydd went to his sleeping cabin and there found his full dress coat with its Nile medals and pulled it on. Clapping on his gold-laced cocked hat he made his way in the darkness to the hatchway.

As he descended he could hear the usual babble of talk and guffaws issuing from the mess-deck; it was a strong custom of the Service that the captain would never intrude on the men in their own territory in their own time, still less do so without warning – but this was no idle visit.

His appearance at the foot of the ladder was met with an astonished silence, men twisting at their tables and the nearest scrabbling to distance themselves. The stench of so many bodies in the confined space, with the reek of rush dips guttering in their dishes, caught Kydd at the back of the throat: it had been long since he had endured these conditions, inescapable as they were for sailors in a small ship of war.

Standing legs a-brace, he placed his hat firmly under his arm and faced them. He said nothing, his hard gaze holding first one, then another. The dim light picked up the gold lacing of his uniform, and when he spoke, he had their entire attention.

'Teazers!' he began. 'I won't keep you f'r long. Now, one of y'r number came aft t' see me, thought fit t' lay an information afore me as was necessary f'r me t' know.'

Furtive glances were thrown and there were awkward shuffles: was there a spy in their midst, bearing tales to the quarterdeck?

'He was right t' do so. F'r what he said was concernin' y'r own captain. He said t' me that there's those who'd believe I'm not sailin' square wi' ye since I had m' sad loss – that I'm toppin' it th' tyrant t' no account.' He paused: apart from the lazy creaking of a ship at anchor there was utter stillness.

'This I'll say to ye. I took aboard all that was said, an' have considered it well. An' my conclusion is, if there's anything that stands athwart *Teazer*'s bows in bein' the finest fightin' ship in the Navy then, s' help me, I won't rest until I've done something about it. I'll not see m' men discontented, an' I won't, y' have m' word on't.'

In the flickering light of 'tween decks it was difficult to make out expressions but the silence told its own story. 'I give ye this promise: at th' end o' the month, any man wants t' ship out o' *Teazer* c'n shift his berth to another. An' that same day, needs o' the Service permittin'. Thank 'ee – an' good night.'

He made his exit. Behind him the silence dissolved into a chaos of talk. About to mount the companionway he hesitated, then turned to a tiny cabin and knocked. Renzi appeared and regarded him. In a low voice Kydd said, 'I'd be obliged, Nicholas, should ye sup wi' me tonight. There's some things I need t' get off m' chest.'

It wasn't until well into the second bottle of wine that Renzi allowed himself to thaw and listen courteously to Kydd's earnest explanations. 'Nicholas, all I could see then was that if'n I wanted t' keep from hurtin' all I needed was t' lay hold on duty an' be damned t' all else!'

'Duty taken at its widest interpretation, I'd hazard,' Renzi said drily. 'To include a zeal touching on engagement with the King's enemies that's a caution to us all.' He looked across at Kydd. 'Tell me, my friend – for it's a matter much discussed below – was it an unholy passion to prevail or the baser impulse to suicide that had you throw *Teazer* across the harbour mouth? Do tell. If I might remind you, it did not seem you were of a mind to communicate your motives at the time.'

'Why, nothing as can't be explained wi' a bit o' logic,' said Kydd, smugly. 'It was a fine piece o' reasonin' by their captain, t' take the gunboats out as they did, an' place 'em out o' reach – so I had t' find a way t' call him off. An' I thought o' you,

Nicholas. You always say as how I'm overborne by logic, so I set th' French wi' a puzzle.

'Th' duty o' the gunboats was to defend th' port an' its craft. They see *Cerberus* an' think t' take her. All I did was remind 'em of their duty. I made a sally at th' harbour as made them tremble f'r its safety. They then have t' make up their mind which is th' higher call on their duty, and . . .'

'Bravo! A cool and reasoned decision worthy of Nelson!' There had clearly been no impairment of Kydd's judgement in his time of madness, and there was every reason to hope for a full restoring of the man that lay beneath.

'On quite another matter, brother,' Renzi began lightly, 'do I see a brightening of spirit, as it were, a routing of melancholia, perhaps?'

'Aye, Nicholas, y' do. It's been . . . hard.' He dropped his eyes.

Renzi noticed the tightly clenched fists; the madness was over but the hurt would remain for some time and he longed to reach out. 'Ah, you will probably not be interested at this time, but that sainted ethical hedonist Jeremy Bentham did once devise an algorithm for the computing of happiness, the felicific calculus, which I have oft-times made use of in the approaching of vexed decisions in life. And I'm bound to admit this day, to my eternal shame, that by its calculations it would seem you *were* right in placing aside the admiral's daughter in favour of . . . of the other . . .'

He trailed off uncertainly but Kydd raised his head with a smile. 'Aye, m' friend, but I had not th' time t' perform the calculations and had t' set a course by my stars as I saw 'em – and I dare t' say I would do it again.'

Renzi's eyes pricked: it had been a hard time for them both but now was the time to move forward. 'Er, your opinion.

What do you consider the captain of this fair bark would pass in judgement over that iniquitous young mariner, Jacko, now in durance vile?' he said languorously, stretching for another mutton cutlet.

'Why, I believe if th' rascal should make his apologies to his lawful commander, I don't think he will suffer for it.' Kydd grinned and raised his glass to his friend.

It was evident that there would be no immediate breakout from Granville so HMS *Teazer* shaped course to Guernsey, raising Sark in the morning. The flagship was back at her mooring in the Great Road and, like her lesser consorts, dressed overall in bunting, but what caught the attention of every man aboard *Teazer*, when the smoke of the gun salute had cleared, was the distant squeal of pipes aboard *Cerberus*, followed by a long, rolling thunder of drums.

'B' glory, mannin' th' yards an' it's all fer us!' came a cry from forward. From below-decks of the flagship her ship's company came racing up, leaping into the shrouds and mounting the rigging of all three masts at once. As they reached the fighting tops they spread out each side along the yards, hundreds of men in urgent motion upwards and outwards. When they were in position the drums stopped and in the sudden silence, atop the mainmast truck at the very highest point of the ship, a lone seaman snatched off his hat, and as he whirled it round disciplined cheers broke out.

Granville was not going to be a great fleet action celebrated by the nation but in Navy fashion these men were recognising their own *Teazer*'s gallantry in a very public way. The figure of Saumarez was unmistakable on *Cerberus*'s quarterdeck and Kydd made an elaborate bow, which was returned at once.

'Pray allow me to shake the hand of a very fine officer!'

the admiral said, when Kydd went aboard to report. 'That was the finest stroke this age, I must declare.' Looking intently at Kydd he added, 'And I do believe that our successful engaging with the enemy has gone some way into laying your own troubles – am I right?'

'Aye, sir.'

'Then it will be Lady Saumarez's pleasure to renew your acquaintance in the near future. There will be a dinner given at Saumarez Park on Saturday in grateful token of our victory at which I dare to say you will be guest of honour, Mr Kydd.'

In *Teazer*, Standish was receiving the official visitors and was conspicuously enjoying the task, quantities of young ladies, it seemed, requiring a personal sighting of the ship that had recently fought so bravely. Renzi, however, went below, taking advantage of the quiet in the great cabin to prepare the ship's papers for her return to port.

The wail of a pipe on the upper deck pealed out: this would be Kydd returning from the admiral. A few minutes later he entered the cabin, but his face was bleak, his gaze unseeing. Renzi understood instantly: this was the first triumph he would have been able to lay before Rosalynd.

Then Kydd noticed him and his eyes softened. 'Nicholas, m' dear friend, do let's step ashore. I've a yen f'r different faces, if y' understands.'

'Why, to be sure. But here are my papers – should our stern captain learn of their neglect in wanton disporting ashore . . .'

They went in plain clothes but their disembarking on to North Pier steps drew immediate attention from the urchins playing about the busy waterfront and there were gleeful cheers and whoops for two sailor heroes of the hour as they stepped out for town.

It was an agreeable afternoon; Renzi was able to direct their course to take in the colour and bustle of the Pollet, the boat-yards and the admirable views to be had from the upper reaches above St Peter Port. Then they supped together at a snug inn with a fine prospect of the castle islet.

They spoke little: Kydd was quiet but Renzi could see that it was part of a process that would end in a new man emerging, hard lines in his features telling of experiences that had not destroyed but changed him, rather as a furnace fires a creation to permanence. Renzi knew that with Kydd's strength of will and depth of character he would eventually come through stronger.

'And so I give you Commander Thomas Kydd, an ornament to his profession and a sea officer whose future can only be bright and glorious in the service of his king!'

Kydd bowed gravely in acknowledgement of Saumarez's fulsome words, while in the splendid room the toast was duly raised by the assembled captains of the squadron, expressions ranging from the hearty and comradely to the envious and grudging. Anointed as the favourite of the commander-in-chief, Kydd could look forward to the plums of appointment on the station.

They clustered about him, exclaiming, laughing, hearing his modest protestations while Saumarez stood watching benevolently. 'I do believe you have now proved yourself, Mr Kydd,' he called, 'so I'm giving you an independent cruise, sir.'

There were admiring gasps and growls of envy from the others and a slow smile spread on Kydd's face – and stayed.

The news raced round *Teazer*. An independent meant that as long as no other was in at the capture of a prize it would be theirs: duly condemned, ship and cargo would be sold and the proceeds would go to the captors – with, of course, a share due to the commander-in-chief.

The atmosphere aboard changed. This was a captain who was demonstrably a favourite of Saumarez, and any lucky enough to be in his ship's company would now share in his fortune. There would be no more talk of mutiny.

Three days later, Prosser returned from the admiral's office with orders. Renzi signed for them and locked them away in Kydd's confidential drawer for his return from shore.

'A cruise t' the west o' Bréhat!' Kydd grunted with satisfaction, picked up an inner packet and looked at it with delighted surprise. 'Do y' smoke what this is?' he said, impressed. 'It's m' first sealed orders, Nicholas.'

It seemed from the superscription that, prior to Kydd's relief of *Scorpion* off Les Héaux de Bréhat, there was a special mission to be performed as specified in these secret orders. They were to be opened precisely at noon the next day when *Teazer* was required to be in position three leagues north-east of St Peter Port, halfway between Guernsey and Alderney, and action taken accordingly.

'Secret orders,' Kydd said in awe. 'We're full stored 'n' watered. Tomorrow we make discovery o' the contents and find we may be under weigh f'r Holland, th' South Seas – anywhere!'

'I rather think not,' Renzi said. 'As you see, we have to be at Bréhat directly following. In fact, it rather exercises the intellects as to what precisely can be done in just the one day.'

Chapter 7

As *Teazer* stood out into the Little Russel passage in the brisk morning breeze, Kydd fought to suppress his emotions. With his mind no longer at severe distraction he was able to take his fill of the sights, and the perfection in the way his ship lifted so willingly to the seas. In the furious rush of events of the last few months he had neglected her but now, with everything set fair ahead, he would take time to renew their relationship.

As if sensing his attention, *Teazer*'s bows rose, gave a spirited toss and, with a thump, she threw a playful dash of spume aft that wetted his lips with salt. His heart went out to the little ship, now so far from Malta, where she had been born.

The cruise was just what was needed to pull *Teazer*'s company together. Kydd turned with a grin to Standish, next to him on the quarterdeck. The officer returned an uncertain smile and occupied himself with his telescope.

Grande Canupe safely abeam, Kydd ordered a north-easterly course and in less than two hours had made the specified position. Savouring the moment, he waited for the eight bells of midday to ring out, then went below.

He'd concluded that, in naval terms, Renzi was more of a captain's secretary than a mere ship's clerk, no matter what was entered in the muster book, and therefore could be made privy to any operational confidentialities. 'It's noon, Nicholas,' he said casually, fingering the sealed packet. 'I do believe I'm t' open my secret orders.'

It was disappointing in a way: just a single sheet of paper folded several times, no enclosures. Still, this was his first time opening such orders and he scanned it quickly. From an anonymous hand he learned that he was to recover a chest from the French coast and keep it safe until he returned from the cruise. Then he would pass it to the commander-in-chief. The entire operation was to be conducted in the greatest possible secrecy.

'We have t' steer small wi' this mission, Nicholas,' Kydd mused. 'Not even Kit Standish.'

Renzi looked at him soberly. 'I can conceive of why it should be so,' he said. 'Supposing it were to contain documents and plans won at great personal cost. The very knowledge that we have it might nullify any advantage we gain from the intelligence – and put to hazard the brave soul who brings it.'

'Aye. It seems th' admiral took pains t' make sure th' orders couldn't be known afore we sailed, an' as far as we can fathom it might all be a reg'lar done thing.' Kydd read the instructions more slowly. 'L'Anse Pivette. I figure that's t' be somewheres south o' Cap de la Hague.' This was the very tip of Normandy to the north. He continued, 'We close wi' a small beach after dark an' lift it off – it's passin' strange it says nothin' about anyone handin' it over. Just the spot, th' exact time an' date.'

'That's as if the bearer wishes to disassociate from us, reasonably it would seem.' Renzi's half-smile appeared. 'I cannot help but observe, dear fellow, that there is something else perhaps we should consider, and that is if we are betrayed, the time and place being known, we will then be delivered into the hands of the enemy.'

'Or this is th' way it's to be done b' those in the character of a – a spy,' Kydd said stoutly. 'We carry out our orders, Nicholas.'

'Certainly,' Renzi said. 'It's just that – this creeping about like a common thief is not to my liking. I fear I'm not your born intelligencer.'

'Rest easy, m' friend, you're not t' be troubled in this,' Kydd said. 'It should be quick enough done.'

The strictures on secrecy meant that besides Dowse, only one other aboard, Queripel, was told the exact location they were heading for, but neither was informed of the reason.

It was not going to be easy but, clearly, the nameless hero who had tracked across the lonely wilderness of the interior to deposit the chest would be counting on them to muster sufficient seamanship to achieve the last lap in its journey.

'Sir, it's a wild an' savage shore,' Queripel said warily. 'I remember passing th' Nez during the peace, glad o' some shelter fr'm the Alderney Race, an' recollect as how there's tidal rocks close by as ye'd be glad to keep off from. An approach b' night? I doubts it, sir.'

Together he and Kydd pored over the charts: to the north beyond the Nez, the point guarding the bay L'Anse Pivette, was the Race of Alderney with the fiercest currents to be found anywhere. As the ebb tide turned, the direction of the water would reverse, flooding in to fill the Race from the wider Atlantic in surging currents that at times could exceed a ship's best sailing speed, a fearful hazard.

Picking up on something Queripel had said, Kydd formed his plan. That evening a small British warship would be seen sailing northward along the coast, probably intending to round the Cape to look in on Cherbourg, as so many had done in this war. Its inexperienced commander would pass the Nez de Jobourg, immediately find himself in the teeth of the Race and, dismayed, fall back into the lee of the Nez to ride out the hours until the tide slackened. For this he would choose L'Anse Pivette.

There was no time to lose. Kydd bounded up to the upper deck and told Standish, 'Ease away t' th' east, if y' please – Cap de Flamanville.' This was a dozen miles to the south of the Nez and would allow them to come up as though on their way to the north.

They raised the odd semi-circular headland in two hours and pretended to look into the tiny harbour before shaping course to the north. It needed careful sail-trimming and continual work with the log over the taffrail to keep a constant speed in order that *Teazer* would meet the Alderney Race at the right tide-state. Kydd hid a smile at Standish trying to contain his curiosity at the activity.

Ahead, the bold and characteristic shape of the Nez de Jobourg firmed in the afternoon sun and Queripel pointed out the features. 'La Ronde,' he said respectfully, of the tail of high rocks extending into the sea at the northern end of the quarter-mile bay. His gaze shifted further round to a tiny beach. 'L'Anse Pivette,' he grunted. It was a good anchorage for anything except a southerly.

Kydd's information was that the chest would be placed behind a rock at the well-defined inner end of the small beach.

He hauled out his watch. 'Tide is well on th' make,' he said in satisfaction. 'The Race is beyond?'

'Aye, sir, no more'n a half-mile or so.'

The shoreline was rugged and precipitous, grey granite and scrubby vegetation, with no sign of life in the soft, late-afternoon sunlight. Kydd trained his glass on the little beach until his eyes watered but could see nothing beyond the dash of ruddy gold sand amid the sombre crags.

The breeze was lightening as they skirted La Ronde and weathered the Nez – full into the making tide of the Race. The current was more rapid than any Kydd could remember: fretful ripples and sliding overfalls were hurrying towards them as far as the eye could see. In the light airs *Teazer* had no chance. With all sail set, the water gurgled past in a fine wake – but she made no headway, the coastline abeam quite stationary, then sliding away as they were carried back where they had come from.

Queripel smiled. 'A calm day,' he offered. 'In a southerly gale, tide agin wind, 'twould amaze, the seas as are kicked up. An' tide with a blow – why, in high-water springs we c'n meet wi' nine, ten knots an' then—'

'Aye. I'll remember,' Kydd said. There might be not a soul to witness *Teazer*'s arrival but if there was it had to look right. 'Helm up an' wear into the bay,' he ordered. The ship found her lee and the anchor tumbled down as the sun set out to sea.

Standish could not hold his curiosity any longer and came up to stand next to Kydd as the sails were furled. 'To anchor, sir? On an enemy shore?'

'The gig an' two hands in th' water after dark.'

'We – we're not going ashore, sir?' It was normally the prerogative of the first lieutenant to lead any party out of a ship.

'No, I am.'

The evening drew in, with no movement seen ashore; this desolate spot would seldom be visited by any other than fishermen.

Kydd felt a thrill of apprehension. This was different from his hot-blooded landing at Granville: here there was time to admire the rugged sunset beauty – and imagine what could go wrong.

Was a troop of soldiers concealed ashore? Did a warship lie beyond the point waiting to come down with the tide and fall upon them? If it appeared while he was ashore Standish had the bounden duty to cut the cable and run, leaving them to the French as spies caught in the act.

A three-quarter moon was low in the sky and it was time. The gig was lowered gently. Two seamen, Cobb and Manley, took the oars, Kydd the tiller, and the boat pulled strongly inshore. As soon as they had left the comforting mass of the sloop he became aware of the evening quiet, just the slop and gurgle of water, the distant hiss of waves on shingle – and the enfolding shadows reaching out to claim them.

The boat nudged sand and Kydd stepped out. 'We'll be back directly,' he said to Manley. Cobb followed him up the beach. The land felt inert and lifeless underfoot, adding to Kydd's unease. He stopped and held up his hand: there was not the slightest sound. He looked about, eyes straining.

The tiny beach ended in a long ledge of rock at the north-western end. They trudged over and behind the rock, in its shadow, found an ordinary oblong wooden case with crude rope handles. Kydd took one end – it was heavy but not impossible for them – and Cobb grabbed the other. Before they lifted it Kydd froze. Was that a tiny scrape, a slither?

With an outraged squawk a large seabird launched itself

past them. Kydd cursed and the two manhandled the chest into the boat. Kydd threw his boat-cloak over to conceal it.

'Go!' he hissed at Manley, and they returned hurriedly to *Teazer*. Standish was leaning over the side in great curiosity. 'Strike it down into m' cabin immediately,' Kydd snapped at the two seamen, and ordered Standish brusquely to get the ship to sea immediately.

He'd done it. As *Teazer* leaned to the soft night airs Kydd had the satisfaction of knowing that he had successfully performed his first secret order and now could concentrate on proper sailoring.

Hauling their wind for the south they tried to make up the time to the rendezvous, sailing between Guernsey and Jersey, taking care to fetch the treacherous Roches Douvres – 'Rock Dovers' to the sailors – in the safety of morning light.

It was a sobering passage. Kydd had made up his mind to learn what he could of the area in which *Teazer* would be operating for the foreseeable future, a maze of shoals, sub-sea reefs, fierce tidal currents and some of the most desolate and forbidding coasts he had ever seen. Added to which there was the lesson learned of these waters early in the war when Saumarez himself had been chased by five French warships and thrown his heavy frigate through the hideous tangle of rocks in the west of Guernsey to freedom, a tribute to his courage and to his exceptional knowledge of local conditions.

Queripel had been eager to pass on what he knew, and Kydd began to accrue knowledge and wisdom. As he did so his respect for those who daily plied these waters increased; any who could keep the seas off this ironbound coast would be a good seaman – including the French. St Malo, an ancient town deep in the main bay of Brittany, had produced daring corsairs for centuries, some even now prowling as far afield as the Indian Ocean. This cruise would not be a sinecure.

Off the wicked tumble of grey-brown rocks that was the Île de Bréhat he saw a sloop hove-to. Her challenge was smartly run up, but Kydd was ready with the private signal. It was, of course, Carthew in *Scorpion* but this time there was no doubting the senior vessel, and as custom dictated, *Teazer* was sent round her stern to respectfully round to for hailing.

'You've taken your time, I observe, Mr Kydd,' he blared, through his speaking trumpet. 'I'd expected you a day or more ago. What delayed you?'

It took Kydd aback: it was unlikely that Carthew had knowledge of his secret orders and in any case it was not to be discussed in such a public way. 'Er, an errand f'r Admiral Saumarez,' he bellowed back. 'All concluded now.'

'I should think so,' Carthew said tartly, then added, 'No French about as I've seen to the westward, quiet in Paimpol and you have *Harpy* to the east'd for a rendezvous here in six days. Any questions?'

'No, sir.'

'Very well. Good hunting,' he said flatly. His bored tone implied disinterest in Kydd's prospects, and *Scorpion* lost no time in bracing round and making off to the north, leaving *Teazer* in sole possession of the patrol area.

At last! It was a fine morning, the winds were fair, and there was the best part of a week to traverse the hundred and fifty odd miles westward to Ushant and back. With no ports of significance to speak of – Roscoff was the largest, but not a naval port, and the rest were mere rockbound tidal havens – it was an unpromising prospect.

But with the autumn roads now impassable by ox-cart,

which could carry several score sacks of grain, it would have to be packhorses, each managing at best only four. Every beast would itself require feeding and tending by a man, he in turn having needs, and this would be multiplied by the five or six days it would take to cross northern Brittany. How many would it take to keep the fleet in Brest, with its thirty thousand hungry seamen, supplied? A humble hoy could bring eighty tons along the coast in a day and go back for more. Dozens of these vessels must now be threading their way westward, trying to keep out of sight from seaward among the craggy islets and offshore sandbars, all helpless prey to a determined man-o'-war.

Kydd gave a passing thought to these inoffensive craft, manned by seamen whose daily fight was with the sea and this dire coast – how hard it must be to have their voyage cut short, their ship and livelihood snatched from them. Then he turned abruptly to the master: 'T' th' west, Mr Dowse.' In the fortunes of war, the merchant vessels had to take their chances as did every other seafarer. Even *Teazer* might suddenly be set upon. There was no room for sentiment.

The coast lay to larboard, its rocks caught in the morning sun with a soft pink tinge and lying in dense scatters or peeping coyly from the waves in a flurry of white. Islands sprawled in groups or out to sea as lonely outposts. This coast had a terrible beauty all of its own.

Teazer sailed on westward, past tortuous inlets leading to huddled settlements: Ploumanac'h and Skeiviec, ancient names from the beginning of time – here was quite another France to the pomp and fashion of Paris. They skirted the ugly jumble of Les Héaux de Bréhat well out to sea, giving best to the small fry cowering up the long river at Tréguier.

'I'd like t' cast a glance at Sept Îles,' Kydd murmured. These were sizeable islands lying offshore, of which the master would be aiming to keep *Teazer* to seaward, but frightened coasters might be skulking among them. They angled towards but from somewhere in their midst the smoke and tiny spat of a small cannon erupted.

'Closer,' Kydd ordered. An antique fort in the centre island was ineffectually disputing their progress; it did, however, serve to draw attention to the channel that lay between it and the mainland. 'An' south about,' he added.

The sloop eased into the passage, with a rose-coloured granite shoreline on either beam and, in the sea overside, an unsettling forest of kelp from the dark depths streaming away with the current. Ahead lay only the odd-shaped high islands of the Triagoz plateau, but the coast had now turned abruptly southwards.

A scream came from the masthead lookout: '*Deck hoooo!* Two sail under a press o' canvas, standing away!'

From the deck it was clear what was happening. Their decision to take the inshore channel had spooked the two into abandoning their hiding-place in the Triagoz for a hasty dash to the safety of Roscoff, only a couple of hours' sailing across the bay.

'I want 'em!' Kydd grated, levelling his telescope. Across the deck grins appeared. 'Mr Queripel, depth o' water 'tween here 'n' Roscoff?'

'There's a channel fr'm the nor'-east . . .' he began uncomfortably.

'Aye?'

'As will serve – but, sir, I have t' tell ye, it's perilous waters hereabouts. Can we not—'

'Nor'-east.' Kydd sniffed the wind. 'It'll do. Bow-lines t' th' bridle an' don't spare th' cordage.'

Teazer seemed to sense the drama and leaped ahead. Every eye aboard followed the motions of the quarry whose terror even at a distance could almost be felt. The knowledgeable made lordly judgements as to the probable prize value, but Kydd was aware that things could change in a trice – a frigate disturbed in Roscoff, a sudden change in wind forcing them on to a dead lee shore.

'We're t' shift course here, sir,' Queripel said awkwardly. 'We must be clear o' th' plateau, else we—'

'They're not concerned t' weather it,' Kydd said pointedly. The fleeing vessels were taking a direct course to Roscoff, no more than ten or fifteen miles more.

'I – I say we must, sir! Th' – th' tide is on th' ebb an' we—'

'They come fr'm hereabouts, they should know—'

'It's th' state of tide, sir! I mislike we ignore th' overfalls o' the plateau. I've seen—'

'Very well. Ease t' larb'd,' Kydd said heavily.

They angled further southwards while their prey flew directly towards the distant smudge of their sanctuary, masts leaning at a precarious angle in their quest for speed. There were groans about *Teazer*'s deck and sour comments about luck.

And then it happened. The leading vessel struck, slewing round in an instant; she was brought to a complete stop, her foremast toppling like a tree at the shock of impact. The other ship, following close astern, shied to one side but raced on desperately.

'Leave him,' Kydd said, eyeing the wreck. He looked at Queripel. 'Can we . . . ?'

'He took a reef rock o' th' Plateau de la Méloine. We have t' keep to the suth'ard or finish th' same – but this one' – he nodded at the fleeing ship – 'he's going t' be a mort more cautious now. We has a chance.'

Teazer was in the deeper channel and forging ahead but the other vessel was picking its way fearfully through the weed-covered menaces – with only five or so miles to go they most definitely had a chance.

Queripel stepped aside and Kydd saw that Renzi had appeared on deck, wearing the wistful, absent expression that showed he had been happily immersed in his books until very recently. 'Ah. Do I see the cause of so much commotion ahead of us?'

'Aye, y' do,' Kydd said. 'Supposin' we c'n catch him before Roscoff.'

'That's Roscoff?' Renzi said, with interest. 'As you'd know, a port of much antiquity. Here it was that Mary Queen of Scots stepped ashore to be married to the Dauphin of France – in the 1540s it must have been.'

'We're goin' t' be in gunshot in just a quarter-hour, Nicholas. Do y' think I should hold fire, f'r fear I might hurt our prize?'

'Of course, she was only five years old at the time,' Renzi went on thoughtfully. 'A barbaric practice, such a union.'

'And a fine coaster should fetch a handsome sum, as'll be right welcome at this time,' Kydd added.

'Yet many would remember first that it was here as well that the Young Pretender, Charles Edward Stuart, came after the calamitous battle of Culloden – spirited hence by a Malouin privateer, I believe, to his final exile.'

But Kydd had his glass up, his attention on the low sea wall coming into view. He stiffened. 'The bloody dogs,' he growled. 'Gunboats!' A gaggle had emerged and were converging on the fleeing vessel. Even if they overhauled it now they could never heave to and take possession.

'We've lost him,' he said, lowering his telescope. He swivelled round and focused on the wreck of the first. It was fast settling – but if they managed to come up on it through the same hazards that had claimed it they could only ingloriously fish out sodden oddments of cargo.

'Carry on t' the west, Mr Dowse.' They had done well on their first encounter; there would be others.

It seemed, however, word had spread that a new and aggressive English man-o'-war was abroad and the few sail they sighted scuttled away rapidly. After an uneventful conclusion to the cruise, during which Kydd had taken pains to discover more of the sea conditions in this forbidding but often strangely beautiful seascape, Guernsey lifted into view.

With his new-won local knowledge he conned *Teazer* himself past Jerbourg Point and into the Great Road. 'A shame we haven't a prize at our tail,' Standish remarked.

'We shall,' Kydd said firmly. The more he knew of these seas, the better able he would be to find their skulking places.

There was no admiral's flag in *Cerberus* but it flew from his headquarters ashore, and their gun salute cracked out in proper style.

Calloway's quarterdeck brace was an exact imitation of his captain's. Kydd had been impressed by how he had handled the promotion; now in a position of authority over his former shipmates he pitched his orders in such a way that none could take offence at the tone or doubt his intent to be obeyed. 'Boat putting off, sir,' he reported smartly.

'Very well,' Kydd answered.

'Two boats, I think,' Standish said, lowering his glass.

It was odd: the first clearly contained an officer and a number of seamen but the other taking position astern of it seemed to carry soldiers. Kydd was ready in his dress uniform for going ashore to report; the boats, however, were heading purposefully towards *Teazer* so he waited.

When they neared, the second with the soldiers slowed and stood off, the seamen laying to their oars while the first made for the side-steps. Kydd felt the first stirrings of unease as the boat disappeared under the line of the bulwarks and shortly afterwards, with the wail of a boatswain's call, the stern face of an elderly post-captain came into view.

Kydd took off his hat and approached with a welcoming smile, which was not returned. The officer briskly drew out a paper and intoned, 'Commander Thomas Paine Kydd? Provost Captain William Fellowes. By these presents I am instructed by the commander-in-chief to make search of your vessel.' He held out the paper – and, unmistakably at the bottom, there was the signature of Admiral Saumarez.

'Er, you . . . ?' Kydd was thunderstruck. Around him the deck came to a standstill, men gaping.

'Commander?' The officer held himself with heavy patience.

'May I know what's the meanin' o' this, sir?' Kydd said tightly, as he recovered himself. 'T' be rummaged like a country trader? This is a King's ship, sir, an' I'm her captain. I'll have good reason fr'm you, sir, afore I allow such a freedom.'

'Are you disputing the direct order of the admiral, sir?' Fellowes said acidly, holding up the paper.

'I'm asking f'r a right an' proper explanation of y'r actions, sir,' Kydd blazed.

'Come, come, sir. You have nothing to fear if you have nothing to hide.' There was no pity in the man's eyes.

The situation was absurd but also in deadly earnest. 'Very well, sir. Do ye require t' begin for'ard? I'll have th' men take up over the hold as soon as we secure fr'm sea.'

Fellowes wheeled round and beckoned to the boat's party,

who lost no time in coming aboard. 'Leave the matter to us, Commander,' he said harshly. The men clambering over the bulwarks were hard-looking, practised in their movements, and assembled in a tight group before the captain.

'You know what to do.' The men trotted off – not forward, but aft, disappearing down the hatchway.

'Sir! I've a right t' know! What is it—' But Fellowes had turned his back on him and was gazing out to the dark bulk of Sark, tapping the paper impatiently against his thigh.

Suspiciously quickly, there was movement again at the hatchway. To Kydd's horror, the men were hauling up the confidential chest he had recovered with such pains and protected with so much secrecy. 'Belay that, you men!' he roared in anger.

They took no notice and Kydd turned hotly on the provost captain. 'Sir! Have y' men stop. That's a chest o' secrets f'r the admiral. Th' greatest confidentiality t' be observed—'

The petty officer in charge touched his hat to the provost captain, ignoring Kydd. 'In th' commander's bedplace, sir, under th' cot,' he reported.

Kydd struggled for words. 'That – that's—'

'A blackamoor tried t' stop us an' we had t' skelp him on th' calabash,' the petty officer added impassively.

'Tysoe! Y' poxy villains! I'll—'

'That's enough, Commander,' Fellowes rapped. 'I have now to ask you to accompany me ashore, if you please.'

Kydd hesitated, but only for a moment. The sooner the business was sorted out the better. The box was still unopened and its secrets safe. Perhaps this was, after all, a long-winded way to get it ashore.

'Very well. An' the chest remains secured, th' contents not t' be seen.'

'Of course.' There was nothing for it but to board the boat, leaving an open-mouthed Standish to complete the moor, then begin harbour routine and storing for the next voyage.

There was no conversation on the passage back; the other boat fell in astern and Kydd realised that the soldiers were there to enforce a predetermined course of action and his unease turned to alarm. This was no simple mistake.

They headed for Smith Street and the headquarters ashore, the seamen bearing the chest following closely behind. Saumarez's flag still flew and Kydd's anxieties began to subside. Soon he would know what it was about.

They entered a small room and Kydd was shown to a single chair on one side while Fellowes sat behind a table. The chest had been delivered intact and lay in the centre. Two marines stood guard over it.

Saumarez strode in. 'Ah, sir!' said Kydd in relief, scrambling to his feet. 'There's been a – a misunderstanding o' sorts.'

Saumarez ignored him. 'Is this what you found?' he asked Fellowes.

'It is, sir.'

Kydd blinked. 'This is th' secret chest. Your chest, sir,' he blurted.

'My chest?' Saumarez said in amazement. 'You think to make it mine, sir?' His voice thickened in anger. 'Open it!'

'But – but, sir, we can't do that.'

'Pray why not?'

Kydd's mind reeled. 'Because, sir, this is the confidential chest y' ordered me t' recover, wi' secret, um, things as can't be shown t' the ordinary sort!'

Saumarez looked at Kydd in disbelief. 'I gave orders? You're attempting to say that I gave orders? No, sir, this will not do! It will not do at all!'

'S-sir!' Kydd pleaded. 'Don't open it in front o' the others, I beg.' Was he going mad?

Saumarez paused, looking at Kydd keenly. 'Then I'll clear the room. All except Captain Fellowes to withdraw and remain outside.' He waited until the three were alone. 'Now we open the chest. Please oblige us, Captain.'

Fellowes cut the cords then threw back the lid. Saumarez took a sharp breath as the contents were revealed – bundles of intricately worked lace and silk goods.

'I – this is . . .' Kydd could find no words.

Saumarez drew himself up, his features suddenly old and weary. 'Take this officer to the blue room,' he said dully. 'I will deal with him presently.'

Kydd tried to make sense of it. In just a single hour his entire world had been turned upside-down. Why was Saumarez denying his own orders? Had the secret chest been waylaid and a substitute made for him to convey unwittingly in its place? How had the searchers known where to find it? Should he send for Renzi? Or wait until things became clearer? There was every possibility that Saumarez was even now finding out the truth of the matter and he didn't want to involve his ship or any aboard unless he had to.

It seemed an interminable wait and his mind wandered to concern over *Teazer* and her condition after her recent voyage. He must have that fore topmast seen to. When it had come down to the deck for exercise the carpenter had shaken his head over a fissure in the timber, and with the worn main tack having been turned end for end already he would need to do battle to win a new outfit for fore and main both. While they were at it, conceivably the chain-pump could—

There was movement and discreet murmuring in the

adjoining room, the scraping of chairs, the authoritative voice of Saumarez.

The flag-lieutenant's face appeared. 'Sir, if you'd be so good as to present yourself . . .'

Kydd followed the officer. Around a long table faces turned towards him, Saumarez at the head, Fellowes to his right – and Carthew, others. Kydd was ushered to the opposite end to face his commander-in-chief.

'Gentlemen.' Saumarez seemed to have difficulty bringing out the word, 'gentlemen, I would have you in no way misled as to the nature of this meeting. It is by way of an inquiry only, and has no legal standing. If there is cause enough shown then such proceedings may follow in due course, but for now I wish only to establish the facts at hand.'

He looked gravely down the table. 'Commander Kydd. You should know that an information was passed to me recently that you were abusing your position as captain of one of His Majesty's ships to set up in trading on your own account, to the detriment of the honest merchants of these islands and to the dishonour of the service.'

'Sir, who told you—'

'Mr Kydd! Although this is no court of law you would oblige me by remaining silent until called upon to speak, sir.' There was an edge of steel to his tone that Kydd had never heard before and he fell silent, but it was an outrageous accusation and he would soon set matters right when the time came: with a commander-in-chief as morally sensitive as Saumarez, it would be an unforgivable abomination that would require the direst penalty.

'My source was anonymous but brought forward facts that left me no choice other than to take further action. I'm sorry to say that the information was in the event proved correct and a search of your vessel has produced *prima facie* evidence to support the allegation.'

Faces gazed at Kydd, some with interest, others neutral.

'In view of your meritorious record to date in the service of the King, I am most reluctant to believe that you could be so far in want of conduct as to take advantage of your position. Therefore I wish to establish to my own satisfaction the true situation.'

There was a stirring about the table as papers were laid before him. 'Captain Fellowes,' Saumarez instructed, 'detail for me your recent boarding of HMS *Teazer*.'

Fellowes inclined his head and made to rise.

'No, no, sir – this is not a formal gathering,' Saumarez said, with a quick glance at Kydd. 'You may speak to me directly.'

'Sir,' he began weightily, reading from notes, 'pursuant to your order of the twenty-fifth, on the sighting of the said vessel and its subsequent mooring I proceeded—'

'In plain English, if you please.'

'Yes, sir. Er, this morning I and a party of men boarded HMS *Teazer* soon after it anchored in Guernsey Great Road. There I—'

'Did you encounter any resistance – discouragement of your action?'

'Er – no, sir. But when advised of the purpose of my visit, Commander Kydd became heated in his opposition to my action.'

'Quite so,' Saumarez said drily.

'But on showing him my authority for so doing he agreed, but attempted to divert my attention forward, away from his cabin, offering to lay open the hold. However, by virtue of the information supplied, my men proceeded straight to Commander Kydd's private quarters where regrettably his servant offered violence to their entry and was forcibly subdued. The chest was found under his cot, as predicted.'

'Were there any witnesses to the seizure?'

'Petty Officer Crowe, or any of his party present, is prepared to swear as to where it was found.'

'And then?'

'It was hauled, unopened, to the upper deck, at which Commander Kydd became considerably agitated.'

'What did he say?'

'I cannot recall his exact words, sir, for the officer appeared incoherent, eventually claiming that the chest was of a level of secrecy that precluded its public display.'

'And it remained unopened until brought here?'

'All concerned will testify to its integrity, sir.'

Kydd's anger rose at the protracted affair and he made to interject but was stopped by Saumarez. 'Commander, are you perhaps claiming that the chest and its contents are in fact for your own private consumption?'

It was a lifeline – but if *Teazer* had been spotted near L'Anse Pivette by the informer, or his ship's company testified to his bringing aboard a mysterious chest, he would be seen to have lied and then . . .

'No, sir, I am not,' he said thickly. 'I'm tryin' t' say—'

'Later, sir. I find I must now establish a further point. Commander Carthew, did *Teazer* arrive at the rendezvous in a timely and proper manner?'

Carthew looked uncomfortable, furtive almost. 'Sir. Er . . .'

'Come now, Mr Carthew, we can easily determine the answer from your people if necessary.'

'Well, sir . . . then not exactly.'

'Sir – your attempt to shield a brother officer does you credit, but we will have the facts, Commander.'

'I'm truly sorry to have to say, sir, we were hove-to off Bréhat in wait for some . . . twenty hours after the appointed time.'

'Thank you, Mr Carthew,' said Saumarez, looking squarely at Kydd. Dropping his eyes, he paused, then seemed to make up his mind. 'Bring in *Teazer*'s sailing-master.'

'Mr Dowse, sir.' The weatherbeaten mariner shuffled his feet but gazed resolutely ahead. He carried his own master's log.

'Information has been passed to me that *Teazer* was sighted two leagues off Cap de Flamanville and again close in under the Nez de Jobourg at the time her orders specifically required her to rendezvous off Bréhat. I note to my surprise that there is no entry in the ship's log to this effect. Can you explain this?'

'Yes, sir.'

Saumarez leaned back in expectation.

'Mr Kydd, he said as how it were a secret mission, like, an' not t' trouble enterin' it in th' log.'

'Do you have the true workings for those days?'

'Aye.' Dowse steadfastly avoided Kydd's eye.

'And?'

'As y' said, sir. We closed wi' the coast after dark at L'Anse Pivette an' took aboard a – a object.'

'Then?' prompted Saumarez.

'Then we made all sail f'r the rendezvous.'

'I see. You may stand down now, Mr Dowse,' Saumarez said tightly. 'Is Mr Standish outside?'

'He is, sir.'

'Send him in.'

Standish entered carefully, his eyes darting about the room. 'Sir?'

'Just one question, Mr Standish. What occurred at L'Anse Pivette?'

Teazer's first lieutenant glanced beseechingly at Kydd, then murmured, 'Er, we anchored in the lee of the Race and, um, the captain took away a boat and two men an' landed on the coast o' France.'

'You mean the captain went ashore alone but for two hands at the oars?'

Standish looked stricken. 'Yes, sir.'

'Did he give any reason?'

'N-none that I can recall, sir.'

'Was he ashore long?'

'He was away for only half an hour or so, sir.'

'And when he returned?'

'In the dark it was difficult to see, if you understand, sir.'

'I will make my meaning plainer. Did he return with any object?'

'It was covered with a boat-cloak, sir.'

'And as officer-of-the-deck you didn't even glimpse it as it was swayed aboard?' Saumarez said irritably.

'It was the chest,' Standish admitted.

'Good God!' Kydd exploded, 'This has gone on long enough! Will no one hear me out?'

With a pained expression the admiral replied, 'I would be obliged if you would refrain from so using the Lord's name in vain. Yet in all fairness you shall be heard. What is it that you want to say, sir?'

Kydd held his temper fiercely in check: things were bad enough as they were without a confrontation. 'Sir. This is y'r chest as ye gave orders f'r me to find an' bring back. I can't understand—'

'Mr Kydd. This is the second time you have made this public accusation and I am finding it difficult to restrain my anger. I gave you no such orders, as well you know, and to be certain of this I have sent for your ship's clerk under escort to bring me *Teazer*'s orders as received that I might verify their contents myself.'

He glared at Kydd, then called, 'Is— What is his name?'

'Renzi, sir.'

'Is this man in attendance yet?

'Sir.'

'Tell him to step in – lively, now.'

Renzi entered; his features were grave.

'You are ship's clerk of HMS *Teazer*?'

'I am, sir.'

'Have you the original orders for the voyage just concluded? Quickly, man!'

Renzi unlaced the folder and handed them across. Kydd craned to see but Saumarez snatched them and scanned them. 'What's this? I see here no reference whatsoever to any secret dalliance, Mr Kydd,' he said sarcastically. 'Pray tell by what means you are able to place such a wild construction on these perfectly straightforward instructions?'

'Sir,' Kydd gulped, 'there were sealed orders as well, an' they—'

'I have heard from my flag-lieutenant that your master's mate Prosser duly signed out on these orders. You, Renzi, were you not responsible for their registering into the ship?'

'Sir.'

'You signed them in directly from Mr Prosser, did you not?'

'I did, sir.'

'And did you see them contain any sealed orders?'

The room echoed its silence.

'Did they? Answer me, sir.'

If Renzi admitted to seeing them it would be to betray Kydd as having allowed him, a mere ship's clerk, access to the highest level of confidentiality. And if he did not, Kydd would have not a single witness to testify to their existence.

'Sir, I signed for the packet but immediately locked it into the captain's confidential stowage,' Renzi said quietly, his face pale.

'Sir—'

'Mr Kydd?'

'Sir. I find it monstrous that I'm being treated in this way. I did m' duty t' th' best o' my—'

Saumarez bowed his head and held up his hand. 'Clear the room,' he said. 'I've heard enough. You will remain, Mr Kydd.'

When they had left Saumarez looked at Kydd for a long moment before he spoke. 'You! Of all the men of promise in my command – to stoop to venal acts as shabby as any.'

Kydd tried to say something but it came out as a mumble.

'And you think to obfuscate and temporise with wild tales that do you no credit whatsoever. I have to tell you, sir, I'm both shocked and greatly saddened by what has passed.' He sighed deeply and rose slowly from his chair. 'And now I have to decide what to do with you.' He paced to the end of the room, then turned. 'In view of your recent valour and service to my squadron I will not proceed in law, Mr Kydd.'

'Th-thank you, sir.' There seemed nothing else to say.

'However, I see no other course than to relieve you of your command as of this hour, Mr Kydd. You are not to return to your ship. Your effects will be sent ashore at your convenience. I will not have you as an example to my fleet. Good day to you, sir.'

Chapter 8

Kydd was very quiet, unheeding of the hubbub that eddied around the inn's taproom. The candle guttered, throwing the lines on his face into deep relief. Renzi felt uneasy. Would this sudden catapult into shame and an unknown future tip him back into unreality?

'Ye didn't have t' do it, Nicholas,' he said eventually, his beer still untouched in the pewter tankard.

'With *Teazer* in an uproar and all ahoo? Not as this would assist in a scholard's ruminations.'

Kydd raised his head. 'Who is . . . ?'

Renzi saw there was no point in prolonging it. 'Kit Standish is made captain and Prosser an acting lieutenant.' The light died in his friend's eyes and his head dropped. Renzi's heart was wrung with pity. That a man could suffer two such blows in succession was grievous. That neither was of Kydd's doing was so much the worse.

'Did they land y'r books in good shape?' Kydd asked unexpectedly, breaking into Renzi's thoughts. He had found an old sail-loft near the boatbuilders in Havelet Bay as a temporary store for their possessions, the familiar objects of a score of voyages on a dozen seas now hidden under drab canvas, waiting for . . . who knew what?

'They did, bless them. Stirk made the boat's crew bear them the full way, then insisted in making a seamanlike stow of them.' He hesitated, then added softly, 'And wishes I might make known to you the true feelings of the ship's company on your cruel and unjust treatment.'

Kydd gave a tired smile. 'You worry I'm ready t' slip m' cable, go astray in m' wits – I know ye too well, ol' friend.'

His head drooped once more – but then he looked up suddenly and, with an appalling crash, both of his fists smashed on to the table. He held Renzi's eyes with cold ferocity. 'If it takes th' rest o' m' life, I'm going t' get revenge o' this. I don't know what it's about, but y' have my oath – someone's t' pay for it.'

Renzi was taken aback. At first he could think of nothing to say; he had his suspicions but it was not the time to air them. He sought refuge in his glass, then said, 'Perhaps we should give thought as to our future.'

Kydd breathed deeply and forced himself into control. His knuckles were still white, and Renzi felt a fleeting pity for the perpetrator when his friend finally found him.

'Er, what do ye suggest?'

'Well, there's nothing to keep us here,' Renzi said, 'and I do recall we have the better part of a year's lease left on number eighteen, all paid for, of course, and a pity to waste it.'

'No!'

'It's comfortable and . . . it's there,' Renzi finished lamely.

'I'm not leavin' here! Not until I've cleared m' name an' been taken back.'

'Tom. Dear friend. You should not set your heart on this. I fear it'll prove a deep and fearful mystery that may well be impossible to penetrate at our remove. Someone is out to ruin you, and has friends . . .

'Consider – although you've been dismissed your ship, they've not succeeded in having you cashiered out of the Service. You're unemployed, but still a commander, Royal Navy, and can be given a ship at any time – but not here while Admiral Saumarez remains in command.'

'I stay,' Kydd hissed. 'If I leave, I've got no chance o' nobblin' th' bastard who did this. It's here there's th' clues, an' here I stay till I've laid him by th' tail.'

'I understand, brother,' Renzi said. 'And since these islands are proving such a singular source of ethnical curiosities, so shall I stay too.'

'I – I thank ye for it, Nicholas. I've taken rooms here as will serve.'

He took a pull at his drink, then said, 'This I don't fathom, Nicholas. Why should Saumarez deny his own orders? He's a square-sailin' sort, treated me right well before.'

'That's easily answered. There *were* no sealed orders.'

'I saw 'em wi' my own eyes, Nicholas!'

'Those were counterfeit, added to the original orders.'

Kydd slumped back. 'Why?'

'As I said, to bring about your fall from grace and ruin in the most complete fashion possible. A masterly plot, it has to be admitted,' Renzi mused. He went on firmly, 'I saw the orders were unopened: Prosser signed for them in due form in the admiral's office and they were still unopened when I took them in charge. This implies that if there was anything untoward it was done in the admiral's office.'

'Then we clap on all sail an' go—'

135

'This will not be possible. Your presence will be resisted. More to the point, it will be to no purpose.'

'I'll sweat it out o' th' buggers – someone knows—'

'It would appear, dear fellow, that anyone having influence in a commander-in-chief's office and acting with confidence and a degree of familiarity, one admiral upon another, does in fact suggest—'

'Lockwood!' Kydd recalled the man's threats when he had chosen Rosalynd over his daughter.

'I cannot dispute your conclusion. He has sworn to destroy you for what he imagines you've done concerning his family, and but for the respect you have already won from Admiral Saumarez, you would now be facing a court-martial and certain public ruination.'

'How . . . ?'

'The motive is established, the method easily deduced. It requires but one corrupt clerk to accept a suitably fat bribe to insert the poisonous forgery, and one smuggler knowing the coast to deposit the chest, and it is done.' He added, 'It's the perfect method, for how do we proceed? Do we know who took the bribe? Confront the admiral's staff one by one and demand they confess? Or minutely examine their motions on the day in question and— It's hopeless, I'm obliged to say.'

Kydd slumped back. 'If you'd have found th' orders when you were called, Nicholas, I'd have waved 'em in Saumarez's face an' m' case would be proved.'

'You will believe I searched furiously, the escort looking on with a certain impatience – but as you can observe, if I confessed knowledge of them by their absence, we'd be in a strange fixation both.'

'Then they're still aboard!'

'I rather doubt it. I personally supervised the removal of

your effects with the intent of their discovery. If you could but remember where you placed them?'

'I – I've tried, damn it, but we were in a moil at th' time, puttin' t' sea an' all.'

Renzi sighed. 'But then it's all of no account. At this space of time, should you produce them now it would be considered a clumsy attempt at exculpation. No, brother, this is as serious a matter as we have ever faced – and I confess at this time I see no way forward.'

Kydd was frustrated and restless. 'I've a notion t' take a walk, Nicholas, clear th' intellects.' Spirited discussion had not resolved the matter, but there had to be a way through.

With his uniform packed and stowed, Kydd was in his barely worn civilian garb, the dark-green tailed coat and nondescript pantaloons feeling odd after his stout naval coat and breeches. He was now a figure of scandal, of wonder – a Navy captain who had been publicly shamed, caught out in a felony and dismissed his ship. To make things even more juicy for the gossips he was the undoubted hero of the recent Granville action. In the street he would be pointed out, gaped at, scorned – and not a word could he say in his defence.

Feeling hot shame he descended the inn stairs, holding to his heart that, no matter what, *he* knew he was innocent of any wrongdoing. The street was in its usual clamorous busyness and Kydd's emergence was not noticed. Gathering his courage about him he turned left and marched resolutely up High Street.

Renzi caught up with him in the more spacious upper reaches. 'I hadn't bargained on such a gallop,' he puffed. 'Do moderate your pace, I beg.'

But Kydd wanted to be away from the town and didn't

slow. Eventually they found the road north, slackened their speed and Renzi found breath for conversation. 'A remarkable island – just a few miles broad but—'

''I' be pointed out as – as who I am, it's more'n a man should bear,' Kydd said, through his teeth. He knew, however, that there was one easy answer: simply to return to England and find anonymity – but that would deprive him of any chance to uncover the truth and reclaim his honour.

Renzi glanced at him sharply. 'Don't take it amiss, my friend, if I remark that few know you by sight, your not having entered upon society to any great degree. I have my doubts there are above a dozen people outside the Navy who know you so you shouldn't overmuch fear the gaze of the herd, if that is your concern.'

'Aye, but they'll find out – an' you will say I'm damned in society.'

Renzi bit his lip. 'Here, this will be so for now, I agree. But in England—'

'I'm not leavin', Nicholas.'

They walked on in silence and after an hour returned. Nothing had been concluded other than a vague intent to go to the admiral's office and do something unspecified. Yet every hour that passed . . . For all they knew, Lockwood's agent might still be on the island preparing to return, still available for unmasking.

It was the worst kind of frustration; Kydd found it hard to contain, and as they passed Government House he turned impulsively to go into the naval headquarters. Their entry was refused but he pushed past the scandalised sentry whereupon they were indignantly ejected. There would be no interrogations.

The evening meal was cheerless and silent. It had become

obvious now that there would be no quick solution and happy restitution – in fact, nothing constructive whatsoever had suggested itself.

In the morning, Kydd excused himself and said he needed to go for a walk alone. When he returned his face was serious. Renzi knew better than to ask; indeed, his own situation was approaching despair, for complete idleness without the solace of his books was difficult.

The day wore on drearily with neither news nor inspiration; eventually, needing to get out, Renzi suggested they head to the tavern where they had shared a dinner before their world had turned demented.

It was a mistake. They had a fine view of the castle islet below, but also a first-class vantage-point to witness HMS *Teazer* win her anchor and stand out to sea, her long masthead pennant whipping in the brisk breeze. It was proof positive that a new commission had begun for her, a new life under a new captain.

Kydd's face was like stone. Then Renzi saw a glitter in his eyes and he had to turn away. When he looked back Kydd was as still as a statue, following the little vessel with his eyes until she spread full sail and made off southward – to the open sea. With infinite sadness, he said, 'I'd be beholden t' ye, Nicholas, should we go back now.'

'It grieves me to raise the subject, brother, but we must take stock of our position.' Renzi and Kydd sat in their usual spot in the snug, to one side of the fire, teasing out their half-pints of ale for as long as they could. It was now five days gone and they were no further forward.

Kydd said nothing, gloomily lifting his grog-blackened leather tankard.

'In fine, it is to remark that our means are not without their limit – my humble emolument as a ship's clerk ceased the minute I quit the ship, as you would know, and for your own good self . . .'

Kydd shifted uncomfortably. 'I'm on half-pay, that's true, but I have t' say to ye, it's spoken for f'r months ahead – I outlaid a fat purse t' those villains in St Sampson t' prettify *Teazer's* brightwork an' gingerbread. I doubt as Standish is appreciatin' it now,' he added morosely.

Renzi turned grave. 'Am I to understand thereby that we are living on our capital?'

'Aye, I suppose it's so.'

'Then – then it's time for a decision, my friend.'

'Oh?'

'Most certainly. And it is simply to establish at what point we will be constrained to recognise our resources no longer allow us to continue our hunt and retire from hence, wounded but whole.'

'I'm not running!' Kydd blazed. 'T' return to m' family wi' such a stain? I'd sooner roast in hell.'

Renzi gave a half-smile. 'Then we must take prudent measures, steps to preserve body and soul through come what may until . . .'

'Someone's going t' talk,' Kydd said positively, 'spend their vile guineas like water, make a noise in th' taverns. An' then I'll hear about it,' he said savagely. 'An' God help th' slivey toad!'

'Very well,' Renzi said, without conviction. 'The first is to secure our living quarters. This fine inn here is no longer within our competence. We must find—'

'Our?' Kydd cut in. 'Nicholas, this is not your fight.'

'In all conscience the odds against you are high enough.

I cannot find it in me to leave you to face alone what you must, dear brother. No, this is now my decision, which you will allow me to make on my own.'

'Tak' it or leave 'un!'

The hard-faced woman turned to go but Renzi stopped her. 'We'll take it, madam.'

'Ten livres on account,' she said, thrusting out a hand from under her shawl. 'An' I've plenty o' Frenchies as'll sigh for such a one!'

Kydd frowned at Renzi, who whispered back, 'The royalists – having fled the Revolution, they're pining in exile here where they can still see their homeland.'

The wrong side of Fountain Street, it was a mansion of grandeur that had seen better times. Now the familiar drawing room, dining room and the rest were each partitioned off with their own noisy family; Kydd and Renzi's domicile was the topmost floor, the old servants' quarters.

'Such a quantity of space!' exclaimed Renzi, stoutly, at the two rooms, a clapboard partition dividing the open space of a garret. Their furniture was limited to a bed each, turned up against the wall, a single table and chair under the window and a seedy dresser. There were bare floorboards and a dank, musty smell throughout.

'Fresh air,' offered Kydd, eyeing the dirty window. 'And a fireplace.' The small grate looked mean and still contained the disconsolate crumbled remains of the last fire, but he rubbed his hands, and said briskly, 'We'll soon have it shipshape. Um, not as who's t' say, but I don't spy a kitchen a-tall. How . . . ?'

Renzi forced a bright smile. 'In course, we as bachelor gentlemen do send out for our victuals, dear fellow. There's sure to be a chop-house or ordinary close by. As to the smaller comestibles there'll be your milkmaid, baker, pieman calling, eager for our trade.'

Kydd looked at the small fireplace. 'A kettle f'r tea an' coffee?'

'Tea will soon be beyond our means, I'm sorry to say,' Renzi said firmly. 'Scotch coffee will probably be available.' Kydd winced. Childhood memories of scrimping in hard times had brought back the bitter taste of burned bread-crumbs.

They set to, and a seaman-like scrubbing from end to end soon had the spaces glistening with damp, the window protesting loudly at being opened, and a resolve declared that they would invest in more aids to comfort when their affairs were on the mend. Meanwhile another chair was needed, with various domestic articles as they suggested themselves.

When evening fell and they set about their meagre repast, the extravagance of a bottle of thin Bordeaux did little to lift the mood. A burst of ill-tempered rowdiness came up from below. Was the future stretching ahead to be always like this?

The night passed badly for Kydd. In just a few months he had come from contemplating a high-society wedding to regretting the coals for the comfort of a fire. From captain of a man-o'-war to tenant of a dirty garret. It was hard to take, and lurking at the back of his mind there was always the temptation to slink back cravenly to England.

But that would be to accept the ruin Lockwood had contrived and he'd be damned if he would!

The dull morning began with rain pattering on the window and leaks appearing from nowhere. Over the last of their tea, Renzi gave a twisted smile. 'I rather think that the occu-pation of gentleman is quite over for us, brother. We must seek out some form of income – of employment suitable to our character, or it will be the parish workhouse for us.'

'I'll never get another ship from Admiral Saumarez,' Kydd said glumly, 'even supposing he's one in his gift. Er, y' haven't seen my hairbrush? You know, the pearl-backed one Mother gave me.'

'I thought it was on the dresser,' Renzi said absently.

'No matter,' Kydd said. 'It'll turn up.'

He reflected for a moment. 'An' it must be admitted, anything of employment as takes me back t' sea is not t' be considered – I'd then be removed fr'm here an' couldn't find m' man.'

Renzi smiled briefly. 'As one of Neptune's creatures, there's little enough for you on *terra firma*, so completely out of your element.'

'I shall think on't,' Kydd answered stiffly. 'May I know, then, what it is you're proposin' to do, Nicholas?'

'It does set a challenge,' Renzi admitted, 'my qualifications being of the most cursory. I do suggest we devote this day to a reconnaissance of prospects, each being free to follow our independent course and exchange our experiences later tonight.'

Kydd headed down to the busy quayside and found the little octagonal building that had been pointed out to him. The genial harbour-master greeted him and made room for him among the charts and thick-bound books. 'What is it I c'n do for ye, Mr Kydd?'

'Kind in you t' see me, Mr Collas. Er, I'd have y' know that I've seen m' share o' sea service—'

'Oh, aye?'

'But at th' moment I find m'self without a ship, an' I thought it might be time t' swallow th' anchor an' take employment ashore, if y' see what I mean.'

There was a careful silence.

'That is t' say, if there's a position open in th' harbour authority t' a man o' the sea that ye'd recommend, I'd be grateful t' hear it.'

'Y' mean a harbour commissioner, inspector sort o' thing?'

'I do.'

'Then I have t' disappoint ye, Mr Kydd. We runs things differently here. No King's men pokin' into our affairs an' that. An' no Customs an' Excise neither. In th' islands trade is king. So it's leave 'em at it to get on wi' their business.

'Now, the most important thing we does is the piloting. T' be a Guernsey pilot is t' be at the top o' th' profession, Mr Kydd. An' afore ye ask, there's none but a Guern' will have th' knowledge t' do it. See, there's nothing like here anywheres in Creation f'r rocks 'n' shoals, and then we adds in the tidal currents, and it's a rare place indeed f'r hazards. Y' learn about a rock – it looks like quite another when th' tide state's different. Y' come upon it in th' fog, see it just the once – which rock are y' going t' tell y'r ship's master it is?'

He went on: 'Currents about here c'n be faster'n a man can run but they'll change speed 'n' direction with the tide as well. It's right scareful, th' way it can be well on th' make in one part an' at the same time only at slack in another. Why, springs in the Great Russel y' can hear th' overfalls roaring – does y' know how t' navigate the far side of an overfall in spate? An' then there's the seamounts. Nasty beasts they are, currents over them are wicked and they change—'

'– with th' tide,' Kydd said hastily. 'I did hear as ye've bought a patent lifeboat.'

'We did. A Greathead thirty-footer, cost us a hundred and seventy pounds so we takes good care of it.'

'And does it need—'

'We keep it at St Sampson.'

Clearly it was of small interest and tucked away safely out of harm's way. Kydd was running out of ideas. 'Do ye conduct hydrographical surveys hereabouts? I'm doubting th' Admiralty has the time.'

'No need. We're well served b' the private charts, all put out b' local mariners as we know 'n' trust. Dobrée an' others, rutters by Deschamps . . .'

'Then buoyage an' lighthouses – surely Trinity House can't be expected—'

'But they do an' all! Ye've probably seen our Casquet light – remarkable thing! Three towers, an' Argand oil wi' reflecting metal—'

Kydd stood up. 'Aye. Thank ye, Mr Collas. Good day t' ye.'

Renzi waited patiently in the foyer of the imposing red-brick building on St Julian's Avenue. The clerk appeared again, regarding him doubtfully. 'Mr Belmont is very busy, but c'n find you fifteen minutes, Mr, er, Renzi.'

A thin and bespectacled individual looked up as he entered. 'Yes?'

The man was irritable in his manner but making an effort to be civil, so Renzi pressed on: 'Sir, at the moment I'm to seek a position in Guernsey that will engage my interests and talents to best advantage.

'My experience in marine insurance will not be unknown to the profession – the barratry case of the *Lady of Penarth* back in the year 'ninety-three, in which I might claim a leading role, has been well remarked.' It would probably not help his case to mention that at the time he had been a common foremast hand in the old *Duke William* with Kydd.

'Since those days I have occupied myself as an officer in the King's service, lately invalided out, and it struck me that I should perhaps consider turning my experience to account and—'

'Tell me, sir, what is your conceiving of a contract of indemnity?'

'Why, sir, this is nothing but that which is defined in the deed.' It was a fair bet that anything and everything would be covered in any good watertight policy.

'Would you allow, then, rotted ropes in an assessment of common average or would it be the particular?'

'Sir, you can hardly expect me to adjudicate in a matter so fine while not in possession of the details at hand.'

Belmont sighed. 'Might I know then if you have written *anything*?'

Renzi brightened; he had passed the initial test and now they were enquiring after his common literacy. As to that . . . 'Sir, since you so kindly asked,' he began warmly, 'I am at the moment consumed in the task of evolving an ethnographical theory that I do hope will be published at—'

'I was rather referring to policies,' the man rasped sarcastically. 'And, as it happens, I'm desolated to find that there is no opening in this establishment for a marine gentleman of your undoubted talents. Good day to you, sir.'

In the evening, footsore and thoughtful, it was time to review matters. Kydd's attempts had led nowhere, although he now had the solace that in Guernsey society it seemed his crime was regarded more as bad luck than anything else, the pursuit of profit by trade a worthy enough endeavour whatever the nature of the enterprise.

Renzi's manners and evident breeding had created suspicion

and distrust and, apart from a doubtful offer as a proof-reader and another as assistant to a dancing master, whose duties appeared to be nothing more than making himself agreeable to lady students, there was nothing.

'I'm to go to St Sampson tomorrow,' Kydd said. 'There are several yards as build fine schooners an' brigs there, an' they'll be sure t' need a projector o' quality, one who knows th' sea an' has met fine men o' standin' in strange parts o' th' world,' he added unconvincingly.

Renzi hid a smile. Kydd engaged in hard selling to thick-skinned mercantile interests was unlikely, to say the least. 'One moment, and I'll jot our ideas down,' he said.

He found paper, but then in irritation turned on Kydd: 'Brother, I have mentioned before that the silver-lead pencil is a fine but expensive piece, and is for my own studies and not for the, er, general use. Where did you leave it, pray?'

Kydd glowered back. 'An' I've heard above ten times o' this wonderful pencil, but f'r now I'm not guilty o' the crime.' He hunted about briefly. 'It'll turn up.'

Renzi paused at the sound from below of a shouted argument reaching its climax in a crash. 'Possibly we should be considering a more aggressive approach to securing our existence.'

'What?' Kydd grunted.

'Why, er, we have not yet consulted the newspaper.'

They sauntered into the nearest coffee-house. Renzi engaged a bewigged attendant in amiable conversation while Kydd sat on a bench and looked around as though waiting, carelessly picking up a recent *La Gazette*. When he was sure no one was watching he folded the newspaper, slipped it into his waistcoat and left, his face burning.

It was a substantial publication in keeping with the prosperous island economy and its study justified the opening of their last claret, for the light was fast fading and, with a single candle at the table, all Renzi would allow, there were many pages of closely printed columns. They set to, trying to ignore the distant squalling of infants and the reek of burned fat and cheap tallow rising to the upper storeys.

It was depressing reading: without appropriate introductions of the usual sort, access to the more gentlemanly occupations was barred, while without experience even the lower trades would not be open to them.

'There's a situation here that may interest you,' Renzi said.

'Oh?'

'Indeed. I see here a vacancy as a shopman for an antigropelos draper, no less.'

Kydd gave a lop-sided smile. 'Being?'

'Well, a seller of waterproof leggings, of course,' Renzi answered lamely. They both tried to laugh, and Kydd reached for the foul-weather flask; there should be some of the precious spirit left from the last stormy deck watch.

'Where's that bedamn'd flask gone to?' grunted Kydd in annoyance, rummaging about. Suddenly he stopped and raised his eyes to meet Renzi's. 'A poxy snaffler!'

'It has to be – but where's a sneak thief going to get in while we're out?'

Kydd had locked everything and he was sure that it was not possible to gain entry.

'Ah – there is one way!'

'Nicholas?'

'At night. We don't batten down all hatches while we're asleep, do we?'

'The scrovy swab! If I lay my . . .' Kydd smiled grimly.

'Bear a fist, Nicholas. I'm going t' rig a welcome as will see us shakin' hands with th' villain b' morning.'

It was easily enough done: the odd length of wood, pieces of string led along the floor, a cunning door wedge. Then they pulled down their beds to retire.

Renzi did not sleep well. It was becoming clear that they were headed into unknown waters: possibly useless penury, certainly life on the fringes of society. He would bear his lot without complaint but now a moral question was arising.

Was he right in acquiescing to Kydd's forlorn search to clear his name? If Lockwood was at the back of it the implication was that he would not rest until Kydd's personal ruin was seen to be accomplished. Therefore even if by some miracle Kydd achieved his exoneration Lockwood would find some other way to secure his revenge. Renzi knew well the lengths to which vindictive men in high places could go if vengeance was their purpose.

But he had vowed to stand by his friend whatever the situation. Therefore, in logic, he must remain.

The bed with its wire frame creaked and twanged as he turned restlessly, but sleep did not come. His mind wandered to his studies: his theory was proceeding well, coalescing about responses to primal needs in differing cultures, but he needed more data. Much more. If only he could lay hold of Baudin's journal, but the French explorer had died in Mauritius and his data was now separated by the unbridgeable gulf of war. Where else could—

Cecilia. Would she wait for him? The thought shocked him into full wakefulness as he reflected on his failure in Australia to forge a life there as a free settler. He had wanted to create an Arcadia of his small landholding for her. Now, his grand plan to complete his first volume for publication to present

149

to her before he felt morally able to seek her hand – where was this, now that his entire endeavour was at an indefinite standstill? What if she—

'Hssst! Nicholas!' Kydd whispered, but Renzi had heard it too. The door-handle was squeaking softly. He lay still. There was just enough wan moonlight to make out gross shadows so the two of them should well be able to handle one – but if there were more?

The door scraped open and stayed for a space. Then the floorboards creaked but Renzi could not see any bulking figure. Instead, to his surprise, he next heard movement from well within the room.

Kydd yanked the string hard. The door banged to and the wedge slammed into place with a triumphant finality. The intruder whirled about and made for the door but it was jammed tightly shut. 'Strike a light, Nicholas, an' we'll see what we've snagged,' Kydd said, with satisfaction, getting to his feet.

The candle flickered into flame, revealing a slight figure trapped against the door. 'Well, now, an' what's y' name then, y' young shicer?'

There was no answer. Two dark eyes watched warily as they approached. The figure was in leggings, a short jacket and a bandanna.

'Answer me, y' scamp, or I has ye taken in b' th' watch.'

The muttered reply was inaudible.

'Speak up, 'scapegallows!'

'P-Pookie.'

A female child-thief? Caught off-guard in his nightgown Renzi took refuge in frowning severely. 'Pookie what, pray?'

Defiantly the boyish figure stayed mute.

'We c'n easily find out b' takin' you t' each o' the families in th' buildin' t' see who owns ye.'

'Pookie, er, Turner.'

Kydd looked at Renzi in exasperation. The harsh penal system demanded transportation to Botany Bay for the theft of a handkerchief and the gallows for a few shillings. Children as young as nine had gone to the scaffold. What had possessed this ragamuffin to take such risks?

'Get rigged, Nicholas, I'm gettin' satisfaction fr'm th' father.'

But there was none, only a listless, irritated mother who screamed threats at the child. 'Only twelve year she has an' all, sir, an' s' help me the bastard ain't even mine!' she whined. It seemed they would not be seeing their possessions again.

'Listen t' me, an' mark well what I say,' Kydd growled, in a fierce quarterdeck manner. 'If'n I catch this scut skulking about our rooms again it's th' beak on th' instant. Compree?'

The coins clinked one by one as Renzi let them drop to the table, his face in shadows from the single, evil-smelling rush dip.

'So bad?' Kydd asked uneasily. He was trying to toast the last of a stale loaf on a brown-coal fire.

At first Renzi did not reply. Then he turned. 'Despite domestic economies of such austerity as would quite put Mistress Hannah Glasse to the blush, it would seem that the end must come soon and with no appeal.'

'Th' end?' Kydd said apprehensively.

'Suffice it to say that on Friday we shall be unable to render her due to our termagant landlady. It should be quite within prospect that our immediate quitting will be demanded.'

'Then . . .'

'Yes.'

Renzi said nothing further and regarded Kydd gravely.

'You're sayin' we're t' be gone fr'm the islands, return t' England?'

'It would seem the time has come, brother.'

Kydd looked away. 'I'm stayin', Nicholas.'

'Where—'

'I'm goin' t' the sail-loft. Th' old fisherman as offered it me has no use f'r it. That's where I'll be.'

'Dear fellow, that's – that's no living for a gentleman. Why, you might well be taken up for a vagrant. It will not do at all.'

Kydd gave a tigerish smile. 'I'm seein' it through. That chousin' toad only has t' say one word out o' place an' I'll have him.'

It was a piteous image: a fine seaman, and honourable, reduced to rags and the shuffling hopelessness of the poor with the canker of vengeance sapping his life spirit.

'Of course,' Renzi said calmly. 'Then I do suggest we begin taking the rest of our worldly goods thence. For myself, there is no question that I burden myself on you further. Instead I'll, er, find somewhere to lay my head. Yes! I have a mind to visit Jersey.'

'Jersey?'

'A Channel Island not twenty miles to the south-east, which, I might point out to you, is larger in area than this present isle and its opportunities as yet untried. Any news I have will be made available to you at St Peter Port post office.'

'Then – then this is y'r farewell, Nicholas,' Kydd said, in a low voice, 'an' I'd wish it were at a happier time.'

'For now, dear friend. When the one meets with fortune I dare to say the other will share in it. Do take care of my manuscripts, I beg. And at any time you will have need of your friend, make it known at the St Helier's post office.'

Chapter 9

It would be easier said than done. Carrying a bundle for his immediate needs, Renzi stepped ashore in St Helier, the chief town and port of Jersey, with the pressing goal of finding employment, however humble, that might serve to keep both himself and his friend from starving while Kydd's all-consuming quest spent itself before they returned to England.

Preoccupied, he had not particularly noticed the castle set out into the approaches to St Helier, which was of considerable antiquity. Other defensive works of a more recent vintage briefly caught his eye: the massive crenellations of a fortification along the skyline above the town, gun towers and signal posts. Jersey had a definite edge of siege-like tension about it. St Helier itself was less steep than St Peter Port but appeared busier.

The mariner in Renzi noted the immense scatter of granite reefs that crowded in on the port and would make it a lethal trap if the wind shifted to the south, unlike St Peter Port, which had handy escape routes north and south. He shrugged:

there would be precious little sea time for the near future – he had to secure tolerable employ.

Renzi found a coffee-house and went in. Seated in a quiet corner he secured a dog-eared copy of the *Gazette de Jersey* and scanned it – much about the tenor of existence, economic health and the general happiness of folk could be gauged from the profundity or otherwise of the concerns expressed in a newspaper.

Here, it seemed, there was feverish anticipation of an imminent assault by Bonaparte, but otherwise the usual run of vanities: theatre, gossip, confected moral outrage. But there was also a sense of boundary, between the incomers and the established residents. Not so different from any society in similar constricted circumstances, he reflected, but without the requisite introductions, nearly impossible to penetrate socially – or for the purpose of gentlemanly employment.

Renzi sighed and put down the newspaper. He had come across just one avenue. There was a naval presence here, considerably smaller than in Guernsey but apparently rating a junior commodore. It might be possible by deploying his experience as a ship's clerk to make himself useful somewhere in the establishment.

He called for writing materials and crafted a polite note offering his services to the commodore's office in whatever situation might prove convenient, sealed it and carefully superscribed it in correct naval phrasing. He had provided no return address, begging that any reply might be left *poste restante* at the St Helier post office, then sat back to finish his coffee.

In the early morning he emerged stiff and shivering from beneath an upturned fishing-boat where he had spent another night on the beach. Trudging into the deserted town his nose led him to a bakery; and for the price of some amiable chatting Renzi went away with half a loaf of stale bread. Around the corner he fished out a hunk of cheese, pared some off with his penknife, then wolfed his breakfast.

The town was coming to life and he wandered through the streets. Like St Peter Port, this was not a poor community – in fact, it, too, showed signs of wealth.

By mid-morning he was ready to continue to seek employment. On impulse he turned back for the post office; Kydd had promised to keep in touch and he was much concerned for him.

There was nothing from his friend – but there was a neatly sealed letter in an unknown hand, bearing a crest he did not know. It was from Commodore d'Auvergne: in friendly tones it invited him to make himself known at his shore address adjacent to the customs house where they would explore possibilities concerning a position. It seemed a trifle peculiar – a flag-officer, however junior, deigning to involve himself in clerkly hiring? But Renzi could see no advantage to be gained by any kind of prank.

At first he thought he had come to the wrong place. The small office, compared to his usual experience of naval headquarters, could only be termed discreet. He had taken some care in his appearance and stepped in purposefully. He identified himself to a clerk, who looked at him keenly but said nothing and ushered him up a cramped flight of stairs to a small room. It was odd, he thought, that there were no uniformed sentries.

'Mr Renzi, sir,' the man announced.

'Ah, do come in, sir,' Commodore d'Auvergne said genially, in barely accented English; he had a round, kindly face but with the high forehead and alert eyes of someone intelligent and self-possessed.

'Thank you, sir,' Renzi said, attending carefully while d'Auvergne leaned back in his chair.

There was a moment's pause as the commodore summed him up. Then he said briskly, 'You wonder why at my eminence I noticed you, sir. That is simple. In the letter your hand betrays you as a gentleman, and your making application for a menial post intrigues me.'

Renzi's uneasy smile brought a further penetrating glance. 'Of course, this would be a capital way for a spy to inveigle himself into my headquarters. Are you a spy, Mr Renzi?'

'I am not, sir.'

'Then?'

'My last post was that of a ship's clerk, sir, lately *Teazer*, brig-sloop. For reasons that need not trouble you, this position has now been closed to me.'

'Clerk? How interesting. It would disappoint me to hear that your removal was for . . . peccant reasons.'

'No felonious act has ever attached to my name, sir,' Renzi snapped.

'Do pardon my direct speaking, sir. You see, your presenting at this time comes as a particular convenience to me.'

At Renzi's wary silence he went on: 'Let me be more explicit. As commodore of the Jersey Squadron I have my flagship round the coast at Gorey. This little office provides an official *pied à terre* in St Helier and my private house is nearby. As it happens, sir, I have an especial regard for those who have in their person suffered in the terrible convulsions of the Revolution – the *royalistes*.'

He looked at Renzi intently. 'Here there are many *émigré* French to be seen wandering the streets, poor souls, some even standing for long hours on the cliffs mooning over their lost land, which is in plain view to the east. I do take a personal interest in their plight.'

Shuffling some papers on his desk he said, 'It is for this reason I maintain an old, contemptible castle near Gorey, which I devote to their cause. Now, there is nothing in the naval sphere available,' he said regretfully, 'but I have recently lost a valued confidential secretary and the creatures offering themselves in his place are – are lacking in the article of gentlemanly discernment, shall we say? Therefore, should you feel inclined, there *is* a post I can offer, which shall be my secretary for *émigré* affairs.

'You have the French, I trust?' he added.

'I do, sir.'

'They are a distracted and, some might say, fractious community. Dogmatic priests, aristocrats insisting on the forms of the *ancien régime*, a thankless task. For this, shall we say fifty livres a month?'

A princely sum! It was more than he had dared hope, and—

With only a single glance at Renzi's scuffed shoes d'Auvergne added smoothly, 'Of course, this will be at the castle – Mont Orgueil, I should inform you – which is at a remove from St Helier, and therefore I feel an obligation upon me to offer you a room there for a trifle in the way of duties out of the normal hours.'

'That is most kind in you, sir.'

'Then may I know when would be an acceptable date for your commencement, Mr Renzi?'

'This is a very remarkable achievement, sir,' said Renzi, standing next to d'Auvergne within the grim bastions of Mont Orgueil, softened with tasteful medieval hangings and well-turned Gothic furniture. The castle, four-square and forbidding on a prominence looking across the water at France, had its roots in the age of the longbow and armoured knights, but with the arrival of cannon, it had been abandoned in Elizabethan times to genteel decay.

D'Auvergne had brought back some of the colour and grandeur, particularly in the part of the edifice he occupied, the Corbelled Tower, now an impressive receiving place past the four outer gates and a higgledy-piggledy final spiral staircase.

The rest of the castle was an eccentric accretion of bluff towers and quaint gateways that led to open battlements at the top. There, stretching over two-thirds of the eastern horizon, was the coast of France – the ancient enemy of England.

D'Auvergne gave Renzi a pensive look. 'I like to think I am its castellan of modern times and I'm rather fond of it. "Time has mouldered into beauty many a grim tower," it's been said. "And where rich banners once displayed, Now only waves a flower . . ." Sad, for there's myriad tales untold here, I'm persuaded.'

He collected himself. 'You shall bed in the Principal Yeoman Warder's room. Don't concern yourself on his behalf, pray – the last he had need of it was in 1641.'

Renzi found it hard to avoid being affected by the atmosphere; the musty stonework of the upper floors had some life and light but other places lurking below in the dark and unfathomable depths of the fortress made him shiver.

D'Auvergne continued, 'There is a small staff. I have had the kitchens removed to this level, else it plays the devil with keeping the food hot. The gate porter you'll find in St George

Tower – be sure to address him as the *maréchal* – his lodgings are found by the King's Receiver and he may claim one gallon of imported wine and a cabot of salt for his pains.'

At length they returned to d'Auvergne's apartment, where he sat behind a Gothic desk, set before diamond-mullioned windows, and steepled his fingers. 'So. You have the measure of my little kingdom, Mr Renzi. What do you think?'

It was impossible to do justice to the sense of awe and unease that this lonely sea-frontier redoubt had brought to him so Renzi murmured, 'Quite of another age, sir.'

'Just so. Er, at this point, perhaps I should introduce myself a little more formally. You see at the recent demise of Léopold, Duke of Bouillon, I have succeeded to that principality and am thus entitled to be addressed as, "His Serene Highness, the Prince of Bouillon."'

Renzi sat back in astonishment, remembering just in time a civil bow of his head.

'You will, no doubt, be more comfortable with the usual naval titles at which I will be satisfied. However, I do insist on the style of prince in my correspondence.'

'Sir.'

'You might remark on it that since my lands are at the moment in occupation by Bonaparte's soldiers, and as the great hall of the castle of Navarre is unavailable to me, I must rest content with Mont Orgueil. This I cannot deny, sir, and it does explain my ready sympathy with the royalist *émigré*, don't you think?'

'It – it must do, sir.'

'Then let us pass on to other matters. Such as yourself, Mr Renzi.'

'Er?' Renzi said uncertainly.

'Quite. I do now require my curiosity to be satisfied as to

why such an evidently well-educated patrician comes to me in the character of the ship's clerk of a brig-sloop – if, indeed, this be so – seeking a form of employment with me. You may speak freely, sir.' He regarded Renzi dispassionately.

'And I, sir,' Renzi said, firmly now, 'am in a state of some wonder as to why you have seen fit to offer me a position without the least comprehension of my circumstances.'

D'Auvergne smiled thinly. 'I believe myself a tolerable judge of men and in your case I do not feel I am mistaken. Your story, sir, if you please.'

To Renzi's own ears it seemed so implausible. Going to sea as a foremast hand in a form of self-imposed exile as expiation for what he considered a sin committed by his family, later to find its stern realities strongly appealing after the softness of the land. Finding a friend such as Kydd and their adventuring together, which had ended with Renzi's own near-mortal fever – but then the revelation of a life's calling in the pursuit of a theory of natural philosophy that in its rooting in the real world could only be realised by taking ship for distant parts, in Kydd's command, to be his clerk as a device to be aboard. 'And unfortunately he has been, er, superseded and at the moment is without a ship,' Renzi added. There was no need to dwell on the circumstances.

D'Auvergne did not reply for a moment and Renzi began to think he was disbelieved. Then, with a warm smile, the man said, 'A remarkable history, sir. I was not wrong in my estimation – and I would like to hear more of you, sir. One evening, perhaps.'

The chophouse was busy, noisy and welcoming after Kydd's morning exertions walking the streets in search of clues regarding his situation. He drew his grego clear of the sawdust floor and eased himself into one of the communal tables, nodding to slight acquaintances. 'Bean Jar, is it, then?' a waiter asked, swiftly disposing of the remains of a meal in the empty place next to him. His customary order of the local dish of lentils and pork, along with bread and beer, would be his only hot meal of the day.

'Aye.'

'Mutton chop is prime – c'n find yer one f'r sixpence?'

'Not today, thank 'ee,' Kydd said. He had felt his dwindling stock of coins before he entered and mutton was not within reach.

He blessed the fact that, while he was known to the commander-in-chief and other potentates of Guernsey, the common people would not recognise the shabby figure keeping to himself in the street as a naval commander so he could pass about freely in the town. But he had found not the slightest lead to help in his investigations, and time had passed. He had to face it. Renzi had been right. The trail had gone cold, his chances of discovering, let alone proving, the deed now vanishingly remote. It was time to call a stop. He would give it just a few more days, to the point at which his means of sustenance came to an end. Then – then he would go home.

Having made this resolution, he felt more at ease with himself, and in a fit of bravado tipped the waiter a whole penny, then marched out into the street. The autumn sun was hard and bright, and on a whim he headed to the harbour where ships were working cargo, seamen out on the ran-tan, and the rich aroma of sea-salt and tarry ropes pervaded all.

On the broad quay he stopped to watch a handsome barque discharging wine; her yardarm and stay tackles worked in harmony to sway up the cargo from her bowels to a growing pyramid on the wharf. No Customs reckoning here: the great barrels would be rolled directly into the mouths of the warehouses, probably for trans-shipping later by another hull to a British port, given that she flew the American flag, a neutral.

A young man stopped his empty man-hauled cart and waved to him. Kydd stepped across and instantly recognised the face. 'Mr Calloway!' he said, in astonishment. 'What are ye doing?'

Calloway doffed his battered cap respectfully, an unexpectedly touching gesture in the surroundings, and said shyly, 'Mr Standish had his own young gennelmen he wanted t' place on th' quarterdeck an' offered t' me as whether I'd be turned afore the mast or be put ashore, sir.'

It was a mean act, but in the usual course of events when a captain left his command the midshipmen and 'followers' would go with him, allowing the new captain to install his own. And Calloway had chosen the honourable but costly move of retaining his nominal rank instead of reverting to seaman and staying aboard. Midshipmen were not entitled to half-pay and thus he had rendered himself essentially destitute.

'An' so ye should have done, Mr Calloway,' Kydd said warmly. The thought of others who had served him so well now under an alien command wrenched at him. 'Er, can I ask how ye fare now?'

'Why, sir, on Mondays an' Wednesdays I'm t' be ballast heaver. Tuesdays an' Thursdays I'm cart trundler to Mr Duval, the boatbuilder.'

Kydd hesitated, then said stoutly, 'Y' has m' word on it, Luke, in m' next ship I'll expect ye there on th' quarterdeck with me. Won't be s' long, an' m' name'll be cleared, you'll see.'

'Aye aye, Mr Kydd,' Calloway said quietly.

'An' where c'n I find ye?'

'Ask at th' Bethel, sir. They'll find me when y' has need o' me.' A floating church in harbour, the Bethel was a refuge for seamen seeking relief from the sometimes riotous behaviour of sailors raising a wind in port.

'I'd – I'd like t' invite ye t' sup wi' me a while, but—'

'I thank ye, Mr Kydd, but I must be about m' duties,' Calloway said, with the barest glance at Kydd's ragged appearance. 'Good fortune t' ye, sir.'

Renzi had not found the work onerous and, in fact, it was not without interest: d'Auvergne seemed to have a wide circle of royalist acquaintances and was in receipt of considerable sums from charitable institutions in England to distribute to the needy. Some of the royalists apparently had pressing personal problems that d'Auvergne was taking care of privately. Several came while Renzi was working with him. At their suspicious looks he would leave the room quietly; such behaviour from proud ex-noblemen was understandable.

Renzi finished what he was working on and handed it to d'Auvergne, who glanced through it and said, with a smile, 'I do fear, Mr Renzi, that we are not making full use of your talents.' He slapped down the papers with satisfaction. 'Tonight you shall come to dinner, be it only a family affair, and then I will learn more of your philosophies.'

Renzi was much impressed by the mansion just a mile out of St Helier, set in a vast ornamental garden with interiors of a splendid, if individual magnificence. D'Auvergne had humorously named the house 'Bagatelle' and proudly showed him the sights inside: scientific specimens, works of art of considerable value with 'relics of injured royalty', which included *objets de toilette* from the apartment of Marie Antoinette smuggled out at the height of the Revolution's horrors.

At length d'Auvergne made his apologies. 'I must leave you now for a space, Mr Renzi, to settle a business at my town office but I shall be back directly. Do avail yourself of my library – I take much pleasure from learned works in which the flower of man's intellect might so readily be imbibed.'

The library was monumental, with some sixty volumes on naval architecture and navigation alone, another hundred or two of *Voyages and Travels*, a well-thumbed Johnson and a recent *Encyclopaedia Britannica*. Seventy more on chemistry, mineralogy and a whole shelf of arcane botany, more on applied mathematics and a complete Shakespeare.

Renzi noted that nowhere was there any tome that could remotely be said to address religion, although there was Voltaire and commentaries on Robespierre and the Worship of Reason. And neither were there the usual weighty classics; Virgil, Caesar, Plato were conspicuous by their absence.

A gloomy inner library contained a mass of volumes and pamphlets on the history of France, obscure references to medieval campaigns and racks of genealogical studies. It was staggering. Renzi estimated that no less than four thousand books were before him in serried array. This was erudition indeed and he looked forward keenly to making their owner's better acquaintance.

D'Auvergne soon returned, and after passing pleasantries over sherry they moved into the dining room. 'My dear, this is Mr Nicholas Renzi, a philosophical gentleman who is doing us the honour of dining with us tonight. Renzi, this is Madame de la Tour, daughter of the Count of Vaudreuil who will perform the honours of the house.' Two children stood meekly by her side and were also introduced.

A shy but warm acknowledgement was bestowed and they sat comfortably at the table *en famille*. 'Do explain to Madame the elements of your study,' d'Auvergne suggested.

Renzi had caught on to the discreet coding: the lady was not his wife. Were the children hers? 'Dear Madame, this is naught but a comparative essay into the imperatives of human existence,' he began, 'as being differing responses to the same . . .'

Madame paid careful attention but remained silent. D'Auvergne asked intelligently about the same aspects of Rousseau's position on the noble savage that had so exercised Renzi in the great South Seas some years ago. Casting a shrewd glance at Renzi, he murmured, 'From your regard for the Encyclopaedists one might be tempted to conclude that your admiration extends to present philosophies.'

'If by that you are referring to the Revolution, then I can assure you that nothing is more abhorrent to me than the spectacle of the glory of French civilisation falling prey to those political animals now in control of the state.'

'Quite so, quite so. We are of a mind on the subject. Napoleon Bonaparte is now consul-for-life and is energetic and ruthless in his own interest – as witness his domination of the state apparatus, the secret police, even his economic machine, which I have certain knowledge has lately replaced the national currency with his own "franc".' He continued sombrely, 'He has now not a single country in arms against him save our own, and therefore has no distraction from his lust to conquer. I cannot recall that our realm has ever lain under a greater menace.'

Renzi shifted in his seat; this reminder of peril was only pointing up his own essential uselessness in the present dangers. To change the subject he asked politely, 'Do satisfy my curiosity on one point, if you will, sir. Just why is it that in these singular times their lordships at the Admiralty see fit to rusticate Sir James Saumarez to these remote islands – a proven fighter if ever one were needed – rather than require him to lead a fleet in the great battle that must surely come?'

'Why, sir, have you not surmised?' d'Auvergne said, with raised eyebrows. 'It is over. He has won his victory. His purpose is complete.'

'Granville?' said Renzi, puzzled.

'Not at all.' D'Auvergne chuckled. 'I talk of a species of silent victory, but for all that, one that will resound down all of time.'

'Sir?'

'Let me be more explicit. In 1794 the French plotted an invasion of the Norman Isles, specifically Jersey. Only the greatest exertions from us and the convulsions on the mainland at the time saved us. Although the Treaty of Amiens ended hostilities in 1802, it became clear quite early that we would be under assault once more, this time by the most formidable general of the age.

'What better move can you conceive of than to dispatch a feared and respected leader of the last war to take station here as commander-in-chief? By his very presence he has discouraged intemperate assault on the Channel Islands and with a simple flourish at Granville he has shown the impracticality of a local invasion. And he did succeed. My intelligence now is that all troop concentrations have dissipated. For the moment we are safe.' He put down his glass and went on: 'So on the strategical side this is what has been accomplished: from Calais far to the east, to the extremity of France in the west, they have no harbour of size in which to concentrate a battle fleet to seize the Channel – except Guernsey, which in course is now denied them by Sir James's silent victory.

'For the French this is galling in the extreme. You see, we in turn do use these islands to our own advantage, which is as a base to fall on their sea lanes with men-o'-war and privateers to paralyse their commerce and attempts to reinforce. And, most critically, to keep close in watch on Bonaparte's invasion preparations – which we are so well placed to do,' he added, with satisfaction.

The mood changed. He lifted his glass and exclaimed genially, 'But then we are neglecting the plaice with our talk. Pray, eat and enjoy – and I have a notion how we might deploy your talents to better effect, Mr Renzi,' he added mysteriously.

Renzi lay awake in his creaking four-poster. A south-westerly was blustering outside against the ancient stone and penetrating draughts had him drawing up the counterpane. He'd been prepared to endure nights under a hedge and feast on scraps but he was now safely immured in a castle, in comfort under a goosedown quilt and reflecting on the conversations he had enjoyed with the reigning flag-officer no less.

There was no real reason for d'Auvergne to have so readily seized on him as a personal secretary – unless for intellectual companionship. Could this be so? And what were those extra duties that d'Auvergne had alluded to? Was he in truth a prince? His thoughts raced on.

Kydd, meanwhile, was living in a sail-loft, vainly trudging the streets in his forlorn quest. Did Renzi have the right to spend his days in such grand surroundings while his friend suffered? On the other hand, with a library of such richness within reach his study might yet take wings – the *Voyages and Travels* alone must be a gold-mine of ethnical facts against which . . .

'Ah, Renzi. Did you sleep well at all?' D'Auvergne was at his desk early, reading various articles of mail. Renzi took his accustomed place. 'I did, sir.'

One letter seemed to be causing d'Auvergne some concern. He lifted his head and spoke unseeingly: 'Oh. That's good.'

He stood up suddenly and paced about the room then stopped abruptly. 'I think it's about time we put you to real work, Mr Renzi. My daily routine does not vary much, you'll see. In the morning I shall be here attending to matters and the afternoon I spend aboard my flagship, *Severn*, devoted to the business of my flag. There she is.' He pointed out of the window.

Renzi glanced at the two-decker of a distinct age peacefully at anchor in the centre of the wide sweep of Gorey Bay below the castle, several smaller vessels moored alongside.

'She's a 44 only,' d'Auvergne said apologetically, 'but, as you can see, Gorey Bay is sandy and open and the only invasion beach worth the name on the island. *Severn* does her duty nobly as nothing more than a floating battery to cover the approach.'

Renzi could well see the convenience of having a commodore's retinue so close at hand with the ability to put to sea within minutes. At the same time it left d'Auvergne free to maintain his interests ashore.

'Now, this is your first duty. I desire you to make known to yourself the whole situation obtaining on the mainland with its problems and concerns. Only when you are privy to the complete picture will you be able to assist me as you should.'

'Er, yes, sir.'

'That is, in Brittany and neighbouring regions – Paris and that gang of regicides you may leave to their evil machinations. And for this I would suggest the French local newspapers, all of which are conveyed to me here. A prime source of insight into a country, your newspaper.'

'Sir,' Renzi said politely. 'Then might I beg the use of your library for the acquisition of background material and similar?'

'I would hope you do, sir.'

Renzi nearly hugged himself with glee. To spend his days poring over those literary treasures – it was too good to be true.

'Oh, and I'm often accused of being mortally absent-minded, therefore I'll take the precaution of advancing you your first month's emolument before I forget.'

Renzi was touched. 'I am obliged to you, sir.' He pocketed the envelope gratefully.

The piles of provincial newspapers were delivered to one of the empty rooms nearby so he excused himself and set to. They were read in market towns by peasant farmers and agricultural factors, yet clues stemming from the fluctuating prices of common produce, and unintended allusions in shrill editorials, revealed that all was not well and ugly dissatisfaction was not far below the surface in Napoleon's France.

When d'Auvergne left for his flagship Renzi scribbled a quick letter to Kydd for collection at the Guernsey post office, enclosing three coins and explaining his good fortune at meeting the Prince de Bouillon without going into detail.

Turning back to his task he heard movement in d'Auvergne's office. Startled, he went through but found only the flag-lieutenant waiting for a message. He seemed surprised to see Renzi. 'Er, Jenkins. You must be the new man?'

'Renzi. Secretary *pro tempore*, I believe,' he replied cautiously. 'Recently arrived. An interesting place – but tell me, is the man in truth a prince?'

Jenkins grinned. 'There's much you'll find odd about our Philippe d'Auvergne, but I have to tell you that, besides the Duke of Clarence, I believe he's the only full-rigged prince in the Service. He was adopted into the line, but a prince for all that.'

'A man of some learning, I think.'

'He is. Did you know he's an FRS?'

Renzi was amazed. Not only a member of the Royal Society, the premier learned society in the land, but a fellow, no less.

'A deep thinker, he's a Doctor of Letters from Livonia and corresponds with the world on everything from mathematics to botany, but amiable enough. Oh, and an Arctic explorer and colonial planter to boot.'

'Has he – is he distinguished in his service career?'

The young lieutenant chuckled. 'I'm surprised you haven't heard! In fine, yes. A front-line fighter in the American war, first lieutenant o' the saucy *Arethusa* and more than a few prizes to his name even before Napoleon. You'll find – oh, thank you,' he said, taking some papers from a messenger and stowing them in his satchel. 'Have to go now – but I think you'll find your work very . . . interesting.'

He hurried off, leaving Renzi in even more perplexity than before.

After two days he felt he had explored enough of the people and the situation and went to d'Auvergne.

'So you feel able to talk about the royalists and their problems. Then pray tell me your observations on the

Chouan risings and what they would mean to the *paysan* and merchant?'

It was apparent that he was being tested but it was not hard to apply his mind to the social effects of a bloodily repressed rural revolt.

D'Auvergne nodded slowly. 'Very good. You have a natural insight into the human condition and that I like. One moment.'

He rose and crossed to the thick oak door, closed it firmly, then returned and produced a letter. 'Now your opinion of this, if you please.'

Apprehensive, for some reason, Renzi picked it up. The eyes never left him as he began to read. 'Why, this is a letter from . . . It doesn't say.' He looked up. 'Sir, this is a private letter. We have no right—'

'Shall we leave that aside for now? Do continue.'

'From – from someone signing himself "little cabbage",' Renzi read out unwillingly. 'It's to another – "*belle poule*".' He looked up unhappily. 'This appears to be from a lover to his *amante*. Sir, is this necessary?'

'Read,' d'Auvergne commanded.

'Very well, sir. We have this person writing – ah, it is to his wife, he mentions the little ones. He is at last to return . . . The time has been hard while they have been separated.' He glanced up in silent protest but at d'Auvergne's stony stare he continued. 'He will treasure the moment he sets foot in the old cottage once more . . . life in a town is not to be compared to a village of Brittany . . . The soldiers of the garrison are arrogant and he has a loathing for what he has to do . . . but he consoles himself that it is for them both, and with his earnings they will close the door on a harsh world . . .' Renzi finished the pathetic scrap. 'Another of

Bonaparte's victims, I think. Doing a menial's work in some army town that will pay better than rural beggary. I do so feel for him and his kind.'

D'Auvergne waited but Renzi would not be drawn. This kind of human adversity was being played out all over the world as war ravaged previously tranquil communities. Why was he being shown this particular evidence?

'I honour your sentiments, Renzi. However . . .'

A premonition stole over him and he tensed as d'Auvergne leaned back in his chair and spoke in the same controlled tone: 'It would interest me to know your reaction if you are aware that the town he speaks of is St Helier, the garrison soldiers from Fort Regent and the man, Stofflet, acting in the character of a baker, is passing details of our troop levels to Decrès.'

Renzi listened with a chill of dismay as d'Auvergne continued, 'Rather astute, really. He could tell to a man the garrison numbers daily by the size of the bread order. And he plans to return shortly with the capability and firing angles of our defences no doubt carefully paced out and written down.'

'A spy,' Renzi said uncomfortably.

'You have an objection to spies, then?' d'Auvergne asked innocently.

'It— He must be taken up immediately, of course.'

'But the practice of spying?'

'I'm not sure I take your meaning, sir.'

'Well, it would seem to me axiomatic that if a covert act by a single individual could result in the discomfiture of many of the enemy then it is not merely morally acceptable, but his bounden *duty* towards those who would otherwise be put to hazard.'

'I do not deny the necessity but the practices of spying are repugnant to me,' Renzi said carefully.

'I really do not see where the immorality lies, Mr Renzi. If, as commander-in-chief at the scene of a battle, I receive intelligence that the enemy will come by a different direction, do I alter my dispositions accordingly or refuse to do so on the grounds that the information was gained by a single person working alone?'

Renzi held his silence, wondering if d'Auvergne was trying to provoke him.

'No, of course I cannot, morally or otherwise. My duty as a commander is to build a picture of the forces opposite me in the best way I can – and if an opportunity arises whereby one of my men might move forward, keep out of sight and note the truth of what these are, then I shall be grateful to him.'

As though it were final proof in a mathematical theorem, d'Auvergne concluded, 'Therefore no one can be surprised that this is carried forward by all nations as a perfectly valid and utile means of acquiring intelligence.'

Pulling himself up, Renzi said cuttingly, 'Sir, before now I have had to perform bloody acts that were logically dictated by the situation at the time and I believe I have never shied from the duty. What I find immoral is the deployment of such as an instrument of policy.'

'In a way, you disappoint me, Renzi. You have not considered your position in logic, which I find is the only method to be trusted for laying the thickets of sentiment and false moral positions. Take the spy himself, for instance.'

Feeling a heat of resentment at having his cherished logic brought into such a discussion Renzi reluctantly followed the reasoning.

'The spy is a brave and resourceful man who goes alone and unarmed into the enemy camp. It has often puzzled me,' he said, as an aside, 'just why we admire and value those who on our behalf do so, while those of our opponents with the same qualities are, on discovery, vilified and must invariably suffer death. An odd notion, don't you think?'

He thought for a moment then continued his main thread: 'Is there, I ask you, any difference *au fond* between ordering a man to stand before the cannon's rage and another who is required to place himself in greater peril within the enemy's territory?'

'It is not in my power to order a man to do anything, sir,' Renzi said, with feeling. 'Let alone—'

'So who in your universe will harvest the intelligence, save you from the guile of the enemy, his conspiracies and malice?' d'Auvergne snapped. 'You have the freedom, bought by others, to walk away from matters of nicety to your conscience and leave their resolution to others. This is neither logical nor responsible.'

'Then do I understand it correctly, sir, that you require me to assume the character of a spy in some affair?' Renzi asked coldly.

D'Auvergne slumped back. 'No, no. That was never in my desiring,' he said wearily. 'Mr Renzi, you have gifts of insight and understanding with formidable intelligence and a rare admiration for the primacy of logic. All this fits you in a remarkable manner for the role of assisting myself – simply lightening the burden, if you will – in the conduct of oper-ations of a clandestine nature against Napoleon.'

Renzi felt the chill of foreboding.

'If you are in any doubt as to their importance, let me disclose to you that I communicate not with Sir James but directly to the foreign secretary of Great Britain, as indeed I have done since the Terror of Paris in 'ninety-two. The work is allowed to be of such sovereign value that I am entrusted with the maintenance of a network in France whose extent . . . is large.'

He sighed raggedly. 'At the moment I have none in whom I can place my trust and I bear the burden alone. It was my hope that in some degree you would feel able to offer me your help – *and* your country, sir.'

'Help?' Renzi muttered.

'To maintain the confidential papers, take up some of the load of secret correspondence, speak with those arriving from France with news – and, on occasion, to favour me with your views in matters compelling a difficult decision.'

Everything in Renzi rebelled against involvement in illicit affairs of deceit and trickery, in the lies and betrayal that must be at its heart. His whole life was predicated on the sure foundation of the honour and moral obligation of a gentleman and he had no desire to immerse himself in such a moral quagmire. 'Sir. I fear that it would do violence to my nature,' he began. 'Notwithstanding your logic and—'

'It's too late for that, Renzi. Whether you like it or no, you are even now privy to information of a most secret nature. But more pressing than that you have been made aware that there is a service you may do for your country to which you are most peculiarly well fitted.'

'Sir, it may well be—'

'Now, it is within your power to turn your back and walk from this room – but for the rest of your days you must live with the knowledge that you have failed when called upon.

'Now, sir, will you do your duty?'

It had been hard to accept that he had been unable to muster any rational argument against the request but he found comfort in observing that the post was only that of confidential secretary taken a trifle further. But he had been wounded by d'Auvergne's polite assurance that there would be no question of personal risk when he had acceded.

Before going further he was curious about one thing: 'On the question of trust, sir, how is it that you are assured my character is as you allege?'

'Oh, on that score, I had your room and small baggage searched, and who but a hopeless scholar would burden himself with Goethe and Locke for light reading?' he smiled.

Renzi returned a thin smile while d'Auvergne opened a business-like chest and found a pair of heavy, intricate keys. 'The records are in the crypt below. I have one key, you the only other. Be of good care, Renzi. People's lives are in your hands with those papers.'

At Renzi's set face he continued lightly, 'Take it from me, dear fellow, it's a quite different and wider moral framework we find ourselves in, but you will discover that being a friend to logic will extract you safely from many a sentimental mire. For example, see if you can overcome your present scruples sufficiently to detect the transcendent moral certitudes in this little exercise.

'I, as a commander, have several thousand lives in my charge and must meet the foe on the battlefield. If I can convince the enemy commander that my attack will come by course A when, in fact, I will come by B, there will be at the close of that day perhaps some hundreds fewer widows left to grieve. How might this best be brought about?'

Renzi shook his head, even more uncomfortable in this world of shades and compromise.

'Well, here is one sure way. Do you charge a brave man with dispatches, emphasising their grave nature and enjoining their safe delivery by all means. He is not to know their false nature and when he is betrayed and valiantly defends them, even to the death, the enemy will be convinced of their authenticity and act accordingly.'

With a tight smile he concluded, 'So, of course, many lives are saved for the one expended. You really cannot argue against that, Renzi.'

And, to his anguish, he found he could not. These were moral quicksands of a kind he had never been forced to confront before, and their serious considering would occupy him painfully for some time to come.

'I would find it . . . difficult, sir. Er, may I know what action you intend in respect of the letter?' It was something *he* could test d'Auvergne with.

'Stofflet, you mean. All actions must be considered, of course – but pray tell, what do you yourself propose, Renzi?'

'He must be stopped, of course. Taken up as a spy?' He remembered the kind, bald-headed baker from whom he had begged bread. Now he knew that the man was married happily, with children he expected to see soon.

'For a public demonstration in these fevered times that there are spies in our midst? I think not.'

'An assassination?' Renzi said neutrally.

'Goodness me, no! Crass barbarism and not to be countenanced by a civilised nation.'

'Then taken up quietly and a strict parole demanded before banishment?' Renzi suggested boldly, remembering d'Auvergne's words about brave men suffering death undeservedly.

'Perhaps not. I rather think he must meet with an unfortunate accident.'

Chapter 10

Kydd trudged up the steep steps. Without noticing, his path had taken him to another level of the town. It was denser settled and had an indefinable rakish air, which focused round a theatre. Idly he went up and read the billboard: 'The *Much Adored* Griselda Mayhew as The Princess Zenobia and the *Magnificent* Richard Samson as Count Dragonheart in *Carpathia, or, Cupid's Trust Rewarded.*'

He turned to go but his eyes were caught by another notice underneath: 'Stage-hands required: none but those able to go aloft and haul ropes heartily shall apply.'

If this was not work for a sailor then what was? A week or so of jolly theatricals and then he could claim as much as – as a whole mutton pie, with the full trimmings, of course, and swimming in lumpy gravy. His stomach growled as he entered the theatre.

A short, sharp-eyed man appeared from nowhere. 'Where you off to, m' lad? Performance not until seven. Not until seven, I say!'

'Oh, er, th' notice said as how stage-hands are required.'

'You?' The man stepped back to take his measure. 'Done it before? A flyman, I mean?'

Goaded, Kydd looked up: two somewhat faded ornamental gold cords descended each side of the audience entrance from a single ringbolt in the lofty ceiling. With a practised leap he clutched the leftmost one and swarmed effortlessly up to the bolt, then launched himself into space for the other and slid down, hand over hand, much as in the distant past he had found a backstay to reach the deck all the quicker.

'I see,' the man said, affecting boredom. 'An' we've had sailors before an' all. Wages 're two livres cash on th' nail each performance, no liquor during, find y'r own prog. Er, can y' start now?'

Kydd feigned reluctance. 'A livre as earnest.' He sniffed, holding out his hand. He had forgotten how much it represented but guessed it must be worth a shilling or two.

'Be off wi' your impertinence! Y'r impertinence, I say!'

Kydd turned on his heel, but the man caught his arm. 'One livre, an' I'll know y' name, sir!'

'Tom Cutlass, m' shipmates call me,' he answered slowly. 'An' yours?'

The man puffed up his chest. 'Mr Carne t' you! I'm th' stage-master. Stage-master, I say!'

Kydd took the money. 'When do I—'

'Be here at five sharp. Y' late, an' that's all ye get.'

Renzi found d'Auvergne at the battlements, staring moodily out to sea, his greatcoat streaming and whipping in the autumn bluster. Renzi followed his gaze and saw a sail against the far-off Brittany shore, then spotted the gaggle of vessels in chase.

The French coast was a distant smother of white from the pounding of the westerly with white flecks of waves vivid in the stretch of water to the dull-grey coastline. It was a hard beat into the fresh gale and the drama played out slowly before them, the hunted craft clawing desperately against the wind, first on one tack, then another, the others straggling astern as it eventually stretched out towards safety.

With stinging raindrops fast turning things into wet misery, Renzi left d'Auvergne to his vigil and returned to his task, collating a number of appraisals, penned by different hands, into a fair summary.

He heard d'Auvergne come back and go straight to his inner sanctum. Then, some time later, a disturbance echoed in the long passage outside his little room – cries, a panting fuss and the loud voice of the serjeant warder. The commotion faded and he heard the drone of other voices, then the chilling sound of a man's sobbing.

D'Auvergne came and slumped in a chair. 'L'Étalon is taken,' he said hoarsely, his face dazed.

It meant nothing to Renzi. 'Stallion' – the code-word for an agent? He murmured something, never having seen d'Auvergne so shaken.

'That toad Fouché,' he went on. 'Betrayal, murder, intrigue – there's nothing he'll not stoop to for his diabolical master, Bonaparte.'

'The minister for police?' Renzi responded. Paris and its deadly state apparatus was not within his remit and he had no wish to know anything of it, but d'Auvergne obviously needed to talk.

'Secret police – the vile rogue! When L'Étalon was betrayed we had time to get him away, but under Bonaparte's orders, Fouché arrested his family one by one. That – that noble being gave himself up to spare them, and in course will be guillotined.'

Renzi avoided the stricken eyes, unable to find words.

D'Auvergne pulled himself together with an effort. 'Fouché is not the problem. He'll serve whoever it's in his interest to pander to. It's Napoleon Bonaparte! This man is not only debasing a great civilisation but drenching the world in blood – to satisfy his own lust for conquest!'

Sitting up suddenly, d'Auvergne cried in outrage, 'Do you know what the contemptible hypocrite plans now?'

Renzi could only shake his head.

'That – that monster! First Consul and titular head of the Revolution who overthrew King Louis – he's having himself declared emperor! Not just king and monarch – but *emperor!*'

'No!' Renzi blurted. That the man could so subvert the principles of the Revolution, and the people tamely acquiesce, was a titanic shift in national allegiances. Clearly Bonaparte was taking every last skein of power into his own hands – the majesty of the state of France for his own personal property.

D'Auvergne's face was haggard. 'Very soon it will be too late, I fear . . .'

'Too late?'

'For – for the last remedy.'

'Sir, I'm not sure I follow,' Renzi said.

'My dear Renzi,' d'Auvergne murmured, and sat down.

Renzi waited silently.

'I'm about to speak on matters of the very direst secrecy.'

Ignoring Renzi's protest he went on firmly, 'I feel able to do so, for some small time ago I received private intelligence regarding yourself that allows you are a fit and proper recipient, Renzi . . . or is it to be Laughton?'

Renzi stared at him, taken aback to hear his real name. He had been Nicholas Renzi ever since he had gone to sea those many years ago.

'A prudent precaution, in my position, you will agree. So you see, sir, I now know of your high-minded self-exile, your distinguished actions at St Vincent and Acre; I learned of the quality of your late studies from Count Rumford himself. Therefore I feel able to treat you as my equal in matters touching the safety of the realm.

'You may have heard of my not insignificant successes in instigating unrest and rebellion among the Normans. This has been due largely to my network of agents in France, who smuggle out information and carry out acts of bravery as needs must. That was in the Revolutionary War. Since the start of this war, Bonaparte has moved with ruthless speed. The secret police are everywhere. One even needs a passport to travel to another city.

'This has achieved its object. Nearly all organised opposition to the tyrant is now broken, scattered. There are agents and sympathisers, but they are in daily fear of their lives. The gates of Fortress France are fast closing, and with them any chance to prevent the cataclysm of total war.'

It seemed so abstract, discussing such a world in an ancient castle with the winds moaning about, but Renzi felt a sense of inevitability as to what would come next. 'Sir, you're speaking of an attempt on Bonaparte's life!'

'No.' D'Auvergne gave a rueful smile. 'Not his life. His Majesty will not have it. He is to be kidnapped.'

'Kidnapped!'

'Yes, Renzi, seized and held. It is a previous plan by others feeling as we do and ready to lay down their lives in the attempt.'

'Does this have the support of London?'

'At the most secret level conceivable, but with the King's proviso that Bonaparte shall be brought out of France alive to answer for his crimes.'

'Sir, may I ask if we are to be involved?'

'We are central to it! Allow me to lay before you the essence of the plot. It is to waylay his coach as he retires outside Paris with his mistress, as he is wont to do. He is to be spirited instantly through Yvelines and Calvados to the coast – and thence by sea to Jersey.'

'Here?'

'Indeed. When I receive word that the plot is to proceed, I shall have an allowance from the foreign secretary to be employed in preparing here at Mont Orgueil an apartment for the reception of Napoleon Bonaparte.'

Renzi felt unreality closing in. 'Um, sir, is the plot well advanced?'

'Certainly. There are some hundreds of brave souls already in Paris, each with his part to play and practised since the summer. You will, no doubt, recognise the name of General Charles Pichegru?'

'Pichegru!' He had risen rapidly to the top of the Revolutionary Army, invaded and subjugated Holland, then subsequently crossed the Rhine with his victorious troops.

'Yes. The only general in history to capture an entire fleet of ships-of-the-line!' It was the stuff of legend: the Dutch battle-squadron had been ice-bound and Pichegru had led a cavalry charge across the frozen sea to seize them all.

D'Auvergne continued, 'He will raise the soldiery, who love him, to take all Paris and declare for the King. In the vacuum that exists at the disappearance of Napoleon, the Duc d'Enghien will be made head of state and regent until King Louis might return to claim his throne.'

'But – but the organisation, the timing?'

'I have told you the essence only. There is much more. If you knew Georges Cadoudal, and that for five months he has been in Paris preparing, you would rest your concerns.'

'Cadoudal?'

'A man larger than life itself – a Hercules of sublime courage and audacity, and one with an undying reputation in the Chouan risings. I myself have seen Georges hold fast a kicking donkey by its back leg – they sing ballads about him in Brittany.'

Renzi found himself utterly at a loss for words.

'There are others too numerous to mention. Chouans who have made the perilous journey from the Vendée to Paris to lie in hiding awaiting the call, those who pass among the people risking everything to bring word of the coup to come. There are even troops of dragoons training in secret in the forests outside the capital.'

'Then – when shall it . . . ?'

'It is essential that the rising is supported at a scale where it may succeed. To this end we must await a final commitment from London. In my communications I have stressed the urgency and fading opportunity. We shall hear shortly, I believe.'

The evening was turning chilly and Kydd was thankful to get inside the theatre. It was now abuzz with excitement and anxious stage hands hurried to mysterious places past the giant curtain.

For too long Kydd's buoyant good nature had been clouded, but the atmosphere of a place dedicated to losing oneself in fantasy was getting to him. Damn it, he vowed, he would enjoy this interlude.

'Hey, you! You there – Tom, whatever's y' name!' Carne's face came round the curtain and he looked irritable.

'Aye, Mr Carne,' Kydd called humbly, and made his way hastily past the seats and on to the stage.

'Come!' The face disappeared, so Kydd pulled back the curtain tentatively and stepped into a dark chaos of props, ladders, improbable scenes painted on vast boards – and an impatient Carne. 'This is y' mate as will teach ye.' Carne snatched a look at a well-thumbed snap-bound book and turned to a wiry man nearby. 'And I want t' block through scene three again f'r Miss Mayhew in ten minutes,' he told him, and left them to it.

'Tim Jones,' his preceptor said, thrusting out a hand to Kydd. 'Look o' the sea about ye, cuffin!' He snorted, then grinned.

'Aye,' said Kydd, bemused. 'Er, quartermaster's mate round th' Horn in the flying *Artemis*.'

'*Artemis*?' Jones said respectfully. 'As did fer the *Citoyenne* in th' last war? Glory be! Well, I was only a Jack Dusty in *Tiger*, had t' go a-longshore wi' the gormy ruddles as ruined m' constitooshun.' He clapped Kydd on the shoulder. 'We's better be learnin' ye the ropes here right enough.'

They left the confusion of the rehearsal for the dark upper eyrie of the fly-loft where Kydd looked down through a maze of ropes and contraptions directly to the stage below. Jones squatted comfortably on the slats, and began: 'That there's Mr Carne, an' he's the stage-master who calls th' show from that book he has. He's in charge o' the runnin' crew, which includes us flymen, an' that scrovy crowd workin' below. Now, here's the griff. When the scene shifts, th' whole thing fr'm clew t' earring goes arsy-versy in a very smart way, an' it's us as does it. How? I'll show ye ...'

Kydd took in the complexity of ropes and machinery that could change their world of enchantment from a sylvan glade to a magnificent palace and back again. He learned of flats and gauzes, cloths and rigging; and of the special whistles that had as much meaning for the stage crew in the complex operations of a scene change as a boatswain's call for seamen in the operation of a man-o'-war.

Carne's hectoring voice rose above the din, and occasionally Kydd caught sight of an actor in fine robes foreshortened by the height as he strode the boards declaiming into the empty darkness. Excitement gripped him: soon the grand play would open – it seemed impossible that the disorderly rumpus below could calm to the breathless scenes he remembered from his last visit to a theatre. 'Will we see Miss Mayhew an' Mr Samson a-tall?' he found himself asking in awed tones.

'Y' might at that.'

A bellow of 'Places! Places!' cut through the confusion. Carne had the company pacing through the new scene arrangement under the director's critical eye and the flymen were soon hard at work on ropes and flats.

There was a last flurry of activity before front of house went to their stations, then a tense wait for the play to commence. The echoing emptiness of the theatre now had a different quality: a background susurrus of rustling and murmuring as the first of the audience took their seats while the reflectored footlights threw magic shadows into the upper reaches.

The noise grew, shouts from rowdier elements mingling with raucous laughter and the animated hum of conversation. The small orchestra struck up with a strenuous overture until anticipation had built sufficiently – and the play began.

It was hard work and the timing exact, but Kydd had the chance to hear and sometimes see the action. At the interval he descended to help with the flats for the second half but was called across by Carne: 'Take Miss Mayhew her refreshment, Tom what'syername.'

He was passed a single ornate crystal glass on a small lacquer tray with Chinese writing on it. A smell of gin wafted up from it as Kydd carried it to the dressing rooms, past half-dressed nymphs and bearded Magyars, in a stifling atmosphere of heat and excitement, with the unmistakable smell of greasepaint.

'*Enterrrr!*' The response to his knock was the same imperious trill he had heard on stage. Griselda Mayhew was at her brightly lit mirror, a vision of a towering wig, flowing gown and caked makeup, but a jolly face with kindly eyes.

'Ah, thank you, dearie!' she said gratefully. 'Put it down there. I'm near gut-foundered.'

She looked at Kydd shrewdly. 'Well, I haven't seen you before?'

'Er, new t'night, Miss Mayhew,' he said diffidently.

'You're no common stage-hand, I'd wager. Gent of decayed fortune, more like. Still, y' came to the right place. Theatre's a fine place t' make your mark. Good luck t' you, cully!'

Blushing, Kydd left. The second half went rapidly, and when the play finished he felt an unaccountable envy for the tempest of applause that followed and the several curtain calls that had him sweating at the heavy ropes. And when the audience had streamed out he felt a pang of loneliness. All he had to look forward to, after these bewitching hours, was the squalor of the sail-loft. He finished securing the rigging as Griselda Mayhew's laughter pealed at Richard Samson's dramatic flourishes with her coat.

She looked in Kydd's direction. 'Did y' enjoy tonight at all?' she called to him.

'I did that,' Kydd said awkwardly, conscious of his shabby appearance as he approached her shyly.

She frowned slightly, then touched his arm. 'It's not my business, but have y' somewhere t' go to?'

Put off-balance Kydd mumbled something, but she inter-rupted: 'I understand, m' dear, we see a lot of 'em down on their luck, like. Well, not t' worry. Look, we're travelling players an' we have t' take a big enough place for the season. Jem just quit, so why don't y' stay with us for a while?' She turned to Samson. 'That's all right, isn't it, Dickie?' she said winsomely.

A fiercely protective eye regarded Kydd. 'As long as ye don't smoke a pipe, m' good man.'

Staggered by their generosity, Kydd took his leave of Carne, pocketed his coins and followed his new friends out into the night.

It was heaven to lie in a proper bed and Kydd slept soundly. In the morning he went diffidently down to join the others but found not a soul abroad at that hour. He made himself useful, squaring away after the wind-down party of the previous evening, to the surprise of the maid-of-all-work, who arrived late and seemed to find his presence unhelpful.

His gear was in the sail-loft and he went out to retrieve those things that would fit into his modest room, reflecting on the strangeness of life that it could change so quickly. When he returned, a young man was holding an angry conversation with a wall and Richard Samson was stalking about in an exotic bed-robe reading aloud from a script in ringing tones.

'Ah, I thought we'd lost you, Mr Cutlass,' he roared, when he spotted Kydd. 'A yen to feel the ocean's billows, perhaps? Or a midnight tryst with a fair maiden? Do come in and hide those things away.'

One by one the others appeared, but it was not until after ten that Griselda made her entrance, the men greeting her with exaggerated stage bows while she sailed in to take the least faded armchair.

'Miss Mayhew.' Kydd bowed too.

'Oh dear,' she replied. 'The others call me Rosie – why don't you, Tom?'

'I will,' Kydd said, with a grin. It had been an entertaining morning, rehearsing cue lines from a script for whoever asked it of him and his spirits were high. 'Ye're starting a new play, I hear.'

'Of course, dearie.' She sighed. 'We open every second Friday with new. Guernsey's not a big enough place we can stay wi' the same all the time.' She looked at Kydd speculatively. 'You're not t' be a stage-hand for ever. When shall you pick up a script?'

'Well, I . . .' A famous actor? Strutting the stage with swooning ladies to either side, the confidences of princes and dukes? Folk flocking from far and near having heard that the legendary Tom Cutlass was playing? 'I'll think on it,' he came back awkwardly.

On the way to the theatre he called at the post office and this time there *was* a letter to collect. It was from Renzi. He ripped it open and three coins fell out. He scrabbled to retrieve them and eagerly scanned the hurried lines. Renzi had met with unexpected success. Soon after arriving he had made the acquaintance of a Prince de Bouillon, whom Kydd took to be an exiled royalist, and had been fortunate enough to find employ in his household as a private secretary. The enclosed thirty livres Kydd could expect every month from his wages.

A lump rose in his throat. With this generous gift he was now free to continue with his quest for as long as he . . . But he had already concluded that he was getting nowhere in uncovering the plot and must give up – must he track about hopelessly for ever? He had a life to lead. He could at least still hope for a ship in England and, in any case, as an officer even of declined circumstances there were genteel niches in society . . . But the instant he left the islands it would be the final surrender to his unjust fate – and Lockwood would have had his vengeance. Was there no middle way?

There were no performances on the Sunday. Some of the players went to Alderney on a visit while others simply slept. Moodily Kydd went to the deserted front parlour and sprawled on the sofa. Unable to escape his thoughts he laid down his newspaper and closed his eyes.

The door opened and the swish of a dress made him look up. 'Do I disturb you, Tom?'

'Oh, er, not at all, Rosie,' Kydd said, hauling himself upright. 'Just thinkin' awhile.'

She looked at him steadily. 'You're not all you seem, m' friend,' she said quietly. 'I've seen a few characters in my time an' you're so different – you've got iron in your soul, a man's man. And something's happened. I don't know what it is, but it's thrown you down where y' don't belong.'

When Kydd said nothing she came to the sofa and sat beside him. 'I may be only a common actress but I know when a man's without a friend t' talk with, an' that's not natural.' She straightened her dress demurely and continued,

'It would be my honour if you'd take me as y' friend, Tom.' Her hand strayed to his knee.

Kydd flinched but, not wanting to offend her, stayed rigid. She withdrew the hand and said quietly, 'So, there's a woman at the bottom of it – am I right?'

'No. That is, she . . . No, it's too tough a yarn t' tell.'

'Tom! We've a whole Sunday ahead. Your secret will stay wi' me, never fear.'

Kydd knew from his sister that, for a lady, there was nothing so intriguing as a man of mystery; Rosie would worm it out of him sooner or later and, besides, he had to talk to someone. 'Well, it's a long tale. Y' see . . .' He told her of the Navy, of his rise to success and command of his own ship; of his entry to high society and likely marriage into their ranks and subsequent fall when his heart was taken by another. And finally the terrible revenge a father was taking on him.

'Dear Lord, an' what a tale! I had no idea. My dear, how can you keep your wits about you while you're reduced to – to this?'

Kydd gave the glimmer of a smile. 'So th' last question is, just when do I give it away an' return t' England?'

'Never!' she said firmly. 'Never! Tom, you're perfectly right – you cannot return without you've regained your honour. It's just as it was in *Clarissa Victrix*, where the hero is unjustly accused of theft an' thrown into Newgate, an' it's only when his lady seduces the black-hearted earl into handin' over the false evidence that he's made free.'

Kydd grimaced, while she went on proudly, 'We opened the season wi' that in Weymouth last year to my leading lady.'

'Twould be a fine thing indeed, should I meet wi' such,' Kydd said tartly. 'I have m' doubts it'll be soon – savin' your kindness, I've no wish t' top it th' beggar f'r much longer.'

'An' neither should you!' Rosie soothed. 'Tom, do promise me y' won't leave us for now. I've a friend – a . . . a personal friend as was, who I mean t' speak with. An' then we shall see what happens.'

Renzi had slept badly: it was either a hare-brained plot by wild-eyed lunatics or the only chance to rid the world of its greatest nightmare. Or perhaps both – and d'Auvergne had made clear that in the event it went ahead Renzi's whole-hearted participation was expected, and on the inner circle.

He had now seen the secret correspondence with London: indisputable understandings and instructions from the very highest and concerned with real military and political commit-ments. D'Auvergne had not lied about his connections and the scheme was under eye by the foreign secretary of Great Britain and the cabinet itself. But just what was being asked of *him*?

Interrupting his thoughts, Jenkins, the flag-lieutenant, popped into his office. 'Thought you'd be too busy to look in at the post office – letter for you, been there for a while.'

It was from Kydd. He had found a menial job, shared lodg-ings, and expressed sincere gratitude for the few coins enclosed. Renzi started a reply but it wouldn't come. The contrast between his friend's decent, plain-sailing world and this insane arena of chicanery, stealth and the desperate endeavour to topple Bonaparte was too great.

Around noon, the cutter from England with dispatches entered Gorey Bay with a package so important that the commodore himself was brought to sign for it.

Shortly afterwards, a grim-faced d'Auvergne laid a letter in front of Renzi. It was from Lord Hobart, secretary of state for war, short and to the point. The plot to kidnap

Napoleon Bonaparte was to proceed with all possible dispatch and in the greatest possible secrecy.

'There is attached an order authorising exceptional expenditures against Secret Service funds at the Treasury and an expression of full support from their lordships. Renzi, do you cease all duties to attend on me personally. This is the gravest affair this age.'

D'Auvergne was in no mood to waste a second. 'We shall meet in an hour, my friend. Your current business should be concluded within that time.'

Renzi worked quickly: no report or appraisal could stand against the stakes that had now been raised. When he entered d'Auvergne's office he was met with a look of dedicated ferocity. 'Mr Renzi. The world knows me as the commodore, Jersey Squadron, and I maintain that position and retinue in my flagship and a small office in St Helier. Some might know that my sympathies with the royalists occupy me on occasions here in Mont Orgueil. Few indeed know of my other activities. As of this moment I count myself officially on leave of absence from my naval duties. It will remain thus until this business is complete.'

'Very well, sir.' Renzi nodded. 'May I enquire as to the establishment you must now engage for this purpose? The line of command, as it were.'

'None.'

'Sir?' Renzi asked, not sure he had heard aright.

'The matter is too grave, far beyond the compass of what is to be expected of a serving officer, the issue much too delicate to entrust to others at this late hour. It will be you and I alone who will bring this business to a head.'

'Sir! It—'

'Consider. The plan calls for a rising in Paris, a co-ordination of forces and an alignment of purpose that is the concern only of those actually there – Georges and company *en effet*. There is little we might do at this distance and our contribution must be to secure and provide what is asked for, and when the time comes to be ready to extract the tyrant by sea from the territory of France.' His eyes gleamed.

'Thus as you will see, our tasks will be limited – but important. Your good self arriving in Jersey has been a miracle, Renzi. We will press ahead together – my office is yours, and my time. We will share the burden and with it the honour.'

This was nothing less than a strident call to join the gathering maelstrom of the great conspiracy. From a reluctant role at the fringe of this half-world he despised he was now being thrust to the centre . . . It was abhorrent to the principles he had lived by – but how could he deny the syllogistic inevitability of the reasoning: that a smaller evil might be justified for the sake of a greater object? Could he in all conscience stand back at this point? This was where logic and morals collided.

'Sir, I shall do my duty in this matter,' Renzi said coldly, 'with due diligence as my health and strength do allow. But I would have you know, sir, that while bending my best endeavours to the cause I find the business of spying and deception both distasteful and repugnant to my character. When this enterprise is concluded therefore, I must quit your service. That is all.'

D'Auvergne nodded. 'As I would expect of you, Renzi. Before all things you are a gentleman and you are now being asked to violate your sensibilities beyond the bounds nature sets for them. However, before we begin the enterprise I must have your word upon it that you will enter in with a whole heart, applying your mind and body to the one end. Do I have it?'

'You do, sir.'

'Good.' He picked up some papers and made a show of shuffling them. 'Now, their first task is that of supply. It is vital to their plan to establish a chain of trusted *maisons de confiance* from Paris to the coast, each to be defended if needed, stocked with fresh horses, food – I've no need to detail this, it is not our concern, but the Chouans will need gold for bribery, arms for the escort. They will have it.' He paused for a moment. 'And you, Renzi, if you will, shall make it so. Your service as a sea officer allows me to place my fullest trust in your ability to perform this duty. Issue your requirements and I will countersign them without question.'

Chapter 11

Although his future was now reasonably secure Kydd felt qualms. All the time he delayed his return to England he knew Renzi would stay by him at considerable personal cost and this weighed on his conscience. In all fairness he must make plans for departure.

At the theatre Rosie made a point of seeking him out. 'Tom, love, I've something for you.' At her coy words Richard Samson's expression darkened but she went on gaily, 'I'll give it you tonight when we get back.'

It was a letter, addressed 'To Whom It may Concern' and 'Strictly Private'. Cautiously Kydd broke the wafer and unfolded the single sheet, conscious that Rosie was watching quietly.

To his surprise the salutation was a firm 'Commander Kydd'. Puzzled – for he was sure he had not mentioned his last name to Rosie – he read on. In friendly tones the writer allowed that an acquaintance had conveyed to him that Kydd was now at leisure on Guernsey, and it had occurred to him this was a circumstance that might well be turned to mutual advantage. If Kydd was inclined to hear further he would be welcome to call at his convenience.

'A Mr Vauvert,' Kydd said offhandedly, 'says he wants t' meet me.'

Rosie assumed a practical bustle. 'You will show me what you intend to wear, my dear,' she ordered.

Kydd obediently brought out his best and only walking-out clothes, canvas-wrapped from their storage in the sail-loft, and laid them before her. The dark-green coat with tails had suffered somewhat with mould but more serious was the spotting on the cream pantaloons. Undaunted, Rosie got to work and soon pronounced Kydd ready to appear.

He marched up to an impressive door in Grange Road and knocked. Rosie had told him that Vauvert was an important figure in Guernsey, a merchant investor and *négociant* of St Peter Port, of some standing, and therefore he could be sure this was not a social call.

He was met by Vauvert himself, an older man of impeccable dress. 'Sir, it is kind in you to call,' he said, his shrewd eyes taking in Kydd's appearance. 'Do come in.'

The house was spacious and dark-panelled in the old style with expensive ornaments tastefully placed. 'Might I offer you something against this cold evening?'

The cognac was the finest Kydd had tasted; this was hardly surprising, he reflected, given the smuggling reputation of Guernsey. 'Tell me, sir,' he began, 'how it is y' know my name.'

'Why, sir, you must understand that good intelligence is a merchant's first requirement if he is to be successful. Your misfortune is not unknown in the fraternity of commerce.'

Kydd coloured. 'Sir! I have t' make it plain that—'

'Mr Kydd, the circumstances are known to me. If you are

innocent I can only commiserate – but if you were informed upon by another less successful than yourself, it is no reflection on your judgement that you were unprepared for such an odious act. Such things do happen from time to time in the conduct of business and you will find no one in Guernsey who will say that the pursuit of profit is in any way morally offensive.'

'But—'

'I rather feel we should proceed to more constructive discussion. Do sit, sir.' The fire had settled to a comfortable heat in the elegant study and Kydd tried to compose himself. If this was a rich merchant seeking a prestige ornament for his establishment by offering him token employment . . .

'Now, Mr Kydd, let me be open with you. To waste the talents of a sea officer of such shining credentials as yourself in idleness would seem to reflect badly on a nation as sore beset as ourselves. The reasons might be debated but the circumstance itself might yet prove of advantage to both you and me.'

He went on: 'I shall be brief. You are a naval officer of proved distinction with an active and aggressive attitude to meeting the enemy. These qualities are one and the same as those required in the captain of a private man-o'-war.'

'A privateer? No!' Kydd spluttered. 'I – it's not possible! I can't—'

'No?' Vauvert said evenly. 'Then I've misjudged you, sir. At a time when your country lies under as great a peril as ever it has, you would spend your time at leisure ashore? Let me point out to you that your King's ship and your privateer are in the same business of reprisal. One is at the King's expense, the other paid for by concerned citizens who seek to make their contribution.'

'Mr Vauvert, you don't understand. F'r a naval officer—'

'And has it escaped you that war by this means costs His Majesty not a penny? The enemy is made to pay for his own destruction. The sale of prizes repays our own contributions and any overplus is to the credit of those by whose exertions and valour they are secured.'

'But—'

'This very house, sir, a not insignificant monument I would dare to say, is itself raised on the proceeds of private cruising in the past age.'

Kydd felt anger mount. The man knew nothing of the contempt a King's officer held for his commercial rivals. He could hear cries of disgust as his fellow officers learned of his fall from grace, see the shaking heads. No, it was simply not possible.

And this was the thing he had sworn *not* to do. Absent himself at sea while his quest remained unresolved? It was the very reason he was delaying in Guernsey. 'No,' he said, with finality. 'It's kind o' you t' think on me, but I'm unable t' see m' way clear in th' matter. I'll bid ye good-day, sir.'

Vauvert's disappointment was plain. 'My carriage is at your disposal, sir,' he said stiffly.

'That won't be necessary,' Kydd said, and left.

But outside his annoyance ebbed. Vauvert's disappointment had been genuine; in a way it was a tribute to the respect in which Kydd was held. The man had probably counted on his agreeing to be a privateer captain, with a fine profit on every prize he brought in.

Not that it would in any way sway— Kydd stopped in his tracks. He was getting nowhere in trying to uncover the plot against him and he probably never would unless he tried another tack. Lockwood had obviously bribed a clerk in the admiral's office, no doubt with the connivance of someone local. And what could be bribed could be *unbribed*! Elation surged: with enough gold in the right places he could achieve anything he wished, including a recanting of the false witness against him. And what faster way to accrue the necessary wealth than as a privateer whose fortune could be won in a single voyage?

With rising excitement he hurried back. He would need to seek leave for employment at sea in the usual way, no doubt, just as he had done for the convict transport to New South Wales. His half-pay would cease immediately, but what an opportunity. Nothing could stand against a determined man with a pot of gold at his back.

The *négociant* was blank-faced as Kydd was shown back in. 'Mr Vauvert, I do apologise, sir, I may have been too precipit-ate in m' departure. I should have enquired more concerning m' prospects in th' venture.'

'I understand, Mr Kydd. It can seem a big step to take when you're not familiar with practices,' he said. 'I'll do what I can to set your mind at rest. A cigar? No? Perhaps more brandy.' A servant appeared with a tray. 'Please let me tell you a little of the business.

'I use the word advisedly, for this is something we must keep always before us. It is in the nature of an investment and for so doing we expect a return – to bear a profit to the investors, at the least to recoup our costs.' He looked keenly at Kydd. 'Now, prudent men of business do weigh the prospects of a return against the risk to their capital, and that of private cruising requires the greatest thought of all. I do not have to detail to a man of your experience the costs of setting a vessel a-swim, but to those must be added consid-erable legal and agency costs, especially if a prize is to be contested in the courts.'

Kydd attended politely, aware that if he was to become a noteworthy privateer captain he must learn as much of these elements as he could.

'It might be said that the chief determinant in success or otherwise of a voyage must be the richness of the cruising ground but I have to tell you that it is not. It is in equal measure the acumen of the financing promoter, and the sagacity and enterprise of the captain.' He smiled at Kydd. 'You are young and daring, it is true, but your recent actions before Granville tell me that this is tempered in no small measure by cool thinking and a practical appraisal of risk. Should you choose to undertake this venture I for one would not hesitate to accept you.'

'Then, sir, you're saying . . .'

'I'm saying only that your suitability for the post is clear. You should understand that the business of any such venture will not be mine to command. The whole will be conducted by a promoter whom we term an *armateur*. He will form an association of interested persons looking to the matter with a view to investment. Should they concur, articles will be drawn up and the *armateur* will bring together the subscribers' funds into a consolidated whole, which will then form the capital of the venture. Their return will be in direct proportion to the measure of interest they have shown by their investment.'

'I see,' Kydd said. 'Then as a captain wi' no investment of my own m' position is—'

'This will be a matter for the articles of association. You can be assured that you will be adequately recompensed for your conduct. Some choose a regular wage, others a portion of the proceeds. It is a common thing for a successful captain later to become an investor in himself, with shares accordingly. These many fine mansions you see here in Grange Road are some intimation of what can be achieved.'

Kydd's pulse quickened. 'Then, er . . .'

Vauvert leaned back. 'Well, it seems I've sparked an interest in you, sir. Shall we say that, if I'm able to receive an expression of your earnest in the matter, I shall approach an *armateur* of my acquaintance to open discussion with a view to forming a venture? Do I have it, Mr Kydd?'

With only the barest hesitation Kydd gulped, 'Aye, sir, ye do.'

He was nearly late for the evening performance. Carne looked at him sharply as he arrived, but Kydd was too excited to care: he was on another plane of existence and did his work mechanically, letting the nervous energy of the theatre wash about him as a surreal backdrop to his thoughts.

It wasn't until the next morning that he managed to talk to Rosie. He told her what Vauvert had said, then added, with a grin, 'So, y' see, if this works f'r me I'm in a fair way t' hauling m' self back t' where I should be.'

'You will, love, never doubt it.' Her warm smile touched Kydd. If all the world shared her faith in him . . .

The next few days were trying, the possibility of great wealth such a contrast to the reality of present penury, but then a courteously worded note arrived: the *armateur* had shown a degree of interest and suggested Kydd meet him.

A time and date was duly agreed: Kydd was aware that everything was riding on this next stage. The *armateur* was a heavily built gentleman of years in plain dress, still with the blocky stance and weatherbeaten features of a professional mariner.

'Le Sieur Robidou is most experienced in these matters,

I'll have you know, Mr Kydd. His success as a privateer in the American war is still talked of and he's trusted by all the merchant houses here in the article of practical costs management. He has some questions for you,' Vauvert told him.

Kydd found himself held in a steady gaze by the calm blue eyes of the older man. 'I'm pleased t' make your acquaintance, sir,' Robidou said, in a voice that was deep and authoritative. 'Ye've a mind to go a-caper, I believe?'

Vauvert interjected hastily: 'Oh, on a caper – it's an old Dutch term for going in search of plunder.'

'Er, I'm considering th' prospects,' Kydd answered politely.

'Might I know what you conceive t' be a captain's first concern in a private man-o'-war?'

Kydd hesitated, then came back stoutly, 'T' keep th' seas without cease until a prize be sighted,' he said, 'an' then t' spare nothing until th' prize is ours.'

Robidou replied in measured tones, 'For m'self, I'd think that the higher is t' take a proper regard f'r the ship an' her fittings as they are the property o' the owners, Mr Kydd. Cracking on in a chase is all fine an' well, but if she strains aloft or carries away her sticks, is she fit t' carry on after th' next prize? An' can ye tell me your outlay f'r a prime main-yard? 'Twould make y' eyes water, sir.'

Kydd mumbled something, but Robidou pressed on: 'Then what would be y'r second-most concern, sir?'

'Why, y'r books of account, o' course, sir,' Kydd replied. 'What is y'r prize-taking without y' know your expenses t' date as must be set against y'r profit? Double-entry, o' course, an' properly shipshape.'

'Well said, sir!' rumbled Robidou. 'So many neglect the same t' the eventual mortification o' their finances. Tell me, Mr Kydd, have ye experience at sea in th' commercial line?'

'I have, Mr Robidou. I was captain o' the *Totnes Castle* in th' colony trade around th' Cape, an' the owners were pleased enough wi' my service.' There was probably no need to explain that it had been a convict transport. 'And I stood by m' brig-sloop fitting out in Malta. A right caution t' see what hookum snivey the chousin' rogues tried at th' dockyard, it not being a King's yard.'

Robidou nodded. '*Totnes Castle* – can't say I've knowledge of her. Now, these Channel Islands, do ye feel comfortable wi' the sea conditions t' be found here?'

'Aye. In *Teazer* we had on board Mr Queripel, an' a taut hand he was at y'r currents an' tides. He was good enough t' allow me t' hoist aboard a mort o' learning o' th' Brittany coast.'

'I know Queripel,' Robidou said. 'A good man. Well, I can see ye'll need to haul in a lot more about the privateer trade, but b' the look o' you, we'll rub along, I'm sure. Mr Vauvert, if we can satisfy Mr Kydd with our articles, I think we have a venture.'

It was no good. He couldn't go on any longer: a privateer captain or a stage-hand – he couldn't be both. But if he stopped working he would be without enough funds to contribute to his lodging or whatever lay ahead.

Rosie was sympathetic. 'My dear, it happens to us all. You're between engagements and embarrassed for means.' She smiled sweetly. 'You shan't leave us on that account.' Crossing to a corner table she touched an odd-looking china cat with an upraised paw. 'If y' have need, just ask Mojo here.' She lifted its head and found him some coins. 'In course, we give him back th' rhino as soon as we're in the cobbs again.'

Kydd felt a gush of warmth. He felt he was sharing in

a tradition that might have been handed down from the travelling players of Shakespeare's time, a custom that helped the needy without causing embarrassment. 'Don't worry, Rosie, I will,' he said. 'An' when m' first prize comes home, we'll have such a hob-a-nob together as will set th' town t' talkin' f'r weeks.'

Robidou's small office was on the top floor of an old ship's chandlery on the waterfront near the harbour and still smelled of the century of sea stores that had once been there. He looked up from a broad desk set under old-fashioned windows with a view out to sea. 'I think it only proper t' tell ye what's to happen afore we can think t' fit out our craft for cruising.'

An elderly clerk scratching away against the wall murmured something but Robidou cut him short. 'No, Samuel, those figures must be presented tonight – we'll not disturb ye.' He took Kydd into another room and said gravely. 'He's preparing our case as will be put t' the investors. It has t' be a fine rousin' one or they'll not hazard their capital.'

Kydd felt a sudden chill: his hopes might yet be turned to dust.

'Don't concern y'self, Mr Kydd, that's business for me. But after we've got agreement we must appoint the officers.'

'The officers?' Surely this was his prerogative?

'Why, yes! I shall be made ship's husband, o' course, but there's the business house in London. We'll need a bond agent – Paul Le Mesurier I'd trust. We has t' find a proctor an' notary public, and there'll be insurance and legal agents t' appoint. But ye won't be interested in this-all, you'll want t' hear about drawing up th' articles of agreement and shares.'

'I do, Mr Robidou!' Kydd said, as heartily as he could.

'Well, curb y' impatience, sir, all in good time. Now after this is signed, we have the venture. I'll be collectin' the subscriptions an' establishin' our credit wi' the Priaulx house – they owns privateers but they'll handle fittin' out for us in return we gives 'em commissions of appraisement an' such on our prizes. When I've done *that* we can go lookin' for a ship for ye.' Robidou chuckled. 'Then ye has t' find a crew as will follow, an' then finally take out y'r Letter o' Marque!'

It was an intoxicating thought: there was every reason to hope that soon he could be once more at sea and, miraculously, as captain! 'When do we— That is, m' ship. Do we . . . ?'

Just how did one go about acquiring a privateer vessel? Go to a builder of privateers? Look in the newspaper advertisements? Impatience flooded Kydd.

'Your ship? A mite impetuous when we hasn't yet an agreement, sir.' Robidou relented with a grin. 'Why don't ye take a walk along the harbour? If'n there's a saucy craft as takes y'r eye, it's possible we'll make an offer. Havelet Bay an' St Sampson, the builders' yards there, might have something t' interest ye.'

Kydd lost no time. There was every conceivable vessel in St Peter Port harbour. Stately barques, nondescript luggers, and at anchor in the Great Road large merchantmen sporting a surprising number of guns a side.

But where were the privateers? Would he recognise one? Those he had come upon at sea were a mixed bag indeed, from large three-masters to the swarms in the Mediterranean not much bigger than boats. There was probably not a single type of vessel that could be classed definitively as a privateer.

His pace slowed. This would not be easy. Were vessels purpose-built to be privateers? If so, what would their characteristics be? Fast craft, probably sharp in the hull with sparring to take a cloud of canvas – but those were the very kind whose sea-keeping was so poor they would have to retire at the first sign of a blow. And as well, in the confines of a sharp-built vessel, where were the prize-crews going to find berths? And stowage for stores to keep the seas for any length of time? Then again, if *he* were the prey, a smart, rakish predator lifting above the horizon would instantly have him sheering away for his life, and it would be a tedious and costly stern chase to go after every prize.

It was something to which he had never before given thought. He looked at the ships working cargoes: what would be their perspectives on the matter? As prey at sea, they would be as wary as any wild animal fearing a fox ranging nearby, so if the privateer seemed one of them on its lawful occasions they would not take much notice of his approach or any manoeuvre that would otherwise seem threatening.

Yes! A ship of respectable size, probably brig-rigged, as so many traders were. Then a sudden unmasking of a goodly row of guns to convince even the stoutest heart that resistance would be futile. This would have the additional benefit that there would be no gun-play to damage prize or cargo. A ship, in fact, not so very different from *Teazer* . . .

There were several that might qualify: as he surveyed the busy harbour one in particular stood out. A black-hulled brigantine of two or three hundred tons, sitting handily on the mud in the tidal harbour to reveal her sweet underwater lines. There were few about her decks; her hatches were on, probably awaiting her cargo – or she was in idleness.

His heart beat faster. Was this the ship that would take him to wealth and respectability – to adventure in the unknown? Casually, he walked round the harbour wall until he was up with her. Close to, she appeared well cared-for, the gear tautly bowsed, lines from aloft properly tarred, decks priddied. All this was a good indicator of her condition below.

He sauntered past to peer at her stern. *Cheval Marin* was painted there in ornate yellow lettering. *Seahorse*: a fine name. A shipkeeper gazed up at him curiously. Kydd walked on: he knew now what he wanted – *if* the investors came to an agreement.

Renzi and d'Auvergne fell quickly into a working relationship based on mutual respect. Together they reviewed the plot, the heroic lengths to which Georges and his compatriots were going merely to maintain themselves at the centre of Napoleon's capital. They traced the route out of Paris that the fleeing carriage and its prisoner must take – west through the meadows and beech forests of the Orne, into the uplands and to the rugged coast, to a secluded but accessible place where the final delivery of the would-be emperor to the waiting vessel could be effected in secrecy and at speed.

That done, it was now necessary to prepare the ground. The secret records of La Correspondance – d'Auvergne's underground network dating back to the days of the Revolution, to the doomed risings in the Vendée with all their desperate valour and treachery – these would hold what was needed.

Renzi placed his candle on the bare table, oppressed by the stifling atmosphere of the ancient dungeon, and crossed to the iron chests. The heavy keys were awkward and the lock wheezed reluctantly, but then he had them: deeds of heroism never to be told to the world, letters of pleading ended briefly in another hand, bald receipts for gold and arms – and the names of those living quietly in the peace of the countryside who had to be informed that service and sacrifice were now asked of them.

He stuffed the ones he needed into his satchel, relocked the chests, closed the grim door and left the room to the dust of centuries.

While Renzi's first requisition was being readied he started on the hundreds of messages that were to go out. Each missive, reaching to villages and farmhouses in a long line to the capital, had to be carefully phrased to avoid implication if it was intercepted but be undeniably authentic.

For Kydd time passed heavily. Then a hurried note came from Robidou to the effect that one of the investors had raised a serious objection. To him as captain? It didn't say, but Kydd knew that Vauvert and Robidou were relying on his name as a daring naval officer to offset his lack of experience. Would this suffice?

Two nights later a letter arrived by hand of messenger. Kydd ripped it open. There was agreement: he was appointed captain, and expected at the office at ten the following morning for the formalities, which would include his acceptance of the initial articles.

Kydd called his friends: 'Rosie! Richard! Raise y'r glasses, please, t' Guernsey's newest privateer captain!'

'Hurrah!' Rosie squealed, hugging Kydd. 'A real corsair! How romantic! We'll come down to the harbour an' see you off on your voyage o' plunder and adventure. You lucky man!'

At Robidou's office he picked up the memorandum and articles of association that were the foundation of his future. It was strange to see before his eyes, in sombre, weighty phrases, the financial underpinning to nothing less than a voyage of predation – but then he remembered that he was a mere employee of the association, the captain of their venture but, nevertheless, a servant of the owners.

This became even more plain when preparation began on the articles of the voyage. There was dignified discussion concerning his emoluments but this was merely a form of politeness: his basic income would be no more than a bare wage. The incentive for captain and crew would be a share in the proceeds of any prize they might take. This was apportioned out and agreed at a five-eighths share to the managing owners, the rest to be distributed among the privateer crew. The captain would receive sixty shares, twice that of the officers; the boatswain, gunner and other valuable members half that again. The common seaman could expect anything from twelve to two shares in accordance with his worth to the ship.

That settled, there was the question of the conduct of the voyage. In the merchant service there were no Articles of War, no regulations or Admiralty Instructions as a comforting guide and sometime refuge from decision. On a merchantman, aside from the venerable customs of the sea, the captain stood alone to rule as he saw fit – and be ready to take the consequences.

There had to be *something* sturdy and bracing in the articles, however, as this was the only binding document for a seaman, who must sign them before the forthcoming voyage. For a privateer it was a particular case: carrying on the profession of war but within the structure of the merchant service. Under Robidou's advice, Kydd compromised on simple clauses that required obedience to lawful orders and refraining from insolence and disorderly conduct.

As to provisions touching on combat, it was no use to

make appeal to King and country. There was but one simple equation: those who flinched in action or showed cowardly behaviour would forfeit their share in the prize. On the other hand the first man to board a resisting prize would be rewarded: six gold guineas for him and one each for the next six; no pillage to be tolerated.

The articles went on to other details: no extra privileges to officers save the captain; a week's wages in advance on signing and a redeemable ticket for shares immediately on prize condemnation; none to suffer loss of wages or prize money if put ashore with illness or injury caused in the line of duty; and all monies due a seaman to be payable within three months of the end of the voyage.

These were clear enough, for Kydd had been master of a merchant vessel before and the legalities of such documents as the Portage Bill, and others concerning the crew, were no mystery to him. He must have impressed, for Robidou sat back in satisfaction and grunted, 'An' if ye'll clap y'r scratch t' the articles we can get th' venture under way.'

The *armateur* pulled out a bottle of malt whisky and glasses. 'Here's t' your good health, Mr Kydd, an' may our enterprise be profitable.'

It was time to find a ship.

'Aye, I did get sight o' one,' Kydd said casually. 'She's alongside by South Pier. Name of *Cheval Marin*. Fine lines she has, trim an' well fettled, wi' a deck as'll take a line o' six-pounders—'

'The brigantine? About two, three hundred ton, a mite over-sparred f'r the Channel?'

'Aye, but not a problem f'r a cruiser.'

Robidou's expression hardened. 'Pray tell me, Mr Kydd, why do ye think she'll make a privateer?'

'Why, she has the size t' discourage valour and looks a simple merchantman well enough.'

'And where did ye say y'r cruising?'

'Gulf of Avranches t' Brest,' Kydd said defensively, remembering the two quarry he had seen from *Teazer*.

'Then ye'll need to think again, I believe. There's two things y' may have overlooked. The first of 'em is, in those waters they're all coasters close in. Shallow draught is what's wanted in chase through shoal waters, bigod, an' that's not y'r *Cheval*.

'Second is, have ye costed the barky? Three hundred tons, a hundred an' fifty crew – puttin' aside th' purchase price, what'll she cost each day o' sea-time? Disbursements in harbour dues, wharfage, repair an' maintenance? Add all y'r other outlay with this an' we come to a pretty sum. Now, how much do y' reckon a coaster prize will yield, figuring on a ready market but fees o' thirty per centum at the least? Not enough t' cover expenses.

'No, sir. It will not do. You'll be wantin' a trim coaster y'self, I'm thinkin', no more'n eighty ton, probably lug-rigged an' country built, a hold well enough f'r a prize-crew. Y' won't need storin' past a week or so at a time.'

Kydd's dreams of cutting the figure of a rapacious privateer putting to sea in a proud craft in search of booty were rapidly fading.

'I did see one as I'll allow is more t' my taste,' Robidou went on. 'In St Sampson f'r repair, a saucy lugger, just y'r size. You'll want t' see her first, o' course. Name o' *Bien Heureuse*, been in th' salt trade this last twelve-month, a common enough sight to the French.'

'What weight o' metal?' Kydd asked dubiously.

Robidou chuckled. 'A Frenchy coastin' craft won't have more'n swivels, so a pair o' small carriage guns'll be enough

213

t' terrify him. If ye're crafty an' go quietly ye'll outsail any deep-laden vessel o' y'r own class, an' then it's how well y' board.'

Kydd's first sight of *Bien Heureuse* was a vessel propped up on the mud near a slip-yard up the coast at St Sampson. Plank walkways were laid to allow their inspection but as Kydd made his way gingerly towards the rearing bulk his heart sank.

Her construction was sound enough, carvel strakes of a thickness out of respect to the rocky shoals and reefs – but so drab. No figurehead or decoration to relieve the sturdy lines, not a touch of gold-leaf or a proud stern-gallery. Her hull was utilitarian tarred black-sided, faded in parts but her spars and rails were varnished, giving an overall impression of unpretentious strength.

They clambered up a wooden ladder to the deck. She was two-masted, really; the third much smaller and well-raked mast right aft was so out of keeping with the others. But at least they soared to a satisfying height, Kydd reflected, and they could probably spread topsails above.

Flush-decked, there was one hatchway forward and one aft: the latter led to what would be his cabin, little more than a hutch with a table and space for a cot, with two tiny skylights above. Forward was a space with curtained-off bunks above lockers, no doubt the officers' accommodation.

Reaching the open air again, Kydd saw that with gratings in the hatches the partitioned hold held good promise of accommodation for prize-crew and there was the usual fo'c'sle glory-hole right forward for the main crew.

Aware that Robidou was watching him, Kydd took his time. If this was to be his command, nothing could be left to chance. He crossed to the shrouds; they were faded to the plain hemp but when he examined inside the strands, there was the rich black of Stockholm tar.

The deck was uncluttered, the lead of the lines from aloft economical and practical as to be expected of a small crew. There would have to be doubled backstays and the like as in a man-o'-war to provide for rigging carrying away in the thick of an action, and other additions would be needed aloft.

Her ground tackle – anchors and cables – had been landed but could be inspected later, as would the suits of sails going with the sale, but all in all . . . 'She'll do,' Kydd said evenly. 'Subject t' survey, o' course.'

The pace quickened: it was made very clear that ships in harbour do not catch prizes, and Kydd spent more of his time at St Sampson.

When he called on Robidou he was asked to provide a completion date for the conversion. 'We're livin' on our capital,' the *armateur* rasped. 'Ye must have crew, but not too quick – they'll be guzzlin' on our account soon enough – but they needs t' plan out their time fr'm when you're askin' 'em to sign on, which'll be less'n a week afore ye sails. An' *that*'ll be as soon as she's fit t' swim.'

Kydd made to leave but Robidou stopped him. 'Aren't ye forgettin' something, Mr Kydd?'

'Er, what's that, sir?'

'If'n ye goes a-cruisin' without it, the world will take ye as a pirate.'

'Ah, th' Letter o' Marque.' It was the legal document that set him loose on the seven seas to board and seize ships going about their business without being accused of piracy. He had never seen one close to but knew them to be of vital importance.

'Do ye know what's t' be done in the applyin'?' When Kydd

shook his head, he passed across the single sheet of an old Letter of Marque from a previous voyage.

It would be no trivial matter. The object, it seemed, was to petition the King through the High Court of Admiralty for a grant of reprisal, the legal conceit being that the petitioner was seeking redress for injury from the nominated prince – Bonaparte – through the seizing of his property, namely ships and their cargo.

This in turn required the production of a warrant from the Lords Commissioners for executing the Office of Lord High Admiral of Great Britain for the granting thereof to the named captain and ship. To obtain such it was necessary to make deposition as to the suitability of such a vessel and its commander, with the owners, tonnage and rig, her principal officers, the size of crew and armament to be strictly specified. Even the number of shot for each gun and the state of her sea stores would be noted.

'Th' suitability of her captain as must appear before 'em?' Kydd had never heard of a naval captain of a privateer – but, then, it was likely that few would wish to boast of the experience. And what of the recent shadow over his naval career?

'That's as it has t' be,' Robidou said impatiently. 'You'll not need t' appear. As Guernseymen we can declare b' proxy, an' we has a London agent who'll weasel th' thing through any shoal waters for us. He knows what he's about, an' we're payin' the devil enough for his pains.'

Kydd read on. 'A bond?'

'Sureties on the commander against his good conduct. I'm askin' Paul Le Mesurier t' stand in the sum o' one thousan' five hundred pounds, as he will, trustin' you'll steer small in the article o' seizin' ships as will fight.'

It staggered Kydd. The princely sum of five years of his total pay as commander was being advanced in trust by a complete stranger on the word of Robidou that he stood to lose if Kydd ran afoul of some bloody-minded Admiralty clerk who judged that his conduct in boarding had been wanting.

Robidou continued, 'Well, now, that's under way, then. I fancy ye'll want t' find a crew.' He paused. 'You'll not know s' many in th' islands – do ye wish t' leave it to me t' find some as'll ship with ye?'

'If y' please, Mr Robidou,' Kydd said.

'I'll put th' word about.'

Slowly the replies arrived on Renzi's desk: a tribute to the skill and dedication of d'Auvergne's network. Concealed in tree-trunks and under bridges, they were retrieved and, at great risk to the carriers, made their way to the coast, then by fishermen and smugglers to Jersey, now to lie in his hand.

The secrets were held in grubby, spidery letters, some as spirals to be uncurled, others folded to minute squares, in innocent shop receipts or letters to relatives. However, great care was needed, for while the old trick of writing in lemon juice and reading it by the heat of a candle-flame was well known, many preferred to use baking-soda and grape juice. This could be read only the once, then would slowly fade for ever, effectively preventing its later use as evidence.

The messages: fervent support, elaborately worded reasons for unavailability, warnings of billeted troops . . . All needed to be plotted against the route and alternative arrangements made.

Chapter 12

Kydd was set up in his rendezvous at the Blue Anchor in St Peter Port in due style, ready to stand a muzzler of stingo to any brave tar who wished to sign on with him for a cruise of fortune westward.

It was noisy, hard-drinking work, but Robidou was sitting next to him and it was clear that he was well respected as a privateersman. Among the first to approach was Rowan, a seamed West Country man with a direct eye and quiet manner. His recent experience quickly saw him signed as lieutenant and prize-captain.

A boatswain, Rosco, was next. Bluff, he had a hard-eyed countenance that Kydd liked. Seamen started to appear; there were some prime hands that would not have been out of place on the gun-deck of a man-o'-war – which was probably where they had learned their trade. Others had the look of the wharf-rat about them, but Kydd could not be too particular as numbers were thinning.

Another experienced officer came up: name of Tranter, he could claim service with the Guernseyman Hamon of the

Phoenix, which had taken twenty prizes in the Revolutionary War; he was made second prize-captain and lieutenant.

More seamen came; some curious, others disdainful. It was hard to make out their mettle when it was overlaid with the traditional independence of the merchant seaman, but this was not to be a long, deep-sea voyage where any real defects of character could matter.

As time passed, Kydd was perturbed that no gunner had stepped forward: he had secured a pair of nine-pounder carriage guns and needed to see they were fitted properly. A merchant vessel was not equipped with the heavy scantlings of timber round the gun-ports to absorb recoil and they would require sea testing to work up to a safe charge.

By the evening it had become evident that while they would not go short-handed they had not been besieged by eager fortune-hunters and Kydd knew he was lucky to have signed his crew. Now it was time to take on the ship's boys.

Their main purpose was to manage the ship when the men were away in prize-crews. Paid at the lowest rate and with but a half-share each they were nevertheless vital – and cheap. They crowded up to his table, eyes shining, ready for adventure. He hoped the reality of a cold autumn sea and an overcrowded ship would not too quickly disillusion them and managed a few words of encouragement to each.

The next day Kydd was back at the *Bien Heureuse*, which was now in the water so he could take his fill of her. Her lugger rig was his main concern as it was seldom encountered in the Navy. This one was similar to a French *chasse-marée*, with its sharply raked third mast and ringsail with jigger boomkin out over the stern, but she had a lengthy bowsprit over her dignified straight stem, English style.

Time was pressing, and there was so much to see to: the

sails had to be in reasonable condition for the weather as it worsened with the season; the running rigging needed to be overhauled – no twice-laid stuff to fail at the crucial moment. And all the time expenses were mounting and Robidou had to be convinced of their necessity.

Artificers and artisans were signed on – the sailmaker, armourer, carpenter – each with shares negotiated and commensurate, all found outfits of tools and spares. The clock was ticking with the hands signing aboard and taking wages.

The Priaulx yard was doing a good job but seemed to have no sense of urgency: it needed goading, and drink money for the shipwrights, who were, of course, in a way of business that in a King's yard they were not. A gunner was finally found: Kevern, a sallow and somewhat nervous young man, who had the unsettling habit of agreeing instantly and completely with anything Kydd said.

By now Robidou was showing clear signs of impatience. Kydd's requirement for more powder and shot was denied curtly; he was allowed the bare minimum of charts and no chronometer. The prize-captain Rowan, however, was unexpectedly helpful in discovering odd rutters and pilots of the waters in French and Dutch.

A small crowd of interested spectators had taken to looking on from the pier, to the hazard of the ship's stores, being prepared there to be struck below. Driven to distraction Kydd was told that the cook had stormed off in disgust at the primitive stove – and he knew only too well that the men wouldn't stand for there not being hot scran on board at the right time.

It was chaos and confusion on all sides as Kydd took refuge in his tiny cabin. It smelled of damp bedding and stale tobacco.

The timber sides were weeping at the join of the transom, and there would be no money wasted on oiling the faded wood of the bulkhead; it remained a drab and pale-blotched sadness.

He held his head in his hands. What had possessed him to take this on? He would have given a great deal to have his friend Renzi with him, now loyally working at menial clerking in Jersey to give him the chance to clear his name. Yet something had prevented Kydd writing to tell him of his change of situation, some feeling of reluctance to admit to his friend his new status as a privateer.

There were more pressing matters: how could he forge this ship's company into a fighting whole when they were complete strangers? Not a soul would he have aboard that he had known more than hours only. He would be again without a friend in the world.

Staring gloomily at the grubby skylight he had a sudden idea that set him to calling a ship's boy. 'Here's a sixpence. Do you find a Mr Luke Calloway as will be at th' Bethel or workin' on th' waterfront, an' tell him th' captain o' *Bien Heureuse* wants t' speak with him. Off y' go, then!' It would not only provide Calloway with a job and a chance at real money but Kydd would have a familiar face on board.

It wasn't until the afternoon that the lad came back, breathless. 'I did fin' a gent b' that name, but he was pushin' a handcart, Mr Kydd. An' when I told 'im what ye wanted, he asked what ship. I told 'im *Bien Heureuse*, privateer!' He puffed out his cheeks in pride.

'Then where—'

'When he hears she's a private ship, he don't want t' know, sees me off,' the boy said, astonished.

Kydd grinned mirthlessly. 'Tell him Mr Kydd has need o'

his services, younker. Another sixpence if he's aboard b' sundown.'

That evening, still without a cook, Kydd welcomed Calloway warmly and, over a hot negus in his cabin, told him of his plans. 'An' if ye'd wish it, there's a berth f'r master's mate on th' next cruise.' Whatever it took, he would get it past Robidou. After all, Calloway was a prime man-o'-war's man and an officer in his last ship. And a master's mate aboard a merchant ship? Well, if the practice was to call mates 'lieutenants' in privateers, then surely he could import other ranks.

'I'd like it well, Mr Kydd,' Calloway said, in a voice tinged with awe.

It vexed Kydd that he was apparently now touched by the glamour of a corsair. He went on sternly, 'In course, as soon as we're rightfully back aboard *Teazer* I'll see ye on the quarterdeck as reefer again.'

'Aye aye, Captain,' Calloway said happily.

'Get y' baggage an' be back smartly. I've a cook t' find fr'm somewhere,' Kydd said heavily, remembering. If he did not find one—

'Er, I do know o' one.'

'A sea-cook? Where?'

Calloway hesitated. 'Over in La Salerie, Mr Kydd. I seen him cook up f'r the boatyard there. See, he's of an age, as we'd say – you'd have t' hide th' grog or he's a devil cut loose, but—'

'He's been t' sea?'

The young man's face cleared. 'Oh, aye! If ye'd lend ear t' his yarns an' half of it true, why—'

'Get him here!'

*   *   *

Then, suddenly, it was time: after a last frantic scrabble to load stores and find missing crew, they were singling up the shore lines. Shouts were thrown at men standing uselessly about the fo'c'sle and the boatswain knocked a man to the deck in vexation. Canvas rustled as it was hoisted on the fore and a sightseer bent to give the bow-line an expert twist and toss into the water. As the wind caught the tall lug and the bow sheered away from the pier Kydd roared the order that brought in the stern painter – and they were on their way out to sea.

Kydd took a deep breath to steady himself: he was back in command and outward bound on a voyage of fortune – free of the land. But this was in a small, barely armed former salt trader, with an untried crew, and in minutes they could be fighting for their lives – or seizing a rich prize.

As they left St Peter Port there had been no fine gun salutes or pennant snapping bravely at the main, the hallowed ceremony of a King's ship putting to sea to meet the enemy. Instead it had been a casual slipping from the pier to catch the ebb, along with all the other small vessels leaving to go about their business on great waters.

Bien Heureuse picked up the breeze and stood out into the channel of the Little Russel. Kydd took care that they carried only small sail until he was happy he knew his ship better. It was unsettling not to have a Queripel or a sailing-master aboard as they headed out past the sombre rocks round the harbour. Probably Robidou had reasoned that if he needed deeper local knowledge he could ask Rowan or one of the others, but for now he must be the one to give orders.

With clear skies and in only a slight lop, they shaped course past the Plattes for the north of Guernsey. 'Where are we headed, Mr Kydd?' Rowan asked, standing by his shoulder, perfectly braced on the heeling deck.

'We're t' quarter th' coast west o' Bréhat,' Kydd said, in a tone that did not invite discussion. However, he planned to delay their arrival on these hunting grounds along the north coast of France as there was a driving need to get his ship in fighting array before their first encounter. He did not want arguments: he felt there was quarry in those regions and, besides, his one and only patrol of the French coast had been there so these were the only waters he knew well.

Rowan looked at him keenly but said nothing.

They reached the north of Guernsey and put the tiller down for a smart beat westward in the direction of the open Atlantic where he would have the sea-room to take her measure.

The fresh breeze strengthened in gusts and sent the lee gunwale dipping into the racing side wake: a lesson learned. *Bien Heureuse* was tender on a wind and would need more men to each mast. Her angle of heel was considerable, even for a fore-and-aft rigged vessel and Kydd found himself reaching for a shroud to steady himself. Approaching seas came in with a hard smack on the weather bow and transformed into solid spray that soaked every unwary hand; she was a wet ship.

He tested the wind, leaning into it with his eyes closed, feeling its strength and constancy. A strong blow from the south-south-west; surely they could carry more sail? He made the order to loose one of the two reefs on the fore – the bow fell off and buried itself in the brisk combers. 'An' th' main, Mr Rosco!' Kydd bawled; there was little subtlety in the lug rig, but this brought a definite improvement in her response at the tiller.

225

He sheeted the little ringsail behind him harder in and was surprised by the response. Not only did she right herself considerably and take fewer seas over the bow but her speed seemed to have increased. And closer to the wind: there were possibilities . . .

He let *Bien Heureuse* take up full and bye again, then tried her going free, downwind. Without a comfortable breadth of beam she felt uneasy, rolling in a regular arc to one side then lurching to the other – not her best point of sailing, and the absence of a weighty cargo low down didn't help.

A crestfallen Calloway appeared. 'Sorry, sir. Purvis is – um, flustered b' liquor an' needs t' rest.'

Kydd grimaced. Their cook, prostrate with drink. As were other crewmen who had disposed of their advances in the time-honoured way. They would have to be roused soon for the setting of watches, then must abide by the ageless rhythm of the sea. In the Navy such behaviour would earn at the least a night in the bilboes – but this was not the Navy.

'Mr Rowan? I'd be obliged should ye take the deck until we've got our watch-bill. Course west b' south f'r now.' Kydd wanted to get the paperwork squared away while the daylight lasted; there were no clear-light spermaceti lamps aboard this vessel.

The motion was uncomfortable in the confines of his cabin, a pronounced wallow that demanded a sustained bracing against the movement. He turned to his papers, hurriedly stuffed into a box. He had not had time fully to digest the 'Admiralty Instructions to Privateers', a specific set of rules enclosed with the Letter of Marque, which by their infraction would result in the bond being forfeited. They seemed straightforward enough, however, in the main to ensure that merchant ships of whatever flag, and particularly neutrals, were not assailed by swarms of ill-disciplined free-booters little better than pirates. From the look of some of *his* crew this was not impossible, Kydd thought wryly.

The other paperwork would have to wait. He swung out of the cabin and then on deck. In the cold evening bluster he saw only Rowan and the helmsman in any sense on watch, with possibly a pair of lookouts on the foredeck, but more probably they were landmen, unable to keep below-decks.

He stumped down to the curtained officers' quarters and found the other prize-captain lying in his cot. 'Mr Tranter, muster all hands f'r watches,' he snapped.

'Bit hard, like,' the man drawled. 'They been on th' turps – we lets 'em sleep it off.' He made no move to rise.

Kydd saw red. 'Out 'n' down – now!' he roared. 'If I don't see ye on deck this instant, so help me I'll have ye turned afore the mast!'

Tranter rolled an eye towards him. 'Y' can't do that,' he said, in an aggrieved tone. 'This ain't a King's ship. We got articles as say I'm a prize-captain.' He contemplated Kydd for a moment more, then slipped down slowly and reached for his watch-coat.

Stumping up the companionway Kydd clamped down his anger. If he was going to have a well-trained crew, instead of a cutlass-waving bunch of pirates, he had his work cut out.

The men came on deck reluctantly, some helped by their shipmates; there were by count but fifty-one, all told. The chill wind whipping in set the unprepared shivering, but Kydd was in no mood for sympathy. He waited until they were still. 'Ye're crew o' the *Bien Heureuse* privateer,' he rasped. 'Ye've signed articles, an' now ye're takin' my orders.'

Apart from some sullen shuffling there seemed to be stolid

227

acceptance; he would show them he knew the customs of the merchant service well enough. 'Mr Rowan, Mr Tranter,' he called importantly. Rowan stepped forward and, pursing his lips, pointed to a level-eyed seaman with his arms folded across his chest. 'Raynor,' he grunted.

The man obediently crossed the deck and stood by him. With a grimace, Tranter moved forward and surveyed the group. He called out a thickset seaman from the back, who shuffled across to him through the others.

It went on: the best men fairly distributed, the unknowns parcelled out. When it reached the boys Kydd intervened. 'I'll take him t' be m' peggy,' he said, pointing to the tallest. He wanted a cabin boy who could stand up for himself.

When the process was complete, Kydd set Calloway to taking down the details. 'I'll have a full watch o' the hands b' morning,' he ordered both lieutenants. It was now up to them to assign their own men to best advantage in the watch that they themselves would lead.

He left them to it and headed for his cabin, relieved that the first steps had been taken in bringing order to the world. No sooner had he sat down than there was a tap at the door. 'Come!' he called.

It was the young lad he had chosen as his cabin boy. 'Well, now, an' ye've nothing t' fear if y' do y'r duty, younker,' Kydd said genially. Was there not something familiar about the youngster?

'Yes, sir,' he replied, not meeting Kydd's eyes.

'I'm sure I've seen ye somewhere about – what do they call ye?'

'L-Leon, s' please ye, sir,' the boy said, shrinking back.

Realisation dawned. 'Be damned, an' Leon it's not! Pookie more like!' Kydd spluttered. 'What th' devil – what d' ye think

228

y'r playin' at, y' chuckle-headed loon?' A twelve-year-old waif of a girl in a privateer, however big for her age?

'I – I want t' be a pirate,' she said stiffly, 'an' sail the seven seas—'

'Pirate?' Kydd choked.

'– t' seize an' plunder, an' then I'll give it to m' ma.'

It was rank lunacy. 'How—'

'I heard as how you was goin' t' be captain o' the good ship *Ben Herses*, an' cruise the seas for—'

'Enough o' th' catblash! You're goin' back t' y'r ma.'

The child's eyes filled. 'Please, Mr Kydd! I want t' be a sailor, see aroun' the world like you do – an' ye did promise us when we signed as we'd be able seamen afore we knew it. That's what y' said.'

Kydd's first reaction was to summon the boatswain and have the girl taken off his hands, but then he sat back heavily. The ship was halfway between Guernsey and the French coast with night coming on: he was not risking those rocky outliers to return in the darkness with a fluky wind. She would have to stay on board for the night.

To return in the morning would be to waste their hard-won westing and result in an ignominious arrival in port to explain that one of the hands he had personally signed up was female. Not to speak of the expense, which would be mounting hourly. And he couldn't land the rascal somewhere to pick up later: there was no friendly territory anywhere to the west of Guernsey. Kydd sighed. 'What can y'r mother be feeling now, y' scamp?'

'Ma?' she said scornfully. 'She's so plagued b' the little 'uns, she'd be main pleased t' see th' last o' me. I been away before, y' know,' she added, with self-possession beyond her years.

'Y' can't stay aboard. What if they finds ye a – a female? Does anyone know?'

'No, they doesn't, Mr Kydd,' she said stoutly. 'Look, I'll be th' same as the others – honest! I'll pull on y'r ropes an' such, just like a man. Don't make me go back.'

Kydd had to admit that she was indistinguishable from a boy in her breeches and plain homespun, and her hair, while long, was in keeping with that of the other ship's boys. Her impish features suggested anything but a demure damsel. Despite himself he warmed to her need to escape dreary poverty for the freedoms of the sea. He made up his mind. 'Be just th' same as the other lads? Take orders wi'out a cackle? Stand up f'r y'self?'

'I will, Mr Kydd,' she said, with fervour.

'Then I'll make ye a deal.'

'Mr Kydd?'

'I don't know ye're a female. Nobody told me. Now, if any aboard find out, ye're taken straight t' this cabin th' same instant an' locked in until we make port again. Y' scavey?'

'Aye, Mr Kydd,' she whispered, eyes shining.

'An' none o' y'r snafflin' tricks either – sailors has a short way wi' thieves.'

'Never, sir. I only did it t' give Ma.'

'Remember – if just a one sees ye're female . . .'

'They won't, Mr Kydd.'

He looked at her very directly, 'And if'n any shows ye any mischief at all, you're t' come t' me directly. I'll not stand f'r it, d' ye hear?'

'Yes, Mr Kydd.'

'Right. Well, *Mr* Turner, let me tell ye of y'r duties.'

*   *   *

230

Morning found them under small sail tossing uneasily in a long swell from the west. Bleary-eyed men were roused from below to meet the dawn. This would be the last time Kydd allowed the ship not to be ready at quarters – or whatever passed for battle readiness in a privateer.

'Mr Rowan!' he hailed. 'I'll give both watches one bell f'r their breakfast an' then we'll turn to f'r some real sailorin'.' It was near impossible to work up a ship's company to effectiveness as a fighting unit in such a short time – but it would be their captain they blamed if they failed to take a prize or, worse, were overcome themselves.

The men left the deck, muttering, and Kydd remembered the cook. Going forward he found the forehatch but, praise be, immediately below it Purvis was at work with his pots and pans on the small portable stove. He looked up cheerily. 'Ho there, Cap'n!' he breezed.

'Everything in hand?' Kydd called down. The stove was rigged over a bed of bricks under the open hatch but how it was possible to bring in meals for scores of men in such conditions was a mystery to him.

'Aye – all's a-taunto, sir.'

Kydd left him to it and returned to his cabin. Inside, an apprehensive cabin boy waited with a steaming dish and plates on a tray under a neat canvas spray-cover. 'Why, thank 'ee, er, Turner.' Clearly the cook had been consulted and together they had managed a hot breakfast fit for a captain. It was a hearty burgoo and toast thick with Jersey butter – Kydd had not been able to afford his usual private cabin stores and knew he was sharing with his men.

'Mr Purvis says as if ye has y'r particular taste he will oblige, Mr Kydd.'

'That's kind in him,' Kydd said. 'Now, you duck below an'

crowd some victuals inboard. I've got work f'r all hands this forenoon as'll have 'em all in a sweat.' He chuckled. The smell of hot food was irresistible and he realised he was very hungry.

Later, restored after his meal Kydd went on deck. He had given it some thought: there was no use trying to bring things along by setting masts to compete or appealing to some sense of nautical excellence. These merchant seamen were used to a sea life very different from the Navy, often with parsimonious owners providing tiny crews barely adequate to do the job, leaving little time or energy for non-essentials.

No, it would be necessary to go about it in other ways. The first was to trust the mates, that they would see to it their men would not let them down.

'Mr Rowan! I desire ye t' exercise y'r men under sail. What do y' have in mind?'

At first it was a shambles, but that was to be expected. Order out of chaos, seamen out of men, the time-honoured sequence when each had to learn the ropes on an unfamiliar ship that did things in its own particular way. 'Different ships, different long-splices' was the old saw. But Rowan proved experienced and wise, and well before midday each point of sailing, every manoeuvring task, any major event to be expected in a chase had been completed to satisfaction.

With a core of competence at the heart of the watch it would now be possible to build on it and start the task of bringing along the ordinary seamen, landmen and boys to their rightful standing and respect as full able-bodied seamen.

After a hearty noon meal of beef stew, it was time to attend the guns. Kevern assembled a crew and they set to on their main armament.

It quickly became obvious that they were paradoxically

both over- and undergunned. A vessel of their tonnage could be expected to mount at least four carriage guns a side. In his desire for the authoritative heavy crash of a sizeable gun Kydd had acquired a pair of nine-pounders. It had been a mistake: they were too long, unwieldy, and their full recoil would send them right across the deck; if they had to reduce charges out of respect to *Bien Heureuse*'s light timbers the weapons would be of no more use than smaller ones.

Kydd realised he should have stayed with more but lighter guns and felt resentful that Kevern had let him go to sea so encumbered. He consoled himself, however, with the thought that a pitched gun-battle was the last thing he wanted. A quick chase and rapid boarding: that was the way to get an unspoiled prize.

They were making headway: the restraining of his Navy instincts and understanding of his men's ways had gone a long way to winning their grudging respect. It was left to see how they would behave in a boarding. Should he begin to exercise with cutlass and pistols?

Along the horizon on the larboard bow Kydd saw, just starting to lift, the low untidy jumble of dark granite islets that was the north of France. There was little time left now to prepare. He took a deep breath. So much depended on—

'*Saaail hoooo!*' An excited whoop from forward shattered his thoughts.

'Where *awaaay*?' he bellowed. The lookout obliged with a pointing finger. There were no tops and ratlines up the shrouds with the lug-rig so he was at essentially the same level.

An excited roar went up and Kydd fumbled for his pocket telescope. This close to the coast, the odds were in favour of it being French and a prize – so soon! His heart thudded as he tried to focus.

They had surprised the ship as it had come round the cliffy headland into full view. No more than three or four miles away it was sailing along the shore on a course past them.

'Steady as she goes!' Kydd called urgently, and rounded on Rowan. 'I want these men out o' sight below – now!' They would play the harmless coastal trader for as long as possible. Nothing would be more calculated to alarm their prey than a sudden alteration towards them with crowded decks.

He lifted the telescope again, gripped by rising excitement. So far the vessel was holding its course, and they would hold theirs, imperceptibly inclining towards until they could make a lunge. His mind clamped in concentration on their relative positions and speeds. They were close-hauled westward in brisk seas while the stranger was driving before the wind, a dramatic contrast of pale sail against a backdrop of the sullen, dark-grey squall front spreading behind it. Flickering white wave crests showed in the darkening water nearer.

Kydd's eyes watered as he stared through the glass. It was a brigantine of sorts, so not a warship, and showed no colours. It shaped course closer to the coastline, opening the distance they would have to cover to intercept.

Offshore there was another of the innumerable uninhabited islets. A white mist was lifting on its far side, a token of mighty seas from the Atlantic ceasing their thousands of miles' travel in the concussive finality of iron-hard granite.

Under the looming dark heights of the squall, the headland merged into misty white curtains of rain. Trying to control his impatience, Kydd judged that their encounter with the brigantine would occur before the rain reached them.

Nothing could be better calculated to pull his ship together as a fighting band than a successful prize-taking.

At the forehatch men unable to contain themselves snatched a look. 'Keep th' heads down, y' blaggards!' he bellowed. The stranger would be wielding telescopes, too.

The offshore island disappeared into the advancing rain curtain and Kydd's gaze turned to the vessel. As he tried to make out more detail its perspective altered, curving ponderously round to take up on a course away, back where it had come. They had been discovered.

'Sheet away, y' lubbers!' he shouted, at the men boiling up from below. The stranger – now the chase – was hard by the wind, clawing as desperately as it could to windward but it had lost much ground and now lay barely a mile ahead. A lazy smile came to Kydd's face: in their panic they had put the helm to the wrong side and now found themselves on the other tack to *Bien Heureuse*. They could not possibly weather the headland.

'We have him now.' Kydd laughed. 'He'll be ours afore sundown.' They would keep to seaward and wait for the chase to come out to them.

Bien Heureuse was lined with eager privateersmen, each hungrily making the same calculation. A sizeable merchantman with a small crew, judging by their tardiness in putting about and taking up close-hauled. Her cargo? Probably returning from Biscay with wine and brandy, risking a quick dash across Baie de Saint Brieuc – a pity for him that a Guernsey privateer just happened to be round the point.

There was no hope for the Frenchman and Kydd wondered why he held on so doggedly. Then the first squall arrived. In a wash of cold down-draught *Bien Heureuse* entered a wall of rain, passing into a hissing roar of water that stippled the sea white in a drenching deluge. It stunned the wind momentarily and the sails hung limp and wet.

They emerged damp and chill but the chase was still ahead and closer. Then another wall of rain closed round them, and the sails, now deprived of a steady wind, flapped and banged. Visibility was reduced to yards, and the seas lost their liveliness as they were beaten to rounded hillocks in the swell.

Kydd squinted into the chaos, which seemed to go on and on. Where *was* everything in this never-ending rain world? Uneasily aware of the treacherous currents surging over unforgiving ground he gave the order to veer sheets and *Bien Heureuse* slowed to a crawl.

The rain volleyed in a loud drumming on their deck, gurgling down the lee scuppers; when it finally stopped, the chase had disappeared. The headland was much closer but there was no sign of the brigantine. Had he successfully weathered the headland? If so, he was away up the coast and could be anywhere.

Then Kydd saw the offshore island again – it was well within reach and would make a perfect place for the Frenchman to lurk out of sight while Kydd went chasing past, then take up on his old course, his voyage delayed only by a few hours.

'Lay us t' wind'ard o' that island!' Kydd snapped. The breeze had picked up and pierced like a knife through his sodden clothes. He shuddered.

'The island?' Rowan said uncertainly. 'Are ye sure?'

'He thinks t' wait out o' sight – he's too lubbardly t' have weathered th' point,' Kydd said.

Tranter cut in: 'I don't reckon he's there at all. We're wastin' time—'

'Get y' men ready f'r a boardin', Mr Tranter, an' *you* stop y' pratin'!' Kydd answered, with sudden anger.

His heart fell at the sight of the rabble in the waist. They were as unlike a naval boarding party as it was possible to be, jabbering, excited men with drawn cutlasses and lurid headgear. Where was the lethal discipline of a sectioned assault? Where the calm weighing of opportunity and deadly resolve?

'Hold 'em there, Mr Tranter,' Kydd called, with an edge of sarcasm. They were up against terrified merchant sailors and the likelihood was that any fight would be minimal.

A nine-pounder was cleared away and Kydd sent Calloway to the forward crew to stiffen them. They were as ready as they could be.

Drawing near, the island seemed the ideal bolt-hole, and at a respectful distance they took time to round the white-fringed weather shore. Kydd kept his telescope up, straining for sight of a naked mast above the irregular lumpiness of the bare rock.

They circled the island in silence, ready for a panic-stricken dash. Nothing. At a loss Kydd carefully quartered the sea. The brigantine had to be somewhere, a little cove perhaps, a hidden river mouth . . . The prey had escaped.

Tranter snorted and stormed below. The men followed in ones and twos, with scornful looks aft.

Kydd caught Rowan's eye. 'Where did he go, d' ye think?'

'I don't think y' give th' Frenchy credit, Mr Kydd. He's one cool hand, waits f'r the main squall, then slashes about t' stay inside it an' passes us close in th' murk an' away off t' Paimpol, cool as y' please.'

It was galling. It seemed these French *matelots* in their home waters were every bit as bold and seamanlike as the English, certainly far from being frightened sheep about to be snapped up by a passing wolf. 'We press on,' Kydd grunted. 'There'll be more – an' I know where . . .'

The Sept Îles resolved out of the grey murkiness as he remembered them from the deck of *Teazer*. The only question now was whether to pass to seaward or take the inner channel. He decided quickly. 'South about, lad,' he told the helmsman. There was no point in crisp naval orders to an officer-of-the-watch in this vessel.

Obediently the young seaman swung the tiller and *Bien Heureuse* headed into the channel under easy sail in the fluky north-easterly, every man on eager lookout, as guineas would go to him who first sighted their prey.

This time there was no gunfire from the old fort – they must appear as innocent as the salt trader they had once been. As they passed through unnoticed, Kydd tugged his coat closer and sighed. He was now a captain again, even if it was of a jackal of the seas. He was under no orders other than his own, with nothing to do but fall upon any sail sighted. No other purpose or distraction; no convoys, senior officers, strict instructions. This was what it was to prowl the seas as a single-minded predator. No wonder the carefree life of a pirate in past ages had—

'*Saaail!*' screamed two men, simultaneously – or was that a seaman and a sharp-eyed boy?

Kydd swung up his glass eagerly. As they emerged from the passage on the other side of Sept Îles he saw a three-masted lugger on the same course. It had taken the deeper seaward route and they had met the other side not more than a mile or two apart.

His telescope told him that the vessel was larger than they

and low in the water – a full cargo? A handful of men stood on deck, no doubt filled with consternation at their sudden appearance. The lugger held its course for minutes longer, then curved sharply into the wind and made for the open sea.

'Go after him, then,' Kydd growled happily at the helmsman. An exultant roar went up from the men busy at the ropes and *Bien Heureuse* heeled sharply. The hunt was on.

'Clear away an' give him a gun, Mr Kevern.' The first would be unshotted and to weather, the demand to heave to. The next would be a ball across the ship's bows. Failing a response to this, there would be a cannon shot low over the decks.

With an apologetic crack the nine-pounder under reduced charge spoke out, the rank odour of powder smoke nevertheless carrying aft its message of threat and challenge. 'Boarders, Mr Tranter,' Kydd warned. In the event of resistance he wanted no delay in the manoeuvre to give their opponents time to rally.

The two ships stretched out over the sea, leaving the lumpy grey islands to disappear into the rain astern with the pursuer straining every line and stitch of canvas to close with their prey. As Kydd watched, he saw suddenly that the fleeing craft was falling off the wind. Then, incredibly, it was turning towards them. Rowan cursed and muttered, 'That there's *Trois Frères* o' St Malo – I should o' known.'

'Frenchy privateer?'

'A Malouin? He is that. Cap'n Vicq, an' he's a Tartar, particular well manned 'n' armed. We'd best—'

'Helm up!' Kydd roared, to the startled man at the tiller, 'T' th' Triagoz!' It was a single near conical rocky islet ahead set in endless reefs but it was the only land in sight – and down to leeward.

With a dispiriting wallow *Bien Heureuse* slewed about for the distant hillock and picked up speed. Kydd thought furiously. The other was a larger ship and almost certainly more experienced – and these were home waters for the Malouin. In these seas it had the edge – with superior numbers and firepower.

Tranter came aft. 'Th' bastard's got us! Tide's on the ebb an' we can't—'

'Hold y' jabber!' Kydd snarled. He had just noticed that the wily Vicq with his slight advantage of speed had eased away to parallel his run for the Triagoz but was closing with every yard. They could not strike for the open sea because Vicq would be waiting there, but on the other hand they were being pressed slowly but surely against the hostile land.

It was the same trick he had used on the Cornish coast to box in another privateer to a rockbound coast – but this time he himself was the victim. The deck fell quiet as each man took in the dire situation. Their captain was the only one who could save them now.

Kydd had no illusions about Vicq. His initial move to flee had drawn Kydd into betraying his true character as a privateer and, further, had lured him into the open sea. Now he had the patience to make sure of *Bien Heureuse* and win the bounty Napoleon Bonaparte had promised to any who could rid him of a detested English privateer.

By definition they could not prevail in an encounter at sea. Therefore they must keep in with the land. He recalled his first sighting of the lugger low in the water; without doubt, this was the outset of a cruise for Vicq with the ship full of prize-crew and stores. Kydd made his decision: with their lesser draught the only course left to them was to head for the rocks and shallows under the coast to try to shake off the larger craft.

'South!' he ordered. Into the embrace of the land – enemy land. Once again *Bien Heureuse* bucketed round, taking up on the larboard tack in a race for life and safety.

Vicq conformed immediately and tucked himself in astern for the chase but when Kydd reached the reef-strewn coast and swung cautiously away to the south-west Vicq angled over at once to keep his clamping position to seawards.

Close inshore the prospect was fearful: granite crags, deadly rocky islets emerging with the falling tide – and everywhere the betraying surge of white from unseen sub-sea threats.

Rowan was sent up the foremast in an improvised boatswain's chair to try to spot imminent perils ahead – a trying task with the mast's manic dipping and swaying in the following wind. Vicq remained at a distance, passing on the outer side of the forbidding Plateau de la Méloine and allowing *Bien Heureuse* the inner passage. In a chill of fear Kydd saw why.

With the wind dead astern the only course was ahead – and into the five-mile stretch of Morlaix Bay. Constrained to keep close inshore *Bien Heureuse* would need longer going round, and with Vicq taking a straight course to cross it there was only one outcome. The two vessels would converge on the other side of the bay and Kydd's sole voyage as a privateer would be summarily finished.

He balled his fists. It was not just the humiliation of craven surrender – for he could not in all conscience consider a fight against superior odds with the crew he had – it was that the investors who had believed in him would now lose every farthing.

His ship's company would be taken prisoner and, as privateersmen, had no hope of release. And, of course, he would be among them. He could reveal his true identity and claim the protection of his naval rank to be later exchanged, but he knew Bonaparte would make much of capturing a commander, Royal Navy, as captain of a privateer. He could never suffer such dishonour to his service.

Although he would not fight, Kydd was determined to resist capture with everything he had. He fixed Vicq with a terrible concentration, noticing he was disdaining the shallows at the head of the bay. This allowed Kydd to weather a menacing central peninsula but it was only delaying the final act.

As they came to understand the meaning of the drama, panic-stricken local fishermen scattered. They had obviously felt quite secure previously, for at the end of the other side of the bay was Roscoff, where *Teazer* had been cheated of her prize.

In less than a mile *Bien Heureuse* would reach the far side. Vicq was on an intercept course under the same wind from astern, which would prevent Kydd's retreat. The climax would occur close in off the ancient port in full view of the towns-folk and the gunboats sallying forth would put paid to any escape.

But the tide had been on the ebb for some time and Kydd reasoned it must now be close to its lowest point. Roscoff harbour was therefore an expanse of mud so neither the gunboats nor any other could be a threat. His spirits rose: the bay finished in the sullen mass of the Île de Batz, three miles long but so close to port that every approaching ship must pass warily round it. If he could think of a way . . .

The harbour opened to view at the same time as Vicq, no more than a few hundred yards distant, triumphantly fired a gun to weather. Kydd saw with a sinking heart that any channel between Roscoff and the Île de Batz was lost in a desolate and impenetrable rockbound maze.

'Give 'im best, Mr Kydd,' Rowan said sadly. 'Ye did y' damnedest for us.' Mortification boiled in Kydd. He felt an insane urge to throw the ship on the reefs to rob Vicq of his victory, but this would be at the cost of lives.

It was time. 'G' rot ye for a chicken-hearted scut!' came from behind.

Kydd swung round to a flush-faced Tranter, who had clearly taken refuge in drink as the chase drew to its inevitable climax. 'Clap a stopper on't, y' useless shab!' Kydd retorted.

'Or what?' sneered Tranter. 'We're goin' t' rot in some Frog chokey f'r years, thanks t' you! A dandy-prat King's man as thinks he's—'

'One more word from ye, an I'll—'

Ye're finished! I'll be takin' no orders from you no more, *Cap'n*!'

Kydd's pent-up frustration exploded in a fist that felled the man to the deck in one. At that moment a shaft of pale sunlight turned the dull grey seas ahead to green; under the surface the black splotches of seaweed now could be seen streaming away from rocks that had lain hidden before and Kydd saw his chance.

The waters of the great Gulf of Avranche were draining fast into the Atlantic with the ebb – but the seaweed was not pointing straight ahead: it was at an angle, crossing their bow, indicating that the current was not going round the Île de Batz but instead between it and the port, racing into the confusion of crags and half-tide islets between that had seemed so impassable.

'Take us in!' he roared.

Nervously the hand at the tiller worked the vessel round the last rocks and committed *Bien Heureuse* to the hazard. The current clutched at the lugger and whirled her forward. Distant shouts came from Vicq's vessel, but as Kydd turned to see what the Frenchman would do, the vessel hauled out for the seaward side of the big island and disappeared.

Clearly Vicq had no desire to imperil his own ship, but he was confirming, too, that Kydd had stumbled on local knowledge of a channel between, and was hastening round to trap him at the other end.

Or was he? Kydd's first instinct was to throw out an anchor and, after a time, double back the way they had come to freedom, leaving a frustrated Vicq to wait for them at the wrong end. But what if the wily corsair had considered this and was at that moment hove-to, ready for an unwary *Bien Heureuse* to track back into his arms? Or did he reason that Kydd would know this and instead press forward?

Distracted, Kydd noticed suddenly that the current was converging through scattered islets on a deeper but narrow passage close to the island – and it was carrying them along at a breathtaking pace. If he had had any ideas of returning it would be much harder the further he went in. And now the tide had receded, exposing vast rock-strewn sandbanks and beaches as they left Roscoff to its somnolence.

There was no easy answer, just an even chance that Kydd would make the right choice. 'Put us in the lee o' that bluff ahead,' he decided. 'We'll stream a kedge b' th' stern.' The craggy cliff-face protruding out from the island with crumbling ruins atop would serve as a temporary refuge, and the ship's bows would be in the right direction if Vicq came after them so that they had to cut and run.

The small anchor splashed down and held. Roscoff was in plain view only a mile back but, dried out, was no threat and the lowering island was, as far as he could see, uninhabited. They were safe, but for how long?

'Get th' boat in th' water – now, y' lubbers.' Vicq was on the other side of the island. He would go and see for himself. Kydd swung over the side into the boat and took the oars. 'Get aboard – jus' you,' he told the seaman holding the painter.

'N-no, not me!' the man muttered, shrinking back.

'Be damned t' ye!' Kydd exploded. 'I need someone t' hold th' boat, y' villain!'

Not a man moved.

'Anyone!' he bellowed.

'Stan' aside, y' dogs!' shrilled a sailor from the group of men forward, pushing through with a swagger. 'I'm wi' ye, Cap'n.' The boarding ended in an undignified tangle of arms and legs, a cutlass clattering to the bottom boards.

'Pookie!' Kydd hissed. 'Get out this instant, y' chuckle-headed looby.' But as the man with the painter saw his chance and let go, the boat was taken by the current and slid away rapidly.

'I'll – I'll tan y' hide, Pookie! I'll – I'll . . .' Kydd said angrily, tugging hard at the oars to bring the boat round. A glance showed that too much time would be lost in a return so he pulled it round and headed in.

Beyond two long islets there was a wide beach and he stroked furiously for it. The boat grounded in the sand with a hiss and he scrambled out. 'Seize a hold on th' painter,' he panted, 'an' if ye lets it float off, I'll – I'll slit y' gizzard.'

'Aye aye, Cap'n.'

Kydd pounded off along the beach until he found a way up to the scrubby top. He stopped and looked back. The figure at the boat was clutching the rope with both hands. He shook his fist; the child waved back jauntily.

A flock of goats scattered at his appearance, and a young

herdsman stared at Kydd open-mouthed as he raced past over the patchy ground to the opposite side.

'Bigod!' Kydd gasped, as he dropped down to look. Tucked in within a headland Vicq was just coming to a light anchor, his sails brailed and ready to loose.

Kydd leaped to his feet and ran back the way he had come, the goatherd still mesmerised by his antics. His eyes sought out the boat – and his heart nearly stopped. It was still there but the little figure was surrounded by others. Faint shouts eddied up from the beach.

He ran down the sand, yelling hoarsely; at least they were not in uniform. While their cries were no French that Kydd could understand, their meaning was plain. The little soul they were shouting at held the boat firmly with one hand and was keeping them at bay with a ridiculously large pistol in the other.

Kydd thrust past, set the boat a-swim, turned it into the waves and scrambled in to take the oars. 'Get in, y' rascal,' he panted, 'an', f'r God's sake, be careful wi' the pistol.'

The child struggled over the gunwales and sat forward as Kydd pulled hard out to sea. 'Didn't matter nohow, it were empty. No one'll teach me how t' load it. Will you, Mr Kydd?'

'Now, look, Pookie,' Kydd panted, 'I thank ye f'r th' service but if'n ye—'

They came up with *Bien Heureuse* and were pulled alongside. While he clambered aboard Kydd called to Rowan, 'He's waiting for us, sure enough.' At the other's grave expression he laughed. 'So we'll disappoint. Cut th' cable an' run t' th' west.'

Ready facing the right way, sail was loosed and, wind and tide with them, *Bien Heureuse* began to shoot through the tortuous channel to the open Atlantic. Nearly overcome with relief Kydd blurted out, unthinking, 'An' see Turner here gets a double tot.'

The go-between with the conspirators in Paris arrived to meet d'Auvergne late that night. 'Le Vicomte Robert d'Aché, this is Mr Renzi, my most trusted confidant.' The man was slightly built, with shrewd, cynical features.

With a polite smile, d'Auvergne went on, '*Le vicomte* is anxious that the shipment of arms is brought forward. How does it proceed, Renzi?'

'The transport from England is delayed by foul winds,' Renzi said smoothly, sensing the real reason for the question was to reassure d'Aché. 'I'm sanguine that it shall be with us within the week, sir. Four hundred Tower muskets and one hundred thousand ball cartridge. We lack only the destination.' Setting in motion the requisition had been an interminable grind but allegedly the arms were at sea; local arrangements must be made.

'La Planche Guillemette. Sign and countersign "Le Prince de Galles" – "Le Roi Bourbon".'

'Very well, sir. As soon as I have word . . .'

D'Auvergne smiled beatifically. 'Excellent. Renzi, do escort *le vicomte* down to the privy stairs. His boat awaits him there.'

Renzi attempted conversation on the way but tension radiated from a man well aware that he was about to re-enter Napoleonic France in circumstances that were the stuff of nightmares.

Chapter 13

Far from showing resentment at his handling of Tranter, who was keeping sullenly out of the way, the crew seemed to have settled. Kydd saw willing hands and respectful looks. He lost no time in setting them to boarding practice; it would be a humiliation, not to say a calamity, if they were to be repulsed through lack of discipline or skills.

He appointed Calloway master-at-arms in charge of practice, and for an hour or two the decks resounded to the clash and clatter of blades while the ship stretched ever westward along a desolate coast. Kydd's plan now was to put distance between him and Vicq, and at dawn be at the point where France ended its westward extent and turned sharply south into the Bay of Biscay. This should be a prime lurking place. All shipping from the south must turn the corner there – up from Spain and Portugal and even further, from the Mediterranean and Africa, all converging on the Channel at the same point.

There were disadvantages, of course: not far south was Brest and therefore the British fleet on station. Few French would be willing to run the blockade and, coast-wise, traffic would be wary. But the pickings were better here than most.

Shortly after three that afternoon they were given their chance: as they lay Portsall Rocks abeam a ship passed into view from the grey haze on the starboard bow. It firmed to an unremarkable square-rigged vessel that held its course to pass them.

'A Balt!' Rowan said, with certainty. Bluff-bowed and rigged as a snow it certainly qualified but when *Bien Heureuse* threw out her colours as a signal to speak she held steady and hoisted the Spanish flag.

'A Baltic Spaniard?' Kydd grunted. 'I think not.' The vessel was near twice their size but its ponderous bulk, rolling along, would indicate neither a privateer nor a man-o'-war.

Calloway stood down his men and came aft. 'Them's Spanish colours, Mr Kydd,' he said.

'Aye, we know.'

'Are ye going t' take him, sir?'

At first Kydd did not answer. This was so different from a war patrol in a King's ship when stopping a vessel with a row of guns at his back was so straightforward.

'Not so easy as that, lad,' Kydd said, then came to a decision. 'Bear down on him gently, Mr Rowan,' he ordered, and the privateer leaned to the wind on a course to intercept. 'Mr Calloway,' he said gravely, 'you're t' be a sea officer in time, an' I'll always remember it was a hard enough beat t' wind'd for me t' hoist aboard how we takes a prize.' Kydd glanced at the distant ship, still holding her track. 'Let me give ye a course t' steer as will see y' through. There's only one thing we're after, an' that's evidence.'

'Evidence?'

'Aye, m' friend. Even y' stoutest courage at the cannon's

mouth an' the bravest o' boardings won't stand unless we has th' proof.' He regarded Calloway seriously. 'The richest ship we c'n take will never make us a prize 'less th' Admiralty Court says so, an' this they'll never do without we show 'em evidence as will convince th' judge t' condemn him as good prize.'

'A – a judge, Mr Kydd? What's t' be th' crime?'

'An' we're talkin' international law now,' Kydd went on, 'as all nations agree on. Now here's the "crime". The one, if we bring evidence that he's an enemy o' the Crown. The other, if he's a neutral an' he's found a-tradin' with 'em.'

'That's all, Mr Kydd?'

'That's all – but th' devil's in th' detail, m' lad.'

'Er . . . ?'

'Ye'll be findin' out soon, never fear.'

The heavily built merchant ship seemed resigned to her fate, bracing aback her foreyards and slowing. *Bien Heureuse* went around her stern to take position off her weather side and Kydd cupped his hands. 'Bring to f'r boarding, if y' please!' he hailed, across the short stretch of water.

He turned to Rowan. 'I'll board, an' take Calloway as m' notary, with three hands t' rummage th' hold,' he said. 'Have a boardin' party standin' by t' send across if I hail.' It was the usual arrangement when not expecting trouble.

Their boat was in the water smartly and Kydd eyed the vessel as they approached. His experience in boarding was extensive but almost all in the Mediterranean and overseas. Here the principles would be the same but the players different.

He had noted that the ship was the *Asturias* as they rounded her stern; her sides were worn but solid and she had the familiar sparse workaday reliability of a merchantman. A rope-ladder clattered down her sides; he mounted nimbly and swung over on to her upper deck.

'I'm Kydd, an' I hold th' Letter o' Marque of a private cruiser.' He offered the paper to the grey-haired man he took to be the master. It was ignored.

'I'll ask ye t' submit to my examination, sir,' he said evenly. The ship smelled of the Baltic: an undertone of pine resin and a certain dankness, which seemed to go with vessels from cold climes.

The man snapped orders at one of the men behind, then met Kydd's eyes coldly. 'I vill, thenk you,' he replied tightly, then added, 'Pedersen, master.' Yards were laid and sails doused to take the strain off the masts while the ship settled to wait, lifting uneasily on the slight swell.

They took to the small saloon, and after Kydd and Calloway were seated, Pedersen left to get the ship's papers. This was the living space for the officers; here among the polished panels and brass lamps they would eat their meals, exchange the comfortable gossip of the voyage. To Kydd, their intrusion seemed an act of violation.

Pedersen returned and slapped down a thick pack of papers. Sitting opposite, he waited with barely concealed bitterness.

'Spanish flag?' Kydd enquired mildly. The master made much of riffling through the pile and finding the sea-brief, the attested proof of ownership. He passed it across; as far as Kydd could see, the title of the ship was vested in Spanish owners trading with northern Europe and, as King George was as yet still in amity with Spain, this, with a florid certificate of registry on Cartagena, entitled it to fly the Spanish flag.

'Your muster roll, Captain.' As a naval officer, Kydd had by this means unmasked deserters and renegades among crews before now. Swedes, several Finns and other Scandinavians – no Danish. Spanish, Italian names, some unpronounceable Balkans – the usual bag for merchant ships in wartime. Nothing there.

He looked up at the master. 'No Englishmen, then, astray fr'm their duty?'

Pedersen returned his look stolidly. '*Nej*.'

So it was a neutral, but this by no means disqualified it as a prize. 'Charter party?' Pedersen found it and passed it over. This was the contract for the freighting of the cargo and might reveal to Kydd whether the owners or its destination was illegal – which would make the cargo contraband and subject to seizure.

It was a voyage from Bilbao to Goteborg in Sweden: varying shippers, each with an accompanying bill of lading and duly appearing on the manifest, all apparently innocent of a French connection. And most papers in Spanish but some in Swedish. But such were the common practices and argot of the sea that there was little difficulty in making it out; Kydd had dealt with far more impenetrable Moorish documents in the Mediterranean.

Watched by a wide-eyed Calloway he painstakingly compared dates and places. Even the smallest discrepancy could be exploited to reveal that the papers were false and therefore just reason to act.

He called for the mates' book. The practice in every country was that the first mate of a ship was responsible for stowing the cargo and maintaining a notebook of where each consignment was placed, generally on the principle of first in last out. Against the bills of lading Kydd now checked off their stowage for suspicious reversals of location while Calloway jotted down their actual declaration for later.

Conscious all the time of Pedersen's baleful glare, Kydd knew that under international law he was as entitled as any warship to stop and search a neutral and took his time. But he spotted nothing.

'Port clearance?' This was vital: clearing a port implied the vessel had satisfied the formalities in areas such as Customs, which demanded full details of cargo carried and next destination. For the alert it could reveal whether there was an intention to call at another port before that declared as destination and perhaps other incriminating details.

It was, however, consistent. A hard-working trader on his way from the neutral but unfriendly Spain, voyaging carefully through the sea battlefield that was the Channel to the Baltic before the ice set in.

No prize? He wasn't going to let it go. There was something – was it Pedersen's truculence? If he had the confidence of a clear conscience he would enjoy seeing Kydd's discomfiture, sarcastically throw open the ship to him as other innocents had done before.

No – he would take it further. 'I'd like t' see y'r freight, Captain. Be s' good as t' open y'r hold, sir.'

Pederson frowned. Then, after a slight hesitation, he nodded. 'Ver' well.' He got up heavily and they returned on deck.

While the master threw his orders at the wary crew, Kydd called Calloway to him. 'We see if what we find squares wi' what's on the manifest,' he whispered. 'Check off y'r details – any consignment not on y'r list he's t' account for, as it's not come aboard fr'm some little Frenchy port on the way.'

'Or any as is missing,' murmured Calloway, 'which he could've landed . . .'

Kydd chuckled. 'Aye, ye're catchin' on, m' boy.'

The thunderous cracking of timbers and goods working in the lanthorn-lit gloom and the dangerous squeeze down amid their powerful reek to the foot-waling below did not deter the experienced quartermaster's mate Kydd had been and he clambered about without hesitation.

Muslin and linen, cased oranges, Spanish wine in barrels; each was pointed out by the mate and accounted for, Kydd's sharp-eyed survey omitting no part of the hold, no difficult corner.

Nothing.

It was galling. There was *something* – his instincts told him so. But what? There was no more time, two ships lying stopped together might attract unwelcome visitors.

Kydd was about to heave himself out of the hold when a glimmer of possibility made itself known. He paused. This would be one for Renzi – but he wasn't here . . .

Slithering down again he worked his way back to the tightly packed wine barrels. He held the lanthorn above one. 'Tinto de Toro, Zamora' was burnt crudely into its staves. He sniffed deeply, but all he could detect was the heavy odour of wine-soaked wood.

On its own it was not enough, but Kydd suspected that inside the barrels was not cheap Spanish wine but a rich French vintage. He squirmed over to the casks closest to the ship's side and found what he was looking for – a weeping in one where it had been bruised in a seaway or mishandled.

He reached out, then licked his finger: sure enough, the taste was indisputably the fine body of a Bordeaux – a Médoc or other, perhaps? He was not the sure judge of wine that Renzi was but, certainly, a cheap Spanish table wine this was not. And he could see how it had been done: they had left Bilbao with Spanish wine on the books as a welcome export, passed north along the French coast, crept into a lonely creek and refilled the barrels before setting sail once more.

He had them! Exultant thoughts came – the most overwhelming being the vast amount the prize would bring, with the sudden end of his immediate troubles, but cooler considerations took hold.

The only 'evidence' was his nose; was this sufficient justification for him to bring his boarding party swarming over the bulwarks and taking the grave action of carrying the vessel into port? The ship's papers were in perfect order and any trace of a quick turnaside would be difficult to prove.

He returned to the saloon. 'Ship's log!' he demanded. Kydd ignored Pedersen's thunderous look and flipped the dog-eared pages: he wanted to see the dates between sailing and rounding Ushant. It was scrawled in Swedish, but again the shared culture of the sea allowed him to piece together the sequence. Light airs from the south when leaving on the tenth, veering to a fresh seven-knot south-westerly within the day – but not to forty-five degrees north before another two days.

'There!' Kydd said, stabbing at the entry. 'Seven knots on a fair wind an' it takes ye three days to cover fifty leagues!' He snorted. 'If'n it does then I'm a Dutchman. Ye put in t' Bordeaux country an' took a fill o' Frenchy wines, as I c'n prove below.'

Pedersen's expression did not change. 'Ef wine are not Spanish, ze merchant iss cheat – not vorry for me,' he snapped. 'An' m' time?' he went on frostily, 'I lost by privateers inspect me there, *two* time!'

'An' may we see, then, y'r certificates?' Kydd shot back sarcastically. These had to be issued by the examining vessel on clearing any vessels boarded, that any subsequent boarding could be waived – and none had been shown to Kydd before he began his inspection.

'An' they'm be French?' Pedersen came back with equally heavy sarcasm. The French did not issue such certificates.

It was no good; the man was lying through his teeth and had been trading with the enemy, but he could not take the ship prize with this hanging over it. At the very least there would be lengthy litigation, which would cost his investors dearly. He had to let it go.

At his desk the day wore on for Renzi. First there was the matter of the arms shipment. It would arrive soon in a store-ship. To preserve secrecy it would be better to make rendezvous and trans-ship at sea to the lesser vessel that would be making the dangerous run into France. This would probably mean smoothing the offended sensibilities of the master and mate, who would be expecting the formalities of clearing cargo in the usual way, and the crew, who would resent the need to open the hold and rig special tackles in an open seaway.

Then there was the task of finding a vessel suitable for the final dash. D'Auvergne had suggested employing a privateer as their season was drawing to a close and one might be tempted to an extra voyage. They were well armed and not afraid of fighting if the need arose and, of course, had the carrying capacity, but Renzi had a naval officer's healthy dislike of the breed: it would mean haggling with near-pirates.

His attention turned to the details of the currency ship-ment: this would be coming from England in a cutter and there would be no alternative to the flummery associated with the movement of bullion. It would necessarily be taken aboard and signed for in the flagship, then released upon signature into the delivering vessel – it was the right of the captain of any naval vessel carrying bullion to claim a 'freight money' percentage and did this apply to the flagship captain? How were the receipt and delivery to be accounted for in a form acceptable to the Treasury? Who would make the clandestine conveyance? Another privateer?

And all the while he worked on these details, he knew desperate men were risking their lives. Wearily, Renzi picked up another sheet from the growing pile on his desk.

Days passed: the area was not proving as productive as Kydd had hoped. Possibly the autumn weather was thinning the flow or another privateer at work in the vicinity might be frightening off their rightful prey.

It gave Kydd time, though, to make another attempt on sea discipline, but he quickly discovered that, without well-tested naval command structures in place, it was really to no purpose – there was no interlocking chain of responsibility linking the seaman on a gun through gun captains, petty officers, warrant officers and so on to the commanding officer, such that at any point his will was communicated in ready understanding straight to that seaman.

But then he was finding that a merchant sailor was in some ways more independent and expected to perform his seaman-like functions on his own; the ship-owner would not outlay good money on layers of command that were only vital in the heat and stress of combat.

He had to make the best of it: his was a merchant ship prettied up with a pair of nine-pounders and gun-crews of untrained amateurs. Enough to overawe small fry but if any showed real resistance . . . He kept his thoughts to himself and focused on where to find that prey. All too aware that every day without a return was draining capital, Kydd kept the deck from first light until dark – and then their luck changed.

Anchored overnight in the lee of a convenient sweep of rocky headland, *Bien Heureuse* was greeted in the chill of the morning by the astonishing sight of another vessel no more than a few hundred yards away. In the darkness it had unknowingly chosen the same shelter as they and was still firmly at anchor when it caught sight of them – *and* the boat thrashing across that Kydd had instantly in the water, with Rowan at the tiller.

It was hardly a ship, more a low, floating barge that was easily recognisable as a store-ship for the Brest dockyard. As the boat drew close, the crew abandoned their efforts to weigh anchor and hastily took to their own boat to escape ashore.

With satisfaction Kydd watched Rowan go alongside and board, his men fanning out fore and aft on the deserted vessel. He had only to select a prize-master and crew and *Bien Heureuse* had one in the bag.

Rowan returned quickly. 'A prize, t' be sure. Dried fish 'n' potatoes f'r the garrison in Brest.' No complications with papers and international law, this was an enemy that was now rightfully theirs.

Kydd sent Tranter away as prize-master, glad to see the back of him; the new captain wasted no time in hoisting sail for the run back to Guernsey, ribald shouts of encouragement echoing across the water. Kydd's chest swelled. Their first prize!

Turning his gaze to sea, his eyes focused on a sail, a good three miles away but an unforgivable lapse in lookouts whose attention had been diverted. Square-rigged, she was hove-to and alone out to sea. Uneasy, Kydd sent for his glass as *Bien Heureuse* won her anchor.

A brig-rig, the workhorse of coastal shipping: she could be anything, but there was something . . . Then, as he watched, the ship got under way again, laying over as she took the wind . . . and he knew for a certainty that it was *Teazer*.

It affected him deeply, this sudden encounter with the ship he'd loved, his first command, where he had experienced the joys, insights and anxieties that went with the honour of being a captain. And the one where . . . Rosalynd had never come aboard *Teazer*, had not seen where he slept, never had the chance to . . .

He crushed the thoughts, but when he lifted his telescope he found his eyes stinging and his glass not quite steady. He forced himself to concentration as she altered her course — and headed inshore towards them.

Kydd had no wish to make contact and snapped at Rowan to hasten the unmooring, but *Teazer* arrived as they were getting under way. Her colours broke at the mizzen shrouds in unmistakable challenge and Kydd had to decide: to attempt a break to the east or await events?

'Luff up,' he ordered, resigned to the inevitable.

Teazer rounded to, backing her fore topsail. 'Bring to, I'm coming aboard of you, Captain!' It sounded like Prosser with a speaking trumpet, giving the same orders that he himself had used. As it came closer Kydd saw an officer in the sternsheets.

He stood back as the man came aboard. It *was* Prosser, stiff in his new lieutenant's uniform. He looked about him importantly, then stumbled in shock when he saw Kydd. 'I, er, I've been sent b' Commander Standish t' examine y' vessel, um, Mr Kydd,' he said uncomfortably.

'Here's m' Letter o' Marque. As ye can see, it's all in order.' Kydd snorted. The brailed-up sails banged and slatted overhead impatiently.

Prosser took it, then looked up awkwardly. 'He means y' full papers – where bound, freight an'—'

'I know what an examination means,' Kydd said cuttingly. 'I now need y' reason why m' vessel is bein' detained after I've proved m' business.'

'It's not like that, sir. Mr Standish is hard on them who don't carry out his orders t' satisfaction, an' he said—'

'Then tell *Commander* Standish as I'm a private ship-o'-war and may not be delayed in m' tasking without good reason. Good day, L'tenant.' He stalked to the ship's side; Prosser's boat was bobbing off the quarter, the men at their oars.

'Boat's crew!' Kydd roared, and gave the straight-armed up and down signal of the naval order to come alongside. A plump midshipman he did not recognise swivelled round in astonishment. 'This instant, damn y'r eyes,' Kydd added.

Hesitating, the young man gave the order and the boat came to hook on at the main channel, the midshipman looking reproachfully at Kydd and his officer by turns.

'Good day t' ye, Mr Prosser,' Kydd said menacingly. Crimson-faced, the man swung over the bulwarks and barked at his men to shove off.

Kydd saw the pinnace clear, then ordered sail to be loosed and *Bien Heureuse* resumed her course. He tried not to look astern, but when he did it was to see *Teazer* brace round and set out in chase.

The high crack of a bow gun fired to weather gave point to her hoist at the signal halliards: 'heave to immediately'. Pointedly it was in the naval code, which no strange merchant ship could be expected to know.

Once again *Bien Heureuse* lay submissively to leeward. *Teazer* eased close alongside, men at quarters next to their guns in plain sight. 'Let everything go by the run or I shall fire into you!' Standish hailed from the quarterdeck, his voice ringing with hauteur.

Kydd bit out orders for the yards to be lowered and tried to keep his anger in check. Was the man showing off in front of his ship's company or was it a deliberate attempt to belittle Kydd in front of *his* men?

The two ships moved together in the long swell, every detail of the lovely *Teazer* before him. The chess-tree was set at such a rake that by so doing it cunningly led the tack clear of both the sheet-anchor fluke and a nearby gun-port – he hadn't noticed this before.

Standing back he waited with arms folded. The boarding party swung over the bulwarks and quickly spread out, a petty officer and six with bared cutlasses, then Standish, glorious in brand-new commander's gold lace and sword.

He took his time, disdainfully inspecting the plain decks, a glimmer of a smile at the single pair of nine-pounders and a cursory glance aloft before he strolled over to Kydd. He did not remove his hat. 'You failed to stop on my lawful order. What is the meaning of this?'

'You, sir, have come aboard my vessel armed, t' th' contempt of the law an' custom o' the sea. What's th' meanin' o' *that*?'

Standish blinked. He had obviously forgotten that in the arcane practices of the sea it was quite in order to board with a party of men armed to the teeth – but the officer in charge should never bear a weapon. 'I may have omitted the observance in this instance, sir, but I do require an answer to my question.'

Several of the boarders dropped their eyes and shuffled in embarrassment.

'An answer? I hove to in th' first instance, an' the order was improper in the second,' Kydd said tightly.

'Improper?' Standish said languidly, moving a few steps away and testing a down-haul. 'I rather think not. As I command a King's ship you shall obey my every order whether you like it or not. That is the law.'

Kydd held his tongue. How long would this charade continue?

'Lieutenant Prosser was within his rights to demand your papers, as well you know,' he went on, and returned to stand arrogantly before Kydd, legs a-brace. 'He tells me you bear a Letter of Marque as a private ship. Any luck?' he asked casually.

'Th' sport is thin—' Kydd said thickly.

'Good!' cracked Standish, with a cruel smile. 'Then you won't miss a few men. Do you muster your crew on deck, I shall press half, I would think.'

'Ye'll press my men?' Kydd choked.

'Are you disputing my right to do so?' He was well within his rights. Prime privateersmen were a favourite target for the press in any form. 'If any of your men have protections then in course they will be left to you.' He went on implacably, 'Do turn your men up more quickly, Mr Kydd. I really don't have time to waste.'

With a terrible intensity, Kydd leaned forward, 'Have a care, Standish. Lay a hand on just one o' my men an' I'll see ye standing afore Admiral Saumarez to explain y'self!'

Standish recoiled. 'You forget yourself, Kydd. You no longer—'

'Oh?' Kydd replied. 'Then I'll be glad t' hear what ye'll be saying t' th' commander-in-chief as ye tell him ye've decided t' disobey his orders.'

'Orders?'

'Aye. His written order that no native-born Guernseyman – as is his own countryman – shall be subject t' th' press. An' everyone aboard is, as they'll swear.'

Standish blinked. 'Is this right? Sir James has never given me a written order to that effect.'

Kydd pulled himself erect. 'Then ye'll be tellin' y'r commander-in-chief as ye haven't had th' time t' hoist in his standin' orders?'

Somewhere Kydd had heard that a Guernseyman had ancient privileges that allowed him to serve the 'Duke of Normandy' rather than the English sovereign, giving him theoretical protection from the press gang. It was unlikely that Saumarez would take kindly to any who trampled the rights of his proud bailiwick – and who would be the one to argue?

'Very well. Mark my words, Mr Kydd. If this is your deceiving, the next time I see you and, er, your private ship-of-war, I will strip you down to the cook, do you hear?' He stalked to the ship's side and signalled to his boat. Impassively Kydd watched him leave.

When the boat was halfway a full-throated shout came from forward in *Teazer*. 'God save ye as a good 'un, Mr Kydd!'

Stirk's shout was taken up in a roar of others. Standish leaped to his feet in outrage, the boat swaying perilously. 'Seize that man in irons!' he yelled. 'And stop your cackle instantly – d' you hear me, you mumping rogues? – or I'll see the whole lot of you up before me!'

Kydd gave a wry smile. 'Loose sail, Mr Rowan. Let's be away!'

Chapter 14

The sport *was* thin. Days later, of three encounters only one had proved fruitful, a tiny but voluble Portuguese with a freight of slab cork that could only have one destination in this part of the world, and time was getting short. Kydd's hopes of wealth were disappearing fast.

Still, he had learned much of the privateering trade and could see that, given certain advantages in the future, there was every chance of succeeding in a handsome way. There would be changes on the next voyage, he would see to it.

Bien Heureuse returned to St Peter Port in the tail end of an autumn gale but the Great Road lay as a welcome triangle of calm away from the port shielding it from the battering of the south-westerly, and the little privateer finally lay at rest alongside the pier.

Kydd made his way smugly to Robidou's rickety top-floor office to receive an appreciation for a good start in the privateering business and to learn when he was to receive his share of the proceeds.

Robidou told him gruffly to wait while he dealt with his

clerk and Kydd contented himself with the fine view over the harbour, including his two prizes.

The clerk was then sent away and, with a cold look, he was bade to sit. It unsettled Kydd – he had expected a warmer welcome. Besides, he wanted to get away to tell his theatrical friends of his adventures.

'Ye've disappointed me, sir,' Robidou began heavily. Kydd's heart sank. 'M' investors did expect much more'n ye found for 'em,' he went on remorselessly. 'I told 'em as ye was th' proven article as an active an' enterprisin' privateersman.'

Kydd's hackles rose. 'Only a couple o' weeks at sea? An' two prizes on m' first voyage.'

'Two prizes?' Robidou said acidly. 'Th' first a store-ship wi' dried fish an' potatoes – how d' ye expect me t' place such a cargo on the market? Potatoes, when we has our own Jerseys that knocks such into a cocked hat? An' dried fish, as is only fit f'r soldiers?'

'The ship?' Kydd tried.

'A store-ship? Worthless! None wants a slab-sided scow as is built t' supply an army. No, sir, this is no prize worth the name.'

Face burning, Kydd said tightly, 'Th' Portuguee – a freight o' cork as can only be bound f'r the French wine ports?'

Robidou sighed. 'He's worse. I'll agree, it c'n only be f'r the French, but the master is savvy, an' knows it's no use t' us. We don't make wine. So he protests th' capture. In course, we must go to th' litigation in an Admiralty court but this takes a mort o' time – and fees. If'n we win, it's only cork we has, not worth a Brummagem ha'penny a bushel, the ship contemptible an' we can't cover the fees. We have t' let him go.'

Kydd bit his lip. 'Can we not—'

'We lets him go, an' must pay him demurrage f'r the delay t' his voyage, a sum f'r his extra vittlin', harbour dues t' St Peter Port f'r his moorin' – an' if we're not lucky he'll lodge an affidavit with his consul claimin' consequential damages! No, sir, ye've not had a good voyage.'

Shaken, Kydd realised that, without any return from prizes, the voyage was a failure. And the investors had not merely lost their outlay but were faced with liability for heavy unforeseen payments to the Portuguese. 'Er, I'm sure th' next voyage'll be capital. Um, I've learned much as will—'

'Mr Kydd. When th' investors hear o' your – *success*, I wouldn't hold m'self ready f'r a next voyage. Good day t' ye, sir.'

Three days later the venture meeting was brief, and Robidou had news for Kydd when he returned the following morning. 'Sir, I have t' tell ye, th' investors did not see their way clear t' renewing an interest in a privateer voyage by any means.'

It was expected, but it stung all the same.

'If ye'll attend on me just f'r a few hours, we'll finalise th' books an' then you'll be free t' go.'

With the paperwork complete, Kydd left, unemployed once more.

'Why, Tom, m' dear!' Rosie discarded her sewing excitedly and ran to meet Kydd, throwing her arms round him with a kiss. 'You're back on land. Do tell me y'r adventures – did you seize any treasure ships a-tall?'

Her eyes were wide in expectancy but she frowned when she saw Kydd's long face. 'Is – is something wrong?'

'No treasure, Rosie, jus' two prizes as are t' be despised, I'm told.' He sprawled morosely in an armchair. 'An' they don't see fit t' give me another voyage.'

'Oh. So . . . ?'

Kydd looked at her with affection. 'So it means, dear Rosie, there's nothing more I c'n do.' That was the nub of it, really; he could return to being a stage-hand and eke out a few more weeks of existence but to what end? 'I'm t' go back t' England now.' He sighed. ''Twas a good plan, but I'm not y'r natural-born corsair I'd have t' say now.' A wave of depression came, but at least he could console himself that he had given it his best try.

'Don't leave now,' Rosie said, stricken. 'You *will* find the wicked dog as did y' wrong, I *know* it!'

Kydd smiled. 'I'm beholden t' ye all for y' kindness but I'll not be a burden any more. I have t' leave.'

'Please don't, Tom!' she pleaded. 'Give it just a few more weeks, an' then—'

'No. End o' th' week, Rosie.'

With dull eyes Renzi took in a report by one Broyeur who was responsible for their security at the Jersey terminus, detailing actions and observations as they pertained to counter-espionage. Endless lines of trailing this or that suspect, suggestive phrases in purloined letters, rumours – and then one word caught his eye: 'Stofflet'. It was followed by a short entry: 'Per order, Friday last. Drowned – no marks.'

The epitaph of a kindly man. Who had . . . Renzi's eyes stung. Rushing in came the memory of the little bald baker taking pity on a hungry stranger and finding a tasty loaf, which Renzi had gratefully devoured. He would no longer serve his ovens or see his little ones. And now where was pity? Where was the humanity? With a catch in his throat he felt control slipping. Why could not logic preserve him from the stern consequences of its own imperatives?

He staggered to his feet, sending the table and its papers crashing to one side. Urgently seeking open air he was soon out on the battlements, breathing raggedly. His fists clenched as he sought the sombre night horizon. The salty air buffeted his face bringing with it a sensory shock. The spasm passed, but left him troubled and destabilised. Since his youth he had found reason and logic a sure shield against the world, but now it had turned on him. What was left to him without the comfort of its certainties?

Sleep came finally to claim him but in the early hours he was dragged to consciousness by a disturbance – shouts, d'Auvergne's urgent retort, men in the passageway. He flung on a coat and hurried there. It was d'Aché, trembling with fatigue, sprawled in a chair and retching, his side blood-soaked to the waist. 'Go, fetch a doctor!' d'Auvergne threw at the men standing about uncertainly. 'The rest, get out!'

D'Aché had risked everything in bringing his message to Mont Orgueil, such was its urgency. 'D'Auvergne,' he said weakly, 'listen to me! We – we have a crisis!' He slumped in pain, then rallied, his eyes feverish. 'Paris – they won't rise up unless they have an unconditional assurance that the British will play their part.' He coughed, and the consequent pain doubled him over until it was spent. 'You must understand, Bonaparte suspects something. The country is alive with soldiers. It is very dangerous. The Chouans sense treachery, that as soon as . . .'

Once they raised the banner, made their throw, they were marked men, and if the plot failed Napoleon's revenge would be terrible. All the more reason to fear that England, the old enemy, might play them false.

'The last moves will be the most critical,' d'Aché resumed, shaking with pain and emotion. 'If anything goes wrong it will be most tragic.'

D'Auvergne nodded. The frenzied dash with their prisoner through the dark countryside, forces closing in on all sides, the final frantic arrival at the coast – and the Royal Navy not there to receive them into safety? He could see it must be their worst imagining. 'They wish a binding commitment of some sort?' he asked.

'A *written* statement of late date under signature of a high officer of state.' Nothing less, apparently, than a document proving the complicity of England in the plot.

'Very well, you shall have it,' d'Auvergne said calmly. He paused. 'And I shall deliver it.'

'No!' d'Aché said hoarsely. 'You are known, you'll have no chance.' D'Auvergne had been imprisoned on trumped-up charges once in Paris during the brief peace and only been released reluctantly after considerable diplomatic pressure from Westminster.

Yet if things stalled now, inertia would set in, causing the whole to crumble without hope of recovery. As if in a dream Renzi heard himself say, 'I shall take it to them.' It was logical. The situation was desperate. He knew of the plot, he could speak knowledgeably of the dispositions and – and he would be dispensable in the eyes of the Government.

'You!' gasped d'Aché. 'They don't know you. They'll think you a spy.' The irony was not wasted on Renzi, who gave a half-smile.

D'Auvergne frowned. 'My dear Renzi, do reflect on your situation. You would have the most compromising document in Christendom on your person that most certainly would incriminate your government. If threatened, your only honourable course would be to – to . . .'

'So who, then, will be your emissary?' Renzi challenged.

There was no reply. 'I shall require a form of password, an expression of authentication as it were, and . . .'

Early on the Thursday morning a knock at the door caught them by surprise. As the only one fully dressed at that hour, Kydd answered. A messenger held out a letter. 'Mr Kydd's residence?' he asked. 'Favour o' Mr Vauvert.'

Rosie squealed in anticipation and rushed over, her attire forgotten. Kydd broke the seal: it was a curt note from Vauvert indicating that if he wished to hear something to his advantage he should be at the Three Crowns tavern at four promptly.

Rosie clapped and snatched the message from Kydd. 'To your *advantage*, Tom!' she cried. 'I knew something would come!'

Kydd did not reply. It was obvious: he was going to be asked to run contraband as a smuggler. No doubt this Vauvert was extracting a fee from a business associate for introducing him. Well, damn it, he would disappoint them both.

'What will you wear, love?' Rosie enthused. 'It could be a swell cove taking you t' see his friends!'

He paused. There was just the tiniest chance that it was something else – but the cold tone of the note fitted that of a businessman holding him at arm's length while he was handed along to another. 'Nothin' special, Rosie. If'n they can't take me as I come, then . . .'

The Three Crowns was a spacious and well-appointed inn, liberally endowed with snug rooms and discreet alcoves with high-backed chairs for those inclined to serious conversation. Kydd entered diffidently, fingering the single florin in his pocket, which was all he could bring himself to accept from Mojo. He hoped that his mysterious visitor would not expect more than a nip of ale.

A few faces turned curiously but he stared ahead defensively and was left alone. Soon after four the figure of a gentleman in an old-fashioned wig appeared at the door, looking in hesitantly. He seemed distantly familiar, and Kydd rose.

The man hurried over. 'I thank you for seeing me, Mr Kydd,' he said, in an oddly soft voice.

For a moment he was caught off-balance. Then it came to him. This was Zephaniah Job, whom he had once arrested in Polperro as a smuggler and then been forced to release by higher authority. 'I'm to tell you how very sorry I am to have heard about your Rosalynd. Such a sweet child, and to be lost to the world so suddenly.'

Kydd gulped, a memory catching him unawares with its intensity. 'Yes, sir, I was – much affected.' He turned away, so that Job would not catch his expression, and willed himself back to the present.

He realised he shouldn't be surprised to see Job there for he was a sagacious businessman with interests in all things profitable – he even printed his own banknotes. Kydd recalled that Guernsey was the main place of supply for Job's many smuggling enterprises. Now he was going to be offered a position operating against his own colleagues by the man he had previously taken in charge for doing just that.

Job gave a polite smile. 'I heard of your privateering voyage just concluded, Mr Kydd. My sympathy on meeting with such poor fortune.'

'Thank ye,' Kydd said. He was damned if Job was going to get a beer out of his precious florin now.

'You seem in need of some cheer, if I might make bold

– will you allow me to press you to join me in a jorum of their finest?'

'Er, maybe I will,' Kydd said warily.

'Very well,' Job said, after the jug was set in train. 'Let me go directly to the head of the matter. I heard about your recent voyage from a common acquaintance and, besides, something of your history while here and I'm sanguine you'll hear me out if I make you a proposition.'

'Go on.' He was in no hurry – he might as well listen to what the man had to say.

'I'm a man of business, not a mariner, but I confess I was somewhat surprised when I learned that having taken on the calling of privateer you were unable to make a success of it.'

Kydd gave an ill-natured grunt but let him continue.

'Therefore, knowing of your undoubted qualities I made query as to the details. And it seems my surmise was correct. For reasons best known to the investors you were constrained to confine your attentions to the small fry, coastal traders and the like.

'I will speak frankly. To me this is not the best exploitation of your talents – speaking as a businessman, of course. Now, I was too late to take shares in your last venture but I have a mind to consider doing so in the future, should the arrangements be more to my way of thinking.'

'Mr Job, that's all very well but I have t' say I've been told there's t' be no second voyage for me.'

Job paused to refill Kydd's glass. 'This is then my proposition to you. Should you feel a blue-water cruise in the Western Ocean to meet the trade from the West Indies and south would better answer, I will invest in you.'

Despite himself Kydd's hopes rose: there was no reason to believe Job would waste his time in impossibilities. 'This

sounds interestin', Mr Job. But I c'n see a mort o' problems.'
There was so much to overcome: a deep-sea venture was an altogether larger-scale enterprise, much more costly – and many times the risk.

'I'm no stranger to privateering, you may believe,' Job said smoothly. 'I find the chief objective is to secure a captain of daring and acumen, the second to ensure he has the ship and men he needs to perform his task. This is essential and must always stand above considerations of expense. Spoiling the ship for a ha'p'orth of tar is false economy, so by not sparing the quality of ship and man, the enterprise does maximise its chances.'

'An' increases th' capital risk,' Kydd said.

'It does, but those considerations you should leave to the prudent investor who, you can be sure, does take full measure of his exposure.' He went on, 'For myself, I will increase my own determination in the venture by one simple means. I intend to take the majority shareholding.'

'Sir, I c'n see how this might be of advantage t' me . . .'

'Might I correct you in the particulars, sir? I do this not for you but in the cause of profit and gain to accrue to myself. I would not do it unless I saw due opportunity, and having witnessed at the first hand your daring and clear thinking when you apprehended the pirate villain Bloody Jacques, then it's my estimation that the investment is as sound as any now open to me.'

'Go on.'

'Besides which,' Job continued, 'I will naturally take reasonable measures to safeguard my position, the first of which is to state that I will in no wise set to hazard my capital without I have a formal proposal from yourself.

'This shall include details of your intended cruising

grounds, particulars of the vessel you desire to employ, the crew consequential on its size, the length of voyage – all the usual considerations in matters of this kind, which I'm sure you understand – and each most carefully costed.'

Kydd held his elation in check. 'Then you shall be the *armateur*?'

'By no means, sir. There are many such available in Guernsey. I shall be content to remain chief investor, should your proposal prove acceptable.'

Playfully, Kydd added, 'An' if I find such will be sufficiently advantageous as will allow me t' delay my return to England.'

Blinking, Job leaned forward. 'Return to . . . ? Sir, that would be to discard a particularly fine business opportunity. Surely you wouldn't—'

Kydd saw his moment. 'I've had m' taste of privateerin' an' *if* I was t' consider another cruise there's t' be changes.'

'Oh?'

'Y' mentioned there'll be no spoilin' th' ship f'r a ha'p'orth o' tar. Is this t' mean I can select a ship of size as can go up against a big Indiaman man t' man?'

'Ah, yes. This is the very point that encourages me in the whole business. As you will allow, a five-hundred- or thousand-ton vessel is an extremely expensive proposition to set a-swim. With you as captain, however, a more modest-sized craft might well be manoeuvred with daring and resource to achieve what in lesser hands would certainly require a larger.'

'You'll grant me, Mr Job, that a grand Martinico-man will never strike t' a squiddy cutter an' must always resist. I should need m' choice o' armaments.'

'Of course.'

'An' men enough t' swarm aboard when th' time comes.'

'Undoubtedly.'

'Articles I'll draw up m'self of a character as will grant me full powers o' discipline.'

'I'm sure that will be possible.'

'I say where we cruise.'

'As long as it is a blue-water venture I'm certain that will be acceptable. The usual clause runs something like, "shall cruise in waters to the west to take such ships as you shall fall in with" or similar.'

'Well . . . that could be agreeable,' Kydd mused, rubbing his chin.

'If you should decide to take this up,' Job said earnestly, 'then news of my firm and sizeable commitment will of a surety excite interest and speculation that will not leave us shy of subscribers to follow in the enterprise.'

'Aye. I see that.'

'West of the Azores is a famous place for deep-water privateering, Mr Kydd. Those of an age will recall Talbot of the *Prince Frederick* in those waters taking two Spanish in fine style. From Bristol to London the bullion took forty-five armed wagons to send it safely to the Tower of London.'

'Well . . .'

'Can I expect your proposal?'

Kydd beamed. 'Aye, ye can, Mr Job.'

He needed a brisk walk along the foreshore to regain his equilibrium while he contemplated the sudden change in his prospects. He had another chance – could he make a success of it? There was rich trade coming in from the Atlantic, but the French were canny and made much use of neutral bottoms. Their allies were largely driven from the seas as well, while the other ships plying the trade routes would be sure to have a vexatious quantity of protective documents. The fabulous Spanish treasure ships were off-limits with the peace still holding, and while there were multitudes of ships afloat, there were millions of square miles of open sea.

But an ocean cruise was a different game altogether from his earlier foray into privateering: a single fat Caribbean trader in sugar could repay their outlay many times over. Two could make him rich. Or none could— He cut short his doubts: this was an opportunity he would take with both hands, all or nothing. However, the proposal needed expertise he did not have, finely judged costing arguments that he would later have to live with.

'Mr Kydd!' Robidou grunted in astonishment. 'What can I do for ye? If it's about y'r settlement then I'll tell you—'

'No, Mr Robidou. It's about what *I* can do f'r *you*.' Kydd knew his man and got to the point. Straight talking, no tacking and veering, simply that if he was given assistance with a proposal he would see to it that Robidou was appointed *armateur* for the venture.

The name of Zephaniah Job was sufficient to get him a fair hearing and Kydd found himself back in the Three Crowns tavern. He ransacked Robidou's experience: the best area for serious cruising was indeed beyond the Azores – close enough to be at a reasonable sailing distance and far enough that receiving convoys and their escorts would not have formed up. There was stirring talk of cargoes: sugar, coffee, cotton inbound – and outbound exotics like mercury destined for the mines, luxury items for the colonies, bullion. And their chances. French, Batavian, Ligurian, all for the taking, but ready for a fight and disinclined to heave to at the order of one half their size.

The discussion turned to their ship. Kydd's instinct was for the manoeuvrability of square rig but with the high pointing of fore and aft. Both men agreed on the type of vessel that best fitted the description: a topsail schooner. Robidou knew of one, just laid up for the winter.

As soon as Kydd clapped eyes on the *Witch of Sarnia* he knew he had to have her. She had been designed and built on speculation as a privateer with a fine-lined hull that took no account of any need for cavernous cargo holds. Low and rakish, there was no mistaking her purpose, but an innocent approach would not be practical with wary deep-water merchantmen, and sailing qualities alone would decide the issue.

She was recently out of the water, propped at the top of the slip and Kydd walked slowly round her, taking in the tight seams, true curves and obviously new construction. This was a sound, well-built and altogether *convincing* craft as a privateer. His pulse quickened.

A rope-ladder hung over her neat stern and Kydd hauled himself aboard. With most of her gear stored and decks clear of ropes it was possible to take in her sweet lines, leading forward to a bowsprit fully half as long again as the main hull.

As she was bigger than *Bien Heureuse* his cabin was roomier – narrow, but longer. There were two cabins a side for officers and a pleasant saloon, which would later double as an examining place. Forward, a modest hold was followed by a magazine and store cabins, a galley well and finely contrived crew accommodation.

It was impressive, as unlike *Bien Heureuse* as it was possible to be, including limewood panelling below and herringbone decking above. Her hull was a wicked black, not from tarred sides but fine enamelling, and with a compelling urgency in her coppered underwater lines, the *Witch* gave an overwhelming impression of a thoroughbred predator.

Robidou looked pleased at Kydd's evident approval, but cautioned, 'This'n is goin' t' be a pretty penny, Mr Kydd. I knows Janvrin and he's not a-goin' t' let this sweet thing go for a song.'

The costing began. Although prepared for a bigger outlay than there had been with *Bien Heureuse* Kydd was shocked as the sum mounted and Robidou's eyebrows rose.

And because it was virtually certain that they would have to fight for their prey, there was the expensive question of armament. A warship had to be equipped to engage in any number of modes: ship-to-ship broadsides, a cutting out, repelling an aggressive boarding, a shore landing – but for Kydd there would be only one: the subduing of a larger ship followed by an unstoppable boarding. And, unlike in a man-o'-war, defensive fire was not required: if the tide turned against them, the slim-lined schooner's response would be to turn and flee, unworried by notions of honour that would have them stay to fight it out.

A gun-deck and rows of cannon were not in contemplation. Instead it would be close-quarter weapons. Swivel guns, a carronade or two capable of blasting a sheet of musketballs across the deck and, of course, cutlasses and a pistol for every boarder. Half-pikes and tomahawks were to be carried by some to intimidate, and among the cool-headed he would distribute grenadoes – two pounds of lethal iron ball packed with gunpowder and a lighted fusee to hurl on the opposing deck. And he could see how the topsail cro'-jack could be made to do service with stink-pots, devices filled with evil-smelling combustibles . . . In all this the object was to spread fire and fear but without causing damage to a future prize.

Fitting out, manning, storing – without Robidou's head for figures it would have been impossible. More work on the inevitable fees, allowances and imposts, and suddenly it was finished. The proposal was made ready, checked and sent in.

An answer came back with startling promptness: a venture association was being convened immediately on the basis of their proposal and Mr Robidou would be invited to act as *armateur*. It was extraordinary and wonderful – Kydd was a captain once more.

His exhilaration, however, was tempered by the fact that this was going to be all or nothing: if he failed to deliver a prize he was most certainly finished everywhere.

The *Witch of Sarnia* was towed to Havelet Bay for fitting out and in the whirlwind of activity Kydd slept aboard and bore a hand himself on turning a deadeye here, stropping a block there. Then it became time to consider his ship's company. Robidou had good advice. 'Should ye want t' have a tight crew as will keep loyalty, I'd find a right hard-horse mate an' trust him t' find his own men. They'll owe *him*, an' he'll owe *you*, so they'll fight th' barky like good 'uns.'

'Ye have an idea o' who . . . ?'

As it happened, Robidou did: the lieutenant on his own last cruise as a privateer. One Henry Cheslyn.

They met at the boat slip; Robidou had been at some pains to prepare Kydd but the sight of the man took him aback. Cheslyn was powerfully built, with a massive leonine head and full beard, and had a deep-sea roll as he walked. Near twenty years Kydd's senior, he had closed, fierce features and flinty eyes in a sea-ruddy face.

'Mr Cheslyn,' Kydd acknowledged. What could he say to one so much older and so much more experienced whom he expected to take his orders unquestioned?

They stood regarding one another until Cheslyn spoke. 'Cap'n Robidou says as ye're no strut-noddy,' he said truculently, in a deep-chested voice. 'An' he reckons ye're sharp. But yez a King's man – ever bin in a merchant hooker blue-water, like?'

'Aye,' said Kydd evenly. 'An' a gallows sight further'n you, I'd wager.'

Robidou cut in apprehensively: 'Mr Kydd took a convict ship t' Botany Bay in the peace, Henry.'

Cheslyn ignored him. 'Says ye've odd notions o' discipline – you ain't a-thinkin' o' goin' Navy?' he grunted sourly.

'Mr Cheslyn. I'm t' be captain o' the *Witch*. She's in the trade o' reprisal. I'm in the business o' finding m'self a sack o' guineas, an' anything or anyone goes athwart m' bows in that is goin' t' clew up fish-meat.

'So there's no misunderstandin', I'm writin' down m' expectations in th' articles f'r all t' sign, an' the one who's t' be m' first l'tenant will be in no doubt where I stand.'

'Mr Kydd knows men,' Robidou interjected firmly, 'as he started a common foremast jack, ye'll know.'

'Aye, well, I'll think on it,' Cheslyn said, with a last piercing look at Kydd before he stumped away.

'A hard man.' Robidou sighed. 'Ye'll need t' steer small with him – but I'll tell ye now, he's bright in his nauticals an' a right mauler in a fight. If y' makes him mate, ye'll have no trouble with y' crew.'

Within three days Cheslyn had assembled a core of hard-ened, wolfish seamen, all of whom, it seemed, were capable privateersmen of his long acquaintance. They packed Kydd's rendezvous, taking his measure silently.

This was not a time for fancy speeches. Kydd spoke to them of Caribbean wealth and South American treasure, of a mighty ocean but a well-found ship, shipmates and courage, spirit and discipline. Any who would go a-roving with him might return with a fistful of cobbs but must sign Kydd's articles and take his orders without a word. He finished. The room broke into a hubbub of excited talk. 'S' who'll be first t' sign f'r an ocean cruise in th' saucy *Witch*?' he roared, above the noise.

They crushed forward, Cheslyn elbowing his way to the front. He raised his eyes once to Kydd, then bent to the book and scrawled awkwardly.

'Mate an' first l'tenant!' Kydd called loudly. 'An' be s' good as t' introduce me to y'r men, Mr Cheslyn.'

For his officers he had brought the one-eyed Le Cocq as his second, a short man but reputed fearless. Gostling, an experienced prize-master, was third. Kydd was surprised when Rosco, the boatswain of *Bien Heureuse*, fronted at the table.

'Y' has y'r chance now, Mr Kydd,' he rumbled, and scratched his name. 'An' I wants a piece of it,' he said forcefully.

With Rosco as boatswain, and a cold-eyed mariner, Perchard, the gunner, he was well on the way to complement – and then Luke Calloway entered. Pale but resolute he stood before Kydd. 'I'd wish t' be wi' ye, sir.' How the young man had heard of the venture he had no idea – rumours must be flying in St Peter Port about this late-season cruise into the Atlantic.

'Ah, there's a berth if ye want it, Mr Calloway,' Kydd said, 'but I have t' tell ye, this is not y'r regular-goin' cruise. We'll be up against th' big ones as'll object t' being taken by a pawky schooner, an' will want t' give us a right pepperin'.'

This was not the real reason: the men he would have aboard were a callous, pugnacious crew and young Calloway would be hard put to handle them.

'Sir, I – I'd want t' ship out, if y' please.'

'Er, Luke, if it's pewter ye're lackin', then—'

'Able seaman afore th' mast would suit main well, Mr Kydd.'

Kydd nodded and threw open the book for signing. Ironically Calloway would probably succeed better at that level without the need to assert himself over the hard characters in the crew, and his seaman's skills were second to none.

It was time for the final act. 'Send in th' boys,' he called to the door. Instantly the room was filled with an urgent press of youngsters eager to ship out in the *Witch of Sarnia*, the talk of the town.

One fought to the fore and stood proudly and expectantly before him. Kydd's heart fell at the sight of Pookie Turner. 'No, it won't do,' he said sadly. 'It's an ocean voyage an' I can't—'

The young face set. 'Cap'n, y' knows I—'

'I can't, an' ye knows why.' Kydd looked pointedly at the eager boy behind.

At the end of the day Kydd sat back, satisfied. These were a dissimilar breed of men to the coastal privateers of his previous experience: tough, competent and professional, deep-sea sailors of one mind – the ruthless pursuit of prey and profit. This alone would make it an altogether different experience. All he had to do was put them in the way of what they desired and they would follow him.

'You're a black-hearted villain!' Rosie taunted him, hearing of Pookie's attempt to sign on. 'Can't you understand? She wants adventure and excitement before the mast, Captain, just like you do. Shame on you!'

'Rosie, I'm never before th' mast in *Witch*, and I'll have y' know this is an ocean voyage wi' a crew o' right cut-throats as any I've seen. It's not right an' proper f'r a young—'

'Y' have ship's boys to do men's work, so if Pookie wants to be a boy why can't she be? Make her y' cabin-boy to keep her under eye if you have to, but I don't think she'll need any o' your protectin'.' Kydd thought wryly of her prowess over the other boys with her fists, while Rosie went on warmly, 'Besides, if *you* don't take her, she'll be back on the streets up to her old tricks. And don't forget her share of the booty. Won't this help her poor mama?'

'It's too late betimes, Rosie. I've closed books an' we sail on th' tide tomorrow forenoon. She's a game 'un, she'll find something else,' he added lamely.

It was a day of autumn overcast, with a brisk wind that fluttered dresses and tugged at hats as *Witch of Sarnia* made ready for sea. A crowd had come to see the smart privateer that was reputedly making a daring foray into the Atlantic Ocean on which much Guernsey money was riding.

They lined the quay, gentlemen and ladies, quantities of curious wharf-loafers and the odd redcoat soldier with his woman. Robidou appeared and pushed through the crowd, waving what seemed to be a book. 'Just been published,' he shouted against the excitement, passing it to Kydd. 'Someone gave it me f'r interest – but I think ye should have it.'

Kydd yelled back his thanks, but there would be precious little time for books. 'Stand by for'ard!' he bawled. As they began to single up the lines his eye was caught by a lone figure standing apart from the others.

With a grin he recognised Pookie who, no doubt, had come down hoping for a last-minute change of heart – so, with an exaggerated beckoning, the *Witch of Sarnia*'s crew was complete. The delighted youngster threw a small bundle aboard, grabbed a rope, twirled round and landed lightly on the deck with a huge smile.

Departure was easy enough in the southerly; sail mounted quickly as lines were let go and hauled in, and water opened up between ship and quay. With Cheslyn by Kydd's side in well-worn sea gear, hard men efficiently handing along tackle falls, and overhead the crack and slap of a topsail spreading along its boom, the schooner made for the twin piers at the entrance.

A knot of spectators on the very end waved gaily, and as they passed close on their way to the open sea the group broke into whooping and shouts. A firework whizzed skywards and another followed. Kydd was touched: his theatrical friends were not allowing him to seek his fortune on the vasty deep without due ceremony. He waved back energetically, which would have produced expressions of horror on *Teazer*'s quarterdeck. 'Kind in 'em to see us on our way,' he murmured to Cheslyn, who had looked at him askance but Kydd, feeling the *Witch* heel as she took the wind at the harbour entrance eagerly seeking the freedom of the open sea, was letting nothing spoil his happiness of the moment.

They passed between the vessels anchored in the Great Road, each with decks lined with interested sailors watching the privateer head out – Kydd knew that the *Witch*'s fine lines would be attracting admiration while her sleek and deadly black form would leave no doubt as to her mission.

Through the Little Russel and leaving the shelter of Herm they met long seas – combers urged up on the lengthy swell by a brisk westerly from the deep Atlantic. Kydd and Robidou had taken the *Witch* out earlier with a skeleton crew to try her mettle, and with one or two changes to the set of her sails he was satisfied and confident in her sea-keeping.

He had discovered that *Witch of Sarnia* had completed only one voyage previously, and that a poor one under an over-cautious captain, but *he* would take full advantage of her qualities – he would have to if she was to have any chance of closing quickly with a prey. His crew were hard-bitten enough, but would they follow into the teeth of a larger crew intent on repelling boarders as he knew a man-o'-war's men would? Could he—

'*Saaail!*' The cry came at the sudden emergence of a size-able ship from beyond the point – and directly athwart their path. It took no more than a heartbeat to realise that the noble lines belonged to HMS *Teazer*. Kydd guessed that Standish had been waiting for him: hearing of Kydd's Atlantic mission he had positioned himself ready for where he must come and was up to some sort of mischief.

'Ye'll 'ware she's a King's ship,' Cheslyn muttered pointedly.

'Aye,' said Kydd, evenly, watching as *Teazer* laid her course to intercept them. He was in no mood for Standish's posturing and gave orders that had *Witch* wheeling about and heading away downwind, mounting the backs of the combers before falling into the trough following in a series of uncomfort-able sliding and jerks.

'What d' ye do that for?' Cheslyn spluttered. 'He's a brig, an' we can point higher, b' gob!' It was true – the schooner had had every chance of slipping past by clawing closer to the wind but Kydd had seen something . . .

'An' what does this'n mean?' Cheslyn growled. 'As if ye're of a mind t'—'

'I'd thank ye t' keep a civil tongue in y' head,' retorted Kydd, carefully sighting ahead. If this was going to work he would need everything he had learned of the frightful rocks about them.

'Be damned! Ye're losin' y' westin' by th' hour – this ain't how to—'

Kydd turned and smiled cynically: beyond *Teazer* was another, *Harpy*, summoned by the signal flags he had spotted, so obviously in place to swoop if they had tried to slip by.

Cheslyn had the grace to redden, and kept quiet as Kydd made his estimations. Astern, the two brig-sloops were streaming along in grand style, shaking out yet more sail with the wind directly behind them. The fore-and-aft rig advantage of the *Witch*, however, was now lost to him, and with the brigs' far greater sail area spread to the wind the end seemed inevitable.

Along the deck worried faces turned aft: if Standish had the press warrants, in a short time any not native-born could find himself immured in a King's ship for years.

Ahead was a roil of white, which was the half-tide reef of the Platte Fougère; Kydd stood quietly, watching it carefully, his eye straying back to the two warships, willing them on. Then, at the right moment, he rapped, 'Down helm – sheet in hard!'

Pitching deeply the *Witch* came slewing round to larboard, men scrabbling for purchase with bare feet as they won the sheets in a furious overhand haul. The schooner took up immediately at right angles to her previous course, now broadside to wind and waves in a dizzying roll – but she was passing the reef to its leeward.

Kydd grinned: he knew *Teazer*'s limits and there was no way she could brace round as quickly when she cleared the reef. Watching her thrashing along dead astern Kydd decided it was time to end the charade. Eyeing the jagged black islets of the Grandes Brayes further on the bow he sniffed the wind for its precise direction. 'Stand by t' go about, Mr Cheslyn.' This time there was no argument and the man stumped off, bellowing his orders.

Kydd thanked his stars for an experienced crew: what he was contemplating was not for the faint of heart. Rapidly assuring himself once again of the exact relative position of the islets, reef and the wind's eye, he gave the order to go about.

Witch of Sarnia did not hesitate. She pirouetted to the other tack and took up quickly, passing into the few-hundred-yards-wide channel between reef and islets – and thrashing into the teeth of the wind where no square-rigger could go.

With a pang for his old command, Kydd saw *Teazer* left far astern as the *Witch* energetically made the north tip of Guernsey and round. It was done. They had won the open Atlantic and the rest was up to him.

The low lines of the privateer meant exhilarating going, but there was a price to pay: very soon Kydd found his new command was going to be a wet ship, knifing through the waves instead of soaring over them; with every second or third roller the decks were thoroughly sluiced.

But the *Witch* lived up to her name. It was remarkable how close she held to the wind and her square sail aloft gave added impetus and, at the same time, a degree of manoeuvrability that required fewer men for the same tasks than a sloop.

The vessel type had originated in England, but it was the Americans who had termed it a schooner and taken it as their own, adding special features. From his time on the

North American station Kydd recognised the deeply roached topsail that allowed it to clear the rigging; the lead of the schooner stay that was like a shroud moved forward, easing pressure on the foremast to spread an expansive fore stay-sail.

Engrossed in becoming acquainted with his lady he failed at first to notice Cheslyn next to him.

'Goes like a witch, don't ye think?' he offered, but the man's features remained stony, and an expressionless Le Cocq stood with him.

'This time o' year, after th' equinoctials, gets chancy,' the big man said cautiously. 'B'sides, the glass is still droppin'.'

Kydd looked at him in surprise. 'Why, if I didn't know th' better, I'd have t' say m' first l'tenant's gone qualmish!'

Cheslyn reddened. 'The *Witch* ain't built f'r heavy weather. An' that there's no lady's puff.' He gestured at the low-lying dark-grey cloud masses across their path.

'A squall or two, I'll grant ye, but this is only y' regular-goin' Western Ocean blash!' Kydd had seen the Atlantic at its worst and this was no threat at the moment. 'I'm t' raise Flores in five days, Mr Cheslyn, do y' like it or no.' If the wind stayed steady from the west they could do this even earlier in one slant to the south-south-west and then they would be at their cruising ground.

He turned and left for his cabin, the prospect of rest suddenly enticing. He closed the door firmly; it was not a big cabin – a high bunk over drawers on one side, a working desk with lamp the other and a neat dining-table at the after end. Mercifully there was a skylight above, with a compass repeat further forward. He ripped off his spray-soaked coat and boots, let them drop carelessly, heaved himself into his bunk and closed his eyes.

The *Witch* was close-hauled and had an angle of heel that could be alarming on first meeting but he wedged himself in familiarly and let the sounds of the sea wash past him. Reaching ever westwards into the vastness of the Atlantic involved an endless repetition of a sudden crunch from the bows followed by a defiant rapid upwards lift, then an eager long glide downward and forward, the hiss of their way quite audible through the hull.

Weariness laid its hand on him and thoughts crowded in, but one in particular would not let go. Unless he succeeded, this was going to be the very last voyage he would make as a captain. Neither the Navy nor others would ever offer him employment again.

A double wave thumped the bows and the schooner lost her stride with an affronted wiggle, which dislodged Robidou's book in the bedside rack. It fell into his bunk. Kydd sat up and opened the little volume. Thomas Hartwell Horne. *A Compendium*. He leafed through. It was an exposition in clear English of the Prize Law of 1793 in the form of a handbook of guidance to privateers and ships-of-war, and it had been published by Clarke of Portugal Street this very year.

One stout passage caught his eye: 'Lawful force may be used to enforce a boarding, it being assumed a vessel cannot be proved innocent otherwise. Contumacious resistance to fair inquiry is evidence of guilt in law, to be followed by just confiscation.'

So, if any objected to his boarding, whatever the circumstances, he had the whole force of the law at his back. And whatever else there was in this little treasure . . .

As he addressed himself to the task of teasing out the practical meanings of the legal rules he barely noticed a tiny knock at the door. It was repeated unsteadily.

'Come!' he called loudly.

It was Pookie, gamely passing hand to hand in the lively motion with a small cloth bundle. 'S-sir, Mr Purvis says as how th' fire ain't lit but wonders if this'n will do.' It was cuts of cold meat, cheese and bread.

'It'll do fine, younker.' The little figure had a pale face and Kydd felt for the effort it must have cost to come below where there was no horizon to steady senses thrown awry by the relentless heave and jerking. 'No – leave that, I'll do it,' he protested, when his carelessly cast aside wet gear was painfully but tidily stowed in the side-locker. 'Compliments t' th' officer o' th' deck,' he added, 'an' because ye have the youngest eyes in th' ship ye're t' be lookout. F'r prizes, o' course.'

The child looked up gratefully and scuttled out.

Kydd resumed his book, munching hungrily on the cold victuals, but he soon noticed a definite change in the rhythm of the vessel, a sulky twist after each lift. He frowned and glanced up at the compass repeat.

North-west? Be damned to it! He slipped out of his bunk, grabbed his grego and made the upper deck. 'Mr Cheslyn? What's th' meaning of—'

'I've taken in reefs an' we're headin' f'r shelter in Falmouth,' he said truculently, against the bluster of the wind.

'Ye've abandoned course!' Kydd burst out in amazement. 'An' without s' much as a by' y' leave?' It was a near treasonable offence in the Navy.

'Take a look f'r y'self!' Cheslyn said, heated, pointing at the layer of darkness near the horizon ahead.

Kydd caught his anger. 'An' what's the barometer say?' he asked dangerously.

'A bare twenty-nine – an' losin' fast.'

Without a word Kydd crossed to the hatchway, then to the saloon where a neat Fortin barometer hung on gimbals. He looked closely: as he suspected the fiducial point had not been set – the vernier would not read reliably without a true datum. He tapped the mercury column carefully and adjusted the levelling screw, then saw the reading was closer to twenty-nine and a quarter inches, a figure not out of place in a southern English autumn.

Snorting with contempt, he resumed the deck. Behind Cheslyn the stocky figure of Le Cocq was flanked by Gostling and the boatswain, Rosco, hovered uncomfortably. No one spoke.

'Who has th' deck?' Kydd said loudly, knowing full well who it was.

'Me,' snapped Cheslyn.

'Get back on course west b' north,' Kydd said coldly, 'an' we'll douse th' fore staysail I think.'

'We reckon it's goin' t' be evil doin's afore long, an' we—'

'We?'

'As every sailor knows, a westerly in th' fall ain't t' be trusted. An' with th' barometer—'

'At twenty-nine and a quarter? What lubber can't do a correction?' Kydd said scornfully. 'I've crossed th' Western Ocean enough times an' I know what I see – what ye have ahead is a parcel o' black squalls only, nothing t' fret upon.'

It was worrying that Cheslyn, a reputed North Atlantic mariner, was having trouble with this weather – until Kydd realised he might have other more mercenary reasons for a quick visit to Falmouth. 'Bear up, there,' he commanded the helmsman. 'Course, west b' north.'

The others flicked anxious glances at Cheslyn, and Kydd

wondered darkly what tales of sea-woe he had been spinning to them. 'This I'll do,' he said. 'Should th' glass fall below twenty-nine before dark I'll put about f'r Falmouth.'

It was not much of a concession – if it fell so quickly he would flee in any event – but he was confident in his reading of the sea and felt it unlikely. But he missed having a sailing-master to fall back on for advice and the comfort of such wisdom at his side. He was on his own and would have to stand by his decisions.

Just as dusk was closing in, the first line-squalls arrived. As he suspected, they were short-lived but with disconcerting venom, short periods of screaming and droning in the rigging, and bucking in the canvas. Kydd knew that behind a series of black squalls was marching in from windward with an abrupt drop in temperature and the wind veering sharply in their wake.

He was determined to press on. The *Witch of Sarnia* was well found, nearly new, and her gear could be trusted. It would be uncomfortable and daunting to some but they would do it. But once deep into the ocean, what if a real Atlantic howler coming out of the unknown fell upon them?

A black squall, heavy with stinging rain, blustered over them; the keening winds that followed brought a shock of raw cold as they bullied at watch-coats and oilskins. Kydd sent below those he could, but realised this might not have been a mercy to any still finding their sea-legs; in the fitful conditions the schooner was skittish and unpredictable in her movements.

The seas, however, were constant from the west, long combers, white-streaked down their backs and as powerful as bulls, coming at them ceaselessly. Kydd ticked off the seconds between cresting: if the time had increased, the swell was lengthening, a sure sign of weather to windward.

Another squall; in square rig, with these backing and veering winds, there would be heavy work in the bracing of yards and at the tacks of so many more sails, but in the *Witch*, with but two main sails, it was so much less.

Some time into the dark hours the wind shifted northerly and at the same time the barometer sank below twenty-nine inches. 'Time t' turn an' run,' Cheslyn said pugnaciously to Kydd.

'In this dark? What codshead would go a-beam in these seas without he knows what's a-comin' at him fr'm windward? We're safe as we go, an' we stay this way.'

The next day dawned on a cold, grey waste of heaving, white-streaked seas and sullen cloudbanks, but no sign of the broken and racing scud of a coming storm. 'It'll blow itself out,' Kydd said confidently. Cheslyn merely stumped below.

There were no sun-sights possible but despite the dirty weather they seemed to be making good progress. With a whole clear ocean ahead they would pick up their position in time. For now, however, Kydd must estimate the extent of the set to leeward caused by the weather coming at them.

The constant motion was wearying, the bracing against anything solid taking its toll of muscle and strength. He sent Calloway to round up the ship's boys, then start a class of how to pass bends and hitches and the working of knots; possibly it would take their minds off the conditions.

They were now well out into the Atlantic and the weather had eased more westerly again. The underlying swell was long and languorous, which might mean anything, but the wind was back in the south-west as a strong breeze streaming in, fine sailing weather for a schooner.

Night drew in with little in the evening sky to raise concern and Kydd read his *Compendium* with interest before turning in. He fell asleep almost immediately; any worrying about just where in this vast desert of sea he might find prey could wait for the light of day.

At some time in the night he came suddenly to full wakefulness and lay in the dark *knowing* something was amiss but unable to pinpoint it. There was nothing, no sudden shouting, no change in the regular pitching and heaving of the ship. The feeling intensified, and a sense of preternatural dread stole over him. He rolled out of his bunk, threw on the grego over his nightclothes and hurried up on deck, his eyes straining into the blackness.

The watch-on-deck looked at him in astonishment. 'Cap'n, sir?' said one with concern, approaching. Kydd tried to make sense of his feelings. The rollers showed white in the darkness, seething past as usual, and the overcast made reading the sky conditions difficult. But *something* was . . .

Then he had it. An almost indefinable continuous low roar at the edge of hearing beneath the bluster of the wind but, once detected, never fading. He froze in horror: a memory from long ago, burned into his soul burst into his consciousness – one night perilously close to the dreaded Cape Horn and . . .

He threw himself at the wheel as he had done then, knocking the helmsman aside, and spun on turns. The little schooner seemed reluctant and frantically Kydd willed it on for otherwise they had but seconds to live.

The roar became audible to the others on deck, who looked at each other in terror as Kydd shrieked, 'Hold! Hold on f'r your lives!'

Then the wind died. In not much more than a breath of

air *Witch of Sarnia* came round into the calm whisper and started canting up – the angle increased sharply and the nearness of a monstrous presence beat on Kydd's senses. 'Hold!' he howled, as the schooner reared higher still and from within the vessel he could hear anonymous thuds, crashing and terrified cries.

The roaring was now overwhelming and suddenly it became a reality. The foaming peak of a rogue wave of mountainous size rolling down on them out of the night like a juggernaut, its feral presence mind-freezing.

Now all depended on whether Kydd's action had been quick enough. As the schooner's bow buried itself in the boiling white of the crest, the wind, which had been cut off by the sheer bulk of the wave, resumed with shocking force – but she was now in the eye of the gale and it blasted equally both sides of the fore and aft sails. By that one fact the *Witch* had been saved from being slammed sideways, to die rolling over and over broadside at the teeth of the wave.

The deluge took possession of the deck and came rushing aft; at the same time the naked, dripping bow emerged spearing skywards before the vessel fell with a sickening crunch into the back of the great wave. Then the rush of water thinned and disappeared over the side before it reached them.

They were through! But at what cost? Men boiled up from below in terrified incomprehension; above the bedlam Kydd could hear Cheslyn's roar, then saw his bear-like shape forward as he restored order with his fists.

The man handed himself aft, his heavy face streaked with wet hair, eyes red. 'The barky's well shook up below, Mr Kydd,' he said hoarsely. 'You keep th' deck, sir, an' I'll take some hands below an' do what we can till day.'

'Very well, Mr Cheslyn – an' thank ye.'

There was a glimmer of a smile, then he left abruptly.

First light showed much the same bleak seascape: white-streaked waves to the horizon, advancing on them energetically, but there had been no worsening during the night. The barometer holding steady confirmed Kydd's estimate that it was but the North Atlantic exercising its age-old right to nastiness. He faced the wind: the centre would be some six points or more out there on his right hand. If he shaped away more south of west he would avoid the worst of the blow and still be on course for the Azores and their hunting ground.

With a sigh of satisfaction he retired to his cabin; they had survived remarkably well, considering, almost certainly because of their new fit of rigging. Between decks the mess was still being cleared away but nothing vital had suffered.

He was peeling off his sodden clothes when the door flew open and a cabin boy raced in shrieking, 'An' it's a *sail*!'

It was pale against the east horizon, and of some size. Excitement swept the *Witch*, even though Kydd knew the chances of it being prize-worthy were not great, given they had not yet reached their hunting ground.

Nevertheless the privateer prepared for a chase, setting topsails abroad in earnest for the first time since St Peter Port and laying her course to intercept. As if scenting the thrill of the hunt the *Witch* lay down under her full sail and slashed along in exhilarating style.

Feverishly Kydd brought his new-won knowledge to mind for if there were to be word-grinding arguments he would be ready now. And if the ship resisted their examinations they would earn a whole-hearted boarding.

Strangely, the vessel did not shy away downwind but held her course under the same light sails and in perfect confidence.

'A gun, if y' please, Mr Perchard.' As the powder smoke whipped along the decks the *Witch of Sarnia* broke her colours at the masthead – the Union Flag of Great Britain.

Their intent must be obvious: why, then, did it not take action? As they drew nearer it became even more perplexing with the ship continuing steadily on, not once varying her eastward course. For some reason her upper rigging was full of men. Putting his telescope down Kydd was certain now that this was a Martinico-man, a French Caribbean trader and therefore an enemy; nearly twice their size, yet not making any manoeuvre to meet the threat.

Cautiously Kydd allowed their courses to converge; then a tricolour rose swiftly up the halliards and instantly up and down the deck-line guns opened with stabs of flame, the smoke carried swiftly to leeward. The lively seas made any kind of accuracy impossible but it was clear to Kydd that they were badly outclassed in weight of metal – any boarding could end up bloody.

Still the stubbornly held course and few sails. Kydd made to pass under her stern at half a mile range – and when the big vessel failed to wheel about to keep his guns bearing on them Kydd understood. 'He's taken th' same wave as we,' he laughed in relief, 'an' is higgled in the top-hamper.' It was the cruellest of luck for the ship, weakened beyond manoeuvring in masts or yards. *Witch of Sarnia* had sighted them before they had found time for a jury-rig to the injured spars. Kydd thought guiltily of the men who had worked through the night as they had, and when blessed daylight had come, so had their nemesis.

But this feeling did not last long: a surging happiness flooded him as he went through the motions of criss-crossing the unfortunate ship's helpless stern until the point was taken and the flag fluttered slowly down. Horne's *Compendium* would confirm that this was rightful prey and, being enemy, he could fear no lengthy legalities before she was condemned as prize. The venture was made, *Witch of Sarnia* had made her first kill – and it had taken minutes only.

Chapter 15

As they glided close into the shore, Renzi felt the calm of the night, an utter stillness broken only by the occasional animal cry and the slap of playful waves on the side of the privateer. 'Here!' the captain grunted, squinting into the anonymous darkness.

'Are you sure?' Renzi asked quietly. The man nodded. By this time there should be two lights showing out to sea, one above the other, but nothing interrupted the uniform blackness of the shoreline. A tantalising scent of autumn woodland and fresh-turned earth wafted out to them.

'Then they've had trouble with the lanterns. If you'll set me ashore now, Mr Jacot?'

'I don't reckon on it, Mr Giramondo.'

'Why—'

'Done this afore. Ain't good t' second guess 'em. If they's found trouble . . .'

An hour passed, and more. Although keyed up with the appalling tension, Renzi mused that this would be his first step on the soil of France since those inconceivably remote days when Kydd and he as common seamen had made their desperate escape following an abortive landing.

Kydd! What was his friend doing now? So true and honourable, one of nature's gentlemen who did not deserve his fate – any more than others in the chaos of war. And he had sworn to stay by him, yet here he was—

'There!' Jacot said, with satisfaction. Two lights had finally appeared in the right place. The captain looked at him questioningly and Renzi realised he was waiting for a decision.

Had this signal been delayed by lantern trouble or had it been made under duress after capture to lure them in? Should he seize courage and proceed, or cancel the mission? 'I'll go ashore,' he said, as calmly as he could. There was no alternative.

The boat nudged into the sandy beach and Renzi scrambled out. It disappeared rapidly into the night and he was left standing at the edge of a wood sloping down to the water's edge. With every nerve stretched to breaking point, he listened. Night sounds, the soughing of wind in the trees, creatures in the undergrowth. And blackness.

At that moment he was in as much mortal danger as ever in his life: the letter sewn into his coat felt like fire, a document of such towering importance that, if he were captured, would result not in his simple execution but in the deadliest torture the state could devise to rip his secrets from him. Then merciful death.

With shocking suddenness a hand clamped over his mouth from behind and his arms were seized on each side. A voice close to his ear whispered, in French, 'A sound and you die!'

Renzi nodded and the hand left his mouth but his arms were held as he was frogmarched into the woods. Unseen sharp forest growths whipped across his face as he stumbled along in the grip of at least two men, others following behind.

Panting at the unaccustomed effort, he was relieved when they reached a small glade and paused. The rickety outlines of an old woodcutter's hut appeared before them. Low words were exchanged, then he was brought forward. The door opened, slammed shut behind him and the impelling arms fell away.

Sensing the presence of others in the hut he kept still. There was a tapping of flint and steel and a single candle sputtered into life, to reveal a large man standing behind a table, silent shadows all around.

'*Qui êtes vous?*' the man said mildly. The accent was metropolitan – Parisian. A poignard blade jabbed impatiently at his throat.

Mustering his best French, Renzi replied, 'Nicholas Renzi, a British naval officer.'

'We were expecting another.'

'*Le vicomte* was detained by his wounds. I come from him with a letter.' Renzi drew back his coat far enough for the scarlet-heart insignia of the Chouans to be seen. A rustle went through the others as they bent to see.

'And here is his token.' He held out his hand, which now bore d'Aché's signet ring.

The blade stayed unwavering at his throat.

'So you robbed *le vicomte* of his ring as well?'

'As a show of his trust in me, he desires further that I should say this to you.'

He took a breath, and in the ancient French of seven hundred years ago the noble lines of 'La Chanson de Roland' echoed forth in the old hut:

> *'Tere de France, mult estes dulz païs,*
> *Oi desertét a tant ruboste exill!*
> *Barons franceis, pur mei vos vei murir,*
> *Jo ne vos pois tenser ne guarantir . . .'*

The blade fell away. 'Robert always did relish his civilisation. I am Henri. You told that well, Englishman. Are you perchance a scholar?'

'You were late,' Renzi snapped.

'It is the situation, *mon brave* – soldiers, gendarmerie, they are in unrest, they stalk the woods. It is menacing outside, M'sieur.'

The candle flickered as another entered the hut and muttered something to Henri. He nodded, with a frown, then turned to Renzi. 'A letter, you said.'

'Sir, I've come to deliver assurance from His Britannic Majesty's Government that all possible support shall be given to you in this decisive hour.' He relieved the man of the poignard that had recently been at his throat and, with swift, savage strokes, slashed open the lining of his coat.

A sigh went round the hut as he passed over an elaborately sealed parchment. Henri broke it open and held it up to the candlelight. 'This is from a Sir Saumarez,' he said accusingly.

'It is,' said Renzi, with a haughty sniff. 'Commander-in-chief and admiral. He owes his allegiance directly to London and his word may be accepted, I believe. Would you rather we delayed by requiring a reply all the way from there?'

'It speaks of aid and assistance but with no detail, no numbers.'

'Sir! You can hardly expect a high commander to concern himself in the kind of specifics a quartermaster might deal with.' The hut was warm and close; Renzi was perspiring but it was more from the knowledge of the colossal stakes behind his every word than the lack of air.

Peering intently at the letter, Henri spotted d'Aché's scrawl across one corner. He looked up suddenly. 'Robert commends us to accept this letter. But we have the biggest decision still. If we—'

'If you rise up and triumph in your plan, where is the certitude that there will be ships and men to join with you in consummating your achievement?'

'Exactly.'

There was only one way to go forward now. 'Sir,' Renzi said, 'it is I who have been charged with the responsibility of ensuring that vessels will be there to receive the tyrant – and, of course, any who wish for any reason to quit France at that time. And I have seen with my own eyes the apartment in the castle of Mont Orgueil that is at this moment being prepared by the Prince of Bouillon for Napoleon Bonaparte. Sir, if you have any anxieties on this matter be pleased to address them to me that I might answer them.'

Would this suffice?

In the light from the single candle, Henri's eyes seemed to glow – with satisfaction or suspicion? Holding up the letter he pronounced, 'By these writings the British Government have implicated themselves in the greatest threat to Bonaparte he has ever experienced. In all the chancelleries of Europe it will be seen that perfidious Albion reaches out to topple its foes by cunning and clandestine means and all might tremble that they are to be next.'

Renzi held rigid. He had done all that could be expected of him and now the verdict on his efforts was to be made plain.

Henri looked directly at him. 'Sir, this letter is a gunpowder keg for your government. That they have seen fit to trust it to our keeping is all the assurance we desire.' He held the sheet to the flame. It caught and flared until it was consumed and the ashes fluttered to the floor. 'In forty-eight hours you shall have our date and places.'

Renzi could find no words and gave a simple bow. A scatter of applause and excited talk was halted by Henri, holding up his hands. 'I would that we were able to extend to you the hospitality you deserve but, alas . . .'

He cocked his head to one side and listened intently. Then Renzi felt an irregular thumping in the ground, a jumble of drumbeats out of synchrony.

'Dragoons!'

The door burst open. '*Les soldats! Nous sommes trahis!*' The hut turned to Bedlam and in the rush for the door Renzi heard Henri bellowing orders. Outside in the Stygian darkness there was a crashing of vegetation as the conspirators scattered in every direction.

Renzi's arm was seized and he was forced to one side. 'Stay with me!' a woman's voice urged, as she propelled him across the glade into the woods and they plunged deeper into the wilder depths flying over bracken and fallen tree boles. Shots popped behind them and the squeal of horses pierced the night air.

Mercifully the terrifying sounds lessened and, panting uncontrollably, they stopped at the edge of a meadow, still and serene in the beginnings of a moonrise. Renzi was confused: they were certainly no closer to the sea but the drumming hoofbeats were going away. 'My brother, he draws them from us,' the woman said brokenly.

'He – he is a brave man,' Renzi said, affected.

'Is his duty,' she sobbed. 'We must go.'

The mad scramble resumed; Renzi, however, now saw that they were going in a wide sweep along the edge of the woods to reach the landing place. Everything depended on his endurance in overcoming pain and exhaustion.

But what if the privateer, hearing the shots and commotion, had considered that this was none of his business and left? Renzi could tell now that a body of dragoons had entered the wood on its far side, not far from where they were.

He stumbled on, aware of the woman's agonised breathing. Then the wan glitter of the sea showed through the trees and they reached the shore. 'This way,' she gasped, urging him to the left.

They rounded a small point of land – and there was a boat, ready afloat and bows to sea. Renzi's relief nearly overwhelmed him and it took his last ounce of strength to reach it. 'You waited!' he panted wildly to Jacot.

The man looked puzzled. 'Why, in course I wants th' other half o' me money, Mr Giramondo.'

Almost spent with emotion Renzi urged the woman, 'Quickly, into the boat!'

'No.' She wept. 'I stay with Henri.'

'Get in.' Jacot pulled Renzi aboard. 'We has t' leave now, Mr Giramondo.' When Renzi looked back, no one was there.

Kydd sent Gostling as prize-master of the Martinico-man; an English port was only several days' easy sail to leeward. The mood aboard was exultant but Kydd knew they had been lucky – the next could well be hard-fought and he insisted on serious practice with cutlass, pike and musket, a difficult task on a pitching deck.

Flores, the furthest flung of the Azores, was raised as

planned, the distant blue-grey peak of Morro Alto reminding him of other times. Having arrived it would now be nothing but hard work; searching, waiting, lurking – Kydd had chosen the area because he knew that merchant masters, at this time of the year, from both the East Indies and the Caribbean, converged north of the island group to pick up the reliable south-westerly trade winds to speed them into Europe.

On the other hand without fighting-tops his single lookout in their tiny crow's-nest on the foremast would have a height-of-eye of only some forty feet, say seven miles to the horizon. Any number of ships at that very moment was certain to be passing either side as they sailed, perhaps only a dozen miles or so away, perfectly hidden.

'Keep y'r eyes open there!' he roared up at the lookout. He had impressed on them time and again that a prize could appear from anywhere – ahead or just as easily approaching from the beam or even crossing astern.

The day ended quietly, and night saw them lasking along under easy sail. Soon after midnight the overcast cleared and a fat, gibbous moon rose. By morning the weather was near balmy with bright sunlight and a glittering sea.

So far south the temperatures were more than tolerable and Kydd was enjoying the utter contentment of flying-fish weather in a well-found craft, knowing that even if the rest of the voyage proved fruitless he had cleared the costs and, judging from Cheslyn's comments, probably produced some return into the bargain.

The ship fell into routine, far from naval in its details but as comprehensive as Kydd could make it in the circumstances, chief of which was practice with weapons.

In another four days they had reached the limits of their beat across the tracks of homeward-bound vessels and put about for the slant to the south-west. Unusually the weather calmed until they found themselves ghosting along in a glaring sea, a luminous band of white concealing where water met sky.

The sun grew higher and warmer. On the bow the mist burned off and there, revealed for all to see, was a ship. Incredulous yells broke out as its delicate image took form. They were sighted in turn, the vessel's masts coming together, then separating as it put down its helm and made off as fast as it could.

It had gone into a quartering run to allow its square sails to fill to best advantage and, in the light airs, the *Witch* was finding it a hard chase. No colours or any indication of origin was visible and the angle of the ship made identification impossible. Their own flag would be difficult to make out, end on as it would be.

As noon passed the situation changed: an afternoon breeze strengthened and the schooner picked up speed over the deep blue of the sea. Within an hour white horses were studding the seascape and, their prey encumbered with cargo, eventual success was assured.

'Larb'd side, do y' think, Mr Cheslyn?' Kydd said amiably. He had closed up his crew to quarters, the small gun-crews at the six-pounders, the rest flinting pistols and edging cutlasses – no martial thunder of drums or bravely waving pennons, simply hard-faced men making ready for a fight.

The anticlimax when it came was cruel. As they fore-reached on the sea-worn ship there was sudden activity among the few on her afterdeck and her topsail sheets were let fly as English colours soared up into her rigging.

Rosco recognised the ship. '*Bristol Pride*, or I'm a Dutchman. Trades wi' Nova Scotia an' the West Country in dried cod an' colonial goods. Reg'lar as clockwork an' this must be her last voyage o' th' season.'

The *Witch of Sarnia* ranged alongside and the Canadian twang of the master floated over the water to confirm that they were indeed on passage from Halifax to Falmouth with such a freighting. Kydd waved and hailed back suitably, aware that the black schooner hissing along so close to them must make a handsome showing.

Nevertheless, this was no prey for the *Witch*. 'Sheer off,' he ordered the helm.

'Mr Kydd!' Calloway called urgently, racing up to him.

'Wha—?'

'There, sir!' He pointed vigorously below the *Bristol Pride*'s bowsprit. The buckler, a blanking piece inserted in the hawse while at sea, had been knocked out and an arm was protruding from the hole, frantically jerking a white shirt.

After a split second's incomprehension Kydd bellowed, 'Stand to!' at the boarders. 'Mr Perchard, a shot afore his bow!'

But they had no stomach for a fight against the numbers that the *Witch of Sarnia* could muster and Kydd quickly found himself in delighted possession of a French prize of three days before. Her English crew, confined to the fo'c'sle, had found means to alert them and now the bilingual Québecois master and his prize-crew were themselves prisoners.

'Some happy sailors going home t' England,' Calloway said mournfully, as they bade farewell to *Bristol Pride*, 'but no prize f'r us, is she, Mr Kydd?'

'No prize,' agreed Kydd, then broke into a fierce grin. 'But for us there's th' salvage on recapture. One sixth o' th' entire value an' no questions asked.'

This was a time for celebration – and relief – for Kydd

had needed to demonstrate faith in himself before the investors and had commuted his entire pay for the voyage into shares, which would accrue to his account if, and only if, the voyage was successful.

The length and breadth of the privateer fell quiet as every man figured his own reward. And Kydd now saw his position in the world transformed: even if they met with no more good luck, he had not only cleared expenses but was well on the way to being far better off than at any other time in his life.

It was astonishing how quickly the balance sheet could change. A cargo ship could carry the equivalent of the complete stock of hundreds of shops, and as prize law conveyed the entire ship and cargo to the captor they were in the same position as a prosperous merchant without the need for capital. It was an intoxicating thought.

But it could all be lost – and in a single day. Should Kydd's examination and sending in of a vessel be successfully challenged and he be cast into damages, then the consequences would be grave: a naval officer had a form of compensation but not a privateer captain.

Then there were the fortunes of war: it was foolish to believe that only merchant shipping was abroad. Sooner or later a vengeful warship might loom and predator would become prey – Bonaparte was incensed at the onslaught of privateers on France's vital trade and was showing no mercy to those who fell into his hands.

And his prizes. Would they arrive safely in an English port or in turn be recaptured, as *Bristol Pride* had been? That would put everything back to nothing and be a total ruination of their hopes and hard-won gains.

Kydd returned to his cabin. Like a pendulum, his mood

changed from awe and delight to despondency. Then the gleeful chatter from his cabin boy, as the place was fussily tidied, restored the balance and he turned his mind to the practicalities of the voyage.

Some ten days of provisioning remained and with only one prize-crew away every reason to press on. Kydd and Cheslyn consulted the charts against the prevailing late-season winds and decided on six days north of the Azores and four south before making for home.

The weather was good, but the sport was not. Day after day in blue seas and trade winds and never a sighting. Could it be because now was the season of hurricanes?

D'Auvergne was solicitous when Renzi returned but the strain was showing in the lines of his face. Date and places duly came; Henri had survived the incident but there was no mention of the fate of any other.

Renzi threw himself into the work. The place of embark-ation agreed on, it was possible to assess from the depths of water the size of ship they could use. Bonaparte and his gaol-keepers would be a sizeable party, and while bulwarks would have to be low, deck space was vital.

Word came that Querelle, the final link with Brittany, was in hiding six miles out of Paris. Georges had the keys of the citadel – his plot was manifestly coming together. Reliant on couriers for their news, however, Renzi and d'Auvergne could only await its unfolding.

The indomitable Pichegru was smuggled into the capital and concealed close by the barracks. Others converged on Paris, and within a city in a fever of rumour, Napoleon was said to have secret police reports brought to him in bed as soon as he awoke.

From somewhere deep in the Normandy countryside Henri sent advice that the tenuous line of escape that linked Paris to the coast was complete. Horses were staged ready, parties of soldiers set to delay pursuits. It was the last act.

D'Auvergne alerted his commander-in-chief; for security reasons the time and place of Napoleon's embarkation were not given out to the fleet, but Saumarez promised that, within a bracket of time, the Navy would be conducting live exercises at that precise spot, brig-sloops inshore, frigates in depth.

The day dawned: a crystal clear winter's morning like any other, the French coast the same iron-grey granite the other side of a cold sea. The hours passed: when Renzi and d'Auvergne sat down at last to dinner, tired and overwrought, they ate without conversation.

At the end of the meal they raised a glass in silent tribute to the men who were undoubtedly at that moment engaged in mortal struggle in Paris and those who would be stretched out in a desperate gallop towards them.

'I should think it time now . . .' Renzi said thickly. He got to his feet; d'Auvergne stood up and stretched out his hand. Renzi grasped it, neither man able to find words. Abruptly, Renzi left to bring back Napoleon Bonaparte.

Every vessel was in position. Discreet light signals were exchanged with the shore and Renzi's vessel closed slowly with the coast. It was a tricky task in seamanship, the flat beach selected ideal for carriages but a tidal trap. Kedge anchors were prudently laid to seaward for if they were to ground on the sand as the tide went out . . .

And they waited. Arrival had been timed for early dark but there was still no sign from the interior. Hours passed and men grew edgy and anxious for they were vulnerable from sea and shore. Midnight approached; the plan called for tight timing and this was an ominous sign.

In the long early hours the tide rose again, and in the deathly silence an hour before dawn, they were close enough to hear shouts and disorder carrying in the stillness. The commotion grew nearer and Renzi knew it could have only one meaning.

With desperate sadness he watched running figures burst from the trees, hurling themselves into the shallows towards the waiting ships. The first made it and were hauled up while others, so pitifully few, broke for safety and followed. 'It's Georges – he's been taken,' gulped one. 'We're betrayed – that vermin Querelle turned informer. It's all over for us – finished.'

The *Witch of Sarnia* passed Flores once more and continued south. After barely a day they sighted something in the west: a tiny blob of white on the rim of the world, a sail. At first blinking in and out of existence, then keeping steady, it seized the attention of every soul. They altered towards it instantly, knowing they had the advantage that as their sails were edge on to the other ship their sighting would be delayed.

Then more and more sail came into view. 'A convoy,' Cheslyn grunted. 'But whose?'

Kydd held his telescope steady and tried to make out clues. Anonymous merchant shipping – blue-water vessels certainly. There was a frigate in the van; a large one, possibly of thirty-two guns, no colours. He swung back to the merchantmen. Nothing remarkable; if they had been closer he would see identifying vanes at their mastheads, numbers in white on their stern quarters.

He began counting the ships – six, eight . . . and that was all. This was very likely not a British convoy; it was a telling comment on his nation's primacy at sea that convoys of sixty or a hundred ships were more the rule.

'Johnny Crapaud,' he said crisply, and while the *Witch* closed with the distant ships he took in the situation. They were running before the south-westerly directly towards the French coast, over a week away. The frigate was protectively at their head and far too formidable even to think of engaging, but if anything happened to it he could take his pick of the brood.

'We stay with th' convoy,' he told Cheslyn.

Easing sheets he allowed the ships to advance on him, edging round as the frigate pointedly took position between the privateer and the convoy and shortened sail, allowing its charges to sail on steadily until they were all past, while still remaining between the *Witch* and her intended victims.

This was exactly what Kydd would have done in the circumstances. They were now astern of the convoy, which was downwind of them, but between them and any prize was the impossible menace of the heavy frigate.

The convoy ploughed on, the frigate on guard and immovably positioned astern. Experimentally Kydd allowed the schooner to ease round the rear of the convoy and begin dropping down towards the van but there was no advantage whatsoever to their fore-and-aft rig in this point of sailing and the frigate kept effortlessly with them.

Kydd eased away and the convoy moved ahead again, the frigate keeping pace with the *Witch* as though on wires. Eventually they took their place astern of the convoy once more and it was time to think again.

Aboard every one of those ships there would be fear of

the privateer dogging them but Kydd could not see how to move against them. He could go tearing downwind to fall on one of the leading vessels but well before he could secure his victim the frigate would be upon him.

On the other hand his advantage of better sailing into the wind was of no use, for the frigate was already on the windward edge of the convoy and perfectly positioned to go to the aid of any as they were all to leeward and in a direct line of sailing.

There was no easy answer. They were only a few days off retiring from the area so perhaps he must let them go – but any accident aboard one of the vessels would make it fall out of line and then it would be theirs; or at night some inexperienced master might lose the convoy and in morning light be found alone on the ocean.

So he would follow in their wake ready to snap up stragglers, like a wolf prowling about a flock of frightened sheep, waiting to catch them off-guard.

They stayed with it through the afternoon and evening. As dusk drew in the frigate, having nothing to fear from revealing her position, hung two lanthorns along the foreyard, three along the main, and settled comfortably in the centre of the two columns of four ships where all might see and be comforted by the bright lights.

There would be no lost sheep, it seemed. The night passed, and the day following, with not the slightest false move by the frigate, which stayed in perfect station between the *Witch* and the ships huddling together. It was a masterly textbook defence and Kydd wryly honoured the unknown captain.

Two more days went by. They were now approaching France, heading probably to a port south of Brest, possibly Nantes or La Rochelle. Still the skilled blocking. But this course was not altogether out of their way and Kydd would stay with them until the last moment, then head for home.

Meanwhile he would take the opportunity to circumnavigate the convoy slowly, taking in details of each ship and making a hypothetical choice of which he would choose as victim. Speculation passed round *Witch* as to their qualities and value, but still the frigate kept careful watch and ward.

As they drew nearer the coast they saw various craft, mainly local traders scuttling from port to port and occasionally a larger vessel. Then, with France a low blue-grey smudge ahead at last, everything changed with the sighting of a single vessel closer inshore: not a particularly large ship, a brig, but purposefully beating out towards them.

It posed a dilemma for the frigate captain: should he abandon his position to windward of the convoy and stand away to intercept the possible threat or remain? If the brig was a warship and hostile it was much more of a threat than the *Witch*, but if he went to meet it and Kydd struck, he would have to claw back against the wind to come to the rescue.

Kydd watched developments keenly. Soon it became clear that the brig was a man-o'-war, a Royal Navy sloop of the type that was carrying the fight to the enemy in such numbers, come out to try its steel, wheeling about the head of the advancing ships in an arrogant show of inspection. It was too much for the frigate, which loosed sail and charged through the convoy towards the interloper.

An electric thrill whipped through Kydd: at last, here was his chance. A cooler voice intervened to point out that if he was caught with half his men on an enemy deck by the returning frigate the *Witch of Sarnia* would be blasted out of the water in a single vengeful broadside.

Eight ships. Three or four miles of sea. Was there time to fall on one of the convoy in a wild boarding, seize and sail off with it before the frigate could reach them? All the crew had to do was to put up a stout enough fight to delay matters and they would be saved. It would be a hard and bloody affair. And he had seconds to decide.

At the frigate's decisive move the sloop had kept its distance and was warily stepping away from confrontation. Kydd's instinct was to secure co-operation from the unknown captain and tackle the problem as a team, but a proud navy commander would never stoop to joining with a privateer.

To the starboard rear there was a medium-sized ship-rigged merchantman, probably hailing from the Caribbean and with no particular attraction other than that she had a modest stern quarter and bulwarks to lessen the dangerous climb aboard. *She* would be his kill.

'Mr Cheslyn, we board!' There was an instant response. He had no need to make bracing speeches: they all knew the stakes – and the reward.

Sheering over to starboard he let the *Witch* have her head. She rapidly overhauled the merchant ship and set her bowsprit to pass down the vessel's outer side. This was no time to check on the frigate's actions for now they were committed and there was no turning back.

Puffs of smoke appeared from along the after deck and were joined by others coming from the tops. A swivel banged, and another. Kydd heard the vicious whip of bullets overhead and felt their thump through his feet as they slammed into the hull.

The gap of water narrowed. 'Fire!' he bellowed. Their six-pounder crashed out, its hail of musket balls sleeting across and, with a hoarse roar, the coehorn mortar joined in, throwing grenadoes among the defenders who scattered wildly.

The two vessels came together with a crash, sending Kydd staggering; men stood to hurl grapnels – one collapsed as he took a ball to the chest but others secured a hold and hauled the ships together while the boarders gathered, brandishing their weapons in a bloodthirsty show.

However, there were cool and brave heads on the other ship and seamen darted out and hacked at the grapnel lines with axes and the vessels drifted apart again.

They had to act or it was all over. 'Wi' me!' Kydd shrieked at Cheslyn, in the crazy noise, and raced forward, throwing over his shoulder at the helmsman, 'Take her in!'

On the foredeck Kydd looked frantically about for the fall of a line from aloft, found one and slashed through it; then, as though he were a seaman atop a yard aloft, he ran out on the bowsprit, which was swinging towards the other ship, clamping the coil of line under his arm.

He felt Cheslyn behind him, and others as well – they had moments only, for their impetus through the water would translate to a deflection out by the shock of impact. He reached the cranse iron at the tip of the bowsprit and paused, passing a hurried bow-line around the fore topmast stay, conscious of the racing water below and, in the other ship, the men tumbling down from the low poop to meet the sudden threat, and then the long spar was arcing over the enemy deck.

Instantly he dropped. There was only one thing he had to do now but would he live long enough to do it? Then he heard Cheslyn's roaring battle-cry above – followed by the man's body knocking him askew, others dropping by him.

Kydd heaved himself to his feet and felt the line tug away

from him. Ignoring the ring and clash of arms around him as Cheslyn parried and thrust to protect him, he threw himself at a kevel-head and passed turns round the thick timber belaying point. The schooner's bowsprit was now fastened to its victim and was thus a bridge into the heart of the other vessel. In minutes it was all over, the defenders falling back in panic at the stream of screeching privateersmen flooding aboard.

Kydd stood apart, watching Cheslyn urgently dispatch men into the rigging and along the deck – then raised his eyes to seek out the frigate. With a lurch of his heart he saw it had skilfully driven the brig clear to leeward, then had worn about instantly and was now beating back ferociously.

They had bare minutes to take possession. Having seen the masterly handling of the frigate Kydd knew it was impossible. Still under full sail, still within the convoy, they had to fight their way out – but to do this they needed to learn enough about the rigging operations of a strange ship to put about without a mistake and there was not the time.

The last of the defenders scuttled out of sight – he was master of the deck but with a hostile crew still unsubdued below. He forced his mind to an icy calm. One thing was clear: this prize was heavy with cargo and would never achieve the swift manoeuvres he needed – and all the time the frigate was thrashing closer.

Defiantly he looked back at the wheel. One of his men held it firmly, not daring to vary the ship's heading until he could be sure of the sail handling. The body of an unknown sailor lay sprawled at his feet.

Then Kydd had it. 'Steady as she goes!' he bawled at the helmsman, and hurried over to stand by him. Cheslyn looked aft questioningly. He had groups of men positioned at the base of each mast but Kydd knew that to go about now was simply too risky. Even missing stays would have the frigate right up with them and . . . He shook his head vigorously and concentrated.

They had just this chance. 'Follow m' motions!' he croaked at the nervous helmsman. As a square-rigger, they were sailing directly before the south-westerly, which gave them their only advantage – they had a wide angle of possible courses ahead.

'Steer f'r th' Frenchy frigate,' Kydd ordered. The helmsman gave a frightened glance but complied, and the ship swung ponderously until it was headed directly towards the ship beating up towards them between the two columns of the convoy.

The man-o'-war did not change its course and Kydd guessed there would be frenzied discussion on her quarter-deck. They stood on stubbornly, but Kydd knew that the frigate captain had only one object – to lay them aboard. He would do his best to oblige.

'Shake out that reef!' he hailed Cheslyn. Sails had been trimmed to achieve an even speed in convoy. Loosing the main and fore-course would give them speed in hand.

The frigate's track did not vary in the slightest and, head to head, the two ships approached each other. Everything now depended on the timing and the placements: Kydd's eye took in not only the menace of the French frigate but the convoy – especially the next-ahead vessel – and he made his calculations deliberately, passing his orders quietly for fine corrections of heading.

Their advance downwind was drawing the next-ahead perilously near, and somewhere on her inner beam there would be a meeting. One or other of the closing ships must give way.

The frigate slashed ahead, straight for them, with no sign of yielding way – but this was not Kydd's concern for at the last possible moment he gave orders to fall away to starboard. Instead of coming to a confrontation their ship instead passed to the outer side of the next-ahead and so close that the pale, shocked faces of the men at the wheel were clear and stark as they bucketed by.

In one move Kydd had placed this ship between him and the frigate as they passed in opposite directions – but the best was yet to come. Enraged by Kydd's bold escape the frigate captain made to bear away closely round the next-ahead's stern, but in his eagerness to grapple gave insufficient allowance for the strength of the fresh winds. In a chorus of splintering smashes, twangs and screams of indignity the frigate made close acquaintance with the vessel's stern quarters and, recoiling, fell off the wind, helpless.

Quickly, Kydd had his new prize angling off into the open sea with *Witch of Sarnia* close beside.

Outside the Three Crowns Kydd stood in a maze of happiness. He was gazing at a poster on a pillar proclaiming boldly:

FOR SALE BY THE CANDLE

At THREE CROWNS TAVERN, St Peter Port, on Monday the next by Ten o' clock in the Forenoon, **THE GOOD SHIP** HÉROS DE GUADELOUPE, burthen about 400 Tons, lately taken by the WITCH OF SARNIA, Letter of Marque, Thomas Kydd, Captain. A remarkable sailer, well found and calculated for the **CARIBBEE TRADE** and may be sent to sea at a Trifling Expence . . . after the Sale, the entire cargo now landed will be set to Auction, inventories may be viewed at . . .

And this was only the first of his two prizes. Hearings had taken place immediately and the evidences of French ownership sent to the Admiralty Prize Court had resulted in swift condemnation as prize and the vessel was now in the process of being sold at auction.

'Mr Kydd, is it not?' a well-dressed man asked politely, removing his hat. 'I believe the heartiest congratulations would be insufficient to express my sense of admiration at your late action. And another prize to your name?'

'Aye, there is, sir,' Kydd answered warily.

'Magnificent! Just as in the old days! Oh, might I introduce myself? Robert de Havilland.' He handed Kydd a card. 'As you may see, I'm a banker and it did cross my mind that should you see fit to favour us with your financial interests then I'm sure that we would be able to offer very advantageous rates to a gentleman as distinguished as yourself. A line of credit against your captures, perhaps? Sovereign investment in Consols at above market—'

'Why, thank ye, Mr de Havilland,' Kydd came back politely, 'but I'm not ready t' change banks at th' moment.' It was truly amazing how many new friends he had made in the few days since his return from sea.

Curious to see proceedings he entered the tavern. It was stifling, packed with merchants watching while the auctioneer droned away on the fine qualities of the vessel under the hammer. A stir went through them when he had finished and an assistant brought a lighted taper.

'Are ye ready, gennelmen? light th' candle!'

The bids were low at first, then from all sides the serious ones came in. 'One fifty t' you, sir – two hundred? Mr Mauger? Two seventy . . .'

Kydd had no idea of the value this represented but was

content to let it wash over him. The bids petered out but all eyes were fixed on the candle and Kydd saw that it was burning down to where a blackened pin with a ribbon had been inserted. As the flame neared, the bids redoubled until there was a staccato hammer of shouts before the pin dropped clear, and the highest bidder was declared the new owner.

Turning to go, Kydd was stopped by the auctioneer, who had spotted him. To general acclamation he announced that they had been honoured by the presence of the victorious captor. Kydd blushed and made a hurried escape outside to an unseasonally warm sun.

He strolled along the parade, nodding to respectful passers-by, and pondered the change in life's direction that had brought him so much. He recalled the smugness of Zephaniah Job at the wind-up meeting, the almost fawning attention of Robidou, the ledger figures that told of his restoration to fortune.

Then there was the respect he seemed to have won from Cheslyn and the crew of the privateer at paying-off time. He chuckled aloud to recall a bold and swashbuckling Pookie stepping ashore playing the corsair to the limit as she took home her plunder to present to her mother.

Would Renzi believe how things had changed? His friend's selfless toil in Jersey to keep him going was now no longer necessary. He would ask him to return but without telling him of his great change in fortune, simply say he was due for a surprise. Yes, he must write him a letter . . .

Kydd then remembered a promise, which he would soon be in a position to keep. He planned to take one of those grand and very comfortable mansions in Grange Road.

A celebration, a great dinner occasion – and the only ones

invited would be those who had stood so nobly by him. As he hurried along to set it in train he imagined the room resounding to Richard Samson's Shakespearian declaiming, the extravagant gown that Griselda Mayhew would flaunt, the studied nonchalance of Carne, who would probably complain at the waste of a good flyman. It would be a splendid evening.

Chapter 16

Renzi was on his way back to Guernsey and to Kydd. He had kept his word and stayed with d'Auvergne until it was obvious there was no more to be done, and then, accepting only what he was owed in wages, he quit the place.

It had been a catastrophe – not for want of courage: there had been every reason to expect a different conclusion but for the treachery of Querelle. The head of the secret police, Fouché, had moved rapidly and, with bloodshed and torture, the conspiracy to kidnap Bonaparte had been comprehensively crushed.

Georges had been taken after a gigantic struggle, the old soldier Pichegru dragged from his bed to the Temple prison. Troops had been sent across the Rhine to arrest the Duc d'Enghien and orders poured out of Paris for apprehending lesser names.

Bonaparte's vengeance was savage: arrests, trials and executions followed swiftly one on another. Georges was guillotined with eleven others, bellowing, '*Vive le Roi!*' even as the blade fell. The Duc d'Enghien was imprisoned and put on trial for his life while Pichegru was found strangled in his cell with a stick and neckerchief, some said to prevent unwanted disclosures at the trial.

It had been a searing experience: Renzi knew he looked haggard and drawn, and that it would take some time to emerge from the darkness of tainted violence. To see his friend again was now all he asked; he remembered the last letter, the reference to his 'surprise', and hoped it would allow some small leavening of Kydd's existence – what means he himself had been able to bring back was not as much as he had hoped.

St Peter Port was unchanged, the waterfront as active as ever. He checked the address on Kydd's letter. Off Fountain Street to the south: quite up to the fringes of respectability – was this his surprise? He found the house easily enough, a somewhat decayed dwelling but of some size.

'Oh?' The strikingly featured woman who answered the door seemed disconcerted at his appearance.

'Madame,' Renzi said, with an abject bow, 'I have no wish to intrude. My recent understanding is that Mr Thomas Kydd is in residence here.'

'Ah!' she said. 'You're naught but a bailiff come after the poor lamb!'

'Indeed I am not,' Renzi said, with the first smile for many weeks. 'I am his friend.'

'You're not Mr Renzi?' she said, incredulous.

'I am.'

She took him by the arm and said warmly, 'Why, do come in! I'm Rosie – he's not living here any more but you'll have such a surprise when y' hear what he's a-doing now.'

* * *

328

An hour later, warmed by a stiff tot and the odd group's open regard for him as a friend of Kydd, he stood in the street outside, bemused at the turn of events. Kydd was the talk of the town and, to a fair way of thinking, a rich man – a privateer captain of all things – still out on his third voyage but expected daily.

Renzi wandered down to the foreshore where they had last walked together. By all accounts Kydd's days of penury were well and truly behind him and his own little contributions would no longer be needed – in fact, the new address he had been given was up on Grange Road, one of the imposing villas that looked down haughtily on the bustling seaport.

It would be a quite different man he would shortly be seeing. Their time together in *Teazer* was over, of course, however brief in the larger span of life. He'd wedge himself no longer in his tight little cabin, musing on mystical paradigms and vaulting theories while the sea tossed about their sturdy bark – and he would be so much the poorer to have to develop his thoughts in some dingy shorebound building.

Renzi shook off his selfish concerns. Now their ways would necessarily diverge, given their utterly different courses in life, and with Kydd busy amassing a fortune as a privateer captain there would be little point in lingering in Guernsey waiting for his infrequent returns.

No, it was time to part. The bleakness returned, threatening to become a desolation. He cast about for something to fasten on to. Was there anything perhaps he could give Kydd to show him how much he had appreciated his friendship? Given his circumstances, it would have to be a forlorn sort of present.

Then a thought struck. There *was* one last service he could do for his friend.

With the prospect of increasing wealth and Kydd's conse-quent high standing in society, there was little doubt that he would now see any resumption of his attempt to clear his name as irrelevant. Renzi had heard from Rosie of Kydd's naïve plan to unbribe the perpetrators. It had no chance, of course, but if he himself by other means was able to get to the bottom of it it would be a satisfying thing indeed to offer his friend.

Renzi strode purposefully along the Pollet to Smith Street and made his way up to the headquarters of the commander-in-chief. Renzi,' he snapped at the guard. 'Confidential secretary to Commodore d'Auvergne of the Jersey Squadron. If you please – Mr Jessop, high clerk to Sir James.'

Being of such stature, the man maintained his own office; Renzi entered, then made play of closing the door behind him and testing the latch. Then he intoned gravely, 'Renzi, sir. We have corresponded on occasion.'

Mystified, Jessop rose to shake hands.

'Sir. I have come on a matter of some delicacy. You are aware, are you not, of the commodore's *other* responsibilities?'

'Um, if you are referring to his activities of a clandestine nature arising from his connections with . . . yes, Mr Renzi, as high clerk to the commander-in-chief I am generally made cognisant—'

'There is no necessity for details at this time, Mr Jessop. The matter under privy investigation at this time merely requires an indication only concerning a possible breach of confidentiality. It may or may not be necessary to take the issue further but for now a simple response will answer.'

Jessop frowned and waited.

'Within the last several months has any communication of

a covert or unusual nature been received by this office from the admiral commanding at Plymouth? Do please indicate with an affirmative or negative only.'

The man's face cleared. 'Absolutely not. As you must be aware this is a commander-in-chief's station and does not have anything operationally to do with a subordinate admiral in another station. Therefore we have had nothing from Admiral . . . Lockwood, isn't it? Apart from the routine and mundane, that is.'

'You can be quite certain that nothing touching on covert operations or deployments—'

'Sir. You can rest assured that anything of such a nature must pass across my desk and there has been no such.'

'Nothing that can require a secret deviation from operational orders, perhaps?'

'Mr Renzi, I myself make up the order packs for captains and there have been no secret orders issued a commander on this station these last six months. As you must know, such operations as might be classed as covert are generally attended to by Commodore d'Auvergne. Of course, *Cerberus* frigate was once diverted—'

'Thank you, Mr Jessop. That has been most helpful. Good day to you, sir.'

So there could be little doubt that Kydd's forged 'secret orders' had not originated from Lockwood. Therefore it must have been effected locally.

Renzi fought down his weariness and concentrated on a careful review of the procedure: he himself had signed for the orders but not sighted them, locking them away in the confidential drawer for the captain's later attention. When Kydd had opened them he recalled that the outer, normal orders had been in a packet as usual, only the secret orders sealed. He did not recall anything singular about the seal.

Surely they could not have been falsely planted in *Teazer* – there had been no signs of a lock forced and, in any case, the idea of any getting past Tysoe for access to Kydd's inner cabin was ludicrous. Therefore the false orders must have been inserted prior to their delivery to *Teazer*.

They had been brought in the usual fashion from the commander-in-chief's office by Prosser, the master's mate, who had signed for them properly. He had presumably then returned without delay in the boat to hand them over.

If at the flag office there had been no secret orders and in *Teazer* there were – there could be only one conclusion: that Prosser had himself inserted them or knew of the act.

Prosser! But what possible motivation could he have had for the deed? Vain, insensitive and no leader of men, he was much more likely to have been led by another. Standish? There was no way of telling. Prosser would never risk his career in admitting anything – he had now his acting lieutenancy. And the principal in the affair would have ensured that all tracks had been been well and truly covered.

It was unfortunate but there was no way forward. As a failed commander Kydd would therefore be for ever under a cloud and— A wave of rage roared through Renzi, shaking him with its intensity. It moved him, as nothing else had, that the gross world of deceit and treachery had reached out and touched his friend.

Renzi knew that unless he did *something* he would . . . But then . . . he realised he could.

The devil that was in him spoke seductively through the storm, plotting a course of action that in its very symmetry was beguiling and deeply satisfying. If the virtuous were to be brought low by an immoral and felonious act, then the wicked should be likewise: in one stroke he could turn the world he despised against itself and at the same time achieve justice for Kydd at last.

Feverishly he assembled a plan. He would need accomplices who wouldn't talk – with his inside knowledge of the shadow world of spies and assassins that would be easy. Vipère and Hyène would now be available; he brought to mind their saturnine, grave-robbing features. Yes, they would do admirably.

Next, a suitable location. What better than the old sail-loft in which Kydd had spent so much time recently? Excellent. Then let the game commence . . .

Sitting at the single table in the dank and empty space, Renzi trimmed the one candle. It shone up with a trembling flame illuminating his face from below with a malevolent gleam. The table was bare, save an open razor in the centre.

He waited calmly. At the appointed hour there was a scuffle outside; a struggling body was forced within and flung to the ground before him, the pinioned arms splayed immovably sideways, the gagged and blindfolded head desperately turning this way and that.

The struggles eventually ceased and Renzi nodded; first the gag and then the blindfold were removed and a terrified Prosser looked about wildly. He tried to rise but was held down. 'For God's sake, Renzi, what's happening?' he choked out.

Renzi watched him writhe. He had no pity for the man's ordeal, called from the warmth of the Mermaid Club on a pretext, then rapidly bundled away blindfolded into the night.

'What're they doing?' Prosser shouted, terror rising. Vipère cuffed him to silence.

Renzi contemplated the creature who had brought Kydd down and who was now trembling uncontrollably, his eyes staring at Renzi's cruel mask of a face.

'You played Mr Kydd false with your poisonous secret orders. You'll tell me why.'

'I – I didn't do it! It wasn't me, I swear!'

Icy anger seized Renzi. 'I've the blood of far better men than you on my hands,' he snarled, with the conviction of perfect truth. 'Yours will not cost me a moment's pause.' He was shaking now at the sudden insight that he really meant it. His hand slid to the razor and, picking it up slowly, he tested its edge.

'You – you're mad!' Prosser gasped, hypnotised by the weapon's gleaming menace.

Renzi rose suddenly, shifting his grip on the razor to a workmanlike underhand. The two others yanked Prosser's head back by the hair.

'No!' Prosser screamed. 'I beg you!'

Renzi paused and the man fell limply. 'H-how did you know?' he said weakly. 'He said no one would ever discover us.'

It all came out. Such a simple, foolish act, conceived in jealousy and hatred but with such consequences – it had been Carthew. When he had seen his position as senior commander and favourite threatened by Kydd, and aware of Saumarez's strict moral code, he had bribed a smuggler to land the chest and persuaded Prosser to tamper with the orders.

There had been no one else. Carthew had promised Prosser that on this remote station Standish would get the ship and he himself would achieve his long-sought lieutenancy. He had been right – and, but for Renzi, he would certainly have got away with it.

But Renzi could see no path forward. Without evidence, without witnesses, there would be no happy ending. In lieu, should he put an end to this reptile's life? He moved forward – Prosser shrieked as the razor went straight to his throat. It stayed poised while a tiny nick beneath exuded a trail of scarlet. 'Your life is now forfeit,' Renzi said levelly. 'My dearest friend has been ruined by your acts. Can you give me any reason why I should not end it?'

He waited for the hysterical babble to trail off, having discovered to his intense satisfaction that Prosser had not trusted Carthew and had stealthily retrieved the actual secret orders, which he still had in his possession.

Renzi pretended to ponder. 'I see – to be produced in court at the proper time.' He reflected further. 'You will observe,' he said, as though to a lecture audience, 'how trivial a task it has been for one in my position to arrange the abduction and death of any I choose. Should you fall in with my demands you may yet escape with your life – but if you fail me I will give orders that will find you out wherever you are and extinguish your miserable existence. Do you understand?'

'Y-yes, Mr Renzi.'

'Then this is what you shall do. First bring the orders to me, with your written confession. Afterwards you shall stand up and testify against Carthew – and only then will you stand quite discharged of your obligations. This is now your choice, sir. How will you proceed?'

'I – I'll do it, Mr Renzi. Whoever you are . . .'

It had been a stiff walk out of town, up by Elizabeth College to Grange Road, and a little further to the Kydd residence, a fine house with many rooms set back discreetly from the road. He passed the gardener, who touched his hat to him as he reached the ornate front door and found the bell pull.

A bewigged footman regarded him disdainfully. 'Sir?'

Fighting down a sense of unreality he said, 'I'm Nicholas Renzi. I saw that Mr Kydd's ship is now in port. Is he at home at all?' He had seen the wicked black lines of the privateer schooner as she had returned to a joyous welcome on the quayside but, for some reason, had refrained from joining the crowds.

The footman seemed unimpressed and held out his hand.

'Oh, er, I have no visiting card on my person,' Renzi said uncomfortably, 'but I assure you I am his good friend and sanguine he will offer me welcome.'

He was shown into a receiving room adjacent to the door by the disapproving flunkey. Renzi settled into a comfortable chair and picked up a *Gentleman's Magazine* to avoid gaping at the splendours of decoration to hand.

It was hard to believe that this was now the residence and home of the young, credulous quartermaster's mate who had sailed with him in *Artemis* frigate on her legendary voyage round the world; the master's mate who had stood with the seamen in the great Nore mutiny, then spurned an admiral's daughter for a country lass at ruinous social cost.

Kydd's sea sense had made him a natural predator and he was clearly reaping its rich rewards. Three voyages now. He was a figure of admiration in an island with a long history of privateering and could command the fawning attention of any he chose – and this was only the beginning.

Had it altered him? Was the open-hearted sailor now a hard-nosed businessman? When each cruise was adding massively to his private fortune, would he deign to go back to life in a humble sloop like *Teazer*? The more Renzi thought about it, the more unlikely it seemed.

Most of all, a gulf now separated them that could not have been greater: Kydd had found himself and would go on to great things, while he could only dream of achieving something in the philosophical line, not a path likely to lead to such riches.

With a sudden stab he realised as well that, as Kydd and his family rose in the world, Cecilia might be placed for ever beyond his reach. His despondency turned to fear.

The gritty rolling of wheels outside told him that soon he would know the worst. Sitting quite still, his pulse quickening, he heard the cries of an ostler and the jingling of harness – then a deeper voice of authority, probably the majordomo greeting his master: 'A pleasant voyage, sir?'

Then the blessed sound of Kydd's hearty voice: 'Not s' pleasant, but a mort profitable, I'd have t' say.'

'Oh, er, there's a gentleman in the receiving room,' the voice went on. 'He gave no card but claims to be an acquaintance of yours. Will you see him or . . . ?'

'He gave a name?'

'Well, yes, sir – a Mr Rancy, sir.'

'Renzi!' The door burst open – and Kydd stood there, utter delight on his face. 'Nicholas!' he cried. 'Ye're here!'

Renzi stood slowly. 'Yes, dear fellow, as you have rightly perceived, I am indeed here,' he said, eyes smarting.

Kydd advanced impulsively and hugged his friend. Then, frowning, he held him at arm's length. 'That rogue the prince o' whatever – why, he's been working ye half t' death. Still, no need f'r that kind o' thing any more, Nicholas. We're rich!'

While Renzi was digesting the 'we', Kydd turned on the majordomo. 'Rouse up th' hands!' he roared. 'We're t' have a right true welcome home t' two heroes o' the sea!'

They moved to the more august surroundings of the spacious drawing room, and Renzi noted how confidently Kydd moved about the sumptuous furnishings. Soon, fortified by a fine brandy, the two friends were slipping back into their old familiarity.

'Then do I take it that your recent voyage might be accounted successful, brother?'

'Aye,' Kydd said, with relish. 'One who thought t' go a-tradin' with th' French colonies – a right Tartar but no match f'r the *Witch*, o' course.'

'So now you have taken the character of a man of means, not to say wealth.'

'Oh, this pile, y' think so? It's on a very favourable lease fr'm a Mr Vauvert, rich cove who's done well out o' investin' in m' cruises.'

'Then this bounteous cornucopia might be said sufficient for your plans now to go afoot.'

'Ah – the plans. Nicholas, I've had time t' think about it. It wasn't really much of a plan t' conceive they'll put 'emselves up against th' law just f'r a few guineas. Foolish t' believe so, don't y' think?'

'I'd be obliged to agree, dear fellow. But what if we could find some other way to right this grievous wrong done to you?'

'Y' mean, lay out the gold t' hire a flash London lawyer as will see me right? No, Nicholas, without we have th' evidence t' show him it just won't fadge.'

'Perhaps then we could find a denizen of the demi-world, an abandoned creature not noted for the delicacy of his morals who would follow the trail wheresoever it led. But who would know such a person?'

'Nicholas!' Kydd exclaimed, scandalised. 'I'll not have dealings wi' such. It's not the place f'r a gentleman, as you y'self tells me!' he said with heat. Hesitating, he conceded reluctantly, 'So it seems I'll have t' face it. There's no way forward. This is m' lot in life, an' if I'm t' be truthful then it's t' say that it's not so hard, an' I'm still fightin' the King's enemies – in a private way, o' course.'

'Umm. Well, do tell me, for my interest, if it were in any wise made possible that at some future date the vile act is exposed and the malefactors brought to a reckoning, would you still desire to set yourself on *Teazer*'s quarterdeck again? To give away the carefree life of a corsair for the stern duties of the Navy?'

Puzzled, Kydd blinked. 'Why, o' course! Why else would I . . . ? Ah, I see – ye're flamming me! Well, Nicholas, let me say ye can be sure that if I c'n think of another plan as'll smoke 'em out, well, I'll do it with all m' heart.'

Renzi paused. A half-smile spread as he felt about inside his waistcoat. 'Well, now, if you're ever to be a commander again we'll have to find a way to deal with these.' Slowly he withdrew a small sheaf of papers.

Unfolding the top one and holding it up, he asked innocently, 'Oh, er, do you recognise this at all?'

'*My God!* Th' secret orders! Where did you . . . ?'

'From the knave who deliberately inserted them into your lawful orders.'

'Who?'

'As instructed by another, who most ardently wished for your ruin.'

'Who, damn it, Nicholas? Was it Lockwood?' Kydd blazed.

'Prosser.'

Kydd slumped in amazement. 'That – that gib-faced shicer? In God's name, why?'

'To achieve his step as an officer.'

'An' who was th' other?'

'The principal was Carthew. In a fit of jealous rage he paid a smuggler to land the chest and used Prosser to falsify your orders. Simple, really.'

Kydd shook his head in wonder. 'That any should be s' low.' He turned to Renzi. 'Nicholas, how did ye . . . ?'

'Oh, merely the application of common logic, and when I enquired it of him he most readily admitted the act. You will find his written confession here, the name of the smuggler, and as well he has agreed to testify against Carthew.'

Speechless, Kydd could only gaze at him in admiration. 'Then – then this means . . .'

'It is over, dear friend. With this evidence your reinstatement will be a matter of formality only, and remembering the particular kindness Sir James Saumarez had for you, I would not be in the least surprised to find him especially anxious to make up in some handsome way for what you have suffered.' Stretching out lazily, he continued, 'And from henceforth your new fortune will set you in the first rank of society, never more to concern yourself with trifles as we mortals must. Not forgetting that your means now will bring you influence and power, perhaps a seat in parliament? It were folly for the Admiralty to ignore such a one.'

Kydd listened quietly, then grinned. 'O' course, Nicholas, if life in a pawky brig-sloop doesn't please ye any more, I shall have t' find a new clerk . . .'

It took another brandy before conversation could resume. With a triumphant flourish Kydd waved the evidence in the air. 'Who'd have thought it? I hold in m' hands just a few squiddy papers, but they're enough t' see me back in command o' dear *Teazer*!' His eyes shone.

'And a nemesis for the wrongdoer!' Renzi added.

'Aye,' Kydd said, his voice hardening. 'Carthew doesn't know it yet but he's found out, an' I'm about t' choke his luff with this 'n! I'll now have my revenge on him, th' dog!'

Renzi gave a saintly smile. 'A court-martial and dismissal with disgrace from His Majesty's Navy, scorn and contempt at all levels and no hope whatsoever of being received by polite society ever again. And, of course, little prospect of employment by any who value probity in character.'

The smile grew wider. 'If, of course, you wish to cast him into damages then you must add penury to his suffering.'

'Enough!' Kydd rose to his feet. 'I'm goin' t' Saumarez – *now*!'

Renzi gave a little laugh, which he tried to smother.

'What?' Kydd grated.

'Oh, nothing. Just the irony of a privateer's revenge setting a right true sea officer back into His Majesty's Service.'

Author's Note

The ancient castle of Mont Orgueil still lies at the head of Gorey Bay in Jersey. The curious may wish to visit and pace the stone floors of the rooms from which Commodore (later Admiral) Philippe d'Auvergne ran *La Correspondance* in those desperate days two hundred years ago. They might then desire to mount the old battlements for the thrilling view of the coast of France, as countless sentries and others have done over the centuries since Good Queen Bess. I would recommend the trip; there have been few of my research locations that have proved so little changed and so genuinely atmospheric.

In fact the Channel Islands are fascinating indeed. St Peter Port is rightly said to be as prime a Georgian city as Bath or Weymouth and a brisk walk up Grange Road will allow the interested to view the splendours of the residences built by successful privateers and grand merchants. The original harbour remains, but within the embrace of a much larger modern edifice; however the fearful sea hazards of dizzying tidal currents and the maze of submerged rocks still have the power to chill.

For the inhabitants of the Norman Isles, as fiercely independent as ever, the loyal toast will always be to the Duke of Normandy. They revere those who have loomed large in their thousand-year history, perhaps none more than Admiral Sir James Saumarez, a grave figure whose integrity and sensitivity ensured that he would always stand in the shadow of other, more colourful commanders. I was gratified to learn recently that there are plans for his memorial, dynamited by the German army, to be restored.

Philippe d'Auvergne's story is a less happy one: at the end of the war, exhausted and in debt, he crossed Europe to enter into his princely inheritance – only to have it bartered away by the Great Powers in the readjustment of borders after Waterloo. He died days later.

As usual, I owe a debt of gratitude to three women without whom there would be no books: my creative partner and wife Kathy, my literary agent Carole Blake and my editor, Alex Bonham. I've consulted many in the Islands, and I apologise for not naming them all. However I would be remiss in not mentioning Dr Gregory Stevens Cox, whose peerless work on the period started me on my quest and whose personal tours stripped away the layers of years; the Lt Governor of Guernsey, Sir Fabian Malbon, who as an admiral and commander-in-chief himself shares my respect for Sir James; and Captain Peter Gill, the Queen's harbour master, whose insightful observations on navigation in those waters informed my writing. My thanks are due, too, to Captain A J Holland,

Nicholas Gold, Peter de Sausmarez and the staff of the Priaulx Library.

I do hope you enjoyed this story: in the next book Kydd will be sailing into shoal waters of quite another kind . . .